CW01426062

DOC SAVAGE

The Wild Adventures of Doc Savage

Please visit www.adventuresinbronze.com for more information on titles you may have missed.

THE DESERT DEMONS
HORROR IN GOLD
THE INFERNAL BUDDHA
THE WAR MAKERS
THE ICE GENIUS
PHANTOM LAGOON
DEATH'S DOMAIN
THE MIRACLE MENACE

(Don't miss another original Doc Savage adventure, THE WAR MAKERS, coming soon.)

THE INFERNAL BUDDHA

A DOC SAVAGE ADVENTURE

BY WILL MURRAY & LESTER DENT

WRITING AS KENNETH ROBESON

COVER BY JOE DeVITO

ALTUS PRESS • 2012

First Edition — May 2012

DESIGNED BY

Matthew Moring/Altus Press

SPECIAL THANKS TO

Lee Baldwin, James Bama, Jerry Birenz, Condé Nast, Jeff Deischer, Dafydd Neal Dyar, Matthew Moring, Ray Riethmeier, Art Sippo, Anthony Tollin, Howard Wright, The State Historical Society of Missouri, and last but not least, the Heirs of Norma Dent—James Valbracht, Shirley Dungan and Doris Lime.

COVER ILLUSTRATION COMMISSIONED BY

Dr. Tahir Bhatti

Like us on Facebook: "The Wild Adventures of Doc Savage"

Printed in the United States of America

Set in Caslon.

For James Bama, who reimagined Doc Savage for a new generation—

And whose artistic vision we are proud to continue....

The Infernal Buddha

Table of Contents

Chapter I

STRANGE PEOPLE

THE MAD MYSTERY of the infernal Buddha, as it came to be called, started east of Singapore, which is a speck of an isle off the lowermost tip of the Malayan Straits. It was a fitting day for a mystery to begin, there being a fog, which was highly unusual for that part of the South China Sea.

Dang Mi, who was destined to play a major role in the unbelievable events to come—although he didn't know it yet—sprawled in the shade of the mainsail on the poop deck of his two-masted Chinese junk, *Devilfish.* The name was a rare bit of honesty. She was as devilish a hellship as ever plied the South China Sea.

From hull to clumsy-looking batten sails, she was also as black as an octopus. A round white orb was painted on either side of her bows, after the superstitious custom of the Orient, which ascribed to such painted eyes the ability to see danger ahead.

Dang Mi had heard of Doc Savage, fabulous man of might, who was also to become embroiled in the mystery about to start. By repute, Doc Savage was a more fearsome foe of evildoers than Scotland Yard, the Royal Mounted and the G-Men put together. Doc Savage had never gotten wind of Dang Mi, so far as the latter knew. Dang planned to keep it that way.

There was good reason for this. Dang Mi was a follower of a very old and exceedingly dishonorable profession. Dang Mi was a gentleman of fortune. That was the polite term for it.

Dang was a pirate. He did not fly the Jolly Roger, nor had he occasion to make a captive walk the proverbial plank, but he was a pirate nonetheless, one of the few still prowling Asiatic waters. The British Navy had pretty much cleansed the China coast of piracy, particularly in the area of Bias Bay—which meant only that the surviving pirates had sought out more welcome waters.

That had all been before Dang Mi's advent in the Malay Straits. He was a relative latecomer to the profession of piracy. And although his crew consisted of a polyglot collection of cut-throats and smugglers—mostly Dyaks and Malays, with a sprinkling of Siamese and Borneo wharf rats—Dang Mi was a white man. An American, to be precise.

Dang Mi's honest name was Hen Gooch—which possibly explained why he didn't mind being known as Dang Mi. In truth, he came upon his Oriental cognomen quite by accident.

A salty cuss by disposition, Hen was free with epithets. But there was one saying he preferred above all others.

"Dang me," he often complained—often enough for his crew to mistake the exclamation for Pidgin English. They thought he was saying, "Me, Dang"—Dang being a perfectly respectable name for a Chinese pirate.

Eventually, Hen Gooch got them straightened out. But not before he decided he liked the sound of Dang Mi for a name. Loosely translated, it meant, "Like a Demon."

It was to be suspected that the numbers of lawful authorities in America—both North and South—and Europe who had designs on Hen Gooch's future, had a little to do with the change of name—not to mention inspiring Dang Mi's preoccupation with sunning himself daily to keep his hide from becoming too white.

There were times he smeared collodion at the corners of his eyes to give them a slanted aspect. He wore his hair long and shaggy, in order to conceal the indisputable fact that the top of one ear had been cut off some time in the past. Back in the

United States, this bit of rough justice branded a man as a common horse thief. Horse thieves are not hanged so much as they were in the formal frontier era, so earmarking them is seen as the next best thing.

Dang Mi was certainly not the first horse thief to adopt a change of career. He was probably not even the first horse thief to turn pirate. But from such humble beginnings, he had certainly ranged far from his native badlands.

Dang Mi's finger had been in many a darksome mystery in its time. But it had never touched anything quite the equal of the enigma of the infernal Buddha.

THE mystery made its advent in the guise of an airplane which came buzzing out of the north.

The instant he heard the plane, Dang Mi bounced up from baking his hide in the brazen Oriental sun. He ripped orders. The *Devilfish's* radio operator got busy.

The *Devilfish,* for all the fact that she was a fat-bottomed junk, and equipped with a brace of old-fashioned smoothbore deck cannon concealed by removable iron shields affixed to her gunwales, had her modern aspects. Dang Mi was an up-to-date rascal. Fastened to the hull was a submarine listening device, as sensitive as money could buy, which could pick up the noise of any vessel within a good many miles and, furthermore, give a general idea of its location. The radio installation was also complete for short or long wavelengths.

"I think the perishin' plane must be off a British Navy hooker," said Dang, who had picked up a sprinkling of British slang during his sojourn in this corner of the globe. "Listen for the noise of a cutter's screws. Sparks, you fish around with the bloomin' radio and see if the plane reports our location."

The interval immediately following was a tense one. The British Navy had of late years inaugurated a disquieting habit of sending a search plane to spot a suspicious vessel and radio its location to a Customs cutter. Dang Mi feared that was happening now.

Aboard the *Devilfish* at the moment were a half-dozen assorted aliens, all destined for surreptitious landing on the Malay coast. Not the least member of this little group was a gentleman known as "Poetical" Percival Perkins, a gangling lad who recited poetry and swindled people with about equal skill.

No, it would be unfortunate if the British customs authorities searched the *Devilfish* just now.

UP until this point, the plane had been a noise in the fog, no more. A throaty, firm noise, such as would be made by a good speed-cowled motor with many big cylinders. The British Navy had such motors, which was, in truth, what had alarmed Dang Mi, formerly Hen Gooch. He had made a study of British Navy planes for the same reason that a burglar entering a strange town looks around to see what kind of uniforms the cops wear.

Dang Mi knew the plane was more likely to see them than they were to see the plane, the *Devilfish* being the larger. This was the case. Abruptly, the plane tilted one wing down and the other up, and began circling their position curiously. It reminded Dang of a big bumblebee swinging on the end of a string.

"Sit tight, you brown blokes," Dang Mi warned his crew and passengers, all of whom had meantime donned conical bamboo coolie hats to look like innocent Chinese seafarers. A few were adorned with appropriate pigtails.

The name of the ebony vessel had been changed for the moment, also, by substituting a canvas strip across the stern nameplate. The identification forward had been altered likewise.

These precautions were old stuff and might fool the British Navy, or might not. These waters are overflowing with two-masted fishing junks, their seaworthiness being first-rate.

"Blast the dang world," gritted Dang Mi, for the moment mixing his Limehouse with his Pumpkin Buttes, Wyoming, from which he originally hailed.

The plane was going to land. It swooped close to the mast tops and the pilot leaned out of the cabin window and with an arm made gestures indicating his intention.

Dang Mi had been blessed by nature with intensely black hair that enabled him to pass for Chinese, Malay or Indo-Chinese as the situation required. He felt like tearing out some of that hair now. The plane overhead did not have the regulation markings, but it was the same type of plane used by the British Navy, so Dang Mi had no doubts.

"Break out Iron Mike," rapped Dang.

IN seaman's parlance, an "Iron Mike" is the telegraph instrument used to signal the engine room crew. The *Devilfish* was hardly large enough to require such a convenience, but Dang liked the appellation.

In this case, Iron Mike was actually a Maxim machine gun. Crew used pry bars to expose the concealed deck well in which it was normally stored, and set it up. When they were done, the bulky, serrated barrel assembly jutted forward of the tripod mount. Hard, ugly with the canvas gullet of a brass catcher hanging empty by the breech. Extra ammunition sat handy in gunny sacks on either side of the weapon.

"No sign of a cutter over the listener," reported the Malay who had been at the submarine detector.

"Plane not using ladio," advised Sparks, a Chinese, whom everyone except Dang invariably called "Spalks."

"Which makes her a bit of all right," leered the renowned Dang. "He ain't reported us. 'Twouldn't surprise me none if he didn't."

Dang Mi's men, all of whom were Asiatics, heartily wished they had never seen the fat, peaceful looking white man whom they had decided was no less than their tribal earth devil come to life, and who was their captain, incidentally, without paying them.

They waved their arms. But they did not wave them fast

enough for Captain Dang Mi, who hauled two nickel-plated six-shooters from leather holsters hanging from his bullet-stuffed cartridge belt, and began to shoot. He fired first one gun, then the other. He pierced an ear here, stung the bottom of a foot there. It was amazingly accurate two-handed shooting.

The pirates waved arms as if lives depended on it, which they conceivably did.

And with that, Dang Mi leathered his smoking pistols and pointed the Maxim at the plane, which was making another trip over the mast hounds. He came down hard on the arrangement which served as a trigger.

The Maxim bucked, stuttered, and hot brass shell casings filled the brass-catcher with a busy clinking. Dang shook so hard he was forced to close his artificially-slanted eyes.

When he opened them he saw that the active half of the bullets had found resting places in the tiny plane's cowl. It was now as perforated as the top of a salt shaker. A piece of Dural metal hung loose, flapping in the slipstream. The plane banked; it went flying away, falling like an autumn leaf.

"Dang!" said Dang Mi. "Her bloody prop's still turning!"

It was. The blades and shiny spinner seemed to have escaped the leaden storm unscathed.

Dang watched with one eye beginning to droop—a nuisance that plagued him whenever the collodion lost its fixative strength. His broad face reflected unhappiness when he saw that the tiny craft was banking again.

"What's he up to?" Dang muttered, shading his eyes.

Then he saw. The plane was coming closer. Its engine began to labor. There was smoke about the riddled cowl.

"He must like catching lead in his snout," Dang muttered.

"In a little while," put in Poetical Percival, "he might alight on that isle."

"Huh?"

Dang looked over his shoulder. There was an island, one of the many dotting this patch of the South China Sea. Through the fog, it was visible as a shadowy hump.

Abruptly, the noise of the airplane motor cut out completely.

"Make for that dang isle quick-like!" Dang shouted. "*Berhenti!* Chop-chop!" he added for the benefit of his mixed crew.

The junk-hands got to their business. The engines kicked into life and the *Devilfish* nosed towards it. It was not going fast enough for Dang Mi, however.

Dang ran out into the open foredeck, paused to judge the progress of the airplane and the distance to the isle. He was close enough to the isle to see, dimly visible through the fog, that there was beach enough to accept a troubled aircraft—if the pilot were brave enough or desperate enough to chance it.

He was. It was immediately evident that the plane would land.

"Drop anchor here!" Dang howled. And without removing the pistols jammed in his belt, he leapt into the sea. He immediately struck out for the isle.

HAD Dang Mi known what the plane was bringing him, and what was to come of it, he would undoubtedly have gotten up and fled, even taking his chances with the British authorities.

But he didn't. So he swam like a man possessed.

He only stopped when the faint shadow of the silent plane passed over his head. After that, he trod water and watched, completely unaware that his lungs were not working.

The pilot attempted to fishtail air speed away, narrowly missed a wingover, pancaked violently, careened along for a time and left his landing gear sticking in the soft ground. The plane shed one wing, then the other. The propeller beat itself into a frightful-looking twist. The plane slid on its belly to a dusty conclusion and the wrecking was over.

A protracted silence followed. Fog and dust, agitated by the violence of the plane's unorthodox landing, hung about the wreck like a creeping dun-colored ghost.

Somewhere inland, a sound like a tiger snarling broke the silence. It might possibly have been an actual tiger, too. There were tigers in these islands. The name Singapore had come from the Sanskrit words, *Singa Purha,* which translated as "The Lion City." Whoever it was who had named the city originally, hadn't known the difference. But Captain Dang Mi and his cut-throats were not thinking of lions or tigers at that moment. They were watching the plane.

As they watched, the cabin door was flung upward, disturbing the hovering spook of fog and dust.

A figure stepped out. A man. He clutched a box of some blue crackle-finished metal. It was large but, from the way the man carried it did not seem heavy. It might have been empty. Except that the man held it with a certain care, one arm wrapped over and around it, as if fearful of the lid flying up.

He paused to look into the gaping cabin.

Then a second figure stumbled out of the wreck to join the first. This second figure appeared identical to the first, except that it did not carry a blue box.

Both figures wore odd garments of a single piece that sheathed their bodies from neck to shoe soles. Black was the color of these garments. They rather resembled atmosphere suits, such as are worn by balloonists who venture into the high regions of the stratosphere, where the air is too thin to breathe. Regulation oxygen apparatus completed the remarkable picture.

They seemed utterly unhurt, and even from a distance, not much perturbed by their near brush with death.

The second figure reached back over its shoulders with both hands and drew up a hood-like affair that matched the rest of the garment as to color and texture, except for the square aperture that left the face visible.

Visible, but not exposed, it became clear when the figure reached over to pull the first figure's weird hood into place. Sunlight glancing off the aperture showed it to be sealed with Cellophane or some other transparent material.

It seemed as if the first figure had required the assistance because he was afraid to let go of the tightly-held box.

Noticing this, Dang Mi had the thought enter his head that there was something in the box that its possessor was afraid would get loose.

He started to swim for the wreck.

That was when matters began assuming peculiar proportions.

Chapter II

BOX BIZARRE

"TWINS!" EXPLODED DANG MI.

That was it. Twins. Girl and boy. Young, white—and as almond-eyed as Manchus. Eurasians. One could almost pass for the other. They stood atop the wrecked plane, braced against the settling of the craft, and looked and acted as if nothing had happened, which was strange, since they must surely know that machine-gun bullets had brought their ship down. There were enough bullet holes in the cowl.

Wading ashore on the sandy beach, Dang Mi mentally chalked up a mistake against himself. These were not British bluejackets.

"Stay back, please," suggested the man-twin in perfect, if oddly accented, English.

Dang Mi was startled into doing so by the utter calmness of the request.

"Who're you toffs?" asked Dang sourly.

"We're the Chans," the pair replied in one perfectly synchronized voice.

"Eh?"

"The Chans. Haven't you heard of us?"

"No," admitted Dang Mi.

"We didn't think you had," they assured him calmly. Their easy way of speaking in unison was striking—not to mention weird. They might have shared one brain between them.

Dang Mi glowered. It was a funny time for kidding, and it

certainly looked as if they were kidding him.

He started forward, his boots making mushy sucking noises in the wet sand of the beach.

"If you come any closer—" the man-twin warned.

"—we will open up the box," finished the girl-twin.

"You wouldn't want that," added the man-twin.

"Definitely, you wouldn't," the girl said firmly.

"Us rovers are kinda like raccoons," Dang announced.

What he meant by that was that he knew it was incongruous that his most intense curiosity should be aroused by the one thing in evidence that was sealed, when there was so much else that he didn't understand.

Dang asked a perfectly natural question, given his avaricious disposition.

"What's in that dang box, anyway?"

"A terrible thing," said the man-twin.

"A wonderful thing," said the girl-twin, her voice blending in with her twin's, except on the middle spoken word.

Dang grunted. "Well, which is it?" he demanded.

"Both," they replied.

"In that case," said Dang, whipping out his pistols, "it's all mine." He started to advance, the dry portion of the beach crunching under his hard heels.

That was when the man-twin whose name was Chan opened the blue box.

He didn't do it right away. First, he threw on his hood. The girl did, too. Hastily, she fastened it about her throat, and went to make her twin's hood fast.

Then, with incredible calmness considering the eerie violence of what next transpired, the man-twin opened the box.

He opened it only a crack. The crack was pointed in Dang Mi's specific direction.

Dang narrowed his one slanted eye at the crack expectantly. He cocked the pistol. He planned to shoot whatever came out of the blue box, if necessary.

But nothing came out of the box.

Instead, the moist white atmosphere of fog surrounding them all began to move. Like a great ghost impelled by an unfelt wind, it surged toward the odd duo. The cottony stuff gathered speed. The Chans were instantly lost from sight, consumed in a ball of the stuff.

As Dang watched, his droopy eye popped open in shock.

One moment, he was striding through a cool world of mist. Then next, it was clear. And the fog was—incredibly—pouring into the blue box as if fleeing the realm of normalcy. There was no mistaking what was happening. The box—or something inside the box, Dang suddenly realized—was consuming the thick fog with greedy voraciousness.

The ball of fog rapidly thinned, revealing the Chans, standing cool, calm and collected. In their coverall garments, they resembled a pair of sleek-skinned ebony seals.

Fleet tendrils of white mist slipped into the blue box. When the last wisps withdrew from sight, the box was clapped shut.

Dang Mi no longer cared by that time. He was running, running for the water with both hands clutching his throat, his pistols tossed carelessly in the sand.

Out of his open mouth came a croaking. One word. He could barely get it out.

"Water," was the word Dang Mi croaked.

When he reached the surf he threw himself in with a great splashing. On his hands and knees, he began drinking brine in great sobbing gulps. This went on for nearly a minute.

When Dang had had his fill, he stood up. He was facing the *Devilfish,* now visible through remarkably clear air that had moments before been befogged. Beyond the ship, not a little ways, fog hung low. It seemed to drift closer, as if curious, toward the clear void that had been so misty moments before.

Poetical Percival Perkins stood on the rail. On either side were Dang's cut-throats. Their eyes were so wide their bland faces lost all Asiatic semblance.

"Drinking raw brine," Poetical Percival called out, "will never turn out fine."

Dang Mi's narrow eyes popped and he made some noises remindful of a man who had a chicken bone crosswise of his throat.

"Ark—ark—wawk!" described his vocal reactions approximately.

"What did you say?" Perkins shouted.

"I said," Dang jerked out, "I was thirst-struck."

"Eh?"

"I said, I was overcome by a dang powerful thirst," reiterated Dang Mi.

"I never heard of a seaman who didn't know enough not to swallow sea water. It'll only make you thirstier, you know."

"I know that, dang it!" Dang exploded. "Never felt the like of it, before. I thought I'd die if I didn't fill me belly."

"You'll wish for death once your belly starts to ache," Poetical Percival offered. Then he looked queer. His expression halted Dang, who was in the act of expectorating salty sea water from his mouth.

"What is it?" Dang demanded.

"I felt it, too."

"Felt what?"

"A sudden thirst."

"If you felt what I felt, you'd have yourself a belly brimming with brine, by now. Mark me, you would," said Dang Mi.

"It's like I hadn't had a drop in days," Percival went on, "but I took a swig less that an hour ago. And it's not hot at all."

Then it developed that the crew of the *Devilfish* were also thirst-struck. They were passing a canteen from hand to hand. When the canteen came to Poetical Percival, he swallowed his share.

Seeing this activity only made Dang Mi all the more eager

to get back to his ship.

"Get a dink down," Dang called. "This isle is hoodooed."

"What happened to the fog?" asked Percival, wiping his mouth on his sleeve.

"I'll tell you, but you won't bleedin' believe me."

"Skies go clear, bring on fear," Percival murmured, and strode to the stern, beckoning to the cut-throats to aid him. They did, and he launched a dinghy. Some of the crew got in and Perkins lowered it to the sea on the opposite side of the ship. Up until the boat was lowered, operations were in full view of the two almond-eyed twins on the plane, for they stood on top of the downed aircraft, which was high enough to see the junk's deck.

"While you're at it," ordered the man-twin in a voice that carried despite his all-enveloping suit, "get another boat over the side, or we'll open the box again."

"And don't think we don't mean it," added the girl-twin.

Dang Mi's brown neck was purple and he glared and made gravelly noises in his teeth.

"I won't," he choked.

"Don't be a damned fool," called the man-twin. "You can reach Singapore in the small boats."

He lifted the cumbersome box for emphasis. That unremarkable gesture was all that was required.

Two dinghies were lowered. Poetical Percival took command of one. He sent it putt-putting toward Dang, who had not moved from where he stood, knee-deep in the gentle surf. He seemed afraid to step back on the island.

The strange pair who called themselves the Chans worked their way down to the beach. The man-twin Chan carried the blue box before him in both hands. Earlier, he had handled it as if it contained something delicate. Now he carried it as if it were somehow heavier than before, and more unwieldy.

THE dinks were beached with a grating noise. The corsairs of Dang Mi stepped out, looking anxious. They muttered among themselves.

Last to step off was Poetical Percival. He had remained seated in the rear, at the motor, his hands out of sight, as the Malays grouped themselves near their chieftain, Dang.

Once Percival joined them, the Chans went to claim the dory. The girl clambered aboard while the man held the blue box in a manner suggesting a shield.

"Give it here, twin," the girl said, reaching out her clumsy-looking gloved hands.

"Careful," said the other, handing over the box. "Don't drop it. Especially with all this water around."

"Water?" Percival said.

"If it falls into water—" the girl said, accepting the box.

"—the world could come to an end," finished the man. His voice did not sound facetious in any way. In fact, it had a grimly-worried timbre to it.

This impressed Dang Mi. "Didn't Pandora have a box like that, so the stories go?"

"You'll be able to reach Singapore in that dink," the man-twin said as he took hold of the steering post of the motor. "Now give us a shove."

Dang and Percival fell to pushing on the dory's prow. The boat backed into the water, became buoyant, and the man-twin sent it puttering around in a circle.

They managed to complete the circle before the girl noticed the dory was filling with water.

The girl gave a very creditable shriek. It would have peeled copra from a halved coconut.

"We're sinking!" she moaned. "Back to shore—quick!"

"Keep the box shut!" the other howled, as he wrestled the steering post around.

"Come on!" Percival shouted, whipping his long form for the beached dink. Dang pounded after him.

"Petcock?" he puffed.

"Opened it before I got out," Percival gasped.

They shoved off and were soon within grabbing distance of the returning dory.

"Get out of the way!" the man-twin yelled. "We have to reach dry land!"

"You'll never make it," Percival retorted. "Surrender the box!"

"Never!" the girl-twin snapped.

"Do you want to world to come to an end?" Percival shouted back.

"What're you tryin' to pull?" Dang asked hoarsely.

"String along," Percival undertoned gruffly. "The box is as good as ours."

Dang shut up. The two boats were on a collision course. Disaster seemed inevitable. The water was sloshing about the dory's interior noisily. It began to wallow.

The Chans, their faces visible behind the clear ports of their protective hoods, wore expressions of utter terror. The girl clung to the blue box on her lap, leaning on the lid, as if she feared it as much as wanting to protect it from the rising waters.

"You've only got seconds!" Poetical Percival warned. "Surrender the box or the worst happens!"

The dory was dead in the water now. The only direction in which it was moving was down—straight down to the bottom.

"Give them the box," the man-twin said in hoarse agony.

"But they're—"

"Do it!"

The box was handed over. Dang took it. It did not weigh much, but it was not light, either. He set it carefully on his lap and placed his elbows on the lid to keep it down. His skin was beginning the crawl, and he wasn't sure why. The box was cool to the touch—too cool.

The twins were scrambling from the sinking dory now. It went down under them and they floated there, treading water.

Poetical Percival produced a pistol and employed the business end to menace the almond-orbed twins. The latter held up their hands, and continued treading water.

"Act in haste, repent in Hell," warned Poetical Percival, indicating with a waggling of his gun that the pair were to come aboard the dink.

The strangely-garbed twins clambered aboard and sat down meekly. They remained in that attitude until the dink was back on the beach and they were all standing on dry land once more.

There, the pair were ordered out of their coverall suits. They complied in sullen, apprehensive silence. Their eyes were a little sick about the edges. They did not take them off the blue box.

Once shed of their unusual garments, they stood clad in nothing more extraordinary than tropical cotton shirts with short khaki pants suitable for a jungle trek. Their skins were smooth and possessed a tint that was something like dusky ivory. Their matching eyes resembled ripe olives. Both sets of orbs regarded their captor with an identical narrow regard that was unnervingly catlike.

"Now what—" began the man-twin.

"—will you do with us?" continued the girl-twin.

"As if we couldn't guess," finished the man-twin.

"If you guessed that we'd dry-gulch you on this godforsaken isle," Dang said, rubbing his already-aching belly, "you guessed dang right."

The lengthening faces of the twins told that this was what they had guessed. Exactly.

"There's ample time," interrupted Poetical Percival, "to commit that crime."

"What good are they?" Dang shot back. "We got the blasted box."

"Do we know what's in it? Besides fog, that is?"

"No," Dang was forced to admit.

"Then they live," Percival said firmly and his eyes met Dang's without flinching.

Ordinarily, Dang Mi took orders from no one, and was further inclined to do something violent to anyone rash enough to suggest what he should do. But Poetical Percival had just raked his chestnuts out of the fire, so he merely scowled and gestured that the white-skinned Oriental twins should be made to accompany them.

Corsairs surrounded the odd pair. They allowed themselves to be marched back to the wreck of their plane under the points of unsettling wavy-bladed Malay daggers called *krises*.

Poetical Percival heaved himself upon the plane in a manner which showed that, for a gawky human beanpole, he was physically strong. Instead of climbing onto the ungainly craft, he went to work searching the plane, probably for loot.

It was then that Poetical Percival Perkins got a hint of the fabulous thing that was the mystery of the infernal Buddha, as it was later known.

Poetical Percival had been inside the plane cabin, rifling it for perhaps five minutes before he popped out. His mouse-shaped mouth was pinched tight. His face was several shades paler than before.

"Better take a look," he told Dang Mi, in his agitation forgetting his rhymes.

Dang put his head in. A notebook was held up to his face, the pages open to his eyes. He began reading.

For some time, he remained as a man in a trance, half in, half out of the ship. He withdrew his head, and he looked wide-eyed, startled. His lips moved as if making words, but the sounds did not come out.

His pirates, who had drawn near, became frightened at this unusual behavior by a man hitherto without fear. The brown men retreated uneasily—but were careful not to flee all the way into the jungle, for the good reason that some of their companions had been shot for trying to escape. They greatly feared fat, innocent-looking Dang Mi, and they were literally his slaves.

"Hah!" Dang snorted. "This stuff don't sound reasonable!"

He had the notebook clutched in one plump fist. He cracked it open and started perusing it from the first page. He kept on reading.

DANG MI did not look up from the words for a long time. His eyes were distinctly popping.

The pirates exchanged ugly looks. One ran a finger along his *kris'* razor edge, then cast a meaning glance at the exposed back of Dang Mi's unprotected neck. Mutiny was in their vicious eyes.

Poetical Percival Perkins made a throat-clearing noise that was entirely unheard by the absorbed pirate chieftain.

Then they all squirmed and looked afraid, and fell to peering at the strange twins. One reached down and touched the Eurasian girl's hair, then drew his hand back as if he had been stung when Dang Mi suddenly yelled, and spun about.

He was staring at the girl.

"Dang my soul, the thing must be true!"

They returned to the *Devilfish* in relays, using the little dink.

Chapter III

INTO THE FIRE

IN DANG MI'S cabin was a hidden safe. A stout one, modern. They locked the strange blue box in that. The notebook they kept out, poring over it for the better portion of an hour.

The almond-eyed Chans stared at them levelly when the pirate pair came slinking into the main cabin, in which they had been kept under guard. Dang Mi and Poetical Percival looked happy enough to purr.

"You've been in Shanghai," Dang accused the Chans.

"Making experiments," said Percival.

"With the Buddha's Toe," added Dang.

The Chans looked at each other, their heads swiveling around as if working off one mechanism. They tried to swap grins. These didn't quite come off.

"So you're wise," growled the man-twin.

"We hope so," said Poetical Percival.

"What are you going to do about it?" the girl-twin asked calmly.

"All we can," said Dang Mi.

There was no more to the conversation. The Chans were hauled forward to a cubicle which was normally a cargo hold, for cargo of a nature that was best locked up, lest the crew drink too much of it. This room, in the present situation, doubled excellently as a prison.

"What'll we do with 'em?" Poetical Percival wanted to know.

He and Dang Mi had formed a partnership. No words had been exchanged to that effect. It was simply understood.

"Keep 'em until we get our hands on this blasted Buddha business," said Dang.

"This thing is big."

"This thing," echoed Dang Mi, "is dang sure to get even bigger."

"Do we open the box?"

Dang shook his head. "Not until we know exactly what it is we're loosing on this poor world." He clutched his throat. "I don't want what happened to me to happen again."

And Dang Mi let his soft body shudder like blood pudding in an earthquake.

IN the cubicle below, the Chans listened to the sounds coming from deck. Noises of a ship being readied to depart. A protracted clanking, grinding noise reverberated. They could feel it from the soles of their feet to their back teeth. The *Devilfish* was weighing anchor.

The busy padding of feet on deck soon abated, and was replaced by the rushing gurgle of water against the junk's awkward hull. The engine voiced a constant, monotonous thrum.

"The captain of this ark is no Samaritan, Mary," said the almond-eyed man-twin.

"What a break for us, Mark," said the girl-twin, wryly.

"They're wise."

"Of course."

"An unscrupulous devil like this could make millions out of it."

The girl nodded. "It's sort of out of the pan and into the fire for us."

"Now, Mary," muttered Mark Chan. "You're hinting again that Startell Pompman intends to freeze us out. I wish you would stop these insinuations."

The girl sniffed.

"I'll stop insinuating," she said flatly. "From now on, I'm going to state it as a fact. Startell Pompman is as big a crook as any man on this boat. When we picked him for a backer, we certainly reached out and got a lemon."

"You can't prove that."

"True, brother, true indeed. But you wouldn't call my suspicions anything less than profound."

Sounds continued filtering down from above. Bare feet slapped and whetted the deck as the crew went about the task of managing the great sepia sails. Commands ripped out in assorted tongues.

At length, the *Devilfish* was under weigh.

"Dammit," said Mark Chan forlornly. "I wish we hadn't got lost in that fog and started to land by this old junk to find out where we were and where Singapore was."

"Echo," agreed Mary Chan.

They sat in silence and gloom for a while. It was hot. The place smelled. They were miserable.

"Whoops!" said the girl-twin unexpectedly. "Cheers and jubilation."

"Eh?"

"I have an idea," said Mary Chan. "Listen."

Mark Chan listened, and heard his twin lay down a neat little scheme—neat if it worked—which was to lead them to Colonel John "Renny" Renwick, and through him to that fabulous person, Doc Savage, although the two prisoners had no inkling that it was going to turn out this way.

THERE was a guard stationed outside the cabin. He was unarmed, there being no need for firearms in order to guard two prisoners. He did have a belaying pin stuffed into the elastic waistband of his loose coolie trousers. It was hidden from sight due to the Chinese habit of wearing the shirt tails untucked.

The Chinese passed his time masticating gum-blackening

betel nut, and squirting red streams of juice from between the gap in his front teeth into a brass gobboon.

Came sounds from behind the cabin door. Splintery noises. In the middle of expectorating a stream of juice, the guard turned—thereby coating walls and floor with blood-colored liquid.

Directly, the sentry heard more sounds. This time crashes. Glass breaking. And pooling out from under the door of the cabin, oozed a pungent brown liquid.

Realizing that the strange prisoners were desecrating the *Devilfish's* stock of liquid refreshments, the guard emitted a cackling shriek and fell to unlocking the door.

The lock surrendered and, pulling out his belaying pin, the guard stepped in.

He experienced two simultaneous inconveniences. His legs tripped him up and something broke over his head and assisted him in completing his tumble to the floor.

He landed on his back, shaking warm liquor out of his hair. He looked up to see Mary Chan extracting another bottle of spirits from the splintered packing case. The one that had shattered over his skull finished its breaking when it struck the floor.

They began a great fight.

By now, the guard knew that the twins had stretched a line made of their belts across the cell in front of the door, and he, like a blind clown, had fallen over it. The cut-throat fought handsomely to redeem himself. Dang Mi was not always kidding when he talked about skinning a man alive. The noise of the fight filled that part of the junk.

Pirates began to yell and run toward the spot. They had heard the war.

"Beat it—Mary!" gasped the man-twin, Mark Chan.

At first glance, it does not seem very heroic to run off and leave your twin engaged in a fight. But there was no question about the nerve of either of these twins. They had demonstrated that. And the girl could see that the guard was wiry and as tough as nails and they couldn't whip him in time for them both to get away. But one might make it. So she tried.

She ducked out, dived down a passage. Ahead, she heard noise. Bare feet smacking companion steps. The passage, of course, had electric lights. Shouting could be heard coming from the other direction. The way to the deck was blocked.

Fine white teeth worrying her lower lip, Mary Chan hesitated. Her liquid dark eyes fastened on an inviting cabin door. She tried it. Not locked. Bounding in, she saw that it was another store room.

There was a single porthole—highly unusual on a junk. She glided to this.

Ship portholes are not normally sufficient to allow a human form to pass through. But Mary Chan was a little trick of a girl, after the Oriental fashion, and too, the *Devilfish* was no pleasure vessel. Contraband such as the junk ran sometimes had to be ejected overboard in a violent and unprofitable rush.

The porthole was of a diameter that allowed her shoulders and hips—the widest parts of her frame—to slip through once she had made the former small by lifting her arms over her head, and sticking them out the open aperture.

Setting both elbows and palms against the outer hull, Mary Chan began applying herself to the task. After that, it was only a matter of wriggling and squirming while shutting out the rollicking sounds of fight and chaos.

The splash she made entering the water went unnoticed amid the commotion of combat. She surfaced and fell into an animated dogpaddle calculated to make the most headway with the least splashing.

Mary Chan had struck out on a swim for shore and what, although she didn't know it, was a quest to enlist the aid of Doc Savage, the Man of Bronze, as he was sometimes called. The beginning of the quest, rather.

SINGAPORE HARBOR has for centuries been noted for

two things, among others. Filthy water. Sharks. The water is not so bad nowadays, since they have taken to hauling their garbage out to sea. But the sharks still hang around. There is a lot of argument about whether or not sharks will attack a human. Some will. Some won't. It depends on the breed. These were the kind that would. But they didn't. The girl swam to shore without mishap. She kept all her clothes on. Modern girls do not wear much that will interfere with swimming. Besides, she would need them when she got ashore.

Singapore Harbor is usually thick with rake-masted junks, canoe-like *tambangs*, canvas-covered sampans called *perahus* and other boats that seldom if ever hoist anchor inasmuch as they serve as houseboats. And there is good holding ground farther out for layover docking.

Mary Chan negotiated between these more sparse anchorages, swimming with a practiced ease that made no more splashing than playful leaping fish. The channel she swam along was suitably dark on an ordinary night, draped as it is in moon shadow.

The murk accounted for no one seeing Mary Chan.

Once ashore, she worked down to the waterfront, coming to a wharf where the double-ended little water taxis used by British soldiers and tourists in cruising the harbor were moored. The coolie belonging to the one she hired was not too curious about the water-soaked young lady who was his fare. The unusual often happens in Singapore. Too, Mary Chan spoke perfect Malayan and the darkness made her ivory skin less obvious.

At the Singapore waterfront, Mary Chan paid him with a bill from a small roll which had been hidden in her hair, and she demanded and got her change, which made the coolie angry.

This put the coolie in a cooperative frame of mind several hours later, when a Cockney Englishman accosted him with questions.

"Hi'm lookin' for a little slip of a Chink girl," explained the supposed Englishman. "Had kinda pale skin, like a white woman.

She'd be likely to be soaked from a swim, she would."

The coolie acted thoughtful, and the supposed Englishman greased his palm with silver. The coolie took hold of his jaw and looked up at the moon, as if prodding his memory. He kept his hand extended.

The Cockney swapped the silver coin for a gold sovereign, the weight of which seemed to have remarkable tongue-loosening properties. Once the coolie had bitten the coin to assure himself it was genuine, his cackling was voluble.

"Thank you, my man," said the Cockney. He waited until the coolie had stepped back into his boat before jumping down after him and braining him with the bamboo pole normally employed to propel the awkward craft.

Kneeling at the almost nonexistent rail, Dang Mi—he looked more like Hen Gooch now—held the slumped form of the insensate coolie out of the foul water while he fished about for his gold coin.

Once he had it in hand, he let the man slide into the water, and calmly counted the bubbles until they stopped.

THE girl had by this time secured a fair lead, but the hour was late, and no great number of people were abroad. There had, in recent months, been a reign of curfews with a deadline at midnight, at which hour citizens had to be off the streets. This had somewhat discouraged nocturnal meanderings, and people had not yet resumed the habit.

Mary Chan understood that she would not be hard to locate by cars cruising the narrow streets, provided she kept moving about. Her wet garments would also attract attention. She chose a dimly-lit restaurant in the business section, one with a lot of ornamental flowers, and ducked into a particularly shadowy cranny without anyone noting anything unusual. Being wise, she ordered food, for she had been without viands for some time. She also bought a local English-language newspaper, intending to pretend to read it while her clothes dried.

The purchase of that newspaper was an act destined to affect a good many thousands of lives. Men were to die because of it. Others were to live. And it involved the man of miracles, Doc Savage, in an uncanny mystery.

Chapter IV
BIG FISTS

THE SIGNIFICANT AND resultful item was on the front page of the *Singapore Gazette.*

DOC SAVAGE ASSISTANT ARRIVES

It has been learned that the American engineer, Colonel John Renwick, has taken up residence in the Raffles Hotel for an indefinite stay.

The name of Colonel John Renwick is one spoken with renown throughout the civilized world. His engineering feats are legendary. In that regard, he is considered almost without peer. He is also a notable adventure-seeker, when he is not engaged in his profession.

For Colonel Renwick is famed as an associate of Doc Savage, worker of seeming miracles. It is taken for granted that many residents of Singapore have heard of Doc Savage.

Doc Savage, Man of Bronze and individual of more or less mystery, is a fellow to whom fantastic things often happen. Little is known of him, because he goes to great lengths to keep out of the public eye. It is, however, well known that he is almost a physical marvel and a mental genius.

Doc Savage's profession is undoubtedly the strangest thing about him. Trouble is his specialty—other people's trouble. He is something of a knight in armor, who travels to the far corners of the earth to aid the oppressed, to right wrongs and to war upon those who operate outside the law.

Doc Savage, it is understood, does not work for pay. Yet, he always had fabulous sums at his command. The source of his wealth is a mystery.

At present, Colonel Renwick is in Singapore to organize construction of a rubber plantation railway. The Hotel Raffles will be his headquarters for the duration of his work here.

There was more of it. The newshawk who had written that story must have been an ardent admirer of Doc Savage. The news story was more about Doc Savage than it concerned Colonel John Renwick.

The item asserted that Doc Savage was a modern wonder man. He had evidently mastered all sciences, from aeronautics to atomic theory. He was called Doc, however, because of his surgical skill. But he was no runty super-brain. His physical development was said to be prodigious.

Mary Chan decided that if half of what was being said about Doc Savage were factual, he was harbinger of what men would be like in the twenty-first century—a combination of Hercules, Sir Galahad and Thomas Edison.

"How very interesting," she said, beginning to murmur to herself. "I had been planning to talk to the British authorities about this. They would know what to do."

She frowned, and read the item again.

"On the other hand," she declared, "I know nothing of this Doc Savage. I have never even heard of him before."

She sat back and contemplated her shapely hand. Her nails needed a do, she decided.

"I've got to stop talking to myself," she announced firmly, "and start doing things."

She paid her bill and commandeered a jinricksaw taxi. Dodging autos, trams, and hurling over the ubiquitous open monsoon drainage culverts, it deposited her before the Hotel Raffles after a bumpy ride that included being dragged up flights of stone steps—much of Singapore being built along vertical lines.

At first, the very British clerk—Singapore is a British protectorate, after all—pretended not to have heard of any Colonel

John Renwick.

"I believe in getting to the point," Mary Chan told him.

"A sterling attitude," agreed the clerk.

"I have only to-night learned of the existence of Colonel John Renwick and, believe it or not, have never heard of Doc Savage, but I believe Doc Savage is the only man who can avert the calamity."

This caught the desk man's attention.

"What calamity?" he enquired.

"The end of civilization," said Mary Chan in an earnest tone of voice.

The desk man stared at her a long time.

Mary Chan asked, "Do you think this is a matter that would interest Doc Savage?"

"Undoubtedly," said the clerk, scrutinizing Mary Chan's attractive ivory-complected face.

"Do you think I could see Colonel Renwick?"

"I should," said the clerk with resignation in his voice, "be afraid to say otherwise."

"Thank you," said Mary upon receiving the room number. It was on the third floor so she took the stairs.

COLONEL RENWICK threw open the door after the second knock. He was a towering hulk of a man who had to look down to see who had come calling.

"Hello, Renny," said Mary Chan, walking in and shutting the door.

Colonel Renwick was surprised. Speechless at first. Then he got suspicious.

"Holy cow!" he said. "What's your game? I never saw you before."

He had a rumbling voice that brought to mind something in a cave, and a long puritanical face that appeared constructed for the express purpose of attending funerals.

"Have a seat," said Mary Chan, taking one herself.

Renny pulled his dressing gown more securely about him.

"I," he said, "am not a ladies' man. I'm going to throw you out of here on your ear."

"Would a million dollars interest you?" asked Mary Chan.

"No," said Renny. "I've got a million dollars. After you get it, it sort of loses its kick."

It was the truth. About the million, that is.

"It's my million," said Mary Chan. "My brother's and mine. They are trying to take it away from us. I think a good many people are going to get killed. My brother first, then others."

"Holy cow!" rumbled Renny again. It was Renny's pet ejaculation, and he applied it to anything that disturbed him.

"The thing involved is—"

Mary Chan stopped. She had glimpsed Renny's hands. Those hands frequently rendered people speechless. They were fantastic fists, being composed of fully a quart of hard bone and gristle. The Cardiff Giant, probably, had possessed such hands.

"Uh-h-h-h," said Mary Chan, clearing her throat. "I—ah, well, I need Doc Savage's help. He can save lives, my brother's for one. And he can give to the world something that, if *it* gets in the wrong hands, might conceivably change the whole course of civilization. *It* could incite wars, cause calamities. The possibilities for trouble are practically unlimited."

Renny stared at her. Closely, critically. He shook his long-faced head slowly.

"I guess you're not," he said.

"Not what?"

"Nuts. You sound like it. But you better line your story up so it makes sense, or I'll be inclined to decide you're an imbecile."

Mary Chan snapped, "It's big. It's bad."

It was. Renny learned that an instant later, when, with a startling crash, the door fell down. The door was rickety, anyway, and three men had hit it with their shoulders, simultaneously.

The trio shoved in. One was a squat Malay wearing a blue muslin turban and a dirty loincloth whose waistband bristled with numerous saw-tooth knives. Another was tall, thin and very white.

But it was the third of the trio whose appearance captured Renny's immediate attention. He was a rather round fellow, evidently white, but possessing the white-brown skin of inhabitants of this corner of Asia, with a pair of very Western six-shooters jutting incongruously from his calloused fists.

The words tumbling from his lips were not in keeping with his exotic appearance, either.

"Have a care, Big Fists. We come for the girl, and there'll be no trouble from the likes o' you."

Renny blocked and unblocked his huge fists. It was typical of the big-fisted engineer that he was going to tackle the trio with his bare hands. He had unbounded confidence in those gargantuan fists, and not without reason. It was Renny's boast that no wooden door had a panel so stout that he could not wreck it with one blow from either fist.

MARY CHAN had been a little soldier up to this point. No tears. No hysterics. But now something went snap, and she let out a shriek and dived for the window. Anyone could see that she was wild for the moment, and was going to jump through the window. It was on the third story, with hard cobbled street below. It might kill her.

So Renny tripped her. She fell, hit a chair, and writhed on the floor, stunned.

In the time it took for Dang Mi to cock his six-guns, Renny reached down and gathered up the Eurasian girl. Sheltering her in his great arms, the big engineer turned and made for a connecting door.

"No guns if we can help it!" Dang Mi warned. "Gun noise'll bring inquiry, sure enough."

A serpentine-bladed *kris* chucked into the door jamb, not

an inch from Renny's elephantine shoulder. Another, following on its ornate hilt, buried itself in the door, just as it clapped shut.

There was a key in the keyhole. Renny turned it. Fists and shoulders began pummeling the door. It groaned and warped on its brass hinges.

The panel was stronger than the outer door, because the Hotel Raffles had remodeled its suites internally of late, using new doors. Despite the energy the raiders put into breaking it down, it held.

Renny laid the girl down on a bed, and went in search of his supermachine pistol, a weapon he normally wore in an armpit holster for convenience. Inasmuch as he was dressed for bed, the big-fisted engineer had laid it aside for the evening.

Renny wrenched the drawer of a night stand open and pulled out the weapon. It was charged with a drum filled with mercy bullets, which had the benefit of rendering a foe unconscious while not permanently injuring him. The tiny weapon had proven very effective in the past, especially for taking prisoners for later interrogation.

This was not one of those times.

Bullets—leaden ones—began chewing through the stout panel. They buzzed about the room like vicious wasps.

Renny, knowing that his mercy shells, which were hollow and filled with a quick-acting anesthetic, were insufficient for returning fire through a shut door, fumbled in the pocket of his closet-hung coat for a drum containing penetration shells.

But the lead storm grew more furious. Holes appeared in the plaster of the walls. A wood chip was shot off the bed post. A pillow kicked, expelling goose feathers.

"Holy cow!" Renny thumped, and saw that the area around the door knob was coming apart under the concentrated hammering of bullets. The key, mangled, shot out of the lock and across the room. It landed very close to the unmoving head of Mary Chan, there in the bed.

Renny may not have been a ladies' man, but he was not one to let a woman lie helpless as bullets ricocheted about her head. Still holding his supermachine pistol in one monster fist, he threw his imposing bulk between the door and the bed.

He was affixing the new drum to the intricate weapon when the panel crashed down. Renny looked up.

In came Dang Mi and his confederates, guns held high.

Dang's guns roared alternately. Bullets slammed into the big-fisted engineer's chest. In response to the leaden storm, Renny twisted, long face writhing in pain.

"Why won't he go down?" Dang howled, redoubling his shooting. "He ain't all that big!"

Then Renny collapsed forward. He struck the bed, rolled off, and came to rest with his head under the bed. Out of his mouth came the most unearthly coughings, wracking his great body.

"He's dying!" Poetical Percival croaked, evidently aghast at the idea.

"Let him die!" Dang roared, sending another slug into Renny's twitching torso. "Get the wench. We'll take her back to Pirate Island."

They got her, carried her down the stairs, and out.

Soon, she was under a blanket on the floorboards of a fleeing sedan, unkind feet holding her down until her squirming abated. The sedan careened through the narrow streets of Singapore, driven by a blue-turbaned Malay with a reckless confidence in the Oriental belief in predestination. Evidently, it was not the ordained day for anyone to be run down, because no one was. Although there were numerous close scrapes.

"Good thing I have me an auto in every port," Dang Mi remarked. "We'll be at the dang dory in jig time."

Poetical Percival Perkins, riding beside Dang, leaned back, but not in a comfortable manner.

"Don't give out a whoop," he remarked, "but we're in the soup."

Dang grunted, "How do you figure?"

"That brick-fisted lad was one of Doc Savage's crew. Doc Savage will gallop down here hell-for-leather to do things about it."

"An' so what?"

"It's a sure sign that we'll have a savage time," said Poetical Percival, oblivious to his own pun.

Dang Mi made a jaw. He was trying to act as if he didn't give a damn. He did not do a very good job of it.

"We ain't left no bloody danged trail," he said. "Doc Savage can't find us."

Poetical Percival shook his head. For the moment, his poetic ways seem to have been jarred out of him. "This Doc Savage is something different. Remarkable chap. The outside world don't seem to know much about him."

"He goes 'round stickin' his nose into what don't concern him," growled Dang Mi.

"Righting wrongs and punishing evildoers," agreed Poetical Percival somberly. "A modern Sir Galahad, or something of the like. He's bad medicine. I've heard plenty about him. This Savage is a man known all over the world as the one to go to if you've got big trouble. When I was in Africa doing a job, I heard them talk of Doc Savage. Believe it or not, the guy is as well-known there as he is over here."

"Dry up!" Dang said suddenly.

Poetical Percival Perkins squinted at the other. Dang, he could see, was a concerned man, despite his disclaimer of any apprehension concerning Doc Savage. Not that he was to be blamed. Percival was a bit on the pins and needles side himself. Doc Savage, Man of Bronze, had a reputation as a miracle worker—and he specialized in unsavory gentry such as Dang Mi and Percival Perkins.

Abruptly Poetical Percival thought of something.

"Wait a minute," he barked.

"Huh?" growled Dang.

"Maybe this Renny Renwick ain't dead," essayed Percival.

"We had better keep an eye on the situation until we're sure."

COLONEL JOHN "RENNY" RENWICK was not only not dead; he was far from being fatally injured. For days, his ribs would hurt him when he moved, but not excessively.

Doc Savage's aides lived always in the shadow of danger, and they had to take precautions. Chain mesh undergarments, made of an alloy metal developed by Doc himself, which they wore almost always, were a part of the precautions. The mesh would stop all ordinary bullets. The one Renny wore—even to bed—had halted the slugs which Dang Mi had fired at his chest.

Impact of the missiles, however, had knocked the breath out of Renny, stunned him. Too, he had not known at what instant during the excitement his attackemrs might start shooting at his head, so he had taken care to fall with his head in the shelter of the bed.

The interval during which the girl had been carried out, Renny had employed in yanking on trousers and shirt and descending the fire escape.

The big engineer paused only to make slashing marks on a long wall mirror with a stick of chalk taken from his coat pocket.

Curiously, the chalk left no visible mark.

The rubber plantation which was employing Renny was furnishing him with a car, a small, fast American coupé—one of thousands of used machines shipped to the Orient every year. He kept it parked in a court back of the hotel. Descending the fire escape, he was almost beside it.

He got out in the street in time to get on the trail of Dang Mi and his cut-throats. Dang's crowd now drove slowly and carefully, for they did not want to interest a policeman. Their machines wound through the native quarter for a time. The motors made sufficient noise to scatter the coolies out of the way.

Renny kept on their trail and, in doing so, exercised a simple precaution or so.

Once he had the opportunity to stop, he sprang out and hastily disconnected one headlight, making his machine one-eyed, and thus changing its character.

Later, he connected the light again, and proceeded normally.

The trail ended on the waterfront, or rather, the automobile portion of it did. It continued across the bay in a motor dory. The dory was one from Dang Mi's pirate junk, the *Devilfish.*

Renny was close enough to make sure that the girl was still in the hands of the gang. He cast about hurriedly for a means of following.

The hour was late, and there was only a single motorized water taxi ferrying passengers across the bay. Several conical-hatted coolies were idling on its seats, playing a card game called fan-tan. To all appearances, the boat was loaded and about to start across the bay.

Renny clambered aboard.

"I will pay fifty cents extra if you take me across immediately," said Renny, who did not want to lose sight of the boat containing his quarry.

"As you wish, *tuan,*" agreed the pilot, employing the Malay honorific meaning "sir."

Renny selected a seat. The pilot took up a long bamboo pole and shoved off. The others continued their card game, unconcerned.

After the motor started kicking, Renny said, "There's a twenty in it if you keep that dory in sight without being obvious about it. Savvy?"

"Yes, *tuan,*" replied the pilot.

Renny sat slumped in his hard seat, knowing that a white man of his bulk would be noticeable even on a night as dark as this. His eyes remained fixed on the motor dory. The bay was crowded with sampans and water taxis, so the ferry should not stand out especially.

He paid little attention to the card game in progress, and

none whatsoever to the pilot in the rear of the boat. This proved to be unfortunate, because the card game suddenly broke up amid a cackling of Malay profanity that threatened to carry clear across the bay.

"Pipe down, you three," Renny rumbled, and so did not hear the swish of the bamboo pole as the pilot swept it around in a circle until it connected with the giant engineer's head with an audible *bonk!*

Renny slumped to the floor of the ferry, out of sight, and the crew fell upon him with hardwood clubs, raining further blows intended to prolong unconsciousness.

If any passing seafarers noted what had happened, they betook themselves discreetly away and kept quiet about it. That was an Oriental characteristic, too.

RENNY RENWICK awakened with the feeling that a number of things had happened to him while he was senseless. He peered around, and was sure of it.

He was surrounded—and no longer on the ferry, but on the deck of a sailing vessel of some sort. He lay on his back and his big arms were tucked up behind him. He could barely feel them, owing to the fact that his great bulk had been pressing down on them for as long as he had been insensate. He was undoubtedly bound, he concluded. He couldn't feel the bindings, either.

Among the shadowy figures peering down on his helpless form, was one he recognized. It was the leader of the abductors, he saw.

Renny shut his eyes. "Of late, I've suspected I'm getting old. I'm sure of it now."

"Not a bit of it, mate. You were right smart. You just came alongside of someone who was a mite smarter. I have friends all along the waterfront, I do."

Renny levered his upper body into a sitting position. For an ordinary man, it would have been impossible. But the gargantuan-fisted engineer was no ordinary man. He blew impatient air from his nostrils and his grunting would have done credit to a bull elephant, but he accomplished it.

Instinctively, the hovering Malay crew took a cautious step backward.

"You won't find those bindings so easy to negotiate," he was warned.

"What's this all about, anyway?" Renny demanded.

"'Tis very simple," the other grinned easily. "I happened to learn how me an' my blokes can get our hands on about the most valuable thing in the perishin' world. A pair o' half-caste twins can show us how to get it. One of 'em got away and got to you and talked, so now we gotta take care o' you."

Renny frowned. He did not like the sound of that.

"The almond-eyed white girl didn't tell me anything that amounted to much," he said.

"You'd lie to me anyway," snorted the man. "Right now, we're headed for Pirate Island."

"Holy cow, why?"

"'Cause, me hearty, we just happen to be bloody piratical! They call me Dang Mi, the Scourge of the South China Sea."

"Never heard of you."

"And that's the way I like it," chortled Dang Mi. "This way, no one will be looking for me special-like if I end up feedin' you to a nice, grinnin' mako shark."

"Holy cow," Renny said again, unhappily.

Chapter V
PIRATE ISLAND

PIRATE ISLAND, AS it turned out, lay near Chinese waters.

These days, Chinese waters were nervous waters. The Japanese were in Manchuria and the British were unhappy about it. In the middle were the Chinese. They were the least happy of all.

Poetical Percival Perkins stood watch in the bow of the *Devilfish* as she ran under sail in the direction of Pirate Island, a good British Army rifle nestled in the crook of one arm. He scanned the dark waters for trouble. The rhyming swindler had been at this post all day and it was deep into the night now.

Various cut-throats had been sent to relieve him. Poetical Percival had sent them away with a surly verse during the day and vicious kicks after the sun had set. He was on edge. There was good reason for it, too.

Poetical Percival Perkins wanted no part of China, because the authorities were interested in standing him before a stone wall and shooting him by way of proving that it is not wise to murder Chinese silver prospectors for their pokes. This was trackless water, and there were no Chinese authorities here. But they were near the coast. The silver markets were also on the coast. It was to flee China that Poetical Percival had booked passage on the *Devilfish.* Not that he had so much silver to market. The real reason was painfully simple. He wanted to get his life to a safe place.

Somewhere in the middle part of the night the Diesel engine

kicked into life. Thinking it meant trouble, Poetical Percival ducked low and scuttled back to the poop deck, clutching his sturdy automatic rifle.

"Trouble?" he demanded of Dang Mi, who sprawled on a throne-like chair set atop the high poop. Despite the late hour, he was wearing a tropical pith helmet that shone in the moonlight.

"Naw," snorted Dang. "We're just home, is all."

Poetical Percival looked about the night. He made faces. It was plain he could see nothing but murk.

"So? How do you know?" he asked.

"Ever hear of black light?"

"Every night is black," muttered Percival.

"I said, 'light' not 'night.' Black light is another name for what they call ultra-violet light. You can't see it except with special filters. Here."

A pair of what appeared to be smoked glasses were handed to Percival. He put them on.

And suddenly, off the port bow, he could see it. A low lump of a thing, lazy with palms. It was an eerie sight because it was ablaze with a kind of grayish light. The island might have been a black and white photographic image projected on the water with an old fashioned magic lantern, except that the palms swayed.

"I set projectors around the beach," boasted Dang Mi. "My Malays turn 'em on every night so's I can find my way home if necessary."

Percival surrendered the glasses.

"Slick trick," he said admiringly.

"I ain't the Scourge of the South China Sea for nothing, my fine friend."

THERE was a small cove and the *Devilfish* put into it.

Chinese junks are ingenious craft. Constructed without a

keel, they instead come equipped with a removable daggerboard. This was lifted out of its slot on the foredeck, back of the foremast, and carried to the bows.

At a guttural order from Dang Mi, the helmsman beached the craft, which had become as flat-bottomed as a lowly sampan. The bow grated on fine, granular sand for a third of its length, stopped.

The pirate crew dropped anchor without so much as a rattle, thanks to care and a lining of rubber around the hawse hole. It was a medieval stone anchor, perfect for anchoring on sand. Sails were struck smartly.

One end of the daggerboard was affixed to the crosspiece set between the projecting catheads at the bow, and the other dropped to the beach, forming an efficient gangplank.

Finally, they began putting off crew and prisoners. A narrow rowboat of a type known as a *kolek* was also carried off, evidently for safekeeping.

The prisoners came willingly enough, inasmuch as people with their hands and feet shackled are more likely to feel better on dry land than on a ship, which after all could sink without warning. Being shackled to a sinking ship was not a position to inspire optimism. So they went willingly, even the big engineer, Renny Renwick.

He stepped onto the beach, his face as pleased as could be. Seeing this, Dang Mi muttered, "Watch that one. He's got something up his sleeve, he has."

Poetical Percival, regarding the giant engineer's fists unhappily, blinked and said, "If he does, it must be titanic."

Neither man understood that his pleased expression, conversely, was an indication of Renny Renwick's unhappiness with his present situation.

The prisoners were guided at the points of *krises* through a riot of tropical trees. Swaying coconut palms predominated. Their feathery crowns shivered in the breeze. Bougainvillea flowers on their vines made splashes of scarlet, pink and magenta.

Pineapples and bananas were plentiful, as were the prickly green jackfruit so remindful of bloated cactus pads. Trembling spider orchids grew in profusion, seeming poised to pounce upon the unwary. The ground was moist and muddy from the recent monsoon rains, and their feet—both bare and booted—made unpleasant sucking sounds as they progressed.

Eventually, the march ended at a cluster of longhouses well inland.

"Put 'em in the guest house," Dang ordered his Malays, pointing to a seedy structure a few rods apart from the rest.

"What about the blue strongbox?" asked Poetical, nodding in the direction of the beached junk.

"We'll move the box when them three are safely ensconced in the guest house," decided Dang.

The guest house was a typical longhouse, a thing like a elongated cabin set on stilts to protect the inhabitants from snakes and other crawling perils of the jungle, with a thatched roof of dried palm fronds.

Rude steps led to the single floor and they were marched up these. Renny, coming last, put his weight on the first step. It groaned. The second step, accepting his weight, creaked loudly.

It was the third step that surrendered to the giant engineer's massive bulk. It splintered, precipitating the monster-fisted engineer into a littered pile of kindling.

"Holy cow!"

Krises came out. Blowpipes, as big around as a man's forearm, were brought to parched lips. Sudden death impended.

A hissed word from Dang Mi staved off disaster.

"Let 'im be!"

"Why not give him what for?" Poetical wondered. "He doesn't know anything about the Buddha."

"I have plans for that human rhinoceros," Dang undertoned, as Renny clambered to his feet.

"Plans?"

"Later, me hearty."

There being no other way to accomplish it, Renny was allowed to employ his gargantuan hands to hoist himself up to the longhouse. There was no door. The steps, a ruin now, were hacked to flinders under wavy-bladed swords.

"That oughta hold them," Dang said, pleased with himself.

"I frown," Percival said laconically. "They could jump down."

"And they'd be jumping into a hornet's nest of blowpipe darts," said Dang in a voice loud enough to be plainly heard by his captives. "Each one poisoned to a fare-thee-well."

The prisoners found grass mats on the rude floor and settled into unhappy attitudes.

Satisfied, Dang motioned for his new accomplices in knavery to follow him back to the cove.

THEIR foot sounds were a brushy rustle for a time, then the cacophony of the jungle reasserted itself. Background sounds of waves creaming on a beach made a continual, lulling murmur.

After a time, Renny spoke.

"Who is he?" he asked Mary Chan. Renny jerked an enormous thumb in the direction of the rather subdued young Eurasian man.

"My twin," Mary Chan said. "His name is Mark. I'm Mary—Mary Chan."

Mark Chan looked disconsolate. Shame weighed down his battered head. His lips were a crushed ruin.

"I'm afraid they beat him," explained Mary Chan. "But it's nothing compared with what will happen to the human race should that devil Dang Mi gets his way."

"You might," Renny suggested, "begin at the beginning."

Mary Chan looked to her brother. Mark Chan swallowed hard and nodded uncomfortable assent.

"I sought you out to ask your help in finding my brother," Mary supplied. "I had hopes that through you I could be put in touch with Doc Savage."

"You know Doc?"

"Actually, I never heard of him before to-day. But I chanced to read of him in a Singapore newspaper after I escaped Dang Mi's boat."

Renny had been rather sanguine about his predicament until now. Startlement registered on his long gloomy visage.

"Holy cow! Never heard of Doc! Where were you raised—on the moon?"

Neither Chan seemed to find amusement in the comment.

Mary said, "We grew up in a remote part of China, with our mother. Our father was rarely home. We were en route by private airplane to seek help when we ditched off the Malay coast. That is how Dang Mi got us. He shot us down."

"Ransom deal?" asked Renny.

Mary Chan shook her head. "No. We were bringing the box out of China. Dang Mi and his men discovered it. One opened it."

Mary Chan actually shuddered at this juncture. Mark Chan simply closed his pained almond orbs.

Renny eyed them and asked a natural question.

"What," he wondered, "is in the box?"

As if linked by a common brain, Mark and Mary Chan averted their eyes. Mark moistened bruised lips. Mary bit into her own red lips.

It became plain that neither was inclined to answer the big-fisted engineer's question.

Renny tried again. "I'm in this fix because you barged in on me," he reminded Mary Chan.

Mary made assorted thoughtful faces. They seemed to become her. She possessed an intelligent countenance and the notches created by her knitting brows and the grim twists of her mouth only added to her exotic comeliness.

Renny noted that her speech, which before contained the

flavor of modernity, seemed, as the unpleasant reality of captivity sank in, to more and more revert to a formal brand of English. This suggested that she was raised speaking Mandarin, or some other Chinese dialect.

Mark Chan caught her eye and a look passed between them that Renny could not read.

"Did you," Mary asked at length, "ever hear of Pandora's box?"

"Sure," Renny grunted.

"The world's evils were imprisoned in a box that a Greek maiden named Pandora was forbidden to open. But her curiosity got the best of her and she stole a peek. After she lifted the lid, all manner of imprisoned evils escaped and have ever since plagued mankind."

"That is a myth," Renny snorted. "Pure hokum."

"True. But the box Dang Mi now controls contains a thing infinitely worse than the horrid evils supposedly imprisoned in Pandora's box."

"Infinitely," Mark Chan chorused.

"If mankind is to survive," Mary asserted, "that box must be wrested back from Dang Mi before he unleashes it."

"Holy cow," Renny thumped, impressed in spite of a natural tendency toward skepticism. In his long association with Doc Savage, he had come into contact with many strange and uncanny things. But the rough shape of the mystery outlined by Mary Chan's words threatened to top them all.

Up until now, Renny had been content to sit and listen to the Chans' unnerving recital. Now he sprang into action. He had been shackled wrist to wrist and ankle to ankle. A heavy span of sea-rusted links connected the two lengths of chain. Renny gathered up the leg chain at the point it connected with the vertical chain. They were heavy. Links clattered in his gargantuan hands, whose freakish size made them seem less ponderous than they were. This was in the nature of an optical illusion. The links were exceedingly stout.

"What are you doing?" Mary Chan hissed.

Renny's reply was only a grunt. Conceivably, it was not even meant as a reply. With no warning whatsoever, he separated his giant fistic blocks.

The chain snapped tight between them. Renny repeated the operation, further along the links. Again, he snapped chain.

It soon became clear that the big engineer was testing each link for weakness. A sudden frown suggested Renny had encountered defeat.

Actually, it meant the opposite. Seizing a connecting ring on one end of a link, Renny held it to a stray moonbeam coming in through a chink in the longhouse wall. The maul-fisted engineer gave a protracted strenuous tug.

His long face reddened from exertion. The tendons at his neck grew thick. Veins bulged along his forehead. Muscles egged in front of his ears.

Their own eyes bugging, the Chans watched this operation.

The ring was not weak. It was merely less strong than the surrounding links. Perhaps the weld was not perfect. Or possibly Renny's muscular exertion was more than forged iron could withstand.

Whatever the truth, the ring of iron gave a sudden, tortured creak, and separated. Renny redoubled his efforts. The ring opened up further.

In a moment, there was sufficient space to allow the connecting links to slip off.

"You are still shackled hand and foot," Mary Chan pointed out in a pent but impressed voice.

Renny proceeded to remedy that situation. His legs irons were stout and very tight on him. There would be no removing those, except with heavy tools.

But the connecting chain offered hope. Wrapping the dangling chain end around the links that were stapled to his right leg iron, the big engineer began to haul with both hands while simultaneously stretching his leg out as far as he could.

Once again, Renny's muscles, tendons and veins showed evidence of inhuman strain. This went on for some minutes to no effect. Perspiration popped from every visible pore.

With a snap and rattle, the leg chain finally surrendered. Renny recoiled from the loosened links. Lashing backward, they narrowly missed his long face.

Shifting on the floor, the giant engineer went to work on the other. Since the leg links now hung loose, Renny dispensed with the chain used to exert force and simply applied the considerable might of his thews to the leg chain itself.

Looping three twists of linkage about his oversized hands, Renny pulled until globules of salty sweat stood out on his strained features.

The Chans, watching this intently, began to perspire in sympathy.

With a brittle sound, the leg chain snapped off the left leg iron. Evidently Renny sensed the moment of surrender. He yanked his head out of the way of the flailing chain. It made a dent in the bamboo flooring. He flung the useless links aside.

Renny sat there a moment in the semi-gloom, catching his breath. His lungs sounded like tired bellows working.

For his part, Mark Chan stared with unbelieving eyes.

Hoisting himself to his feet, Renny rumbled, "Wait here."

Mary Chan gasped. "But—where are you going?" she asked.

"To find that durn box for myself."

"You cannot conceive of the danger it represents."

Renny said nothing. He was a tower of elephantine muscle in the jungle dark. His hands were still linked by chain, but he could use them in a limited way. Walking was no longer an impediment.

Carefully, he lowered himself to the ground, paused, then started off. Evidently, Dang Mi's warning of poisoned blowpipe darts was so much jungle gas.

Mary Chan called urgently after him.

"Whatever happens, do not open that box! If the thing inside gets out, *the world will start to end!* Do you understand? Once it begins, there will be no stopping it!"

If this rather fantastic warning made any impression on the hulking engineer, it did not show in his manner.

Renny was soon lost in the undergrowth. The lapping of waves resumed and the jungle seemed to slumber uneasily.

The Chans waited in the darkness, eyes wide, ears alert. They wore the expressions of persons suffering under a death sentence.

Chapter VI

THE MIRACLE MAN

NEW YORK IS a metropolis mixing affluence and poverty. Great apartment houses exist shoulder-to-shoulder with the seediest slums. Common citizens take the subway, while others are chauffeured around in the swankiest of limousines.

One such machine hurtled through the canyons of Manhattan as the day was drawing to a close. Its size and appointments indicated that it belonged to a person of means. In the driver's compartment, the chauffeur wore the crisp gray of his rank. A voice in his ear bellowed out:

"Faster, Maitland! Time is of the essence."

"Yes, sir."

The chauffeur poured on speed and took corners with utter unconcern for pedestrians. He ran lights, horn blaring. Taxi cabs darted out his way. Trolley cars braked to a halt to avoid him.

Bowling through a busy intersection, he blew past the traffic cop with such haste that the officer's cap was knocked off. By the time the officer had recovered his headgear, the limousine was out of sight.

The officer thought better of calling headquarters. No telling how high up the occupant of the limousine rated. Returning his whistle to his mouth, he resumed directing traffic.

"Some of these swells think they own the town," he grumbled.

The limousine lurched onto Fifth Avenue, and began barreling toward a skyscraper that among those crowding mid-town, towered over all others. Over a hundred stories high it reared, its spire catching the fading afternoon light.

"There!" cried the limousine owner. "That is the building. Snappy!"

The chauffeur bore down on the gas pedal. An intersection lay ahead. This time the traffic cop stationed there was not looking the other way. He saw the big black car exceeding the speed limit and blew a blast on his whistle. He stepped into the path of the limousine and lifted a white-gloved hand.

"Go around him, Maitland."

But it was too late for that. Traffic was closely packed. There was no turning.

The chauffeur depressed the brake. In the rear compartment, the owner was thrown forward in the seat cushions. This did not improve his temper.

The cop approached the driver, saw that he was only a uniformed flunky and held his tongue. With his nightstick, he tapped on the back window until it rolled down.

"We got a speed limit in this town," he announced to the occupant within.

"I am in a great hurry, my man."

"I could see that. Give me your name."

"I am on a life or death mission."

"So they all say," growled the unimpressed officer. "Now what was that name?"

"I have urgent business with Doc Savage."

The cop looked up from his notepad.

"Doc Savage, you say?"

"Yes, he is expecting me. And if he learns that you are interfering with our business, there is no telling what he will do!"

The cop was a savvy specimen. He knew the reputation of Doc Savage, knew also that he did not throw his weight around.

"Tell you what. I'll write up your ticket, and if Doc Savage says it's O.K., the commissioner will tear it up. They're good pals, from what I hear."

From the rear compartment, the limousine owner gave vent to a string of inarticulate noises. It was evident that this was a man who did not like to be kept waiting.

Patiently, the cop wrote the ticket, tore it off his pad and presented it to the fuming occupant.

"Any kick, take it up with the police commissioner. He's a good egg."

The limousine got under way once more. This time it proceeded at a more decorous pace.

From the rear, the owner voiced his opinion of the minions of the law in general and one officer in particular. He was not kind in his choice of words.

NOT many city blocks from this scene, an old woman was making her way through the maze that was Manhattan.

She was a frail thing. She craned her head upward often, her faded eyes seeking the imposing pinnacles of the great metropolis. A flowered hat shaded her fading eyes.

Sometimes, she would catch the eye of a passerby, and offer a friendly, "Hello." This marked her as a newcomer to Gotham. Such pleasantries did not pass between strangers in New York City. Each time, she was coolly rebuffed.

When she came to a street crossing, the old woman seemed to find the speedy traffic daunting. Since she walked with painful slowness, this was understandable.

She waited a long time for the traffic to thin before venturing to cross.

Half the length of the block there was a store given over to the handling of camping equipment for boys, and in the window display was a pup tent, various kinds of packsacks, camp cook kits, and scouting uniforms. And the elderly woman discovered this window, stumbled over to it, and stood with her nose pressed to the window.

Her manner was pathetic, and her thin lips rolled in as if to keep back an emotion, and a trace of moisture came into her faded eyes. Her lips moved, but what she said was audible to no one but herself. "Poor Billy," she was mumbling. "He liked to camp out."

Finally, she dragged a handkerchief across her eyes and went on.

Soon she came upon a cop, big, hearty, and Black Irish to the bone. The cop's name was Finnerty. He was the traffic cop who had had his uniform cap knocked off by the speeding limousine. The old woman did not know this; only that the cop looked friendly.

"Excuse me, sir," quavered the old woman in a voice that had the flat twang of the far west. "I have lost my way to a doctor's office."

"Now, what's his address?" the cop demanded in a bluff voice that made the old woman wince.

"I'm not certain," said the old woman. "Savage is his name."

"Doc Savage!" the officer exploded.

"Yes," said the old woman, recoiling a little from the violence of the officer's ejaculation.

"So that's the fellow you're hunting? Well, that makes a difference."

Snatching his whistle, he blew a terrific blast, causing the halting of traffic. Motorists screeched to a stop. One was a little slow with his foot and slid into the intersection, interfering with crosstown traffic. Horns blared.

Red-faced, the traffic cop got in the middle of the tangle and undid the knot. After he had accomplished this—and incidentally bawled out the slow-to-react driver—the officer came back to the old woman.

"Let me walk you across the street, mother," he said in a suddenly solicitous voice.

The old woman, blinking at the sight of both flows of busy Manhattan traffic standing still so she could cross safely, allowed the cop to pilot her to the other side.

"That kind of gives you an idea of how important the big bronze guy is," the cop declared. "Even the mention of his name causes things to happen."

"You—mean—"

"Sure, Ma'am; Doc Savage. The Man of Bronze. Clark Savage, Jr. No matter what name he goes by, everybody in this burg knows who Doc Savage is. Maybe everybody in the whole world, too."

The old woman seemed not to know what to say to that.

Finnerty lifted a wind-reddened finger and aimed it between rows of buildings to one spire in particular.

"See that building there? It's the tallest in the world."

The old woman squinted hard into the snappish wind. "Yes."

"That's where you can find Doc Savage. Way up on the eighty-sixth floor."

"It looks like a long walk," the old woman said in a pathetic murmur.

"Take the trolley. Here comes one now."

The cop lifted an arm and flagged down an approaching trolley car. He escorted the old woman inside and, wonder of wonders, dropped a nickel into the box for her.

"Thank you, sir."

"Any friend of Doc Savage is a friend of the law's," called the cop as, with a clanging, the trolley resumed its route.

The conductor was also very helpful. He stopped the trolley, not at a posted stop, but at the corner nearest to the spire in which Doc Savage, whom everyone seemed to know, held forth.

From there it was a short walk.

THERE was a doorman, who very courteously held a door open for the elderly woman, and a cigar stand clerk who pointed to an elevator that was off in a corner, away from the banks of lifts that seemed to fill the modernistic marble-and-brass lobby. The elevator whisked the old woman upward with such speed she all but lost her breath. It deposited her on a lower floor.

There was a door from which bright light seeped through a pane of ground glass. There was no name on the glass, only a number.

The old woman approached, her chin trembling with anticipation. There was a bell-push and she pressed it. The buzzer was not loud, but the door instantly opened.

A wasp-waisted man with the handsome chiseled features of a stage actor and dark, penetrating eyes greeted her.

"Are—are you Doc Savage?" the old woman asked.

"My good woman, I am merely one of his associates, Brigadier General Theodore Marley Brooks."

The old woman blinked, impressed. Doc Savage must be an important personage indeed if a brigadier general considered himself merely a subordinate.

"Take a seat, if you please," invited Brigadier General Theodore Marley Brooks.

The old woman entered. There was an anteroom, of good size, and beyond it, visible through an open door, a man sat at a desk. He resembled, to the crone's age-weakened eyes, a bull gorilla in a very disreputable suit.

She took the nearest seat. It was one of the few vacant chairs in the anteroom. The others were occupied.

The man who had greeted her conducted each person in his or her turn to the adjoining room where the homely gorilla dealt with them. Most persons were disposed of with alacrity. Others remained with him behind the closed door for long minutes.

No one, so far as the old woman could determine, were granted an audience with Doc Savage.

It soon came to her ears that the handsome man was known familiarly as "Ham." When he was called Ham, the handsome one frowned severely, as though that was something he would permit only with intimate friends. This waspish man, touchy about his name, was especially notable because of his attire. He was dressed in the absolute height of fashion, complete with morning coat, striped trousers, spats and a neat dark cane, which he kept tucked under his arm.

He looked very injured of dignity when the homely fellow at the desk hailed him as "Hey, you overdressed shyster lawyer!" He favored the homely individual with a dark frown.

And a bit later, when the homely man at the desk, in a moment of relaxation between interviews, picked up a shiny nickel and turned it in his fingers and chanced to remark that the five cent piece was bright enough to see his own reflection in, the dapper one advised unkindly, "That's not your reflection. That's the buffalo."

The pair evidently did not get along sociably, and the homely fellow was either called Lieutenant Colonel Andrew Blodgett Mayfair, or "Monk," a nickname which certainly fitted him. He was an industrial chemist of note—one of the best, despite his unlovely looks. Ham—otherwise Brigadier General Theodore Marley Brooks—probably had the most astute legal mind ever produced by Harvard Law School.

The old woman, to bide the time while she waited, took stock of those who had arrived before her.

Many seemed to be cut from the same worried cloth as herself. They looked ordinary in their manner, dress and appearance—except each carried with them some burden of the soul. They waited with studied patience.

Some of the visitors were of a different class. One of these made a particularly overbearing display.

The gentleman was paunchy of waist, ruddy of face, and wore pince-nez nose glasses to which were attached a dark ribbon. He had a pompous manner about him, and seemed to be accompanied by his chauffeur. He did not wait his turn, but strode over and whacked the desk in front of the homely fellow with a domineering fist.

"My man, I am not accustomed to being kept waiting," he said importantly. "I must see Doc Savage immediately. There happens to be a matter of millions of dollars involved."

"Yeah?" Monk said, blinking tiny eyes. "Millions, huh?"

"Exactly." The other put out his chest until it was nearly as prominent as his stomach. "I are prepared to pay up to—ah, one quarter million dollars for Doc's services, in the position I intend to offer him as head of a syndicate."

The rotund gentleman seemed fully aware of how important such money sounded, and he stood waiting for the homely Monk to turn meek.

"Get the devil back in line and take your turn!" Monk said in a small, unimpressed squeak. "Money don't talk around here. It whispers. Generally, we can't even hear it." Then, as the demanding fellow seemed about to explode, he roared, *"Get back in line, I said!"*

THE blustery one was so taken aback he was at a momentary loss for words. Stiffly, he said, "You are obviously busy. I shall return on another occasion. But mark me. Doc Savage will hear of your lack of cooperation."

With that, he departed in a huff, liveried chauffeur in tow.

The interviewing proceeded, finally coming to the patient old woman's turn. Called into a private office by the homely ape of a fellow, she was invited to sit down.

"My name is Martha Holland," began the old woman. "Mrs. John Holland. I am Billy's grandmother. His mother and father have passed away, and I—"

"What seems to be the trouble?" Monk Mayfair asked by way of opening the interview.

"Why, it's my little Billy—" The old woman suddenly choked up. She dabbed at one eye. "He—he is not—well."

"What's wrong with him?" asked Monk.

"The doctors do not know. He suffers from spells."

"Spells, eh? Where is Billy now?"

"At my hotel. The Gotham. He is resting. He—Billy appears to be... failing." The old woman's voice choked at the last.

Monk leaned back in his desk and a procession of expressions walked across his unlovely visage. They made him resemble a gorilla contemplating an impassable river. His eyes, sunk deep in pits of gristle, lost their humorous twinkle. His generous mouth warped. At one point, he tugged at an ear that had once been perforated by a bullet.

Observing these facial contortions, Martha Holland felt an overwhelming urge to flee the room.

At length, Monk's thought processes settled down and he keyed a desk annunciator.

"Doc? It's Monk. I got a nice old lady here who claims her grandson's been suffering seizures. Says the doctors can't do anything for him. It all sounds legit to me, which is why I'm callin'."

The loudspeaker reproduced a voice that, while not loud, conveyed a sense of restrained power.

"Where is the boy now?" asked the unmistakable voice of Doc Savage.

"Hotel Gotham."

"We will go there directly," said Doc Savage.

"Right," said Monk, snapping off the instrument. He got up, saying, "Come on, grandma."

Martha Holland stood up, clutching her flowered hat.

"That—that is all there is to it?" she blurted out.

"Heck," said Monk. "Hardly anyone ever gets to meet Doc in person. But this is a special case."

They went out through a side door and took an elevator to the sub-basement. The elevator dropped with such suddenness, Martha Holland had to be assisted out when the cage settled to a stop.

"Special lift," Monk explained sheepishly.

The sub-basement was a garage. There was an assortment of vehicles, ranging from a milk truck to a sombre sedan streamlined to the ultimate degree.

Doc Savage awaited them at the sedan.

At first glance, he did not seem to be the giant he soon proved to be. He was tall, but so symmetrical was his muscular body that an illusion was created of a less towering individual.

Only after she was presented to the big bronze man did Martha Holland understand that Doc Savage was a veritable colossus.

The Biblical Samson shorn of his beard and cast in bronze might conceivably have resembled Doc Savage. He also brought to mind Hercules, if the latter could be transported forward in time, given a modern haircut and garbed in a quiet brown business suit. His skin had been kilned by tropical suns until it possessed the sheen of polished bronze. His hair was of a darker hue. It lay straight and fitted his head like a metal sheet.

Most arresting of all were the Man of Bronze's eyes—Martha Holland understood now why they called Doc that—for they were a fascinating golden color. Eagles possessed such orbs. No eagle had eyes so vibrant, however. They were like pools of flake-gold held in suspension. They seemed to whirl hypnotically, but this had to be an optical illusion of some kind.

Monk spoke up. "Doc, meet Mrs. John Holland."

"Can you do anything for my Billy?" the old woman asked in a quavering voice.

"We will see," said Doc. His voice resonated with a quiet compelling power that made one come to full attention.

They got into the sedan. It came to life with hardly a rumble of engine. Doc wheeled it to a corrugated steel door. It was down. But as the nose of the sedan neared it, it hoisted up.

"Infra-red projectors in the hood trip a relay switch," Monk explained.

The old woman looked impressed through her worry.

The car eased out into the street, merging smoothly with traffic.

The ride south was not long. Doc Savage asked Mrs. Holland a series of quiet, probing questions designed to elicit the most information via the fewest words.

By the time they pulled up before the Gotham hostelry, Doc had ceased his questioning, lapsing into a solemn silence that might have portended ill.

The Gotham was no fleabag, but neither was it one of the city's finest hotels. Possibly in the gaslight era it had been an establishment of worth, but now it served as a residential hotel for those unable to afford typically exorbitant Manhattan apartment rentals.

The cramped old elevator creaked as it toiled upward.

Billy Holland greeted them at the door. Cheekbones stuck out of his pale, hollow face, but his eyes flew wide at the sight of the bronze giant stepping into the room.

"Gosh! I know you! You're Doc Savage!"

Doc bestowed a rare smile on the young boy. "That's right."

The lad appeared to have trouble with his coordination. He staggered as he walked, and his breathing was not right.

"Billy, Mr. Savage is here to—to—" The old woman's voice caught.

She was unable to get the words out, so overwhelmed was she by the prospect that her only relative would be cured.

Doc directed the boy to lie out on the bed. He had brought a traditional black doctor's valise with him. Out of it came instruments no more sophisticated than the customary stethoscope and rubber hammer for testing patient reflexes. The bronze man used all of these, and checked the boy's pulse in the customary manner.

Most often, however, Doc employed his metallic fingers to thump the weak boy's chest.

When he was done, he asked a simple question of Martha Holland.

"Has this boy ever been exposed to tropical diseases?"

"No. He was born and raised in Indiana. But my late husband had a bout of malaria during the fuss in Cuba." The elderly woman mustered up her best posture. "He was one of Teddy Roosevelt's Rough Riders."

Doc Savage shook his head firmly. "Malaria can only be transmitted through the bite of infected mosquitoes," he imparted. "It is impossible for the boy to become exposed to any such tropical disease merely through contact with an infected person."

A relieved look touched Mrs. Holland's care-worn features.

Doc raised the lad's head and began searching his scalp with careful fingers. Very quickly, he discovered something. Metallic fingers took hold, came away with a fat black thing, which waved tiny legs.

"Wood tick," Doc explained, disposing of the insect in a bottle of solution.

Mrs. Holland shrank. "Oh, no. Mercy!"

Doc cleaned and bandaged the small wound where the tick had taken hold with its stubborn jaws.

"If my diagnosis is correct, he is suffering from tick paralysis, as a result of a toxin carried by the creature. It is sometimes a fatal malady. At any rate, it has been caught in time."

With that, Doc dug into his valise. He extracted a hypodermic needle, charging it with a clear liquid.

Monk asked, "What's that, Doc?"

"Sedative," said the bronze man, rolling up the young boy's sleeve.

Doc cautioned the boy, "This may sting."

"I'm not afraid."

As it turned out, it was old Martha Holland who had to avert her eyes as Doc Savage administered the injection.

When he was done, the bronze man patted the boy on the head and addressed Billy's shaken grandmother.

"You will see improvement in a few hours. He should recover fully in a week. Now that the toxin is no longer flowing into his bloodstream, there is nothing to worry about."

The old woman appeared to be at a loss for words. Tears brimmed her soft eyes. She took Doc Savage's hand in both of hers, wordlessly, unable to express a profound gratitude that had rendered her incapable of speech.

Then she rushed over to little Billy's bedside.

"It's a miracle," the old woman sobbed.

With that, Doc Savage packed up his valise and motioned for Monk Mayfair to follow him quietly from the room. It was typical of the bronze man that he did not wish to remain after doing some good work for the betterment of the human race.

On the creaky ride down, the hardboiled Monk Mayfair took out a violent-colored handkerchief and gave his nose a vigorous honk.

"Cold coming on?" asked Doc.

"Nah," sniffled Monk. "What you did back there just got to me, that's all. Just don't let that shyster Ham know I got busted up over a kid."

The bronze man said nothing. His metallic features were inscrutable. But there were tiny lights in his ever-active flake-gold eyes. An observer intimately familiar with Doc Savage might have ascribed an emotion to those whirling flakes. But Doc Savage was not known to succumb to feelings.

They returned to the skyscraper aerie in a satisfied silence.

Chapter VII

THE MAGIC MUMMY

DANG MI WAS examining the steel strongbox with the air of a mongoose regarding a cobra. He ran fingers along its cool blue crackle finish, as if seeking some clue as to the nature of its contents.

"These Asian artisans have some mighty clever ways o' riggin' a trick box," he muttered.

Beside him, Poetical Percival Perkins regarded Dang with an uneasy mien.

"Opening that box," he said, "means you have rocks."

Dang eyed him villainously. "Eh?"

"In the head, I mean."

"I ain't aimin' to open it," Dang said. "Yet."

"Your face," Perkins sniffed, "expresses a different trace."

They were standing about the box, which had been taken from the *Devilfish's* safe and deposited here away from the water, in a jungle clearing where stood a stone-ringed natural well. This well provided Dang and his cut-throat crew with drinking water whenever they were holed up on Pirate Island for extended periods of time.

"I'm thinkin' we should know what we got here," Dang was muttering.

"The book gave us a look," Perkins reminded.

Dang looked up from the weird box that had been the center of so much turmoil and his eyes fell on one of his blue-turbaned Malays.

"We know what the dang thing is supposed to do. But we ain't seen it in action yet."

"I, for one, will shun," said Perkins. "The privilege, that is," he added.

"Well, Dang Mi, Scourge of the South China Sea, ain't afraid o' no box," the former Hen Gooch announced, giving his colorful trousers a hitch.

Lapsing into the Malay tongue, he rapped out stiff orders.

The Malay on the receiving end of these orders actually flinched. He began backing away.

At a signal from Dang, his compatriots fell upon him. Subduing him, they stripped him of his ripple-edged *kris* and shoved him toward the box.

"Open it!" Dang rapped out in Malay. "But wait until we get clear."

"Are you daft!" Perkins cried. "You don't know what will come abaft!"

Dang took him aside.

"I figure it this way, see? He cracks open the box and the thing inside gets him before he can throw the lid all the way back. The lid falls and the thing is locked up tight again."

"What if it doesn't work out that way?" wondered Perkins.

"It will," Dang said confidently.

"You don't know that—any more than a rat."

"Who gives the orders around here, me hearty?" Dang asked, one hand dropping to the butt of his holstered six-shooter.

Perkins showed himself uneager for a showdown. He took a step backward and, reverting to type, murmured, "You're the boss, so it's your loss."

They retreated into the jungle, leaving the Malay pirate with the mysterious box. He hunkered over it, his half-naked body a-tremble.

Once they moved back a hundred yards or so, they took shelter behind an outcropping of rocks.

Dang unlimbered one of his six-shooters and then the other. With both hands he lined up on the tremulous Malay.

Lifting his voice, he bellowed, "Open that dang box!"

The quivering corsair hesitated.

Whereupon, Dang commenced shooting at his feet the way villains are wont to do in the Western movies.

Snapping and snarling, bullets kicked up sand and dirt dust around the Malay's feet. He broke into a spasmodic jig.

While Dang was prodding him to obey with bullets, Poetical Percival Perkins happened to notice the footprint not three yards away.

It was a rather large footprint. It had sunk into the soft jungle loam fully an inch. That meant a heavy person. The size of the boot also suggested a giant.

Mouth dropping open, Perkins whirled and shook Dang Mi by the shoulder. It happened Dang was in the midst of loosing a shot. Perkins threw off Dang's aim.

And a bullet meant to clip the naked heel of the pirate lackey ordered to open the mysterious box instead drilled clean through his head.

The unfortunate one flopped backward, falling to the ground. There he twitched in his pitiful death throes.

"Dang!" roared Dang Mi. "Why'd you up and go do that?"

Perkins laid a narrow finger against his thin lips and used the opposite finger to indicate the deep indentation in the shape of a large man's foot.

Dang squinted at this footprint.

"Not many men have feet that size," he muttered, looking about warily.

"If there aren't two, then you know who," Perkins breathed.

"THAT ungrinnin' galoot, Renny, got loose and he's around here somewheres," muttered Dang.

"Indeed, and agreed."

Dang made his eyes beady. He looked like an Asian version of a Western badman.

"Get the box," he growled. "I'll cover the fort."

"You're a sport," Poetical Percival Perkins said dryly. But he did not hesitate. He came out from behind the cover of rock, his face wearing a relieved expression. It was evident he did not wish to see the blue container opened at all.

Picking his way down toward the well, he came to the box.

Kneeling, Perkins took hold of it in a firm grasp.

"Grant me the grip," he muttered, "to make no slip."

With infinite caution, he raised himself to his full height, the box balanced carefully in his nervous hands.

Like a man moving in a lead-weighted diving suit, he turned and began to tramping back to Dang Mi's position.

He got no more than a dozen paces when a tower of gloom reared up from a brushy growth and laid heavy hands on his shoulders.

"I'll take that," a low deep rumbling voice said.

Poetical Percival Perkins froze in mid-tramp.

Then all hell broke loose.

FROM the rocks, Dang Mi let out a howl as he recognized the imposing form of Renny Renwick accosting his confederate.

The Malays emitted their own assorted screeches of surprise.

And Poetical Percival Perkins, shocked in spite of himself, happened to lose his grip on the box.

"Oh!" he gasped.

The world seemed to stop for a moment. If there was the breath of something living, that breath ceased.

The box slipped from Perkins' shocked fingers. They fumbled. Some reflex kicked in and he made a grab for the falling hunk of metal.

Renny's big hands lunged at the same time.

"No!" cried Perkins.

Both men had hold of the box now. They tugged. Renny, being the stronger of the two, seemed the certain victor.

Then out from behind the outcropping of rock, poured Dang Mi and his piratical horde.

Dang fired in the air. Three shots. He knew that to bring down either struggling man was to unleash the unknown thing in the box.

At that point, Renny wrestled the object from Perkins' long fingers, tucked it under his arm and plunged back into the jungle.

A chase ensued—wild, noisy, punctuated by shouts and shots.

Poetical Percival Perkins was the second one to blunder into the jungle, hot on Renny's heels. What impelled the long, lathy swindler to such action was unclear. Perhaps he feared that the giant engineer, in his ignorance, would seek to open the box.

In any case, by the time Dang Mi and his excited crew reached the jungle, there was no sign of Renny Renwick, Percival Perkins or most importantly, the mysterious blue container.

That did not stop them from searching.

"Fan out!" Dang cried in Malay. "Find them! Find that dang box! Dang your hides, don't fail me if you value your worthless brown skins!"

The pirate band broke in all directions. There was no system to their search. They thrashed about, beat the bush and tripped over gnarled roots, accomplishing little.

One pirate, thinking he was sneaking up on a skulking foe, slashed down with his straight-bladed *parang* and took off a fellow corsair's hand.

Much bleeding and screaming resulted until Dang trooped up and straightened things out by shooting the maimed pirate dead.

Calmly, Dang Mi broke the action of each pistol in turn, reloading from his well-worn cartridge belt.

When the dying one had settled down, they heard the unnerving cry.

It started off as one of those long, extended screams. The kind of screech a man makes when he sees death beating down on him. Only this scream was cut short before it could achieve its promised volume.

The outcry did not choke off so much as it died. It started off with building volume, cracked, became a parched croak, then trailed off like a fading ghost's cry for life.

There was the hint in the air that the scream continued in a much reduced fashion after it failed to register on their sharpened ears. Possibly this was an aural illusion.

Fixing the sound's location, Dang started toward it.

He ran, plunging through bramble and brush, six-guns waving wildly.

Then he saw the fog and jerked to a stop.

Behind him, his Malays did likewise.

"I feel thirsty," he muttered.

Carefully, the pirate chieftain advanced.

"Dang!" he muttered. "I hope the thing didn't get out of the gol-dang box."

But it seemed that way.

Ahead, there was a ball of fog—the white ghostly fog that had previously attended the opening of the mystiferous box. But it was thinner this time.

Swallowing twice, Dang wavered between curiosity and abject flight. In the end, curiosity won. For a pirate, Dang Mi did not lack intestinal fortitude.

Dang sent a corsair ahead. The worthy hesitated, too. Dang impelled him along by sniping at the heels of his bare feet.

The Malay came back a moment later, babbling excitedly. But he was healthy, so Dang plunged ahead.

In time, they came to a place where there was more dirt than there was jungle—strangely dry soil, given the recent monsoon rains.

And there they found the box. It sat on the hard ground. The crackle-finished lid was shut. Possibly it had been opened and had fallen back of its own accord.

It certainly seemed that way from the attitude of the body lying before it.

It was a long body. A man. Or something that once had been a man. It lay face down. It was impossible to see exactly who that man had been. But through his clothes, it was immediately clear that whoever the unfortunate one had been, he was no more than a lifeless husk now.

The clothing hung on him as if on a scarecrow. The back of the neck was exposed and below the nape of the neck tendons stood out. Not in exertion, for the body was lax, but because all muscle and moisture had departed the tissues beneath the skin.

The skin too was an unhealthy gray tone. It looked dry, old. In places it had cracked in a manner suggesting alligator hide, or half-shed snakeskin.

The wrists projecting from the shirt sleeves were mere bone over which dead dry skin lay stretched as tightly as a drum.

Above the wrists, the hands were clenched tight. They were bony and all out of proportion to the wrists below.

Seeing this, Dang Mi let out a whoop and a holler.

"He's dead! That coconut-fisted son of a sea cook has gotten himself salivated! Curiosity killed the cat for us!"

Dang fired two jubilant shots into the air by way of celebrating.

Striding up to the mummy of a man, Dang Mi gave it a generous kick. The ribcage actually crackled like a dry woodpile.

"Our troubles are over! Renny Renwick is as dead as an old-time Egyptian pharaoh." Turning to his gawking Malays, Dang Mi added, "And if you blokes know what's good for you, you'll watch your step, else I might turn you all into mummies, too."

With that, Dang holstered his six-shooters and reclaimed

the box containing the unknown thing that had, apparently, reached out of its box to turn a living man into a desiccated, be-wrinkled corpse.

His pirates followed him at a respectful distance, their eyes peeled for the still-missing Poetical Percival Perkins.

Chapter VIII
THE PLUTOCRAT

THE TIME WAS several days later. Autumn had settled in.

A brisk wind howled around the spires of the city. It whined past the cornices and setbacks of the tallest skyscraper in Manhattan like a prowling banshee in search of souls to torment.

And in the offices where those who desired to lay their troubles before Doc Savage were interviewed, Monk Mayfair was speaking.

"I don't give a whoop if you're the owner of the whole country!" Monk yelled. "I told you before that you'd take your turn seeing Doc. And that still goes!"

The homely Monk was addressing the portly fellow who, purely by chance, had been present the day when the old woman, Martha Holland, had paid her visit. The man of affairs had returned to attempt to bluster his way to Doc Savage. The fellow was becoming angry, apparently thinking he was being made sport of.

"You must think I'm the biggest fool on earth!" he yelled.

"Nonsense," Monk replied shortly, "You're only of medium size, ain't you?"

This being a sample of why fellows who thought they were important often had compound spasms after trying to get past Monk to see Doc Savage about some trifling matter. Not that Monk did not use good judgment. The resolution of the matter of Martha Holland and her afflicted grandson, Billy, demonstrated otherwise.

The overbearing fellow glared indignantly through his pince-nez spectacles.

"I," he said, "am C. Startell Pompman."

"So you've said several times," Monk snorted.

"I am—"

"I know," grunted Monk. "The cemeteries are chock full of guys who figured the world couldn't get along without them."

"I have a matter of utmost urgency for Doc Savage," C. Startell Pompman insisted.

"That so?" the homely chemist said skeptically.

"I am prepared to offer a significant sum to engage the bronze man's services."

Monk bellowed, "I told you before, Doc ain't for hire!"

"This is profoundly important. Supremely so. It—"

At that moment Ham Brooks, who had the interviewing trick for the day, poked his head out of the interview office.

"Next!" he announced.

Blustery C. Startell Pompman bowled past Monk Mayfair and accosted Ham Brooks at the door.

"I, sir, am next—and it is high time that I was seen!"

"We're very democratic here," Ham retorted, ushering the rotund businessman in. Ham was in the act of shutting the door behind him when Monk Mayfair laid a huge paw—the word fit—against the door and barged in, saying, "I wanna hear what this noisy windbag has on his mind that's so all-fired important."

Coloring crimson, Startell Pompman took his seat. "You look to be a man of means, Mr. Brooks." He offered a business card. "I am in the import-export business, specializing in the Orient."

"Go on," invited Ham.

"Recently, I chanced to purchase a remarkable—ah—curio in China. I believe it to be very valuable. Very. Regrettably, it was stolen from me under circumstances that point the finger of suspicion at two individuals I foolishly took into my confidence."

"So far," Monk said, "this ain't very interesting."

Ham glared at Monk. "Hush, you tree-ape."

Monk glowered back.

C. Startell Pompman cleared his throat.

"What is this curio?" Ham inquired smoothly.

"Ah, I would rather not say."

"Why not?"

"Because of the danger this curio presents to the world."

Monk snorted derisively. Ham made a prim mouth.

Startell Pompman filled the skeptical absence of conversation with sheepish words.

"I realize how melodramatic this sounds, but the entire world is in peril if this—object—is not swiftly recovered."

"I am sorry, but without more to go on, I cannot bring this matter to Doc Savage," said Ham. His dark eyes appraised the blustery plutocrat silently.

Startell Pompman had been deferential in a reticent way when addressing Ham. Now he reverted to type. His pink-flushed face purpled. One plump hand came smashing down on the desk. An inkwell jumped in response.

"I demand to be heard by Doc Savage!" he roared. "This is important! It is vitally important! And I will not be denied!"

"That does it!" said Monk. "Out, damned spot!"

The homely chemist bent down and picked up the chair Startell Pompman had been sitting in. Chair and occupant came off the floor. Monk showed that this feat of strength strained his apish musculature only by the grunt he gave as he bore the belligerent businessman to the exit door.

At that moment, the outer door buzzed and Ham came out of his chair to see who it was.

An express delivery agent stood there with a steamer trunk. It was a very long trunk. The labels and customs stamps plastered all over it told of its travels.

It was addressed to *Doc Savage, New York City*. Such was the fame of the bronze man that the steamer trunk reached its destination with no more elaborate address than that.

Seeing the trunk, Monk set the chair containing a frightened Startell Pompman on the floor with a jar.

"What's this?" he asked.

"It came express," explained Ham.

"We expectin' anythin'?"

"I will ask Doc."

Picking up a telephone, Ham dialed the bronze man.

"Doc, a steamer trunk just arrived for you," the dapper lawyer reported.

"I will be right down."

The sound of the bronze man's voice caused Startell Pompman to climb to his feet and retreat to the inner office. As Monk showed the waiting supplicants to the power of Doc Savage from the room, this action was not noticed.

"We're closing early," he announced. "Come back to-morrow."

When some objected, Monk said, "Doc has a lot of enemies. Bad ones. Some of them like to mail us bombs. This could be one of them times."

This sent everyone scurrying. Monk closed the door on the last malingerer.

DOC SAVAGE arrived moments later. He examined the box briefly and said, "No return address."

"Could be anythin'," Monk opined.

"We will subject it to the usual tests," decided Doc.

Monk wheeled out a portable fluoroscopic device. The trunk was upended and placed behind the screen. It was very light, weighing, it seemed, hardly more than an empty steamer trunk. But a dry rattling told that the trunk was not empty.

Normally, when fluoroscopic devices are employed, they are used to expose the innards and bones of a living human being.

In this case, the bronze man and his aides were checking to see whether or not the trunk housed an infernal device.

Taking turns, each man applied his eyes to the viewing port.

They were more than a little startled when the rib cage of a human being showed in stark black-and-white on the ground-glass screen.

"Jove!" Ham gasped.

Monk pushed him aside, leaned in, peered. "Blazes!" he squeaked.

Doc went next. The bronze man reacted in no outward manner. He had been schooled to control his emotions. Nothing registered on his metallic face, but the air was instantly permeated with a weird sound. A low, exotic trilling note.

Difficult of description, it had a definite musical quality, although it followed no tune, and was as unnerving as the sound of the winds coursing through the spires of Manhattan, although infinitely more unreal. The eerie evanescence finally trailed away to nothingness. Throughout, it had possessed a peculiar quality of seeming to come from everywhere rather than from any particular spot.

A bystander would not be entirely sure the bronze man had authored it. But he had. It was a small unconscious habit the bronze man exhibited during moments of mental stress.

Doc manipulated the fluoroscope and determined for himself that all the trunk contained was a human being, presumably dead, and some packing material. Satisfied, he switched off the device and tipped the trunk onto the floor.

From a pocket of his vest, he produced a steel pick. After first checking for the telltale wires of a booby-trap, and finding none, Doc went to work on the lock. It surrendered so quickly to the bronze man's manipulations, he might have been employing a key.

Crouched beside the trunk, Doc threw open the lid.

The body had been cushioned in common excelsior. Even so, it was not sufficient to preserve it from damage. The head lolled to one side on an obviously broken neck. Fingers had come off one hand. They were very long fingers.

It was clear than the man had been dead a very long time. His skin was dark and shriveled. Ancient dead men pulled from moldering tombs have this grisly aspect, where all moisture has leached from the rigid body, leaving only leathery skin over hollow bone.

There was no telling who the dead man might have been from scrutiny of the face. It was a leathery mask of jerked beef. The eye sockets were dry holes. The teeth were all that looked new. They gleamed like dice. One tooth showed the glint of gold wire.

"Who would express us a mummy?" wondered Ham.

Doc said nothing. He was examining the cadaver's clothes. They were rugged, of modern manufacture. The pants were duck, the shirt a light cotton drill reserved for tropical climates.

Monk, monkeylike curiosity on his apish face, eyed the mummy from different angles.

"You know, that mummy has mighty big mitts."

Contrarily, Ham said, "They appear of normal size to me."

"Look how big they are hanging at the ends of those skinny wrists," Monk pointed out.

"That is because the entire body has shriveled," Ham sniffed. "There is almost no muscle tissue in the human hand, so there is less shrinkage."

"Baloney! That dead mummy has meat-hooks almost the size of—"

The thought hung in the air. Ham looked at Monk and the hairy chemist returned the look. Their faces lost color as a cold, unsettling thought took hold of them.

"Are you thinkin' what I'm thinkin'?" Monk breathed.

Doc Savage then spoke. His words were calm and controlled, but they had the impact of a dropped anvil.

"These clothes," the bronze man said with no evident feeling, "belong to Renny Renwick."

Chapter IX
WARNING IN BLACK

A SICK SILENCE hung in the room.

Monk stared at the inert mummy of the oversized hands with his eyes bugging out like peeled grapes. Ham Brooks, for once, was struck speechless.

Only Doc Savage appeared unmoved by the prospect that their comrade in arms was dead. He stripped the shirt from the mummy, breaking several bones despite taking great pains not to cause further damage to the fragile travesty.

The dryish snappings made Monk wince and Ham Brooks turned green as an unripe apple.

"Renny..." Monk gulped. "It can't be him."

Ham gestured with his dark cane. "Notice the untanned circular patch on the left wrist. This person wore a wristwatch."

"Yeah," Monk said thickly. "Recently, too. So he ain't been a mummy for very long."

Doc examined the shirt labels. Then he went to the cuffs. One cuff had a slightly frayed seam. Doc popped this and out came a bit of what looked like chalk.

Ham gulped. "That—that's a piece of the special chalk we use to leave messages that can only be read by ultra-violet light."

The bronze man then removed a boot. Inside, he discovered a label.

"Renny's?" asked Monk.

Doc nodded. "Renny's." The bronze man stood up. His eerie trilling filled the room once more. It possessed a wondering quality this time.

"When did we last hear from Renny?" he asked quietly.

"About a week ago," supplied Ham.

"This mummy," Doc said, "appears to have been dead at least a month."

"Then it can't be Renny!" Monk whooped.

Doc said, "The circumstantial evidence indicates that it is. More tests are in order."

"What could have mummified Renny so quick?" demanded Monk.

"You are a chemist. Have you any thoughts?"

Monk scratched his nubbin of a head. "Well, something would have to take all the moisture out of body. Maybe if he was… cooked over a slow fire. Say, look at his hair. There's no singe marks."

Ham frowned distastefully. "I do not like to speak of Renny this way."

The bronze man shut the lid tight and lifted the trunk in both hands, saying, "We will conduct further tests in our lab setup."

The speed elevator took them to the eighty-sixth floor.

They stepped out into the corridor, Doc Savage conveying the steamer trunk atop one Herculean shoulder as if it were weightless.

"Just one moment," a blustery voice intruded.

They whirled.

A large man had been loitering in the corridor, face flushed and perspiring profusely. He dabbed at his florid countenance with a monogrammed silk handkerchief the color of lemons, replaced his rimless pince-nez glasses. He spoke up.

"I am C. Startell Pompman, Mr. Savage. I have been attempting to see you for several days without success."

"You get out of here!" Monk raged.

"Permit me a moment…."

Doc let his golden eyes rest on Pompman, nodded, and said, "Follow us."

The plain bronze door bearing the name CLARK SAVAGE, JR. in modest letters opened, apparently of its own accord.

Doc Savage entered first. Bones rattled with a dry grisly sound inside the steamer trunk that had come from the Orient.

Most persons privileged to enter Doc's sanctum usually gawk and rubber-neck at the well-appointed reception room, the massive library, and finally the scientific laboratory as they passed through them. But Startell Pompman was oblivious to all even as Doc set the trunk on a work table in the huge white-walled lab.

"Tell us your story, Pompman," Doc invited as he went to work with a fluoroscope device much larger than the one previously utilized.

"As I told your men, I am an importer, specializing in curios and artifacts. One unusual specimen—ah—came into my possession in China during the present difficulties over there."

Doc was taking X-ray pictures of the mummy while Ham paced and fidgeted, shifting his ever-present cane from one manicured hand to the other. Monk had remained in the reception room to make telephone inquiries of Renny Renwick's last movements.

Pompman continued. "I do not know what this curio was made of, but it resembles crystal, but is intolerably cold to the touch. Moreover, it is a substance never before seen on earth."

Ham Brooks looked at him incredulously.

"Or so I believe," Pompman amended.

Doc paused in his work and looked up.

"Why do you think that?"

"I base this assumption on it's—ah—properties."

"That is not much of an explanation."

"I am being careful with my words, Savage. During the course of experimenting with this substance I hired two individuals to assist me. They betrayed me. They absconded with a portion of the artifact, to what end I do not know."

Doc had resumed his work. He was, of all things, taking fingerprints of the mummy's surviving fingers. First he inked the fingers. Then he applied them to an ordinary police fingerprint identification card such as are employed by the Department of Justice's Bureau of Investigation.

"Your story so far is composed of drama, not facts," the bronze man observed.

Startell Pompman mustered his dignity with a haughty lift of his chin. "I fear betrayal. This is a highly delicate matter. I am requesting your help in recovering the lost portion of the artifact."

"We do not normally engage in business difficulties such as you describe," Doc said absently.

"But there is more to this than I can reveal."

"Is your life in danger?"

"No," Pompman admitted.

"Then we cannot help you."

STARTELL POMPMAN made fat fists at his sides and seemed on the verge of becoming volcanic once again. The sight of the bronze man going about his work in deep thought seemed to dissuade him from launching into a further diatribe.

"Would it change your mind if I told you I have reason to believe that your man Renwick may have been reduced to that terrible state by the missing piece of my lost curio?" he asked in a throaty tone.

Doc's trilling wavered briefly. He stifled it.

Ham rushed up and demanded, "What are you trying to tell us, fellow?"

Startell Pompman swiftly changed his tune.

"I—I could be mistaken of course. But what happened to that mummy is something I have seen before."

"Where?" asked Doc.

"In Shanghai. It was horrible."

"I don't believe you!" Ham snapped. "You are saying this to capture our interest, not because it is true! You are desperate."

Doc interjected, "Your story does seem convenient."

Startell Pompman sputtered inarticulately.

Monk Mayfair barged in at that point saying, "Doc, I been in touch with British authorities in Singapore. They tell me Renny was discovered missing after a fight in his hotel five days ago. His room was busted up and everything. He ain't come back for his... duds."

All eyes went to the mummy on the table. Doc had performed a localized dissection, evidently to expose the stomach and its contents, but was presently examining the fingerprint card under a microscope.

They crowded around him.

"Are they—Renny's?" asked Ham.

Doc shut off the microscope. "Impossible to tell. The tips of the fingers are too badly shriveled to make useful impressions. But I discovered this item tucked into the excelsior packing of the trunk."

One bronze finger pointed to a square of parchment of some kind. In what appeared to be octopus ink was brushed a short message in bold strokes suggesting a stick had been used to inscribe them, Oriental-style:

> SAVAGE:
> UNLESS YOU WANT TO BE TURNED INTO A MUMMY, LAY OFF!

The note was unsigned.

"Lay off!" Ham ejaculated. "Lay off what?"

"There is insufficient information to make conjectures on that score," Doc Savage advised. "But the situation bears investigation."

"Whoever wrote that," Monk growled, "don't know us very

well."

Doc walked up to Startell Pompman.

"If what you say is true, it is quite a coincidence that you should show up at the same time that this mummy reached us."

"I have been trying to see you for days." He levered a chubby arm at Monk and Ham. "Those two buffoons repeatedly rebuffed me. Were I you, Savage, I would fire them forthwith!"

The bronze giant said nothing to that. He did not believe in descending to personalities.

"We are setting off for Singapore immediately to look into the disappearance and possible death of our comrade," Doc said calmly. "It is up to you whether or not you care to accompany us."

"Will you assist me in my quest?" Pompman demanded.

"If it ties in with whatever has befallen Renny, yes."

"Then I will go, for this is very, very important. Of stellar import, I would venture to say."

That settled, Doc Savage went to a far section of the vast laboratory and shifted certain glasses on wall shelves. As a result, the entire panel valved open, and another revealed a sizable capsule suspended in a tube, much like a pneumatic tube, only on a larger scale.

The suspended car was shaped like a bullet pointing earthward. A hatch stood open, disclosing an upholstered interior.

Doc motioned for Pompman to enter. He looked hesitant, perhaps intimidated by the awareness than the capsule hung suspended over some eighty-six stories of void.

Monk gave him an ungentle shove, and he went sprawling aboard. The others joined him. Lastly Doc Savage stepped aboard and closed the bullet car's door. By some mechanical means, this caused the outer door to close, sealing the giant pneumatic tube.

Doc said, "Hang on." Everybody reached for grab straps such as are found on modern subway cars.

With a roaring *whoosh,* the capsule dropped straight down. It seemed to fall forever, abruptly right-angled in a horizontal direction and the passengers were all thrown violently around. The interior of the car was padded against such buffeting. It helped only insofar as to prevent bruising.

At the end of its run, the car ran at a gentle upward incline, stopping with a series of noisy clicks.

The hatch popped and Monk was the first to clamber out.

"Some roller coaster ride, huh?" Monk said. "Once Doc works out all the bugs, whizzers like that one will carry folks between New York and China in an hour flat."

Startell Pompman had to be helped out. His plump knees had turned to rubber.

"What was that contraption?" he wondered breathlessly.

Monk beamed. "I call it the flea run. That go-devil that brought us here operates by compressed air."

"A go-devil is a floating device used to clear clogged oil pipelines," Pompman remarked.

"I kinda grew up in the Oklahoma oil fields," Monk admitted.

Pompman discovered that he was in a cavernous space resembling an aircraft hangar. There were all manner of craft hangared here, ranging from a true gyroplane to various pursuit and transport planes. All were amphibians. A large part of the hangar was partitioned off, and Startell Pompman got the idea that this housed a dirigible or airship of some kind.

Doc went to a big tri-motored flying boat. It was painted bronze. They prepared it for take-off, removing chocks from the wheels and stowing metal storage cases aboard.

When preparations were finished, the hatch shut closed and the bronze man in the pilot's bucket was starting the engines. They filled the hangar with a great reverberant thunder.

The giant transport ran its tail about, and slipped down a concrete apron into the water. Great riverward doors opened to allow this. They operated in response to a radio signal from the cockpit.

Once on the water, Doc turned the craft into the wind and opened the throttles. The streamlined ship thundered along, got on step, and vaulted skyward like a great bronze eagle.

"Next stop," Monk called out, "Singapore!"

Chapter X

MESSAGE IN BLUE

FROM NEW YORK CITY to Singapore in the Orient is over ten thousand nautical miles.

Doc Savage pushed his flying boat non-stop to San Francisco, refueled there, and made the hop to Honolulu, Hawaii, across the Pacific in record time. Rarely did the bronze plane drop below two hundred and seventy-five miles an hour. At times, the three giant engines approached three hundred miles per hour. Tailwinds helped.

Inside the streamlined ship, the cabin was electrically warmed and soundproofed to a degree that permitted ordinary conversation. Doc Savage evinced little interest in that. He ran the great motors with the throttles pushed to their pins, seemingly immune to fatigue.

Monk and Ham spelled one another in the navigation bucket.

"This bus sure travels," Monk muttered sleepily.

Ham queried, "What say, Doc, why not get a little sleep and let Monk and myself carry on?"

The bronze giant shook his head in the negative. He seemed determined to push toward their far destination in the shortest possible time.

Portly C. Startell Pompman kept to himself. In time, the sheer monotony of their voyage began to wear on his nerves and he struck up a conversation.

Ham was seated beside him. It was night over the twinkling Pacific, with the sea and sky a black mirror. Pompman turned to the dapper lawyer and remarked, "Studying the stars?"

Ham blinked his dark eyes. "I was merely attempting to see how many constellations I could identify by sight," he sniffed.

Pompman clasped puffy fingers over his ample middle. "I myself am a student of the firmament."

"Is that so?" Ham drawled in a disinterested voice. He had shown no sign of warming up to the big bluff businessman.

"Indeed. I am also a student of human nature, and the character of men. Take yourself, for instance. By reputation, you are one of the most brilliant minds in your chosen profession."

Ham's sharp features came away from the window. Interest showed in his expression. "I am given to understand so," he admitted.

"You are also a fastidious dresser. A veritable modern Beau Brummell."

"I take justifiable pride in my appearance," allowed Ham.

"And so you should. You are a man of renown. It is only appropriate to cut a proper figure. It is incumbent upon a man of your station in life, and education."

"I consider myself fortunate to count myself among the most noted alumni ever to come out of Harvard Law School," Ham returned, warming to the subject.

"Quite so. With your keen mind and clever ways, I will wager that you were born in the month of May, or possibly June."

Ham's voice grew thin. "Why do you say that, my good fellow?"

"As I told you," said Startell Pompman, "I am a student of human nature. And of the stars."

"You are an amateur astronomer?" questioned Ham, puzzled.

"Not quite. I study the stars, true. But my interest is not in heavenly bodies, but in their effect upon mankind."

"Are you speaking of... astrology?" asked Ham.

"I prefer a more dignified term, namely, Solar Psychology," confided Startell Pompman.

"Do tell," said Ham thinly. Abruptly, he excused himself and got up.

Going forward, the elegant attorney tapped Monk Mayfair on his burly shoulder.

"I will take over now, ape."

"It ain't your turn yet," growled Monk.

"Nevertheless, I think you should listen to what our guest has to say about your personality," Ham informed him.

"What's he been sayin'?" grated Monk.

"I refuse to stoop to such language. Why don't you ask him yourself?"

"I'll do just that," said Monk. Hoisting himself out of his seat, he worked back to the rear on bandy legs.

"What've you been tellin' that shyster about me?" demanded Monk without preamble.

Startell Pompman said with injured dignity, "Merely that I am a student of personality. I have been observing you. I would wager that you were born in the month of April, if not May."

"What makes you say that?" Monk demanded.

"The way you carry yourself. Your bullheaded attitude. You are a man who charges into things. You seize opportunity by the throat. Obviously you—"

"I might seize you by the throat if I took a mind to," growled the hairy chemist.

"Spoken like a true Taurus."

"A—what did you say?" muttered Monk.

"You are undoubtedly born under the sun of Taurus. It is written all over your bovine face."

"My face ain't none of your business," Monk retorted. "So mind yours before I pop you one."

Monk rushed forward to the cockpit.

"This guy's an astrologer!" he bellowed over the engine vibration.

Doc Savage said nothing.

Ham offered, "It is a superstition I take no store in. Hence, my invitation to you to keep the bounder company."

Monk barked, "Out of that seat, shyster. I'm reclaimin' my due."

"Nothing doing!"

They began arguing, but Doc Savage cut them off.

"Monk, get in touch with the authorities in Singapore. See if any late word of Renny has been learned."

"Gotcha, Doc." Monk repaired to the radio station, got busy at the dials.

"I do not like that Pompman person," Ham muttered. He lapsed into silence. The mention of Renny Renwick had reminded him that the hulking engineer's fate was entirely unknown. Ham addressed this concern.

"Doc, do you think that mummy we left back in New York is—"

"The evidence is so far contradictory. But Renny's fate remains uncertain."

A worried frown troubled the dapper lawyer's eagle-like profile. "But it does not guarantee that Renny remains among the living. He has been out of communication for a deuced long interval."

"It might be best," replied the bronze man gravely, "to be prepared for any eventuality, come what may."

Several minutes later, Monk spoke up from the radio set.

"Singapore police say they're still lookin' for Renny. But so far they admit that they ain't got a clue."

Gloom descended upon the spacious cabin. No one spoke.

Reluctantly, Monk returned to the empty seat near Startell Pompman. He had something on his mind.

"Astrology," he said flatly, "is a bunch of hooey."

Pompman eyed him aridly. "I beg your pardon?"

"You heard me. Hooey. Hokum. Otherwise known as the bunk. The stars are far away. They don't affect people. And that's that."

"I am curious," said Pompman. "What is your leader's birthday?"

"What's it to you?"

"Idle curiosity," replied the other suavely. "I confess that the tell-tale indicators pointing to his composite solar personality so far elude me. It is as if the big fellow partakes of all twelve signs of the Zodiac." Pompman made a harrumphing sound deep in his being. "Patently impossible, as we all know."

"Ask Doc, if you're so durned interested," mumbled Monk.

"I shall—in due time." Startell Pompman lapsed into silence.

Monk Mayfair stared out into the night. He was a practical soul, and began wishing that he had brought along his pet pig, Habeas Corpus. But there had been no time to collect the remarkable shoat from the apish chemist's penthouse digs. Doc Savage had also cautioned against it, which meant that the bronze man had already divined that they were all flying into a peril too terrible to risk bringing the pet.

THEY stopped over in Manila, in the Philippines, just long enough to take on aviation fuel, after which they resumed the arduous hop to Singapore, which is a substantial island at the tip of the Malay Peninsula.

Dawn found them dropping out of the Malayan sky. Doc Savage slanted the thundering transport plane in for a landing on Singapore harbor. He dragged the bay twice to warn the covered *tambangs,* bumboats, and assorted fishing craft to clear a path. They did.

The landing was smooth and when the laboring engines shut down, the silence was uncanny owing to the fact that they had become long accustomed to their song and vibration.

Doc nudged the gliding flying boat toward a jetty dock that had been made ready for them.

A contingent of British constabulary—Singapore was a British protectorate—were present to greet him. They stood assembled in their impeccable white uniforms like an honor guard.

Unusual deference was shown the bronze man and his aides. Doc had done the English government a good turn a time or two. They all but saluted him.

A police machine was made available, and they were whisked through crowded streets toward the Raffles Hotel. Assorted coolies and fowl scampered to get out of their way.

They arrived before the entrance to the Raffles Hotel in time to behold an interesting sight.

Two coffee-colored Orientals in blue turbans and tropical whites were exiting the side entrance, carrying a long wall mirror, evidently lately removed from a suite of rooms.

Doc Savage took note of them, and began to approach.

At sign of the big bronze man striding toward them, the two turbaned gentlemen almost dropped the mirror.

One spat something at the other and they tried to pick up the pace. But the mirror—it included the ornate gilt frame—proved too heavy to maneuver with any speed.

Doc Savage called out to them to halt in perfect Malay.

"Berhenti! Hilo-matt!"

Carefully, they set the mirror down and one held it while the other drew from somewhere on his person a weapon that was a cross between a short sword and a very long knife. A Malay *parang.*

The knife wielder spat something pungent at the bronze man.

Doc Savage stepped in, feinted, and the blade began to describe dazzling circles in the early morning sunlight.

Somehow—the bronze man seemed hardly to move—the knife began pin-wheeling into the air, and the knife-man found himself looking at his suddenly empty fist. The expression on his face plainly showed that he had no idea what had become of his *parang.*

Doc caught the hilt as it came back down, made a conjuror's pass, after which the blade disappeared from sight. It appeared magical. In fact, it was a maneuver known to stage illusionists as a "vanish." The blade now reposed along Doc's forearm, held in place by his coat sleeve, the hilt hidden by his closed fist. So fast did the bronze man's hands move that all onlookers were confused by what had transpired.

The man shrieked, wheeled about, and attempted flight.

Metallic fingers drifted out and seized the Malay by the linen collar. Doc Savage lifted one great arm and the man was comically running on air, as if in a movie-house cartoon.

That brought the other Malay close to panic. He dropped the mirror. It struck the ground with great noise and force. Naturally, it shattered.

Then the man did an inexplicable thing. He plunged into the broken glass and attacked it as if to complete the job of destruction.

The glass was as sharp as daggers. Indeed, broken glass is sharper than any knife. With surprising speed, the man was bleeding from many cuts about his body. Instead of this dissuading him from doing any worse damage to himself, the Malay confederate picked up a particularly vicious shard and swiftly slashed one wrist. Gore gushed out in a flood.

Still holding onto his prisoner, Doc reached down and pulled the unfortunate man clear.

It was too late. An artery had been severed. Turning pasty as a brown ghost—if there could be such a thing—the man went limp in the metallic giant's grasp.

Doc rapped, "Monk. Get the lantern from your case." Monk had brought along a case of special equipment. He ran back to the police machine and brought back a folding camera of a thing. He opened it, disclosing a purplish lens.

Monk and Ham surrounded the crimson-stained mirror.

"You know what to do, Monk," the bronze man directed.

Monk and Ham got between the sun and the shattered mirror

and made shade. Monk then pressed a button. Nothing seemed to happen.

But among the blood on the fractured glass, eerie blue letters showed. The words inscribed were difficult to read. They appeared to say:

PIRATE IS

"That is Renny's handwriting," Ham breathed.

Doc nodded. "Investigation should show that this mirror was removed from Renny's hotel suite."

"But what'd he mean by 'Pirate Is'?" demanded Monk. "Is what?"

Ham Brooks separated his slim stick, revealing it to be a sword cane, and applied the tip of the blade to the nose of Doc Savage's captive, saying, "I'll wager this beggar knows."

If he did, they did not learn it. For, amazingly, the Malay took the tip of Ham's sword into his mouth and impaled his tongue on it. Perhaps he saw the sticky brown substance coating the point. Perhaps not. But he was soon insensate in Doc Savage's clamping grip.

"You tort!" Monk squawled. "Look what you done!"

"I did nothing!" Ham snapped back. "He did it—to himself."

Ham carried an antidote to the sticky anesthetic, but seemed unconcerned as to the fate of the door thief. Doc lowered the unconscious one to the pavement, where a slow red wormlet crawled out of his open mouth.

Addressing the amazed police, Doc Savage inquired, "The Macassar Strait is infamous for pirate activity. Is there a locality there known as Pirate Isle?"

"Pirate Island," corrected a constable. "It lies far beyond the Gulf of Siam, in the Tiger Islands of the South China Sea. Beastly bad place. Den for red-handed rotters, corsairs and cut-throats. I can provide you an excellent marine chart, showing its precise location."

Doc nodded. Turning to his men, he imparted, "We will go

there."

"His Majesty's Constabulary offers its service and its protection to you, *Tuan* Savage."

"That will not be necessary," said Doc Savage. "We will handle this matter ourselves."

The police politely deferred to the bronze man. They conveyed the party back to the waiting seaplane and, after Doc supervised refueling operations, the flying boat was climbing back into the brilliant blue sky.

"This new development could mean that Renny is still alive," Ham offered hopefully.

Just to be contrary, and not because he believed it—or wanted to—Monk Mayfair groused, "Don't mean any such thing. They could have hauled Renny off to Pirate Island before... doin' what they done to him. Them heathens was just coverin' their tracks, is all."

Doc Savage offered no opinion on the subject. His metallic face remained composed and unreadable.

Chapter XI

YELLOW PARADISE

NIGHT WAS CREEPING over the disreputable spot known as Pirate Island.

In the harsh tropical sunlight, the island had been a riot of blinding hues—orchids of incredible beauty and variety decorated the verdant isle. Wild fruit hung ripe and heavy from barbaric-looking trees of all descriptions. Too, wildlife crept and crawled with an abundance that dazzled the senses of those unused to its splendid luxury.

All that was fading now as the sun dipped below the water like a tired face falling into slumber.

If the dying of day presaged a lessening of the humidity that had plagued the daylight hours, the first part of the evening failed to live up to that promise. If anything, it felt warmer. Mark and Mary Chan lay on thin pallets on the rough floor of the rude longhouse structure that had been erected on stilts. Its principal and perhaps only virtue being that its stilt construction held it well above the ground, which was prone to flooding in the violent monsoon rainstorms that characterized this part of the globe. Additionally, they served to hold its occupants high above the various lizards and insect vermin which prowled the vicinity for food.

A snarl from somewhere near brought that unsettling fact to mind.

"Sounds like a tiger," Mark muttered, dark eyes switching about.

"Yes, a tiger," Mary agreed. Her voice was subdued.

They were both thoroughly dispirited.

For a week now—longer it seemed—they had been held captive in this longhouse. At first they had been fed. But the feeding had been punctuated by many questions.

The questioner had been Dang Mi, the so-called Scourge of the South China Sea.

The trend of the interrogation had been the nature of the inexplicable thing in the steel strongbox with blue crackle-finish.

Mark and Mary had resolutely refused to reply in anything other than dire and cryptic parables.

"Anyone who opens that box," Mark had warned, "might as well say a prayer to Satan first."

"Because that will be the next person he meets," added Mary.

Dang Mi was a practical soul. He did not put any stock in a Satan or in a literal realm over which he presided. But he had experienced the power of the unknown thing in the box. So he did not openly scoff.

"That—that devil in the box turned that hulkin' Doc Savage assistant into a mummy," Dang revealed.

Mark had ground his white teeth at that news. Mary had gasped. Neither spoke. Words lingered in their throats, unuttered.

"So I shipped the cadaver all the way to New York by express, just as a way of warnin' Doc Savage to lay off," Dang finished.

Mark began, "Do you really think—"

"—that Doc Savage will not rush to this spot?" finished Mary.

"He don't know what spot to rush to, the bronze bloke don't," Dang Mi said, lapsing into British vernacular.

"And you do not know what to do with that box," Mark pointed out.

"Nor will you ever," Mary chimed in.

Dang Mi eyed the similar siblings with a villainous orb. He

rocked back on his high boot heels, broad face ruminative.

"Tell me somethin' I don't know."

"Why should we?" Mary countered.

"So's I don't scrag one of you," Dang illuminated.

Mark and Mary exchanged uneasy glances.

"Promise?" Mary asked.

"Cross my wicked heart and hope to plunder," Dang Mi said somberly, placing a palm on his chest.

"There is another box," Mark volunteered.

"Worse than this one?"

"Far worse" agreed Mary.

"Tang has it," Mark revealed.

"Tang?"

"That is all you need to know," sniffed Mary.

Dang Mi felt of his blocky jaw. "Tang, eh?"

Mark nodded emphatically. "Yes, Tang. And if he isn't stopped, the world may perish in a way no prophet ever predicted."

"Is that why you were headin' out Singapore way to meet Doc Savage?"

The strangely matched pair said nothing. They did not have to. That was why they so desperately needed to reach the Man of Bronze. It was written on their ivory faces.

Dang Mi withdrew at that point. That was when the feeding stopped.

Twice a day, Dang reappeared. Once after sunrise and again before sunset, to ask questions. He seemed hesitant to bring harm to either of the almond-eyed twins.

This day, Dang had come at the early hour. But by the time evening fell and melted all the color away, he had not.

"Do you think we have been left here to die?" Mary asked Mark.

Mark searched the fading surrounding with worried eyes. He did not reply. Plainly, he did not know what it meant.

Things prowled through the underbrush. Heavy things.

Crocodiles perhaps. Snakes for certain. Pirate Island was crawling with snakes, or perhaps it was vice versa. A significant portion of their early diet while in captivity had been reptile meat. At first they had refused any of this noisome repast. But after a day or two, any meat proved better than no meat. And at least it had been roasted for consumption.

Two hours past the last light, a strange hissing filled the night air.

"Serpent!" Mary gasped.

Mark shook his head. "No. It comes from above."

The roof of the longhouse was thatched. But they could peer up through breaks and chinks in the rough thatching created by the pummeling monsoon rains of the summer now passed.

There was only a thin sliver of a moon, and this admitted faint moonlight. But it was enough to spy a great dark shape passing overhead.

Mary drew in her breath and seemed to hold it within for a very long time.

"It looks—like a giant bat."

Mark whispered, "No bat. That was an airplane."

"But I heard no motor."

"Silenced," decided Mark.

Excited now, Mark studied the sky where the first star points were emerging. He craned his head, listening first with one ear and then the other.

"Is it coming back?" asked Mary.

"No. It's not coming back." Mark Chan's low voice seemed to collapse and then he followed suit, letting all the strength flow out of him. He let his pent form drop to the floor like a deflating tire.

"Could that—have been—Doc Savage?" wondered Mary.

"If it was," Mark replied in a weak, disillusioned tone, "he has passed over us."

Mary, too, seemed to deflate at that point. She lay down.

They were shackled, hands and feet. A hawser chain wound around their waists linked them together so that if one escaped, the other would have to follow. And all that loose chain would rattle.

They did not attempt escape. They were certain that Dang Mi's pirates were picketed out of sight. They did not know where. It was possible that they were surrounded, but since they could not know for certain, any direction in which they attempted flight could prove calamitous. They knew that. So they did not try.

NOT long after the hissing aircraft passed overhead, Dang came bustling up. He was alone. Sometimes he came alone. Other times he had two of his crew along. Different members of his motley band came at various times. Early on, Poetical Percival Perkins had been one of them. But after the first visits, he had not shown his lean brown face again.

Mark and Mary understood that was because Dang Mi did not wish for any secret they divulged to fall upon listening ears. Of his crew, only Perkins spoke English. That was probably why he had not been seen in a week.

When Dang dragged the bamboo ladder which lay against a nearby kapok tree over to the longhouse and set it in place, he was muttering under his breath.

Climbing the ladder, he poked his head up and demanded, "Either of you hear a plane flyin' overhead?"

Mark and Mary looked up, but said nothing. Their placid ivory-hued faces told it all.

"Could be that was Doc Savage," Dang muttered.

Again Mark and Mary said nothing.

"If it was," Dang continued, "he ain't stopped here."

Neither twin contradicted him.

"And that means any hope you two had of bein' rescued just went whistlin' on in the general direction of China," Dang decided.

"The pilot might circle back," Mary ventured bravely.

Dang shook his head. "He ain't even slowed down any. He ain't wingin' back. So maybe it's time to talk turkey."

Mark and Mary looked blank. Evidently their grasp of American slang was not perfect.

"What I mean is," Dang clarified, "your last hope just went away. Doc Savage is searchin' for the ones that salivated Renny Renwick. He ain't got a clue to this place. So let's confabulate. Get me?"

Mark and Mary evidently did not.

"Spill! Savvy? Talk!" roared Dang.

Mark offered, "Tang wants the box you have."

"If he brings his box," warned Mary, "it will cancel out your box."

"The devil in your box is not as powerful as the devil in his box," added Mark. "It is vastly greater."

"If Tang comes," questioned Mary, "what will you do then?"

Dang Mi plainly did not know. He laved his lips with a tongue so dry that it almost sounded like a cat licking a sheet of sandpaper. He did not fancy this sudden talk of devils.

"Then I guess I might as well kill you both," he decided at last.

Mark and Mary did not reply to that. A paleness descended over their oval features until they began to resemble a set of identical ivory cameos displayed in an open locket.

Dang added, "No sense riskin' having prisoners any longer. We got to get back to buccaneerin'. I'm thinkin' that the thing in that box can help me in that work. Maybe if I come alongside of a ship and throw the box over onto the other deck, what's inside will suck all the juice out of the other crew."

"If you do that—" began Mark.

"—who will put the horrible thing back in the box?" finished Mary.

Dang Mi made strange faces. "Hadn't considered that angle,"

he admitted thickly.

He massaged his blocky jawline thoughtfully and said, unnecessarily, "Wait here."

Scrambling down, Dang retreated into the close-pressing foliage.

"Are you thinking what I am thinking?" Mary asked her twin brother.

"I'm thinking he's going to bring the blue box here and set it before us, then attempt to open it with a bamboo pole or switch to see what happens."

"Undoubtedly," agreed Mary.

They lay on their backs awaiting their fate. Their breathing became hoarse and rapid, as their imaginations went to work on their frayed nerves.

Before long, a head poked over the level of the floor. It was unnerving, for the owner of the head made no sound approaching.

In the thin moonlight, the eyes of the new arrival were strangely luminous.

For a brief moment, Mark Chan, looking at them, thought that a tiger had clambered stealthily up the bamboo-pole-and-banana-tree-fibre lashed ladderwork as big cats are wont to do in search of a meal.

But these were not yellow like a tiger's orbs. They were golden. Moreover, they were human—if eerily so.

Utterly without sound, the new arrival came up the ladder and towered over them.

He was a giant. Even in the murk, his size and musculature was overwhelming. It was something to take the breath away.

Quietly, the big man came over and knelt, examining their shackles. The face of the man was much like a mask cast in metal. It betrayed no emotion. Only the golden eyes moved, and their movement was a kind of animated whirling. It picked up in speed as if the brain behind the golden eyes were calculating furiously.

The big bronze man was testing the length of chain that connected Mark to Mary Chan. He felt along the linkage, evidently found a link he favored and stepped on a section of the chain, while simultaneously exerting pressure with both hands.

The man's arms were bare, and as he strained, the muscles and tendons of his forearms seemed to spring into life like coiling serpents of sinew.

The link separated, then broke. It was an eye-popping display of brawn. Chain collapsed onto the grass matting with barely a sound.

Mark spoke first.

"You are Doc Savage!" he breathed.

A bronze finger touched parted lips in a gesture for silence.

Then the metallic giant helped them both to their feet. He did this with the same strong hands. They felt like warm metal to the touch.

Once erect, Mark and Mary expected the bronze man to make short work of their remaining shackles. Instead, Doc Savage heaved first one and then the other twin over his broad shoulders and, showing no sign of strain, carried them over to the waiting ladder.

Pausing, the bronze man tested the top rung with a foot, apparently did not like the groan that was produced and simply stepped over the edge, landing on the soft jungle floor with hardly a perceptible jar.

In this strange fashion, the Chans were borne off into the murksome jungle.

DOC SAVAGE bore the helpless pair for a considerable distance with an ease and soundlessness that made them both think they were being carried off by a creature born of some preternatural realm.

Coming to the water's edge, he deposited them at the mouth of a shallow lagoon.

The moon by this time had climbed higher in the sky. The bright crescent seemed to stand wavering on the lagoon surface, a turbulent mirror to the untroubled lunar body above.

Setting the chains down upon a pair of rocks, Doc went to work on them. This time, the bronze man resorted to means other than main strength.

Reaching into his shirt, he drew forth a pair of glass vials, somewhat resembling test tubes, but smaller in size. These were capped by corks that resembled hard rubber.

Unstoppering one, the bronze man poured the liquid contents onto the spots where the shackles were loose and not touching skin. Then, ripping off his rolled-up shirt sleeves, he wrapped them about the wrists where the links were cramped.

Presently a pungent odor billowed forth. Magically, the links began melting.

"Acid?" Mary asked.

Doc nodded. His flake-gold eyes were intent upon the dissolving operation of the acid. Once, a droplet of molten steel spattered as if off a hot skillet and the amazing bronze man jerked Mary Chan's left wrist out of harm's way.

When Doc was done, all that remained were the bracelets on their wrists and ankles. They were inconvenient, but would not hamper movement much. He let them be.

"Can you both swim?" he asked quietly.

"Yes," affirmed Mark.

"Like seals," avowed Mary.

Doc nodded. "My plane is anchored not far from here. We will swim for it."

"But we saw your airplane fly on hours ago," Mary protested. "How did you come to be here?"

"Parachute," said Doc. "Been scouting the island for the last few hours. Came upon a camp."

Mark frowned. "That would be Dang Mi, the buccaneer, and his crew."

Doc Savage asked, "Have you seen any sign of a long-faced man with very large fists? His thunderous voice would be unmistakable."

Mark nodded. "Renwick."

"He perished," explained Mary.

Doc Savage's lips parted as if about to speak. A tiny trilliation seemed to start, but was quickly stifled.

Mark and Mary stared, began looking around, thinking a night-roosting bird had been startled awake.

"Never mind that," Doc Savage rapped. "Into the water."

Creeping down to the water's edge, they slipped in. Soon, they were wading out up to their knees. Fortunately the water was very warm.

This part of the lagoon was choked with reeds—cattails and bulrushes. They pushed through these. They felt as stiff as broom straws. The sea floor underneath was soft and muddy to the touch.

Suddenly Doc halted. He had been in the lead and his great arms swept back in a warning motion. Mark and Mary halted, eyes widening.

They could see nothing

The bronze man's flake-gold eyes were roving among the cattail reeds, alert and penetrating.

For the reeds were moving!

Mark and Mary saw it too. Not all the reeds were moving; only some of them.

Reaching down, Doc Savage grasped one of the nearest, which was not moving. He wrenched it from of its natural anchorage, brought it up to his face.

Examining it for the barest moments, he undertoned, "Back!"

There was such a quiet urgency in his metallic voice that Mark and Mary turned around without questioning the wisdom of retreat.

But it was too late.

Behind them, reeds were quivering unnaturally.

Moving with a speed that was unhampered by the fact that he stood thigh-deep in water, Doc Savage overhauled the retreating twins and got in front of them.

With an abruptness that brought a startled shriek from Mary Chan, the water around them exploded upward!

Blue turbans shot out of the water, under which were faces both dark and ferocious.

Brown hands came into view, thorned with short wavy swords.

"Membunuh mereka semua!" a man shouted. "Kill them!"

Another shrieked, *"Kamu mati!"*—"Die!"

As one, the Malays fell on Doc Savage and his freed captives.

The bronze man's fists cracked out, found jaws, broke same. Teeth flew from shattered mouths, some white, others black from chewing the betel nut.

The attackers outnumbered Doc four to one. In less than a minute, the bronze man had whittled their number in half.

He was hampered somehow by the need to yank some of the fallen attackers out of the water, lest they drown in their insensate state.

Soon, Doc's metallic hands were filled with unconscious corsairs, with no place to deposit them safely.

A pirate made a move for Mary Chan. Mark Chan got in between and, using his steel bracelets, intercepted the wicked edge of the knife that was actually a short sword.

On the third try, the pirate drew blood. Mary screamed, then launched herself on the Malay.

Perhaps it was her wild shriek. More probably it was the force of her lunge, but the pirate suddenly backpedaled, lost his footing and fell backward into lagoon water.

Mark jumped after him and held him down with hands and knees, while the man struggled and emitted bubbles that told of his life ebbing from him violently.

Seeing this, Doc Savage warned, "No killing."

Mark Chan ignored that. He seemed intent upon drowning the worthy who had attacked his sister.

Doc Savage came in and, with the toe of his boot, upset Mark Chan. He rolled off the villain, who then scrambled to a half-standing position and fought madly for air. It was as if he could not get enough of it.

More cut-throats came. They had obviously been lying on their backs in the water, breathing through the straw-like reeds until Doc had almost stepped into the ambush.

Hands clutching corsairs, herding his charges before him, Doc Savage reached the relative safety of shore.

From the lagoon, additional rovers splashing noisily toward them. They raised polyglot Cain. This brought reinforcements from land.

A remarkable figure resembling a cowboy under a pith helmet emerged from the jungle. He wore a pair of six-guns strapped to his middle.

"Dang me if you ain't Doc Savage himself," he boomed out.

His pistols leaped into his hands and he trained both barrels on the giant man of bronze, then shifted to the Chans.

"I could split both of their skulls before you could release my hearties and do anything about it," he said conversationally.

It was the truth.

"So if you don't mind," he continued, "keep holdin' my bully boys until we get this fracas all straightened out."

Dang Mi paused as if waiting for Doc Savage to make speech. But the bronze man remained silent.

Dang muttered, "I guess that means you and me see eye-to-eye on one thing: You are my dang prisoner."

Again, Doc Savage offered no comment. But as more pirates emerged dripping and grinning from the lagoon to surround him, his lack of resistance told the entire story.

Mary Chan looked to the bronze man and, seeing that he was declining to fight, choked back a sob of sorrowful defeat.

Dang Mi grinned in the moonlight and cocked his six-shooters carefully one at a time, as if preparing to take careful aim.

"Let's you and me go for a little stroll," he gritted. "Since you went to all the trouble o' comin' here, we might as well palaver."

Chapter XII

THE BUDDHA OF ICE

THEY WERE MARCHED inland at the point of Dang Mi's matched revolvers.

By this time, Doc Savage had released his burden of helpless Malays. They stumbled along, clutching bruised ribs, and moaning.

The bronze man appeared stoic during this procession. His eerie orbs continually scanned their surroundings as if in search of a means of escape. Nothing appeared to elude his attention.

Once, while taking a turn along a narrow jungle trail, Doc gave a sharp warning.

"Ular!"

Hearing the Malay word for snake, Dang Mi almost jumped out of his hand-tooled boots. He lost his tropical pith helmet.

A particularly venomous viper had been crawling along the path ahead. Its color was a vague gray in the dark, thus the serpent was not discernible until the bronze man pointed to it.

Dang Mi stepped up and with cool precision shot the head off the viper. Then he made a show of blowing gunpowder smoke off the barrel.

"You got eyes like a cat," he said with just a trace of admiration. "But I'm a pretty fair shot, wouldn't you say?"

"Fair," Doc admitted. He did not sound impressed.

This stirred Dang Mi's ire.

"You know who I am, don't you? Dang Mi, Scourge of the South China Sea."

The bronze man said nothing.

Dang cocked a meaty thumb at his own chest. "I'm a bloomin' pirate. Blackbeard ain't got nothin' on me."

"You are Hen Gooch, of Wyoming," Doc quietly countered.

Dang Mi blinked. One revolver slipped from suddenly limp fingers. The other looked about ready to follow it to the ground.

Shaking off his surprise, the erstwhile Hen Gooch scrambled to get his precious pistol out of the dirt. He took a firm grip on both revolvers.

"It ain't healthy to spill a man's secrets in front of company," Dang barked. Under his breath, he asked, "How'd you cotton to that?"

"Your speech, no matter how you disguise it with British slang, betrays your Wyoming upbringing," Doc informed him. "Also, you walk bowlegged, like a man who had spent much of his youth in the saddle."

"That's fair figurin'," Dang allowed. "But how'd you know I was Gooch?"

"Your face once appeared on a wanted poster," Doc related. "Your attempt to disguise your eyes with collodion is an old trick. But you have not the almond-shaped orbs of a true Oriental. Nor is your dyed skin the correct color of someone from this part of the world. Then there is the matter of the slice taken from the top of your right ear—a traditional Western method of branding horse thieves still practiced in some localities. Hen Gooch stole his first horse at the age of fourteen."

Dang Mi made squirming faces of guilt.

"Just the same," he husked, "let's forget all about ol' Hen Gooch, get me? I got a proposition for you."

"And that is?"

Dang indicated the twin Chans with a shiny gun barrel. "These two have presented me with a trick box. I need you to figure out how to work it."

"Box?"

Mary Chan spoke up. "We were flying to seek out British scientific authorities, Mr. Savage. But I heard that Mr. Renwick was in Singapore, so we sought him out instead. Or rather I did after this beast captured my brother. We hoped to carry the box to one who could unlock its secrets. Only you, of all men in the whole wide world, would understand what it portended."

A faint trace on concern touched the bronze man's normally impassive lineaments.

To Dang Mi, he said, "You have this box?"

"Dangdest thing you ever did see. I don't know what it is, but it's somethin' powerful. Terrible, anyway. Just like the filly said."

"What is in the box?" asked Doc Savage.

Mark and Mary Chan exchanged glances. Their similar faces told that they did not know how much to divulge.

"Have you ever heard of the Buddha of Ice, Mr. Savage?" asked Mark Chan.

"Never," Doc admitted.

"It is an amazing thing," said Mark.

"Simply awful," Mary chimed in, nodding.

"The Buddha is in the box?" queried Doc.

Mark shook his head quietly. "No. Only its toe."

Doc regarded them. "That does not make much sense."

"You're tellin' me," spat Dang Mi. "But keep talkin'. Sounds like we're gettin' somewheres."

"That is all we wish to say," Mary Chan said thinly.

Mark Chan nodded in agreement.

"In that case," said Dang Mi, prodding both twins with his hard pistol barrels. "March!"

The unenthusiastic procession picked up where it left off.

The rest of the journey was uneventful. They came at last to a cluster of ratty huts that were erected on stilts.

A fire was burning. Over it hung an iron pot, bubbling merrily.

"Let's all eat," Dang Mi said suddenly. "Maybe some grub

will loosen our brains for some serious thinkin'."

Lapsing into a Malay dialect, Dang ordered his pirates to assemble a meal.

Out of pits covered in cool rocks, they excavated boxed foodstuffs. Hunks of some pale blocky meat were unwrapped from wax paper and oilskins.

The smell that came forth was pungent and unappetizing.

"Ugh," said Mark.

"Python steaks," Mary said distastefully.

"They have been feeding us snake meat since our first day of captivity," Mark explained.

"*When* they fed us," Mary said unhappily. She pinched her nose to keep out the unwelcome odor, mouthing, "Phaw!"

The steaks were roasted on makeshift spits while Doc Savage and the Chans were forced to wait nearby. Stores of potent Chinese wine were excavated. They had been buried in earthenware jugs, and sealed with ordinary corks. These were popped, the jugs upended and passed around in a ritual that would have been familiar to Kentucky moonshiners.

Chains were brought out of brass-bound wooden chests. They were affixed to the wrists and ankles of the big bronze man. He submitted without outward resistance.

The Chans were rebound as well. Their Oriental features, normally placid, descended into gloom.

The steaks were braised in big palm leaves that were set over open coals. The moisture in the leaves kept them from burning up, but they did shrivel somewhat under the scorching heat.

The python meat cooked up with remarkable speed, translucent meat becoming a tan hue.

The pirates ate first. They fell upon the steaks with great relish, as if partaking of a succulent delicacy. No doubt the wine helped.

When the repast was offered to the prisoners, the Chans declined.

Doc Savage, surprisingly, ate a portion. He did so as if in need of nourishment. It could be noticed that he chewed his food slowly and methodically, and if he found the meat distasteful, it did not show on his thoughtful bronze features.

Dang Mi stamped over to look down upon him.

"You're a funny bird. Most folks don't take to python the first time. It's kinda what you call an acquired taste."

The bronze man continued chewing in silence.

Dang Mi studied him at length.

"Bring that dang box," he said at last.

The blue strongbox was brought out and laid before the bronze man. Mark and Mary Chan seemed to shrink from it.

Doc Savage studied it as he chewed his food. It had the look of a strongbox of solid workmanship. Other than the azure-hued crackle surface, it appeared to be unremarkable as to construction and dimensions.

"If I open this," Dang Mi explained, "the same horrible thing that happened to your lad, Renwick, will overtake you."

Dang Mi watched the bronze man's face for signs of fear. He saw none.

"Don't you want to know what happened to him?" he asked at length.

Doc said nothing.

"We shipped you his corpse. Did you get it?"

"That mummy was not Renny Renwick," Doc said simply.

"What do you mean, it weren't! You saw his clothes. The wristwatch was his. And them oversize fists."

Doc shook his head in the negative. "The hands were big, but not as large as Renny's."

"How could you know that!" Dang exploded. "They was shriveled into mummy hands."

"The finger bones were too small to be Renny's," said Doc Savage matter-of-factly. "Furthermore, the mummified man wore his wristwatch on his left wrist. Renny habitually wore his timepiece on the right. Lastly, examination of the contents of the stomach revealed chili peppers. Renny was violently allergic to them and would only eat them under extreme duress, if at all."

"Regular Sherlock Holmes, ain't you?" snorted Dang.

He made worrisome faces and began to pace to and fro. Dang was thinking. The process of thought contorted his wide features.

His voice became sly. "If I open that box, the thing what lives inside will suck out all your juices the way a spider drinks of a trapped fly's moisture."

Doc Savage continued chewing. But his eyes were on the closed box as if attempting to penetrate its tough surface.

From time to time, he touched his chest as if to crush a gnat or other jungle pest. But it was night. There were few gnats.

Abruptly, Doc Savage stood. From a pocket somewhere about his body, a flat metal object dropped. He appeared not to notice this.

Dang Mi leaped to seize it.

Raising this prize to his face, he examined it curiously.

"What is it?"

"What does it look like?" Doc returned.

"A dang camera."

"That is a very good guess," said Doc.

Dang Mi turned the camera device over and over in his hands, and commented, "The lens is a funny color. It's purplish, almost black."

"It is a special lens."

A slow grin overspread Dang's wide features.

"I get it," he said. "For taking pictures at night."

Doc did not disabuse the pirate of that deduction.

After a moment, Dang Mi set the camera down on a flat rock and got back to business.

"As I was sayin', if I open this box, all hell's gonna bust loose. And it won't be pretty. No siree."

Dang Mi retreated a few paces, picked up a knob-headed cudgel known locally as a 'Penang lawyer,' and stole up behind the box. He carefully tapped the lid with his shillelagh twice.

The sound brought forth was dull, hollow. It told Doc Savage nothing about the contents of the mystery box.

"If I use this to crack the lid, *bing!* You three will shrivel into mummies. What does that tell you?"

"Nothing," Doc Savage admitted.

"It is the truth," Mary Chan undertoned.

"The absolute truth," echoed Mark. "If that lid is so much as raised a hair, we are all doomed to die an unnatural death."

"A supernatural death," insisted Mary.

"Or at least an agonizing one," Doc Savage offered. "Whether or not it cannot be explained remains to be seen."

Dang chortled, "Now you're talkin', Savage. You're supposed to be the wizard to end all wizards. If I let you live, will you help me crack the secret of that dang box?"

Doc Savage seemed lost in thought. When he finally spoke, he said, "I cannot unravel the riddle of that box unless I have seen it in operation."

"You want a demonstration, eh?"

"Yes. The properties ascribed to it do not make any sense. No known substance or material could leach the moisture out of a living thing in the way you describe."

"That's the first reasonable thing you have uttered," Dang Mi said happily.

Doc came to a decision. "Very well. Hand me the box."

"No tricks now!"

"I will not endeavor to open it," Doc promised. "I merely wish to examine its construction."

With evident reluctance, Dang Mi picked up the box and handed it over to the bronze man of few words.

Doc took it. Even manacled, his hands moved freely, so great was their innate strength.

First, he weighed it in one hand, transferring it to the other and hefting it again.

"Be careful!" Mark Chan gasped. "If it spills...."

Taking the container in both hands, Doc next felt of its construction. It seemed to be made of ordinary galvanized steel, but it was heavier than its apparent construction, as if what it housed was weighty beyond the size of the concealed contents.

Putting an ear to the box, the bronze man motioned for quiet. He listened for quite some time and when he stopped, it was evident that he was puzzled.

At last he admitted, "I have no idea what is held within this box."

"You don't, eh? Well, ain't that too bad. Because now you're gonna hafta open it."

"No!" Mark Chan exploded. "To open—"

"—is to die!" echoed Mary, aghast.

Dang snorted. "Naw. I lifted it a crack, and I didn't croak. But I was sure mighty thirsty afterward. You, Savage, will open it, taking care to look inside. If you fall down, my men will make sure the box gets shut tight and we'll give you a man's share of water to get over your thirst. For I promise you, it will be a right powerful thirst."

Doc Savage seemed to consider this proposition for fully a minute. His golden eyes ranged over to the flat rock where sat the strange camera whose very dark lens was pointed toward the evening sky.

In reality, he was listening intently.

Finally, Doc spoke. But the words coming from his lips, while distinct enough to be discerned, were unintelligible.

Dang Mi blurted, "What?" blankly.

Doc Savage seemed to repeat his statement.

"I can't make out a word you're sayin'. What lingo is that? It's not Malay. It—"

A hooting came from the jungle growth. Gun-muzzle flashes

threw palm boles into sharp relief. Dropping their food, startled corsairs leaped to their feet.

Turning at the waist, Dang Mi grabbed for his holstered pistols.

Doc Savage took the uncanny box and leaped backward, at the same time, calling to the others. "Scatter!"

Mark and Mary Chan did not need any further encouragement. They broke in two directions.

Whirling back around, Dang Mi observed the Chans separate.

Of the bronze man, he saw nothing. It was as if Doc Savage had vanished. Utterly. His going smacked of the supernatural.

For a careful moment, the self-styled Scourge of the South China Sea was hesitant, not sure how best to react to the sudden melee.

First, he aimed at Mary Chan. Then, apparently deciding that his surviving chivalry prevented him from shooting a woman, shifted his aim toward her twin, Mark.

Feet flying, Mark Chan was in full retreat. Dang cocked his revolver with a deliberate thumb, laid the gun sight on his target, hesitated.

Evidently now Dang decided that he could not shoot a fleeing man in the back. That hesitation cost him his opportunity. With a series of crashing sounds, Mark Chan disappeared into the underbrush.

"Dang it all! Where's Savage?" barked the buccaneer chief.

The pirate band was milling about, grabbing up knives, swords and assorted pistols. This took a few moments.

In those moments, three figures burst out of the underbrush.

They came on, firing. The blare of the pistols in their hands was awesome, almost deafening.

For they were firing Doc Savage's supermachine pistols, the amazing weapons which discharged lead so fast that a submachine gun sounded slow and stuttering by comparison.

Corsairs fell, wailing. Others lit into the brush. They lost no time in doing so. One stumbled into the campfire and ran shrieking in circles, arms flailing, his clothing ablaze.

Seeing this, Dang Mi coolly took aim and shot the man through the skull, effectively quenching his misery.

Blowing powder smoke from the upraised barrel, Dang then went in search of Doc Savage.

He did not get far.

A tremendous maul of bone and gristle swung in his direction, knocking several teeth loose, and him flat.

LOOKING up, Dang saw towering over him a long countenance that was terrible in its forbidding wrath.

"Reckon you remember me," rumbled Renny Renwick, the big-fisted engineer.

"How'd you get loose?" Dang gasped, feeling of his askew jaw. It already ached.

Renny reached down and gasped Dang by the collar, lifting him to his feet, then off his feet, which dangled in the air. Renny shook the pirate as a tomcat would shake a caught rat.

"Loose," promised Renny, "is how your teeth are going to be after I get done with you."

Mindful of his throbbing jaw, Dang Mi considered that threat, then said thickly, "I ain't got my guns no more. They're plumb in the dirt."

The big engineer kicked the nearest six-shooter away with a great booted toe.

"So I see."

Renny looked around. Not far away Monk and Ham were piling into an assortment of privateers, Asian variety.

Grinning broadly, Monk was employing his superfirer to mow them down like a thresher. They wilted in rows, like cane under scything corn knives.

Ham Brooks had his sword cane unsheathed and was engaged

in a fencing duel with two Malays wielding broad-bladed *parangs*. He was a ludicrous sight in white cotton ducks and a pith helmet. But as he slashed and parried, his thinner blade drove back the two attackers. It was a dazzling display of sheer swordsmanship, an object lesson in the value of skill versus the brute force of the heavier blades.

Pinking one and then the other, Ham swiftly rendered them both unconscious.

Satisfied, the dapper lawyer went in search of another foe.

Momentarily distracted, Renny failed to notice Dang Mi shake a dagger from one blouse sleeve until a cool steel thorn was suddenly lying athwart his jugular vein.

Dang gritted, "I call this turnin' the tables. What do you call it, Big Fists?"

Renny raised a bony globe of a free fist as if weighing his chances. Knuckles whitened tensely.

"I sliced more throats than Carter has little pills," Dang warned.

Renny subsided. His fingers remained fisted, however.

Lifting his cavernous voice, he thumped, "Monk! Ham! Hold up a minute."

"I'm just gettin' warmed up," Monk said with bloodthirsty enthusiasm. The air around him was a cloud of gray gunsmoke.

"If you don't want to watch me turn into a human fountain, you listen to this cockeyed bucko here," rumbled Renny.

Monk stopped shooting and took in the situation. He appraised it with a glance and began licking his lips the way a nervous dog does. His narrowing eyes showed that he had calculated the odds of interfering and decided the risk to Renny was too great.

Instead, he barked, "Ham! Hey, shyster, lay off!"

Ham Brooks punctured a lunging pirate in the arm and the latter seemed to fall into a swoon.

Turning, he, too, took in Renny's imminent peril.

"Just drop your blasted pig-sticker and we'll see where discretion takes us," Dang Mi promised.

Monk and Ham laid down their arms. Reluctance was etched on their sweat-smeared faces.

Dang Mi beamed. "Fair start. Now call your leader back here."

Monk and Ham began speaking at once. Ham's cultured voice rang out with distinct clearness.

"Doc! Trouble!"

Monk's squeaking voice overlapped the dapper lawyer's shouting and was unintelligible.

Dang barked, "One at a time. And no tricks! I figure you got yourselves a lingo you use to talk back and forth in secret. That's how Savage fetched you up, ain't it?"

Both men went silent. Dang had hit the nail on the head.

Doc Savage emerged from the jungle foliage so silently and unexpectedly that even his men were caught off guard. Dang Mi was equally spooked by the bronze man's sudden materialization. He started slightly, drawing a faint bit of blood from Renny Renwick's throat.

"I surrender," said Doc Savage. He was no longer clutching the crackle-finished strongbox.

Chapter XIII
SNAKE HUNT

DANG MI WAS pacing before a long log of hardwood on which sat Doc Savage, Monk, Ham, Renny and the Chans.

All were shackled now. The quantity of leg irons and associated chains required to bind the quartet had strained the reserves cached in the pirate camp, and a runner had to be sent to the black-hulled junk, *Devilfish*, anchored in a cove for more.

After the chains were made fast, Dang Mi confronted Doc Savage.

"Where," he grunted, "is that dang-blasted box?"

"Safe," replied Doc.

"That ain't the answer I was askin' for," Dang growled.

"That is the answer you have," returned the bronze giant. In the firelight, he looked utterly unafraid, even bound in heavy chains as he was. Noting Doc's mighty musculature, Dang had employed a length of hawser chain to weigh down his legs. No human being could walk, much less run, weighted down by the rusty links as Doc was.

Dang abruptly holstered his six-gun and gathered up one of the supermachine pistols confiscated from Monk and Ham. He examined the mechanism.

"Nothing beats a good old-fashioned six-shooter," he muttered. "But this do-jigger looks right handy."

He trained the long barrel at Renny Renwick.

"You! Where you been hidin' all this time? My men have

been beatin' the bushes for you. Thought the lagoon crocs had gobbled you up for sure."

"Guess," invited the big engineer.

"Tell me, or I blast you to perdition with this gimmicky gun."

Renny's puritanical lips compressed.

Seeing no evidence of forthrightness, Dang Mi began to pull back on the firing lever.

Then he hesitated. Noticing the big engineer's boots, he decided that they looked water-logged and discolored. Curiosity aroused, he approached, bent over, and used his nose like a bloodhound. He recoiled from the odor.

"Smells like you've been in a bilge!" Dang howled. "You been stowin' away in my junk, you big jugheaded lummox?"

"Seems that way," Renny admitted. "Don't it?"

Dang Mi appeared to take great offense by this. His features gathered up in a kind of convulsive snarl. Lips peeled back off teeth that showed deep staining of tobacco chewing mixed with betel nut.

"If I'd caught you on my junk," he bellowed, "I would have made you walk the plank over a clutch of crocs! A man's ship is his dang castle. And I ain't just any man. I'm Dang Mi, Scourge of the South China Sea! You hear me?"

"I hear you," replied Renny calmly. "Just not enthusiastic about your reputation."

The boastful pirate looked for a moment as if he would blow the top of Renny's head off, but a commotion behind him brought his head corkscrewing around, followed by his thick body.

"What's the dang tribulation all about?" Dang demanded of his pirates.

A Dayak began gobbling in his native tongue. He was pointing excitedly at the body of a Malay who had been felled by a machine-pistol burst.

"What do you mean, he ain't scragged?" Dang exploded.

"He's down and out, ain't he?"

Storming over to the fallen buccaneer, Dang examined him critically. He grunted, "Still breathin'." Ripping open the other man's native shirt, Dang discovered a series of bruises flecked with scarlet. He touched these. Still wet.

"Unless he turned bulletproof," muttered Dang, "somethin' ain't right here."

Doc Savage explained the matter to him.

"Mercy bullets," he stated.

Dang blinked. "Eh? Talk sense."

Doc explained, "My men employ ammunition of a type that is not lethal. Your crew members will come to in about an hour."

Dang looked at the complicated pistol in his hand. "So perforatin' that grim galoot with the concrete fists wouldn't do any good. Is that what you're sayin'? He'd just wake up later."

Doc nodded slightly. "The shells are hollow and filled with a chemical potion that produces near-simultaneous unconsciousness. Impact of the shell breaks it enough to cause a flesh wound, releasing the anesthetic into the bloodstream."

Monk and Ham had been silent up until this point. Now the dapper lawyer spoke up. "The worthies I stuck with my sword cane will also revive."

Dang grunted, "Not much on killin', are you boys?"

"Doc's got a rule against that," offered Monk.

"Well, unless he wants to see some bloodshed up real close," Dang Mi warned, "he'd better come across with some words I wanna hear. What about it, bronze guy?"

"The box is in a safe place," Doc repeated. He was looking Dang Mi dead in the eye and the flake metal in his irises were whirling steadily, like a golden snowstorm.

Dang Mi noticed this phenomenon and approached.

"You got funny-lookin' eyes," he said. "I ain't never seen the like."

"Explain how you knew to ambush us at the lagoon," Doc

invited.

Maybe it was his piratical pride. Perhaps it was the slight hypnotic power exerted by the big bronze man's steadily whirling orbs, but Dang Mi stuck out his chest and began to pontificate.

"I never exactly gave up lookin' for this brick-knuckled pest here," Dang began. "I had me hearties picketed here and there, watchin' the *Devilfish*, and a couple of grottos where I thought he might be lurkin'. When I came back to the longhouse where these twin half-castes were chained, I found them gone. Sent runners in all directions to look and spread the word. It didn't take long."

A satisfied smile wreathed Dang Mi's broad brown face.

"One of 'em spotted movement in the jungle and we figured the Chans were making for water. So we laid in ambush, Malay style."

Doc nodded as if that confirmed his own suspicions. It had been partly a fluke.

Dang added, "We found the parachute you used to drop out of the sky high up in a jackfruit tree, where you concealed it. You did a fair job o' that. But a monkey got into the shrouds and started pickin' them apart. When we come across them, they were dangling mighty free."

Ham inserted archly, "Did you hear that, Monk? One of your brothers, no doubt."

Dang Mi suddenly stepped over to the dapper attorney and slapped him with the barrel of his own superfirer.

"Don't you interrupt me!" he raged. "I don't fancy being interrupted!"

Monk started to laugh, as if enjoying the spectacle of the immaculate lawyer getting a dose of his own medicine.

Then the apish chemist stomped down on one of Dang Mi's boots with sufficient force that toe bones crackled.

Emitting a squawk that would have done credit to a howler monkey, Dang dropped his machine-pistol and grabbed at his mashed foot, hopping about in circles and fighting to wrench the boot off.

Monk saw his chance. He reached for the compact weapon and trapped it with both handcuffed paws.

"Don't nobody move!" he gritted.

Dang Mi could not have cared less about the command. He continued his hopping and howling.

This brought startled pirates running up, fists bristling with assorted blades.

Monk let loose with his superfirer. It hooted. Mechanism shuttled violently. Smoke and steel casings jumped out—an astonishing amount of the latter and an equally surprising number of the former. These intricate guns could expel violence.

Corsairs collapsed or fled madly. Some managed to do both.

Shrieks of *"Orang liar!"* rang out. In the Malay tongue, they were calling the apish chemist a wild man. He was living up to the compliment.

Monk did a good job of cleaning up on the rover crew. But his luck ran out when the drum ran empty. With an unnerving finality, the busy breech ceased shuttling. The weapon fell silent.

By that time, Doc Savage had lunged from his log seat and fell upon Dang Mi. He used his head, butting it against the pit of the pirate's ample stomach.

Dang Mi gave a fresh howl and bleat of surprise. He got himself organized and made a wild grab for his tormentor's head.

Doc faded backward, unscathed.

Dang blinked. He was dumbfounded to discover that he had Doc's bronze-haired scalp in his hands.

Pirates were surrounding Doc Savage now. Blades and bullets threatened. The bronze man subsided.

Dang Mi turned the scalp over in his hands, saw that Doc Savage still possessed his natural hair, and seemed at a total loss for words. His mouth made shapes but no sounds.

Turning the scalp inside out, Dang discovered it was a steel form on which a layer of realistic bronze hair was anchored.

"This thing's like a dang-busted helmet!" he complained.

Doc said nothing. The skullcap spoke for itself. The metallic giant wore it as a safeguard against serious head blows.

Breathing heavily, Dang Mi gathered himself up, lurched to his feet. Wincing with each step, he began to issue orders in a confused mix of Malay and Dyak dialects.

Of the prisoners, only Doc Savage could follow it.

"What's cookin', Doc?" asked Monk.

Doc said, "We are to be taken to the pit."

"That so? What kinda pit?"

"They are not saying," supplied Doc. "But apparently it is well known to the crew."

They were marched in a single file, chained together like slaves. Doc Savage had to be uncoupled from the hawser chain beforehand. This was done with all the respectful care of a zoo keeper entering a lion's cage at the feeding hour.

The group progressed through well-worn jungle paths. Once they passed a tree festooned with green bananas, and Ham Brooks elbowed Monk Mayfair to call attention to them.

"Too bad they are not ripe," he said waspishly. "You could climb that tree and have a fitting last meal."

Monk growled wordlessly, which meant he was very upset indeed.

They skirted a fair-sized pool that looked as if it was filled with India ink. Its surface stood placid as pitch.

"Tar pit," Renny muttered. "The same kind of snare that trapped mastodons and sabertooth tigers in prehistoric days. Worse than quicksand, if you fall in."

"Or get thrown," suggested Ham.

"Not a bad idea," said Dang Mi. "But that ain't what I got in mind. Keep movin'!"

They marched onward.

THE pit proved to be a natural ravine, not very large, but deep enough to contain a half-dozen men comfortably. The floor had a moist, claylike consistency. Here and there red bones protruded from the muck, suggesting that past prisoners of Dang Mi had met their end therein.

Monk, Ham, Renny and the Chans were prodded into the declivity at the points of pistols and blades. A bamboo ladder was employed for this purpose, then withdrawn.

Doc Savage was not among their number.

Dang Mi addressed the bronze man.

"I can see your men are gettin' all their starch and sand from the sight o' you. So I'm gonna cut you down to size. And incidentally coax you into givin' up that dang box."

"The box is too dangerous to fall into your hands," Doc stated plainly.

"It's on my island. I'll find it, and if I don't, you'll tell me its whereabouts," promised Dang Mi. "Mark my dang words."

Leaving Doc's friends under guard, Dang Mi marched the bronze giant into the jungle.

Doc Savage noticed that the contingent of corsairs which accompanied them carried long poles to which were affixed noose-like lengths of hemp. Evidently, there were on a hunt of some kind.

"Devices such as those are often used to snare wild game," Doc observed.

Dang Mi stuck out a proud jaw. "This island is a perfect hideout because it's a-crawl with varmints of all varieties," he said. "British Coast Guard don't venture here. Also, they fear the Scourge of the South China Sea."

"You have been making a fair account of yourself so far," Doc allowed.

"Fair!" roared Dang Mi. "I captured you twice, ain't I? You call that fair?"

"Fair enough," allowed Doc. "You captured me, but failed to take into account my men, who had landed in the water and taxied to Pirate Island."

A scowl crawled across the pirate's wide face. "That reminds me: How *did* you summon your men? Don't say you didn't, because I know you did. It was that dang camera, wasn't it?"

Doc Savage saw no reason not to divulge the truth, thinking that he might learn more if he engaged the braggarty buccaneer in conversation.

"The 'camera' was in reality an ultra-violet light projector," he elaborated. "My men carry in their equipment cases special goggles, which allow them to see that otherwise invisible light. You conveniently pointed the camera upward, so that its shine could be detected."

"Invisible light, eh?"

"One way of putting it."

Dang puffed out his chest. "I use it myself."

"That," said Doc, "is how we recognized Pirate Island from the air. Your ultra-violet projectors were left on."

Dang's face fell. "But how'd they know to use them goggles?"

"Radio."

"Don't moonshine me. No radio set has been built small enough to carry on a man."

Doc did not contradict him. He still toted the compact transceiver on his person.

"Remind me to have flogged the brainless bloke who left them turned on," Dang muttered darkly.

Up ahead, a Malay suddenly called out. His clucking cries were excited. *"Ular sawa putih!"*

"Move, you slant-eyed heathen!" Dang shouted at his crew.

The leading group of pirates rushed ahead. Some of those in the rear hung back, while a few moved cautiously ahead to join their fellows.

Dang urged Doc forward. Doc picked up his pace with an easy swing.

The corsair complement arrived at the scene of the excitement soon enough.

By torchlight, they beheld an unnerving tableau.

A group of Malays had flushed a Burmese python out of the brush. It was a monster, fully thirty feet long and as pale as alabaster. An albino specimen, obviously, its hide displaying a pattern of white diamonds along its intricately-scaled back. It flicked out its rubbery tongue at rapid intervals.

They were employing the nooses to capture the muscular reptile by the head and tail. Their idea seemed to be once it was caught, they would pull in opposite directions, uncoiling the struggling serpent.

This appeared to be a sensible plan. In execution, however, it quickly went awry.

They got the head all right. The ivory-hued serpent opened its mouth wide and made inarticulate hissing sounds of outrage. Myriad hooked teeth showed, designed for fastening upon prey. The tail bunched and coiled wildly. For all its girth, the python was active.

It wound a looping coil about the waist of one hapless Dyak. He uttered a sound that was unforgettable, and the coil constricted tightly.

Others rushed to the aid of the flailing fellow. Powerful curved fangs seized one would-be rescuer by the forearm.

He howled, unable to tear loose, and was soon caught up in another loop composed mostly of scaly neck.

Now, two unhappy pirates struggled in the irresistible coils.

Nooses were dropped. Serpent-bladed *krises* came flashing out.

"Don't kill it!" Dang Mi exclaimed. "We need that critter for the pit!"

There was some backtalk. Hot words flew back and forth while the two trapped worthies began to grow feeble in the obdurate coils of the mighty reptile. They emitted weak bleating sounds. Eyes began squeezing shut in surrender to inexorable death.

Doc Savage intervened then.

Lunging forward, he reached the python head. Doc stayed in front of the snake, away from its twisting body.

Moving in, Doc grasped the serpent by the neck bones, and his strong bronze fingers began to probe and manipulate, tendons standing out like iron rods.

This operation took several minutes, in which the furious python endeavored to snap at and bite Doc. The bronze man evaded each attempt with what seemed to be practiced ease.

It was as if Doc had been battling bull pythons all his life.

The trapped men went down, writhed, and their writhing grew looser and looser until they were still.

After a minute or so, the python began to subside. Its ghostly form relaxed. Doc released the now-limp head, letting the python down to the jungle floor. It lay supine, its diamond-scaled sides heaving like bellows.

When he was finished, the metallic giant stood up. A casual observer could easily discern that Doc was not in the least winded.

Several corsairs fought to extract their brethren from the coils, which had not yet relaxed. Even in slumber, the constrictor would not let go of its prey. The rescuers fell back and began cursing the serpent, calling it, *"Hantu ular sawa."*—"Ghost python."

Doc Savage pushed these pirates aside as if they were hapless children and exerted his mighty muscles. Bronze hands seized heavy loops of snake, heaved them aside.

One pirate was thus extricated. He was barely breathing.

The other wretch was likewise rescued from the brink of extinction.

Doc bore one pirate under each steel-thewed arm and deposited them in an open space. He went to work on them, testing bruised ribs for breaks, and employing proven methods for restarting regular respiration.

When it was all over, Dang Mi approached cautiously and

the degree to which he was impressed by the bronze man's physical prowess was written all over his beamy face.

"I was plannin' to dump you into the pit with that dang-busted python," he said slowly. "Now I see I'm gonna have to rethink this whole dang operation."

He looked like a man who had recalculated his future and discovered it to be far bleaker than he'd ever imagined.

Chapter XIV
THE PERIL PIT

DANG MI SURVEYED the torpid albino python while assorted unhappy expressions crawled and fluttered over his broad-beamed features.

At length, he made a decision.

"Bring that dang thing anyway. You, Savage, you get in the middle where it's thickest and help carry the brute."

Doc Savage regarded the situation as if considering his options.

Dang Mi helped him along by shooting up dust before his feet. When that failed to move the bronze man, he coolly shot the brains out of the most injured of the two rescued pirates.

"I don't brook no objections, mate," Dang growled.

Seeing no point in courting injury, the metallic giant seized the enormous snake about the middle and hefted it to the height of his waist.

The other cut-throats—those who still possessed locomotion—took firm hold of other portions and in this muscular manner the snake was straightened out and held aloft.

The march was cumbersome. The pirates stood much shorter than Doc Savage, and so were forced to carry the dead weight on their shoulders.

Nevertheless, they got underway successfully.

It was the deepest part of the night and the jungle was unutterably quiet. Palms rustled vaguely. That was all.

Tropical bats known as "flying foxes" flew overhead, silent

and watchful, in search of jungle insects to consume. The crescent moon had climbed as far as it was going to and peered down thinly at the shaggy hump of land known as Pirate Island.

The going was difficult. Doc Savage seemed tireless. Not so Dang Mi's cohorts. From time to time, one stumbled, forcing the procession to halt long enough to allow him to get organized.

Dang showed increasing impatience.

"Make haste, you heathens," he snapped in their native tongues, in which he showed a rough fluency.

As they moved along, Dang kept his half-slanted eyes open.

"I'm thinkin' you must've stashed that infernal box somewhere close to this spot," he grumbled.

Doc Savage vouchsafed no reply. His flake-gold eyes were very active, however.

"Once I get my hands on that contraption, there won't be any stoppin' Dang Mi. Dang my sunburnt hide, there won't."

Before long the oppressive heat, combined with ceaseless exertion, brought the burdened pirates stumbling and sinking to their knees.

Carefully, Doc let the pale snake down to permit a moment of rest. He looked unaffected by the arduous trek.

Dang Mi whipped out a superfirer and shot two laggards.

"We ain't stoppin' for nothin'!" he roared. "I want that box, and this is how I'm gonna get it."

Seeing that there was no reasoning with the man, Doc Savage took up the python in two metallic hands and draped the long constrictor serpent across his powerfully-muscled shoulders.

Saying, "Come on then," he continued on his way.

Eyes popping out of his head, Dang Mi watched the Herculean bronze man walk away as if momentarily forgetting that he—Doc Savage—was his prisoner.

His pirates were struck dumb by the sight.

"*Gangsa syaitan*," one breathed. "Brazen devil!"

"Not human," another muttered in his mother tongue.

"Belay that," Dang Mi thundered. "He's human. Or close to it, anyway. Come on—follow him. *Chop-chop!*"

The pirate cohort of Dang Mi followed after the bronze giant with a nervous alacrity. It might be seen that they were losing some of their respect for their captain, while fear of the bronze man was growing apace.

Eventually, they came to the guarded pit. Doc Savage stood over the rim looking down at his men, the insensate serpent still draped across his shoulders.

"We're okay, Doc," Monk called up. "Is that breakfast?"

The others were also present. Ham stood with Renny. The Chans were hunkered down in the manner of their Asian ancestors, placid faces composed.

There was an unconscious pirate lying in the pit with them.

"What happened?" Doc demanded.

"This one accidentally fell in," Ham explained, "and Monk brained him with his shoe!"

"I was half asleep, and I thought he was a wild boar or somethin' that had fallen in," Monk explained blandly.

"Out! Get out, all of you!" bellowed Dang Mi. "And you, the hairy one. You carry my bully boy out with you!"

They clambered up, Monk lastly. He dropped the senseless man from his long hirsute arms. The corsair landed on his face.

Monk spanked his hands together, as if satisfied that he had accomplished something worthwhile. Dust flew from them.

Dang Mi turned to Doc Savage.

"Get down in that pit and carry that blamed python in with you."

Doc Savage did not immediately respond.

So Dang Mi signaled to his men and the bronze man was unceremoniously pushed into the pit. It took five rovers to do it and it might be suspected that Doc, had he simply made a greater effort, could have stood his ground indefinitely.

Landing, Doc untangled himself from the limp python and

found his feet. He looked up, meeting the pirate leader's eyes with metallic regard.

"How long until that python wakes up?" demanded Dang Mi.

"That will be up to the python," Doc ventured.

"Well, in that case we're gonna wait as long as it takes. Everyone settle down. It may be a long night."

It was. The night crawled along like a tired thing.

Jungle sounds kept them awake, even if the situation was not exactly conducive to sleep. Monk dropped off once or twice. Ham elbowed him awake, disturbing his snoring.

"Can't a guy get some shuteye?" Monk demanded of Ham.

Ham undertoned back, "Do you want to miss the escape?"

Monk blinked slumber from his tiny eyes. "Huh?"

"Doc's been acting deucedly passive," Ham explained. "I think he's got something up his sleeve. We should be ready for it."

Over the course of the next few hours, Dang Mi called down threats upon the heads of Doc Savage; the bronze man seemed unmoved by it all.

"When that dang monster reptile wakes up, it will be quite an occasion," Dang suggested. "A regular rhubarb."

Monk snorted. "I've seen Doc fight pythons before. A whole nest of them. That snake is outnumbered."*

Thinking back to the events of the night, Dang Mi seemed to take the hairy chemist's words seriously.

He sent a runner to the junk *Devilfish*, after first whispering hushed instructions.

After a time, the Malay came back carrying a pair of good old American boxing gloves that were tied together by their rawhide lacings.

Clutching these, Dang Mi climbed into the pit personally.

"Put out your hands," he invited.

---

* *See* Python Isle.

Doc did so.

Dang jammed one glove into Doc's right hand and stuffed his left into the other.

When that task was accomplished, he began lacing the gloves tight so they could not be easily removed.

When he stepped back to survey his work, Dang Mi chortled, "Let's see you stun that snake with your fingers covered up with those leather babies."

"Your idea is that I cannot render the python unconscious by chiropractic manipulation?" Doc questioned.

"I don't know what you just said exactly," Dang admitted. "But I think you got the general idea."

Doc Savage shrugged as if unconcerned. He started to turn away.

Then one gloved fist lashed out and rocked Dang Mi's head back on his shoulders. The rest of him followed. The pirate chief landed on his back against the rim of the pit and slid insensate to a sitting position.

No second blow was required. Dang was out.

Rifles poked over the edge of the pit and Doc Savage was ordered to step away from the fallen corsair leader.

Doc obliged them.

Two men scrambled down and heaved Dang up on their shoulders, clumsily bearing him out of the pit.

DAWN was creeping on when Dang Mi sat up and began shaking his head violently. A few seconds of this convinced him that it was exactly the wrong thing to do. He became violently sick.

Water was brought to him cupped in a palm frond and he drank of this greedily.

"What happened?" Dang muttered, looking around.

"*Gangsa* devil, he sucker-punch your lights out," Dang Mi was told. "Down you go, senseless."

Dang winced. "Is the dang snake awake?"

"Not yet, O brave one."

"Well, it can't be long. Come on, let's get down to serious business."

So saying, Dang Mi started to climb to his feet. He got half way, then his knees went wobbly, as if they were balloons filled with water. He sat down hard.

"Help me up, dang it!" he raged.

Two pirates performed the duty. When Dang was back on his feet, he took an experimental step, tottered. It was as if he had lost his sea legs, except that he was safely on dry land.

Stumbling over to the pit, he found several of his men hunkered down in the dirt instead of attending to guard duty.

Dang broke up this activity with a sturdy kick of his boot. Pirates scrambled to their feet.

"What the dang-blasted hell are you up to? Gamblin', when you should be guardin'!"

"We were wagering on the fate of the demon man of bronze," a Dyak explained.

"Yeah? What odds?" asked Dang Mi, who like to gamble himself.

"Fate favors the man that be-bronze, it is believed," Dang was told.

Dang looked about ready to explode. His face flushed, then darkened, then flushed again. If steam could be emitted from a man's ears, as it sometimes is in movie cartoons, Dang was about to burst forth with scalding clouds of it.

"No man can stand up to a bull python when there's no way out," Dang bellowed.

"He is a man of much magic," one pirate insisted.

"I'll magic him!" Dang blustered. "Two of you get down there and strip him of his clothes. Two more of you, follow me! We're going foragin'."

THEY were gone an hour and when they returned they carried in a galvanized steel pail a concoction that looked as if it were composed of equal parts cranberry juice and tree sap.

Setting this down, Dang Mi unholstered his six-guns and trained them into the pit.

"A ladder is comin' down and you're comin' up," he growled. "No tricks. We wanna see if we can revive that python."

Bare-chested now, Doc Savage climbed out of the pit. The boxing gloves still encumbered his powerful hands. Dang Mi inspected the lacings carefully. They were tight, showing no signs of tampering.

While this inspection was going on, two Malays climbed into the pit with the sloshing steel pail and several natural sponges.

Unseen by any of the prisoners, they began slopping the potion onto the dozing white python's scaly hide. They did this carefully, running out thick strings of the stuff from the back of the head to the tip of the tail. Juice ran down both sides.

With sticks, they prodded the snake onto its long spine, exposing its pale belly. They repeated the operation, taking care not to spill any of the red stuff on their own persons.

Through it all, the snake slumbered oblivious.

When the pail was empty, they brought it back up, taking the same care as if even the dross at the bottom of the pail was something they dared not splash about.

Bowing and cupping their hands in unison, they indicated to Dang Mi that it was accomplished.

"Now back into the pit, Savage," Dang ordered. "We just gave that snake a great big bath to wake him up. It won't be long now."

Dang paused. He eyed the bronze giant. "Unless you care to break your dang silence?"

Doc Savage shook his head. He got back down into the pit. He managed the ladder just as well going down as he had coming up, in spite of his encumbered hands.

Whatever the cranberry-colored concoction was, it did not appear to act rapidly. For another hour or so, the alabaster serpent slept on. The sun began to grow hot and the juice commenced steaming. Exotic birds came to life. Somewhere a tiger snarled.

Dang Mi watched the proceedings with eager eyes.

"That bug juice we concocted should do the trick," he told one of his men.

The other nodded sagely. "Yes. Even drying as it is now, it will be fatal to the touch."

Dang fell to whispering. "So even if Doc Savage does figure out a way to fend him off, all the snake has to do is rasp his scales against him here and there and Savage will come into contact with the poison. Paralysis starts right off. It won't affect the snake because he's covered in scale. But porous human skin is a different matter."

They watched as the dazed constrictor snake began to stir.

Doc's men were nudged over to the edge of the pit to watch.

Dang Mi lifted his voice.

"Hey, Savage! This is your last chance. When the snake is done with you, your men go in, one at a time. You know how a python operates. It wraps itself about a man's chest and commences to squeeze the life out of him. They say the last thing you hear before you stop breathin' is your rib-cage cracklin' like kindling."

Doc Savage appeared not to be listening. All of his attention was upon the stirring reptile.

FIRST, the tail began to jitter. Then the white head came up. It took a while for the major portion of the python to come to life. The ghostly gleaming coils began to roll and writhe, causing the cherry-red coating to drip and splash like so much blood. The great serpent's mouth yawned wide, disclosing a pale inner mouth and two rows of impressive teeth.

Amber eyes raised on a wedge-shaped head began pointing

in the direction of the Man of Bronze.

Doc set himself.

But the python did not approach. Its orbs had a filmy quality, as if it were sick. The triangular head writhed about, as if seeking something else. Its thin whip-like tongue flickered in and out.

Reptiles by reputation have a lazy way about them—at least when they are not motivated by hunger. This one seemed to partake of that legend.

It writhed and curled in on itself, slowly forming a mound like a coil of fat rope. When it had accomplished this, the python pulled its head in and closed its gemlike eyes.

It was soon fast asleep.

Dang Mi roared, "Get up, dang you! Get up and fight like a man!"

But the gory reptile refused to respond. It continued to slumber peacefully.

A cheer went up among the pirates. Money quickly changed hands. Congratulations were called down on the bronze man in many languages.

"The ghost snake is afraid of the bronze devil! It will not fight!"

"The golden-eyed giant has the touch of gold! Nothing can withstand him!"

Seeing that the tide was turning against him, Dang Mi shouted, "Fetch up a tiger. Go on! Get a net from the boat and bring back a hungry man-eater. I don't care how many of you brown blokes get mauled in the process."

A contingent of pirates reluctantly betook themselves away.

It was full light now and any tiger in the vicinity would have returned to its den to sleep off his evening meal, if any. Tigers are nocturnal by nature.

Dang Mi called down to Doc Savage, "I ain't through yet. Not by a long shot."

"The poison you used might have worked," Doc pointed out.

"But for one thing."

Dang stared. "Poison! Who said anything about any poison?"

"Easily recognizable by its coloration. Never mind that. The concoction has the property of a crude anesthetic. The snake is simply sleeping off a dose."

"So it wasn't afraid to fight you after all?"

"You will have to ask the snake about that," Doc replied dryly.

Dang Mi looked angry enough to chew nails and spit out corkscrews. "Around these parts," he gritted, "my dang word is law. You are makin' of yourself an outlaw by defying me."

"Your men are not as loyal as they once were," Doc pointed out.

"I think I will shoot me somebody," Dang decided, giving his trousers a violent hitch. "That's it. I'll shoot me somebody and maybe that will cure what ails me."

Turning to a pair of cut-throats, he barked, "Bring me that bucket-fisted palooka of a landlubber."

Renny Renwick was produced forthwith. His sunburned hands hung at his sides like a pair of well-cured hams.

"If I had a plank," Dang announced, "I would make you walk it. So we'll have to make do. Blindfold?"

The towering engineer shook his lugubrious head.

Dang asked, "Last cigarette?"

"Save it for your own hanging," Renny returned dourly.

Dang continued, "The reason I'm executin' you is this: You got away from me. I don't like that. Not one bit. So I gotta make an example of you to keep my men in line."

Renny made an elaborate business of expectorating onto the ground in front of Dang Mi's boots.

Then the long-faced engineer was violently turned around so that his broad back faced the pit.

Dang angrily kicked dirt onto the wet patch. Holstering his pistols, he set himself like an old-fashioned Western badman.

"When you say, 'draw,'" growled Dang, "I will slap leather

and ventilate you."

"Holy cow! What makes you think I'll say draw?"

"You just did!" Dang chortled, and out came his revolvers. He fired each in unison.

The gun blasts were loud, jarring, coming as unexpectedly as they did. Gunsmoke gushed forth in surprising quantity.

Two bullets struck Renny Renwick in the chest and back he toppled.

The unprepared engineer landed awkwardly on the nape of his neck and began coughing. Crimson spurted out with each expelling of breath.

Above, Monk and the others came off the ground and had to be beaten into submission. The hairy chemist flung long arms about, bowling down assorted buccaneers, before giving up at the points of sharp *krises*. He erected his hairy hands over his head.

As Renny seemingly coughed out his life, Doc Savage glided over to him.

There wasn't much the bronze man could do, hampered as he was by the tightly-tied boxing gloves. He touched Renny on the head, the shoulder, and seemed to offer words of comfort. These were not heard outside of the pit.

Sooner than it seemed possible, the big engineer gave what sounded like a final convulsive shudder and his heaving chest subsided. All respiration seemed to cease.

Doc Savage stood up. He fixed Dang Mi with his golden gaze.

"That was murder," he accused in a deep tone like a struck gong.

"Naw. It was an execution. And what would you expect? I'm dang piratical, I am."

The bronze man's metallic eyes were strangely stark, as if the irises had congealed the way ice freezes up in winter.

Seeing that look, Dang Mi took an involuntary step back

from the pit rim. There was something terrible in those orbs—so terrible that Dang abruptly changed his mind about calling for Monk Mayfair to be shot next.

"Bring those two iron-headed half-breeds," he ordered. "Since we don't have the box and they don't know where it is, we don't need 'em anymore. Might as well scrag them, too."

Chapter XV

THE UNCANNY

WITH BRUTAL EFFICIENCY, Mark and Mary Chan were hauled to their feet and frog-marched over to the edge of the ravine that served as an execution pit.

Mary walked with measured steps, testifying to the fact that her feet had not been bound as an infant, as was the usual Chinese custom with female babies.

Mark did his best to look brave, but his eyes kept switching to the face of his sister, who now appeared to be doomed.

"Very sorry, Mary," he murmured.

"Not your fault, Mark," she whispered back.

They were stood at a spot not far from the place where Renny Renwick had been cruelly gunned down.

"Any last words?" Dang asked, holstering in his pistols.

"Just two," said Mark.

"Only two," added Mary.

"Wah Chan," said Mark and Mary in unison.

"Say again?"

"You heard us," said Mark firmly.

"Wah Chan will hear of this," Mary warned.

"Don't think he won't," asserted Mark.

Dang Mi put out a belligerent jaw. "What do you two know of Wah Chan?"

"What do children know of their father?" returned Mary.

"You funnin' me? Wah Chan is the biggest generalissimo

who ever took on the Japanese. You say he is your daddy?"

"Not just saying," Mary sniffed.

"It is fact," insisted Mark.

This gave Dang Mi something of a pause. He licked his lips. He shifted his feet back and forth. He winced as he put too much weight down on the foot that Monk Mayfair had crushed.

"Wah Chan has a mighty fierce reputation," he ruminated. "But he's up in Manchuria. Manchukuo, the Japs call it now. If the Emperor's boys didn't hang him for a bandit by this time. Wah Chan don't worry me none. We ain't never likely to go over into his neck of the Asian woods."

Having decided that, Dang set himself.

"Guess I can't repeat my quick-draw trick on you, too," he said in a disappointed tone. "So I reckon I'll just slap leather whenever I feel like it."

Mary closed her eyes and seemed to go away within her thoughts.

Mark bravely stepped in front of his sister, and stuck out his chest, as if it were bulletproof.

At that propitious moment, the pirate detachment assigned to fetch a live tiger put in a boisterous return appearance.

There were five of them and they carried a snarling bundle of striped fury in a big wad of Manila netting. The moist scarlet scars covering their arms and bare legs told part of the tale.

"Pak Belang!" they cried proudly, using a popular nickname for the local species of tiger. Translated, it meant "Uncle Stripes."

Dang's broad face lit up like a child's at Christmas. "Well, well, looks like we have our tiger."

One of the arrivals boasted, "We dig two pits. Hide in one, place raw meat in other. Wait until *harimau* climb in. Drop net into other pit. Break down dirt wall in between and capture him. Very upset *harimau.*"

Harimau was the Malay word for tiger.

Dang Mi began grinning from ear to ear. His hands came

away from the butts of his holstered pistols.

"Just carry that angry critter over and pitch him in, net and all."

The tiger was duly dumped overboard. It landed in a tangle of netting. The striped feline fury began fighting his way out. It was not easy. Like myriad fishhooks, its unsheathed claws kept getting caught in the Manila seine.

Ignoring the Chans, Dang wandered up to the edge of the pit and peered down.

"Did you hear that, you bronze devil? Let's see you fight your way out of this predicament." Lifting his voice, he cried out, "I wager five hundred Hongkong dollars against the life of Doc Savage!"

The betting began in earnest. When it was settled, the pirates gathered around the pit to watch the festivities—that being what they considered the bloodthirsty event to come.

"Just to make it more interestin'," Dang decided, "here come some reinforcements."

Dang gave the Chans an ungentle shove and in they toppled.

Doc Savage moved to their side. He wore only his whipcord pants.

"Stay here in this pocket," he directed.

"We have no chance against that beast," Mary said. She looked scared, *was* scared. Brave in the face of a bullet, she seemed to lose all courage when confronted with the imminent prospect of being mauled by a man-eater.

All eyes were on the tiger in question. It used its gleaming fangs and its razor claws to worry the netting. Gradually, it succeeded, shredding the weave.

Crawling out, the feral feline began to pace angrily, tail twitching. Its savage mouth opened in a snarl, whiskers bristling. A guttural growl escaped its white-furred throat.

As tigers go, it was no Hercules. Either it was a runt specimen, or the animal was not yet fully grown. That did not mean that it was not dangerous. The contrary. This particular tiger was only a measure larger that an American cougar. Cougars are notorious man-killers, and this sinuously-lean specimen looked as ferocious as any full-grown Bengal tiger out of India.

The tiger surveyed his surroundings, ears twitching angrily. It could be seen that one of its upper fangs had lost its dagger-like point—no doubt in combat with another animal. Amid its profuse stripes, healed scars showed as fleshy furrows where no fur grew.

No one doubted but that this particular tiger was a bantam brawler. He had earned his stripes, natural and otherwise.

DOC SAVAGE set himself before Mark and Mary Chan. Renny Renwick's prostrate form lay behind them, unmoving.

The big engineer had shown no sign of life since his last, and seemingly final, convulsion.

The tiger made a slow reconnoiter of his end of the pit, discovered no way out, and turned his sullen attention their way. Eyes as yellow as citrine surveyed them coldly.

Leaning down, Dang Mi laughed. "After he's done with you, the others go in. That tiger will feast for a week or longer on your miserable flesh."

Doc ignored him.

"Still time to talk turkey, Savage," the pirate chief reminded.

Doc looked up, and said something that could not be clearly heard.

Dang blinked stupidly. "What?"

Doc repeated himself, but a hoarse snarling coming from the tiger blurred his words.

Dang drew closer to the rim. He cupped a hand behind his disfigured ear. "Say again?"

Abruptly, Doc Savage leapt. There was no preliminary coiling or tensing of leg muscles. He simply jumped up from a standing position, and gained the rim of the pit.

His goal was not escape, however. It was Dang Mi's legs. Hands hampered by boxing gloves, Doc gathered both calves in his metallic arms. Gravity took care of the rest.

Doc and Dang fell in a pile. Dang landed atop the bronze man and despite his complete surprise at the sudden turn in his fortunes, the pirate leader was no slouch when it came to preserving his skin. Kicking dirt at Doc's eyes, he made for the ladder.

Renny Renwick lashed out with a stony-knuckled block of a fist and Dang fell on his face, and after that looked dazed.

"I was waiting for something just like that," rumbled big-fisted Renny, coming to his feet. His face grew so mournful that only close friends would know he was beaming internally.

"You are not dead?" gasped Mary Chan needlessly.

"Bulletproof vest," said Renny, tapping his chest. "I bit my tongue when I was shot, drawing blood. Doc whispered for me to put on a show, like I was dying. Dang bought it all, hook, line and sinker—the stinker."

Ringing the pit edge, the assembled pirates let out a roar. Some appeared to be cheering on the tiger. Dang had not made many friends among his wicked crew.

Hastily, the ladder was withdrawn, stranding Dang Mi. Why, was a matter of conjecture. But the inspiration had come from one of the pirate band. Perhaps one who possessed aspirations to become the next Scourge of the South China Sea.

Pacing, the impatient tiger began to stalk them.

Doc Savage padded forward to meet it. When confronting danger, the bronze man believed in the direct approach.

The tiger had the same idea. He slinked forward, baring discolored ivory teeth. White whiskers erected on either side of his black, white and orange dappled face.

Doc Savage took up a boxing stance. His leather gloves made both fists look as absurdly large as Renny's. The man-eater appeared unimpressed. It released a throaty growl, low and prolonged.

Without any further ado, the feline pounced! There was no advance warning. It simply shot off its stringy hind legs.

Spectators roared their excitement, thrust wavy blades high over their heads.

Braced on muscular legs, Doc appeared set to meet the tiger's charge. At the last possible moment, the bronze giant ducked, permitting the surprised animal's own momentum to carry it over Doc's head, and away. Its passing stirred bronze hair.

The tiger rolled as it landed, snarled, gathered its cinnamon-colored anatomy together. It came on again, running hard.

Leaving the ground, the feline stretched itself out for its full length, bared fangs lunging for Doc's throat. Its fierce eyes were fixed on the bronze man's throbbing jugular vein.

Doc dodged, blocking with his gloved fists, and so avoided the snapping fangs. The tiger went sailing on past, assisted by a helpful kick to its hindmost portion. It landed in a black-streaked ball, rolled wildly, and found his footing, claws extending from splayed paws.

The crowd howled its utmost. Some whistled lustily. Money changed hands.

Tiger expressions are not easily read. But the look on this specimen's face began to express feline frustration. Its fierce head swept around, ears twitching, amber eyes searching for fresh prey.

During the commotion, Monk and Ham had leapt into the pit and took up positions around the Chans. Monk's furry fists were bunched and ready. He looked ready to jump into the fray. Noticing this, Doc gestured for him to keep his distance.

Unexpectedly, the tiger made for the dazed figure of Dang Mi, the pirate. Dang gave a bleat of fear, and began clawing the clay pit walls in a frenzy.

Stepping up boldly, Doc intercepted the tiger before he could seize upon other, more vulnerable prisoners. He caught the tiger's active gaze, met it with his own golden regard.

This time, the agitated animal employed feline cunning. It began circling his prey, eying the bronze giant all the while. Doc shifted about, stepping in similar circles to match its movements, always keeping his foe before him, careful to stay between the tiger and the other prisoners.

Tigers are creatures of habit, Doc Savage knew. A preferred method of attack was to seize their prey by throat or nape of the neck, employing their powerful jaws to break the spinal column, thereby bringing a victim down. Thus, the bronze man's efforts were concentrated on evading that unpleasant fate.

A quickening pulsing of nostrils was the only thing that betrayed the tiger's next move.

Uncoiling like a tawny spring, it executed a clean leap. A wild growl suggesting that it was about to snatch up a victory froze the blood of all onlookers.

Moving like liquid metal, Doc Savage flowed to one side. What happened next showed that speed alone does not settle contests, nor are tigers slow learners.

Seeing it would miss, the tiger swiped out and managed to hook one paw in the bronze man's right shoulder. Claws pierced flesh. Scrambling for purchase, the tawny fury gained Doc Savage's broad back. Digging in with foreclaws, it hung onto Doc's shoulders, hind claws madly shredding hide off his lower back. Gore flowed.

A flicker of shock stabbed the bronze man's eyes.

Bellowing lustily, Monk charged up. Doc rapped out a warning. "Keep clear!"

Reluctantly, the apish chemist skidded to a stop. He bounced on his bowed legs like a trainer urging his fighter to stay in the ring. Low growls issued from his thick throat.

Twisting about, Doc flailed with his handicapped fists, endeavoring to pry the killer cat loose. No good. Finger strength was what he needed. But for all the good they did him, his iron digits might as well have been set in stone.

Claws went to work, tearing, rending. Scarlet scars became visible on the bronze man's muscled back. Had the tiger been clinging to Doc's chest, he would have been disemboweled by the furiously ripping rear claws.

Jumping up and down like a bull gorilla, Monk howled red wrath. "*Ye-e-ow!* I'll murder that mangy cat!"

As a match for size, Doc Savage had the advantage. But the tiger was one of nature's more vicious killers. It possessed an animal strength that no human, not even the Man of Bronze, possessed in comparable measure.

Recognizing this, Doc changed tactics.

Bunching shoulders, hunkering his head downward, Doc strove to protect the nape of his neck from the tiger's fangs. Moist hot breath stirred his hair as the bristled mouth yawned open. A growl suggestive of appetite issued forth.

Throwing out his arms, Doc pitched backward. He landed smack atop of the astonished feline. The bronze man was no bantam weight. Over two hundred pounds of steel-thewed brawn crushed the tiger into the dirt. This made an impression on the stunned animal. Claws retracting from human muscle, it gave forth an unnerved shriek.

With a mighty shrug, Doc flung the startled feline off him, regained his footing. That maneuver succeeded, but at the cost of some skin.

Climbing shakily to its padded feet, the dazed tiger padded angrily to and fro, as if contemplating its next move. Angry eyes never left his metallic antagonist. Now they held a wary light.

Back bleeding profusely, Doc set himself for the next round. He watched the tiger's tail and eyes, which would give away its intentions.

The black-banded tail commenced switching back and forth, cold eyes crowding together, almost crossing. It was panting now. Snorting black nostrils twitched furiously. Unmistakably, the slash-marked body—it was dappled with the bronze man's life fluid now—began gathering its remaining vitality for a mighty bound.

Instead, an amazing thing happened.

Doc Savage pounced first!

IT was probably an experience entirely new to the feline. At least, it behaved as if its world had been turned upside down.

Recoiling, it backed away, growling, ears folding flat against its skull, scarred flanks heaving.

Doc advanced confidently. The bronze man began crowding the tiger against one earthen wall. Snorting and spitting, the tiger shied off and tried to slink away, possibly to consider its options.

Discovering none, it peeled back its whiskered mouth to its widest, exposing its full array of fangs. A warning growl issued forth. It lacked its full measure of conviction.

Monk pitched in with a bloodcurdling roar of his own.

It put the tiger's vocal display to shame, seemingly adding to its discomfit.

Doc kept coming, gloved fists held chest-high before him.

Cornered, the tiger did the only thing left to it—it came on in a flashing, tawny leap!

Doc Savage walked into it, shooting out one arm, then the other, popping the tiger on the proverbial button. One boxing glove landed smartly on the broad black nose, followed by the other. It was the old one-two punch perfected by pugilists. Barely any interval separated the impact sounds.

Tail over teakettle, the tiger was hurled backward, to land in a limp heap of red-streaked fur. It did not rise again. Only its tail twitched. Then it, too, lay down and ceased moving.

A wild cheer went up from Dang Mi's cut-throat crew. They began chanting.

"Savage! Savage! Savage! *Tuan* Savage, Scourge of Tigers!" was their cry.

Thus it was when Doc Savage climbed out of the pit, the pirate band cupped their hands to their blue turbans and salaamed respectfully in his direction.

"Lay down your arms," he told them in the language they knew.

Strangely enough, they did. Monk and the others were summarily released. After scrambling up the restored ladder, Monk picked out a pirate at random and batted him off his feet with a hairy paw.

"Next guy who tries to stick me with a knife," he growled, "there won't be enough left of him to snore."

Renny helped Mark and Mary Chan out of the pit.

Doc Savage removed the boxing gloves that had proved to be more of a boon and a blessing than Dang Mi had ever imagined. He did this by taking first one lacing knot, and then the other, in his strong white teeth, biting down hard and parting the cords easily, showing that he could have done so at any time.

Lastly, Dang Mi was hauled out of the pit and stood before the bronze man.

He was now a miserable excuse for a corsair. Both holsters were empty and the collodion smear that had given one eye an Oriental cast had melted, making him look lop-eyed, if there was such a thing.

"What are you going to do with me?" he mumbled through crushed lips.

"Somebody fetch a plank," Monk growled.

"They hang pirates in these waters," Renny reminded.

"We can fashion a noose out of that netting," Ham suggested.

Doc Savage seemed to consider possibilities.

"If you cooperate, your life will be spared," he said at last.

Dang Mi narrowed sun-squint eyes. "By who?"

"By us. We will take you back to the States, where you will be attended to."

"And iffin' I don't?"

"You will be turned over to British authorities to face their brand of justice," the bronze man assured him.

Dang Mi suddenly felt of his neck.

"I got ancestors that were hung for horse thieves. No, thanks."

Doc eyed him levelly. "Then you will behave?"

Dang peered around at his erstwhile crew. They returned his regard without outward warmth. One made a point of expectorating on the ground.

"Don't look like I got much of a dang choice," he admitted glumly.

Turning to his men, Doc Savage said, "Our next order of business will be to recover that strongbox."

"Where is it, Doc?" asked Ham.

Instead of answering, the bronze man led everyone out into the jungle. Monk and Ham and the others recovered their superfirers and were using them to herd the pirate crew along. They didn't require much herding. Not having understood the exchange in English between their former leader and the bronze giant, they had concluded that Doc Savage was assuming command of the *Devilfish* and was about to captain them to victories both glorious and innumerable.

The trail led to an area where there were several jungle ponds created by rainwater pooling in depressions in the earth. Water lilies scaled the placid surface under which tadpoles darted like limbless black imps.

"You submerged it in water!" Mary Chan gasped.

"Knowing what it could do?" blurted Mark Chan, goggling.

"It was reasonable to assume that no one would think to look for it underwater," Doc explained. "And I took into consideration the waterproofing of the container."

Hearing all this, Dang Mi muttered, "Dang and double dang...."

He was looking down into one pool. It had a brilliant green film on it like pond scum. In the jungle, water does not remain pure for very long. Teeming flora and fauna make certain of that.

Doc Savage started to wade into the pool.

"I'd be careful was I you," cautioned Dang. "*Buayas*—that means crocodiles—sometimes lurk in these swimmin' holes."

This mention of crocodiles bought uneasy expressions to the faces of those who overheard.

"I've lost more than a few of my hearties to crocs," continued Dang, warming to the subject. "They up and lash out of the water with their tails and knock a man into the pool with them. Sometimes they just grab hold of an ankle and yank a bloke underwater, drownin' him before even botherin' to eat him."

"Enough," said Doc. He began to wade in.

Dang Mi watched him intently. His dark eyes tracked ahead, the way a man plots the progress of a plane by observing its direction.

Without any sound or warning, Dang sudden plunged in.

"Croc! Over there! Crocodile!" he howled wildly.

Machine pistols came up. The others tried sighting on the unseen reptile. But Dang was making such a splashing commotion that the placid green water turned turbulent.

Doc Savage's flake-gold eyes raked his surroundings. He saw no moving shapes.

"Not there," Dang cried. "Over there!" He pointed to a specific spot, where a water lily sat placidly.

A splash erupted from that locality.

None saw the well-aimed stone that shot from Dang's hands before he jabbed a pointing digit. Their eyes were on the purported reptile.

Only half convinced, Doc lunged for the spot.

Dang suddenly turned frog. He threw himself onto the scummy water and began to kick feet toward the first shiny thing he spotted. It was the strongbox, lying there in the silty pool bottom, a wavering metallic-blue gleam.

Doc Savage realized the subterfuge almost at once. He shifted position and made for the same spot.

It was a race that the bronze man was not certain to win.

This time he did not.

The reflective effect on sunlight in water was deceptive. It showed the box to be in a relative position that was slightly illusionary when one looked down into the pool.

Dang Mi, swimming underwater, experienced no such optical deception. He arrowed like a seal toward the box, reached it first.

What he intended to do was never known. But what Dang Mi accomplished in the last moment of his life became etched indelibly on the brains of all who witnessed the awesome, uncanny event.

Dang's questing fingers brushed the box, upsetting it. In toppling, the lid jarred loose. Just a crack. No one knew that. Only Dang.

Only a crack, but what followed was unforgettable!

FIRST came a noise that could not be easily described. It possessed the noisome qualities of a sucking sound, all agreed afterward. But mixed in were other auditory sensations.

Perhaps Jonah made such a noise when swallowed by the Biblical whale.

Next, the pool began to boil. It was not a boiling that could be ascribed to heat, although it certainly was hot. This was an altogether different kind of boiling—furious, unsettling, and sudden in a way that shocked the senses.

A fog began forming about the pool in rushing aerial streams, as if all the surrounding moisture were being irresistibly summoned by the inhabitant of the mysterious metal container.

Abruptly, everyone was running for their lives. Running partly from instinct, but also because it seemed as if all the oxygen, all the heat, all of everything had abruptly been removed from the immediate environment.

Even Doc Savage veered sharply and quitted the vicinity.

Perhaps he had some inking of what was to come. For the moment Dang touched the box, the bronze man seemed to reverse course.

They ran. All of them. Ran and ran and ran.

And as they ran, they made horrible croakings in their throats—throats that were suddenly parched and dry. Throats that ached with a pain that suggested strained vocal cords.

But their yells had nothing to do with any pain.

It was as if all the moisture was being wrenched from their organs, their lungs, their very inner tissues.

Behind them, the boiling jungle pool abruptly went quiet. They heard this, but did not witness it. No one was looking in the direction of the pool. Furiously they were trying to get as far away from the boiling body as humanly possible—as if their very existences depended upon wild, mindless flight.

A weird silence attended the quieting of the jungle pool.

Chapter XVI
THE TOE

RUNNING AS FAR and fast as they could, the group—consisting of Doc Savage and his men, the Chans and the remnants of Dang Mi's pirate band—eventually reached the edge of a large watering hole.

They plunged in.

Immersing themselves, they began to drink. The water was clear and fortunately not briny. Otherwise matters would have turned out far worse than they did. Drinking salt water is not recommended.

Taking great greedy gulps, they drank their fill. More than their fill. Monk immersed his entire head and seemed determined to engulf as much of the reservoir as possible. Ham was only slightly more refined in his imbibing.

After possibly twenty minutes of this, they dragged themselves back on dry land. Dragged because they were very, very weak.

Doc Savage's amazing vitality seemed to withstand the influence more tolerably than the others. But even the mighty Man of Bronze looked sorely affected. Doubtless, his recent blood loss contributed to his debilitated state of being.

He lay on his back in the sand gasping for breath, and enjoying the satisfaction of a stomach full of water.

After a while, Doc sat up and looked at his bronze forearms intently.

His expression told that he did not like what he saw. Pinching a bit of bronze flesh between fingers and thumbs, he pulled it upward. It distended with an elasticity that was disturbing.

The pinch of flesh was slow returning to its normal contour. The bronze man also noticed that the pores of his fine-textured skin were visibly distended.

Doc's flake-gold eyes became filled with eerie stirrings. Ham was beside him.

"I feel as though I couldn't get enough water—not even if I drank an entire ocean," he complained.

Doc explained, "We have been subjected to something that rapidly leached the moisture from our bodies, potentially with fatal consequences if it were not for one thing."

"Yeah, what's that?" asked Monk Mayfair thickly.

"The fact that the box was immersed in a large volume of water, which absorbed the brunt of its influence upon the surroundings. Otherwise, it is doubtful that we would be numbered among the living at this moment."

Mark Chan offered an unsettling thought. "And that is the smaller of the two boxes."

"The other is much larger," Mary gasped out.

Doc eyed them. "You have witnessed this phenomenon before?"

Mark nodded grimly. "Yes. It is terrible."

"What dwells within the box is more terrible still," Mary chimed in.

"Describe the thing in the box," Doc requested.

"It is something new," said Mark.

"New?"

"Never before seen on the earth," clarified Mary.

"What is it?" pressed Doc, shifting his position carefully. With his thirst in retreat, his bloodied back began aching.

Mark shook his head tiredly. "We do not know, exactly. But it is terrible—more terrible than the worst substance known to man."

"If not brought under control," rejoined Mary, "it could wreck the world."

Doc Savage's trilling piped up as if agitated. He lacked the strength to make it in full measure. He was still very weak.

They lay on the sand for the greater part of an hour. Although their primary discomfort was lack of water—this despite their prodigious swallowing of fresh water—they seemed to have difficulty with their respiration.

"Lung tissues desiccated," Doc decided.

"Huh?" croaked Monk. He sounded like a deep-throated frog.

"He said our lungs are so dried up, we are having trouble with our breathing," enlightened Renny.

That sounded like a satisfactory explanation for their predicament. They were too flagged to doubt it.

Ham thought of a question.

"If that mummy that was shipped to our New York headquarters was not Renny, who was it?"

"A pirate named Poetical Percival Perkins," grunted Renny.

"Any pirate who went by that moniker deserves anything he got," Monk decided at last.

"He opened the box and was turned into a mummy so fast he never knew what hit him," Renny related. "I swapped clothes with him, so Dang would think I was the one who got it."

"What *did* hit him? That's what I want to know," rasped Ham Brooks.

"The Buddha's fury," imparted Mark and Mary Chan in unison.

Everyone looked at the twins strangely.

"This is not the benevolent Buddha of old stories," said Mark.

"This is a wrathful Buddha," agreed Mary. "He is a glutton for water."

"And souls," intoned Mark.

The Chan twins shuddered as if they were connected to one another by an invisible cord. Thereafter, they lapsed into a morose and uneasy silence.

AFTER an hour of this, Doc Savage climbed to his feet and began to trek inland. He motioned the others to remain well behind him. This, they were more than glad to do. No one knew what lay back at the pool and none wished to experience twice the sudden and inexplicable thirst that had almost sucked the very life's moisture out of them.

Doc Savage advanced with utmost caution. The air by the water was steamy. But as he penetrated further inland, that quality of moisture seemed to shrink. It was as if all the steam had evaporated out of the air, leaving nothing behind it. In fact, there was a touch of coolness to the air coming into his lungs.

Doc employed almost every sense—sight, smell, touch and hearing. Trees as he drew closer to the vicinity of the jungle pool began to look unnaturally dry. Some had cracked their entire length, exposing the inner pulp.

Pirate Island boasted tropical fruit in plenty. Bananas, coconuts, jackfruit, spiny-hulled durian fruit, red rambutans and scarlet mangosteen predominated. All of these tasty delicacies hung dried and shrunken on their vines.

Orchids, of which many grew in profusion, had shriveled into tiny knots that hardly resembled dried flowers. Only their ripe colors told that they had once been tropical blossoms in full bloom.

Everywhere, leaves and palm fronds had collapsed into tiny dry fists.

The farther Doc got to the area they had fled, the thirstier he became. He had begun his journey already thirsty, so this sensation of a growing thirst was one he did not recognize right away.

But as it grew more acute, he pressed himself to go on.

The thirst soon became uncomfortable, then unendurable.

Without any outward hesitation, the bronze man reversed himself and quitted the zone of unnatural dryness.

Coming upon his men trailing not far behind, Doc shook his head firmly and, gesturing with lifted hands, said, "Too dangerous."

They needed no more discouragement than that. They too were suffering a growing thirst, mouths and tongues as parched as the once-lush vegetation. They reversed course, seeking the psychological comfort of the water's edge.

"It would be too bad on any pigs down by that jungle pool, huh?" Monk suggested, then watched Ham's features assume an angry flush.

The dapper lawyer detested pork in any form, which motivated Monk to raise the sensitive subject now and again. Why, was a long story.

Back at the lagoon's edge, Doc and his men held counsel.

"We have equipment back at the plane that might be useful here," Doc pointed out.

"What about these pirates?" Ham wondered.

"I will order them to stand guard, but avoid the zone of desiccation."

Doc issued orders. There was no dissent. Their numbers had been appreciably thinned by the bronze man's various activities. In fact, there were three fewer of them now. Possibly some had failed to escape the sudden phenomenon at the pool and now lay dead and desiccated in the jungle somewhere.

Doc Savage led his men in a meandering way along the sand-fringed beach of Pirate Island. The sand was very white, and glittered in the sunlight like crushed pearls.

Ham Brooks mused, "By now, that Startell Pompman must have radioed for help. We told him if we weren't back by a certain time to do so."

"Who is Startell Pompman?" asked Renny.

"A blustering blowhard of an astrologer," said Monk. "He tagged along with us. Or Doc let him, I guess."

Ham explained, "He wanted Doc's help on a matter."

Satisfied, the big-fisted engineer said nothing more.

The bronze amphibian was anchored far out, around a hump of land where it would not be seen—except from the vantage point of that hump.

Evidently, it had not been, for it rode its sea anchor, undisturbed. The wings shimmered slightly in the rollers and sea breezes pushed its tail around in lazy half-circles.

A small collapsible rubber raft was located in a copse of kapok trees, and carried to the shore. This is what had ferried Monk and Ham from the seaplane.

They got into it now and began paddling up to the gently bobbing aircraft.

As they approached, they spied something that brought a growl from Monk Mayfair's throat.

"Hatch door open!"

Doc Savage stopped paddling and said, "Wait here."

He slipped into the water, began swimming, and soon reached the plane.

Clambering aboard, the bronze man was insidc for only brief moments.

When he emerged, it was to wave the others in.

Soon, Doc was helping his men climb aboard.

"Deserted," Doc reported. "The radio was left on."

Monk began searching the plane interior as if expecting to find Pompman hiding under a wicker seat—an impossibility, of course.

Ham asked, "Do you think he was picked up by the British?"

"Impossible to tell," Doc reported. "There is no sign of a struggle, nor did Pompman leave a note."

Doc looked concerned. But after a thorough search, he seemed to dismiss the matter of Startell Pompman from his immediate thoughts. Instead, he ordered the rubber raft brought aboard and the hatch sealed.

Snapping the powerful motors to life, he recalled the sea

anchor with the press of a button; electric motors in the nose did the hauling.

A seaplane on the water is an intractable thing, requiring equal parts seamanship and piloting skills. Doc Savage now proceeded to make handling the unwieldy flying boat seem a casual matter.

Booting the big aircraft about, the bronze man nosed it in the direction of a convenient lagoon, gunned the motors, throwing it up on the beach with practiced skill. The nose of the hull beached itself.

They clambered out.

Doc Savage came last. He was carrying a set of boxes as large as steamer trunks, one under each powerful arm. His amazing vitality appeared to be returning. During his reconnoiter of the jungle pool, the bronze giant had made and applied poultices to his back wounds, using his remarkable knowledge of jungle botany and medicinal herbs. Healing had already commenced.

Renny reached out monster hands to help him with one container.

"Good thinking," said Renny, suddenly realizing what the big boxes contained.

CARRYING their portage inland, Doc Savage and Renny reached the outer zone of the dry area. The bronze man began unpacking the two trunks.

The first thing to emerge was something that resembled a space helmet as envisioned by Hollywood movie producers. It consisted of a clear bubble composed of a substance devised by the bronze man himself, a material having the composite qualities of glass and metal.

The bulk of the outfit looked more like a futuristic version of a deep-sea diver's suit. It lacked the lead boots and belt weights, but the two oxygen tanks strapped to the back were substantial, each good for an hour of underwater breathing.

This entire ensemble was an invention of Doc Savage. Although it looked like something designed for undersea exploration—and could indeed serve that purpose in a pinch—it was apparent that it was a high-altitude suit, of a type far in advance of those employed by stratosphere balloon explorers to test the limits of man's penetration of the upper atmosphere where there is no oxygen and the inhospitable cold is inimical to life.

With Renny's help, Doc Savage donned this suit. It was all of a piece, with gauntlets and boots separately affixed by an ingenious coupling mechanism, to insure a tight seal.

The helmet attached to a cuirass of an affair that fitted over the shoulders. Renny hooked up the oxygen tanks, which strapped onto the suit's reinforced back.

Checking about himself, Doc Savage indicted with lifted hand that all was well.

Then he began to trudge into the dangerous zone.

The going was slow, thanks to the bulk and weight of the stratosphere suit. But the intolerable thirst that had plagued him no longer tugged at his throat.

Doc took his time. To stumble and fall would have placed him in the same position as an upended turtle—unable to rise without assistance.

Along the way, he explored. The bronze man found one dead pirate, as he expected to. The man was a shrunken, shriveled corpse like that of a mummy that had died long in the past. His eyes were dry, empty sockets. In his gaping mouth what must have once been his tongue, was now a mass like a tiny dry sponge.

Grim of countenance, Doc pushed on.

When he came to the jungle pool that had been so green with slime and verdant growth, Doc Savage stood stock-still.

His eerie trilling piped up and the surprise lacing it was a mixture of curiosity and wonder. It echoed in the clear dome encasing his bronze head, but penetrated no farther.

The pool itself was more in the nature of a crater now. The floor lay cracked in the manner of a sun-baked desert during

August. Death Valley had something of that look.

Of course, this was not a desert, but a tropical jungle. Such dryness was impossible here. But there it was.

In the crater, Dang Mi lay curled up, more like a worm than anything that had once been human. He was a shrunken twist of a thing, resembling a huge piece of beef jerky. Even his crossed leather gun belts had shriveled to strings.

Doc Savage leaned over with care and plucked him off the crackle-finished box. The former captain of the *Devilfish* seemed to hardly weigh anything at all. No trace of moisture was evident in his eyes and the bronze man remembered that ninety percent of the human body consisted of water. So this was no surprise.

The strongbox under him lay in the pit of the crater. There were a few dead dried fish here and there. They hardly resembled fish, but that's what they were.

With utmost caution, Doc Savage took hold of the blue container. He straightened his entire body.

Doc stood looking at it, and perspiration began to form on his face. This was created by the close-fitting atmosphere suit. But it might also have been the film of fear.

For one of the few times in his life, the Man of Bronze was confronting a thing that baffled him utterly. He stood there a while, possibly torn between caution and curiosity.

In the end, his scientific curiosity won.

Holding the box up to the level of his golden eyes, Doc lifted the lid a crack.

Nothing seemed to happen.

Gingerly, Doc lifted it still more.

He took pains to hold the box so that the early morning sun shone directly into the aperture.

What he saw within gleamed like a fragment of crystal.

Nearby, a roosting bird plummeted from a branch, giving a death cry that was strange, forlorn.

Feeling no ill effects himself, Doc thumbed the lid still farther upward.

The interior of the box was lined with a glassy greenish substance Doc Savage immediately recognized as jade. It was cunningly contrived, so that when closed, it formed a waterproof and airtight seal. That explained why it had been a safe repository for the artifact that lay within.

This did not explain the artifact. It was a rounded stump of a thing, as clear as crystal, but of no clearly understandable shape.

One end tapered down to a rough surface that suggested that it had been broken off a larger piece of the same substance.

The other end was rounded, polished and appeared to have been carved. There was an outline etched into one surface near the top of the fat end. This was an incised square.

The entire thing resembled nothing so much as the big toe broken off a crystal idol of some barbaric type, the incised square, the outline of a toenail.

Having seen all that was to be seen, Doc Savage carefully closed the lid, made sure it was tight, then tucked it under one arm.

As he walked back to the clearing where his men waited, his metallic face was grave.

Chapter XVII
TALE TERRIBLE

HAM BROOKS, LEFT to guard the prisoners, spent much of his time questioning Mark and Mary Chan.

"You say that you were on your way to see the British authorities, when Dang Mi shot down your plane?" he inquired.

Mark replied, "Yes. But we were separated."

Mary added, "I escaped Dang Mi. In Singapore, I read of Doc Savage. This caused me to change plans. I decided that he was the man to beseech for aid—the only man in the world capable enough to smash the menace of the Buddha of Ice."

"Jove," exclaimed Ham. "You speak of it as if it were a devil incarnate."

"It is an infernal Buddha," advised Mark. "A thing of incalculable evil."

Mary nodded energetically. "If not checked, it will ruin the world."

"In what manner?" asked Ham, impressed in spite of himself.

He kept one eye on the pirate prisoners, but they seemed content to hunker down in a circle, jabbering among themselves.

A few produced dice and began playing what appeared to be an Asian form of craps.

"I think," said Mark, "that we had better wait to tell the full story."

"Yes," added Mary. "Doc Savage should hear the full story. Then he will know what to do."

Ham frowned thoughtfully. His dark eyes glowed with an interested light.

Doc Savage, trailed by Renny and Monk, emerged from the jungle not long after. Renny was carrying fresh clothes scavenged from the plane.

The bronze man toted the crackle-finished strongbox, which contained the thing so terrible that all the corsairs shrank from sight of it.

"They're sure scared of whatever's in that strongbox," muttered Monk.

"They should be," boomed Renny Renwick. "It's bad!"

Doc Savage found a flat hump of stone and set the box carefully atop it.

Slowly, he began divesting himself of the stratosphere suit, starting with the spherical helmet.

Monk took this from his hands and placed it on the ground.

Together, he and Renny helped the bronze man out of the gauntlets and thick boots. The rubberized suit itself took considerably longer, owing to its sealed construction. As Doc emerged, it could be seen that the suit consisted of several layers, some for insulation against cold, others designed to repel water and other hazards.

When Doc Savage stood free of the thing, he was sweating. Oddly, his bronze hair was undisturbed. It had unusual qualities, not the least of which was a kind of natural waterproofing.

Doc padded over to Mark and Mary Chan and suggested, "It is time to hear your story in its entirety."

"It is not a pleasant one," Mark began.

"Nor a simple one, either," Mary added.

Doc studied them a moment. He could see the way in which Mary Chan's feet were arranged that they had not been bound in the traditional fashion when she was very young. This suggested that she had been raised outside of Chinese society, which is many ways still smacked of feudalism. In her dress and manner of speaking, she appeared to be rather modern, yet still touched by the East in her thinking.

"Start at the beginning," Doc Savage suggested.

"We are the children of Wah Chan. Perhaps you have heard of him?" Mary began.

Doc nodded. "Talk out of China suggests that he is a warlord in the Manchuria region. He started out as a bandit, but is now fighting the Japanese occupiers of North China."

"Exactly," confirmed Mark.

"But we never knew that our father was a bandit, you see," contradicted Mary. "For we spent our young years in Hongkong, after which we were sent away to the States to be educated. We are geologists."

"Graduates of the Colorado School of Mines," added Mark. "After earning our degrees, we returned to China. By that time the Japanese had come. And it was terrible."

"Very terrible," agreed Mary. "Our father, Wah Chan, made us stay in the city of Shanghai while he was organizing against the Japanese army. He was in Nanking and other conquered places, harrying the Japanese there."

"But no matter how hard he fought, he and his *Hung-Hutz* band," continued Mark Chan, "Wah Chan could not repel the occupiers. He was growing disheartened. Very."

"Then came Tang," said Mary.

"Tang?" asked Doc.

"A monk," clarified Mark.

"The most evil monk you could ever imagine," Mary elaborated. "He had been schooled in a monastery in Tibet, some said. But he was too wicked to remain a good monk. And so he was exiled."

"They say he wandered the Gobi desert for years, living off the barren land like a yak, drinking fermented mare's milk and growing to hate the world," Mark offered.

Mary Chan nodded in agreement. "Something happened in the *Kara-Kum*—the Black Gobi Desert. Something strange,

Mr. Savage."

"It was said that Tang entered the desert as fat as the Buddha himself," Mark related. "But when he came out, he was a lean, wizened devil, looking very little like the gluttonous monk who had been exiled."

"Stick to the facts you know," suggested Doc Savage.

"One day the monk Tang showed up in Shanghai, clutching a box of jade," continued Mark.

"The box which contained the Buddha of Ice," added Mary.

Doc Savage indicated the blue container. "That box?"

Mark shook his head emphatically. "No, that box is merely lined with jade. This is a different box entirely. But it contained what that box contains, only more of it."

"That was when the Buddha of Ice was whole," added Mary.

"Keep going," Doc advised.

Mark did so. "The wicked monk Tang was going around boasting that he possessed a power terrible enough to drive the Japanese out of China, if only someone would ferry him up to Manchuria to bring it to bear on the occupiers."

"We heard this wild tale, Mr. Savage," Mary inserted. "And we investigated."

Mark nodded. "The jade box Tang possessed was fitted with an eyelet on its lid, to which he had affixed a long cord. He would set the box down and from a safe distance, open it."

Mary wrung her delicate ivory-hued hands. "Birds would fall dead from the sky, their bodies parched," she said. "Dogs howled and perished of thirst on the spot. It was terrible."

"Very terrible," agreed Mark solemnly.

"And worse things were demonstrated," insisted Mary. "When a criminal was taken in the town square to be beheaded, Tang offered to spare the executioner the toil of cleaning up the beheaded man's life blood."

"So Tang set the box before the trussed man and opened it as before," related Mark.

Mary hissed excitedly, "The man became as a mummy—in less than a few minutes!"

"That was when the Buddha of Ice was not so powerful as it is now," Mark finished.

The others had crowded around as the story grew protracted in the telling. They began making thirsty faces. Monk took a swig from a canteen. Possibly this was a psychological reaction to the Chans' account.

"Go on," encouraged Doc.

Mary took up the tale. "We contacted our father by radio. He said he would come. And he did."

To which Mark added, "Tang and my father Wah Chan conferred over the thing in the box a day and a night. My father wanted to know what was in the box, and all that Tang would reveal was that it was a Buddha carved from a crystal unlike anything ever found on earth. He said he had unearthed it in the Gobi. But he would not say any more."

"Our father wanted to examine the Buddha of Ice, to determine what made it so terrible," Mary offered. "We tried to figure out a way to study it, but it could not be safely removed from the box."

"Each time someone tried," Mark said with quiet sincerity, "the man quickly succumbed to an awful thirst that stripped his physical form of all moisture."

Mark and Mary Chan looked uncomfortable. It was obvious that coolie labor had been employed to test the advisability of opening the box, and those who had volunteered had perished in the manner described.

A warm breeze came off the ocean, ruffling and stirring myriad palms trees, whose crowns shook like spindly giants throwing their shaggy heads about. Insects droned lazily.

"Continue," said Doc.

"At length, Wah Chan and Tang came to terms," Mark recounted. "Dad would ferry the box to Manchuria. He commanded a vessel—a five-masted junk. They were to sail up the coast to bring awful destruction to the Japanese army."

"But before this could be accomplished," Mary added, "another party entered the bargain. A trader from America. One who spoke excellent Mandarin and Cantonese. He appeared one day in the International Settlement section of the city."

"This man recognized the terrible potential of the Buddha in the box and attempted to buy it from my father," Mark husked. "But father would not sell it at any price. So he tried to bribe us."

"But we would not be bribed," Mary said firmly.

Mark nodded. "He implored us, saying that the thing in the box would be a boon to science, and could be used to fight floods, and accomplish other needed wonders."

"This made perfect sense to us," Mary admitted. "And we fell upon a scheme to obtain a sample. Through his contacts, this man acquired a pair of up-to-date atmosphere suits from Russia, in the expectation that they would protect us, which they did."

Mark hesitated. "So we... borrowed the box outright."

"We half succeeded," Mary corrected quickly. "During the borrowing, the Buddha fell out of the box, and was broken. We failed to get away with the Buddha, or the box."

"But the toe became ours," said Mark.

Doc Savage's eerie trilling slowly saturated the surrounding air. It carried with it a flavor of the Orient, hinting at its origins stemming from a period in the bronze man's childhood when he had been schooled by a Hindu yogi in the subtle secrets of emotional self-control.

"The toe is what lies in that box?" Doc asked.

Mark Chan nodded vigorously. "Yes. Only the toe. But you see how terrible it is."

"There's that word again," rumbled Renny. "Terrible."

"They are gonna wear it out," growled Monk.

Mark and Mary Chan ignored the interruption. Their Eurasian features remained composed and very sincere.

Mary said, "Because the Buddha had to be sealed in its box immediately, lest it mummify others, the loss of the toe was not immediately noticed."

"Tang and Wah Chan took the Buddha of the box and set sail for Manchuria," continued Mark. "That is the last we have heard of it."

"But we secretly rediscovered the toe, and managed to transfer it to another box, one equally safe to carry it," Mary elaborated.

Mark Chan frowned. "That is the box we employed."

"The man who lusted for the Buddha later sought to bargain with us for it," explained Mary.

Mark nodded in agreement. "But we would not bargain. This man then offered to back us financially, the better to conduct our experiments."

"We considered this," admitted Mary Chan. She colored slightly, skin blushing a sun-burnished ivory.

As if connected, Mary's twin brother also acquired a slightly abashed facial hue.

"But we would not surrender the box, or what it contained," said Mark. "So a bargain was struck. Our backer furnished us with an aircraft, with which we would fly the box safely out of China."

"We agreed to rendezvous with this individual, at a certain place at a specific time, in the United States," elaborated Mary.

"But in truth, we wished to carry the box to the west, where the best scientists could study it and unlock its secrets."

A look of fear came over Mary's ivory features. "Then came the trouble, when Chino-Japanese tensions reached a high point after the student anti-Japanese riots and the other unfortunate incidents that brought Japanese Marines onto the streets of Shanghai patrolling in their steel helmets with fixed bayonets."

"We fled China at that point," said Mark. "That was when we sought the counsel of the British authorities, only to be captured by Dang Mi and his cut-throats. Fortunately, Mary managed to escape and came upon your assistant, Mr. Renwick."

"In the confusion of Shanghai," Mary moaned, "we lost track of our supposed benefactor."

"Who is the man who attempted these thefts?" asked Doc Savage.

"A fat man," said Mary.

"A very fat man," agreed Mark.

Mary nodded solemnly. "His name is Startell Pompman."

"Blazes!" howled Monk. "That windbag ties into this after all."

Ham eyed Doc Savage. "But you knew that all along, didn't you?"

Doc nodded. "It was too coincidental that Pompman should show up at our headquarters at the same time that the boxed mummy arrived from Singapore. A tie-up seemed likely."

"So where is that windy stargazer?" Renny demanded.

"We will endeavor to locate him at once," Doc Savage said firmly. "Once that is accomplished, we are flying to China."

"For what?" wondered Monk.

Doc Savage's voice took on a level quality. "The Buddha of Ice must not be allowed to operate unchecked. It is far too dangerous to remain in a warlord's hands. We must find it and seize it, and if possible discover some way to destroy it."

No one disputed Doc Savage's assessment of the situation. They had seen for themselves the irresistible power of the Buddha of Ice—or at least the portion of it contained in the blue strongbox.

Doc Savage rapped out swift orders.

"Monk, you and Ham comb the island. Renny and I will search the pirate junk."

"What about these buccaneers?" asked Ham Brooks.

Doc advised, "They look sufficiently cowed for the time being. Best we bring them along. They know the innards of the craft and can assist in the search."

"I know a couple of good hiding places, too," muttered Renny. "I spent enough time holed up in that cockeyed tub."

"What about us?" asked Mary Chan.

"Given the many perils of this island, perhaps you would be safest in the amphibian," Doc suggested.

That settled it. They got themselves organized and broke into several groups.

Mark Chan proved to possess the ability to pilot the rubber raft to the waiting amphibian. This was accomplished first.

While Monk and Ham, backed by a handful of compliant corsairs, began a thorough daylight search of Pirate Island, Doc and Renny reached the black-hulled junk, wallowing at anchor.

It was a very seaworthy craft, Doc realized after climbing aboard. For in spite of its villainous crew, it had been kept in tiptop shape.

They worked their way into the cabins, the hold and every other nook and cranny. There were many of these. The interior construction of the typical Chinese sailing junk is ingeniously compartmentalized. Further, Dang Mi, when he had been among the living, had outfitted the large vessel with all manner of hiding places and storage larders. They found many rifles placed there, along with boxes of ammunition for the big Maxim gun, stacked lead balls for the antiquated deck cannon, and gunpowder stores. Other, less savory, implements of the corsair trade also came to light.

There was some booty in Dang's former cabin. This ranged from jewelry confiscated from seagoing vessels to sacks of coins of all denominations, representing many nations. Bottles of a Shanghai wine called *ng ka pay* and another sorghum brew labeled *Mui Kwai Lu* were in evidence.

"Look at all this swag," thumped Renny. "This pirate racket really pays swell."

"If you happen to be the head corsair," noted Doc dryly.

A careful search of the junk's below decks turned up no sign of Startell Pompman. They even checked the bilge. Doc did this, Renny having had more than his fill of the unpleasant place when he had hid out in its malodorous confines. Nothing was found.

In the end, they climbed topside to the deck and surveyed the surrounding water.

Renny had found an old-fashioned spyglass and opened it, telescope fashion. He was using this to reconnoiter the surroundings.

Training the glass inland, Renny almost dropped the tube from his gargantuan paws.

"Holy cow!" he thumped.

A finger no less sizable that a hot dog leveled out at the jungle's edge, indicting a pristine white beach clearing.

Doc Savage followed the pointing digit.

A ludicrous sight came waddling out of the foliage.

"That him?" Renny hazarded.

Even without the aid of the telescope, Doc Savage's keen vision identified the preposterous apparition.

It was C. Startell Pompman. And somehow he had managed to stuff himself into Doc Savage's stratosphere suit!

Worse yet, he was bearing in his round arms the blue crackle-finish box that contained the Buddha's Toe!

As they watched, Pompman began to pry open the lid!

Chapter XVIII
PARLEY

HAD DOC SAVAGE and Renny been faced with a small army of men equipped with the finest and most modern of automatic rifles, they would have stood a chance.

The ebony junk was honeycombed with hiding places and stout teak and mahogany timbers that might turn any number of bullets.

But the force with which they were now being threatened was not a tangible thing. It couldn't be deflected, unlike lead. Nor was there any substance at hand that was proof against the power that lay within the square steel box.

The lid continued lifting.

Renny muttered a weak, "Holy cow!"

Doc Savage sprang to an ammunition box and extracted three grenades. He selected one.

Throwing back one arm, Doc let fly.

The bronze man's throw flung the black pineapple clear of the junk and well onto shore.

It landed, not by accident, against Startell Pompman's domed head. The helmet did not shatter. Conceivably an ordinary bullet might not break it.

But it was enough to startle the fat man. When he looked down at what lay at his feet, the oblate plutocrat emitted a sound that was not audible beyond the confines of the helmet, but the way his mouth formed a surprised "O" indicated that he had gasped.

Renny waited tensely. Nothing happened.

"A dud!" he grunted.

But that was not the whole truth of it.

Doc Savage lifted his voice. "The next grenade will be armed," he called out. Jungle birds leaped from sprawling kapok trees at the sound.

Startell Pompman looked up from the grenade at his feet and over to the one Doc Savage held high overhead.

Something in his heavy features conveyed disbelief that Doc Savage could successfully repeat his feat, if attempted.

So Doc left fly with another grenade.

This one struck Pompman on his metal-sheathed shoulder.

That was proof enough that Doc Savage wasn't making an idle claim, but could make good on his threat.

"There is a microphone and loudspeaker on your suit," Doc directed.

Managing to move the box to one arm, Pompman found the rheostat control. He turned it.

"I am not giving up this box," he announced.

"Can you fly a plane?" Doc inquired.

Pompman's prolonged silence indicated that he could not.

"This is not a place you would want to be marooned in for very long," Doc suggested.

Pompman seemed to understand that. He nodded in dejected agreement.

Doc said, "Truce?"

"What sort of truce?"

"Surrender the box and we will take you back to civilization."

"The stars are with me to-day. They say it is an auspicious day to bargain."

Renny exploded, "Holy cow! He thinks he holds all the cards."

"He holds one very impressive trump," Doc Savage said quietly. To Pompman, he called, "We have a Mexican standoff."

"What do you mean by that?"

"You have the box," Doc told him, "but the oxygen supply to that suit is limited. And I previously exhausted one tank. Once the other gives out, you must remove the helmet in order to breathe. Did you fail to think of that?"

Startell Pompman's ruddy face fell so far that it was evident that the unhappy thought had never entered his mind. Absently, he reached up to adjust his eyeglasses, and reacted with surprise when his pudgy fingers bumped the helmet glass instead.

"Do we have an understanding?" Doc questioned.

"That we do, my dear Savage."

"We will be down directly."

Renny asked uneasily, "Doc, what if he opens up the devil box on us?"

"He could have done that by now. And at this distance we would be helpless."

They clambered down the daggerboard gangplank. All but the pirate cohort, whom Doc had instructed to remain on board. The latter showed no love of facing the man on the beach, or his fearsome box.

Once on dry land, Doc and Renny approached with understandable caution.

The box remained sealed in Startell Pompman's ample arms.

"One false move, gentlemen, and I will give you a taste of thirst," Pompman warned. *"So to speak."*

"Already had mine, thanks," Renny said dryly. He blocked and unblocked his enormous fists nervously. He looked as if he wanted to use them, and very violently.

But Startell Pompman's eyes were on Doc Savage.

"Hand over the box and we will give you our word that you will not be harmed," instructed the bronze man.

"What will happen to me after that?" Pompman asked.

"We are bound for China," said Doc. "You will have to accompany us."

"And after that?"

"After that, you will be turned over to the proper authorities at our discretion."

"The Chinese authorities?"

"American. But you will be treated humanely."

Doc Savage did not say that he had no intention of surrendering Pompman to U. S. justice, but to a peculiar reckoning of his own. There would be time for that concern later.

"Very well. I am a reasonable man. I herewith surrender."

With that, Pompman carefully handed over the box.

Doc Savage took it. He noticed that it appeared heavier than it had been before.

"Did you use this?" he demanded.

"Only to discourage vipers and other predators that happened along in my path. I fancy that we could dine on crocodile jerky, if we had any appetite for such."

"Holy cow," grunted Renny. "A gourmand."

Doc Savage took firm hold of the box and bore it inland. He employed both hands.

Renny herded Startell Pompman along, after helping him out of the helmet. "Just in case you get any ideas," he explained.

But escape seemed to be the last thing on Startell Pompman's active mind. His piggish eyes kept skating over to the box Doc Savage carried. Now that it was no longer in his possession, he seemed to fear it greatly.

"Don't dare drop that," he encouraged. "I daresay that I am in a rather vulnerable spot."

"And I think we'll let you keep that suit on," said Renny. "It will keep you from getting any funny ideas about flight."

"Zounds!" bleated Pompman, fluttering fat fingers. "Farthest thing from my mind, I assure you."

As they walked along, Doc asked, "How did you locate the box?"

"In the simplest manner possible: I was observing you from afar. I saw you bury it under the rock. When I realized that you had left the suit behind as well, I saw my opportunity."

"How the heck did you get into it all by yourself?" demanded Renny.

Pompman cleared his throat noisily. "I have done some deep-sea fishing in my time. Not that the task was easy. But I managed. My motivation was enhanced by my peculiar predicament."

THEY came upon Monk and Ham before long. They were, as usual, quarreling. The nature of their argument was not clear, owing to its verbal violence.

At the sound of Doc's approach, they broke off, Ham sheathing his sword cane, which he had recovered some time before.

"Where you find *him*?" Ham wanted to know. His cultured voice dripped disdain.

"He found *us,"* grumbled Renny. "You two might learn some day to shut your yaps and open your ears. He almost got the drop on us."

"Did get the drop," Pompman corrected.

"But lost it, I see," murmured Ham, walking around the man, marveling at how he stretched the atmosphere suit to its utmost limits without apparently bursting any seams.

"Very clever," he murmured. "But what if you had failed to secure every seam?"

"We never did find that out," Renny rumbled.

"My stars!" said Pompman, blanching.

"Now that we are all assembled," Doc Savage decided, "it is best that we be on our way."

"What about all them blasted pirates we collected?" Monk wanted to know.

Doc Savage looked pained. It was impractical to take them along. But neither did he wish to release them to British Crown justice, where they faced certain hanging.

So Doc gathered them together and explained the way of

things. He spoke excellent Chinese, which was the common tongue of the corsairs.

"Jen fei sheng hsien shu neng wu kuo?" he began. "Who but the sages are free from faults?

"Chin k'ou, yu yin," one replied, meaning that the bronze man's welcome speech was like honeyed words issued from a golden mouth.

"It is a wise man who sees the error of his ways," Doc continued. "Riches benefit a man when he may keep them. But not when his life is forfeit for the taking of another man's wealth. For what good is gold to a man who occupies an early grave?"

The pirates saw the wisdom of Doc Savage's argument. They also felt of their necks uneasily. They vociferously agreed to set sail for parts unknown and seek an honest living, or as one of them put it in flowery Chinese, "*Ko mien hsi hsin,*" which literally meant "to skin one's face, and wash his heart." In other words, they solemnly vowed to reform.

With that promise ringing in the humid jungle air, Doc Savage allowed them to take possession of the *Devilfish* and sail where they would.

"Not exactly a perfect solution," Monk muttered, eying the bronze man.

"No doubt some of them will fall back on their word," Doc admitted. "But the greater portion has been through an experience worse that any of them ever imagined. They have been scared into reconsidering their former ways."

"If not," rumbled Renny, "there are plenty of nooses for any necks that don't."

That seemed to settle the matter.

They left Pirate Island by rubber raft and rejoined Mark and Mary Chan on the anchored amphibian.

Neither half of the twins was delighted to set almond eyes on Startell Pompman. Both sets of orbs narrowed in the fashion of threatened felines.

"If it were not for that scoundrel," Mark Chan accused, "we

would have only one problem, not two."

Mary Chan said nothing. She merely stared daggers at the uncomfortable fat man.

Startell Pompman took a seat in the rear of the plane as Doc and his men readied the amphibian for take-off. This was accomplished in short order.

Soon, the ship was skimming through rollers, then crashing along wave tops with a violence that threatened to shake the wings loose from their roots.

Moaning, it vaulted into the sky.

Presently, they were volleying northeast, in the direction of the China coast.

"I just thought of somethin'," muttered Monk, eying the blue crackle-finished box, which Doc had temporarily locked in an equipment case.

"With what, you fuzzy lunk?" said Ham.

"What if we go down? What happens then?"

Startell Pompman answered that. "The thing in the box could conceivably gorge itself on the entire Pacific Ocean."

"Nonsense!" returned Ham Brooks.

Monk looked to Mary and Mark Chan.

The latter responded. "Every time the Buddha of Ice drinks, it grows in volume. The greater it grows, the deeper its thirst. The larger it becomes, the more water it can consume."

"It could drink the entire Pacific," intoned Mary Chan. "Drink it down to the last drop."

"Holy cow!" Renny exploded. "Could that be true, Doc?"

At the controls, the bronze man offered no opinion. It was better not to say anything. He had never felt so apprehensive about any cargo he carried in his supremely eventful and dangerous life.

Instead of speaking, Doc grimly advanced the amphibian's throttles.

Chapter XIX
THE COMET CLUE

THEY REFUELED AT Saigon, in French Indo-China, and again at Hongkong, where the British authorities showed Doc Savage great deference.

They also wished to know what business the bronze man had in China. They were polite about it. "Veddy" much so. But it was plain that they expected straight answers.

Doc Savage told them, "We are searching for a generalissimo named Wah Chan."

Which was the truth. Just not the entire truth, of course.

The British bluejackets were not completely satisfied with that explanation. Then Doc produced the Chans.

The half-caste twins told a story of fearing for their father's life, going as he did from bandit chief and leader of the dreaded *Hung-Hutz*, to a nationalist fighter of Japanese.

That, the Brits understood.

"We want this bounder, Wah Chan," they said. "To whom do you presume to turn him over?"

"Wah Chan will be dealt with according to his just deserts," promised Doc.

That seemed to satisfy the British authorities. Vague as his words were, the bronze man was trusted by the Crown. He had done the British monarch many a past service.

Doc next asked for any information they had.

"At this moment, we have none," he was informed forthwith.

Then Doc asked about a radio report he had heard during the flight from Saigon to Hongkong.

"A Japanese cruiser is said to have been discovered drifting in the upper South China Sea," Doc related. "Reports are that no hands were found on board."

"That is true. The boat was boarded, and found deserted. A jolly new *Marie Celeste* mystery, wot?"

"What disposition was made of this vessel?" asked the bronze man.

"None. It was allowed to drift away. It is a Japanese problem."

"I would like to search that vessel. Can you provide its present location?"

WITHIN the hour, they were back in the air and hammering over the vast wrinkled expanse of the South China Sea. It was littered with fishing junks and sampans, as well as other coastwise merchant traffic, their delicate sails resembling floating moths.

In back, Startell Pompman was bestirring himself. He had avoided all conversation with the Chans, and they had likewise returned the favor.

But now he was overflowing with talk.

"In Solar Psychology," he began, "the sign of Gemini is known as 'The Twins.' That is because those born under the auspices of Gemini are often duplicitous of mind. They possess sharp tongues and are given to prevarications."

No one commented upon this casual utterance.

Pompman went on, "I am not asserting that all Geminis are thus afflicted. Nor am I impugning the good natures of twins. I am just pointing out plain facts as the ancients have handed them down to us."

His meaning was clear, however.

Renny recast it into plain English.

"If you're trying to convince us that the Chans here are speaking with forked tongues, you can stow it," he rumbled.

"So far, all you have contributed to the proceedings is a load of hot air—none of it valuable."

"Tut-tut, my dear sir," clucked Pompman, waving his plump, womanish hands in the air. "Pish-tosh."

Ham interjected, "If you're still trying to convince us that Mark and Mary Chan tried to gyp you out of the thing in the box, the Buddha's Toe, save your breath. That is not the story that they are telling."

"Let me remind you that I sought out Doc Savage in the first place, flying at great expense from Shanghai to Manhattan for that noble purpose," Pompman said flatly.

"And they had roughly the same idea," grunted Renny. "It was their bad luck to run on to Dang Mi and his cut-throats."

The plump plutocrat eyed the big engineer with one eyebrow cocked superciliously. "Are you certain of that, my good man? How do you know they were not in league with that blackguard, and simply had a falling out over the Buddha's Toe?"

Renny folded his map. He had been doing the navigating, assisted by radio bearings which Ham had taken.

"I like their story the way they tell it," he snapped.

Pursing his lips, Startell Pompman fell silent. He steepled fat fingers over his portly paunch, and a deep frown descended upon his heavily-jowled face.

Mark Chan picked up the conversation at that point.

"Having failed to achieve his unworthy aims, this man thought he could induce Doc Savage to assist him," he said pointedly.

"Perhaps he feared we might do the same," chimed in Mary, "and simply raced to beat us. A fast China Clipper would make the Pacific crossing more rapidly than we could in our little plane."

Forward in the cockpit, Doc Savage was monitoring his compass, while Renny called out bearings.

"Should be coming up on that drifting Jap cruiser any time now," the big engineer remarked.

Not fifteen minutes later, Doc Savage reported, "There it is."

Throwing the laboring amphibian into a slanting dive, Doc set the plane down. The Pacific was well named at this point. It was a very smooth landing, owing as much to the state of the seas as Doc's landing skills, which were considerable.

Doc asked Monk to accompany him. They set down a pneumatic rubber raft and sculled over to the becalmed cruiser. It flew a Japanese ensign—a solar disk radiating red rays against a white field.

"Looks like a big blood-soaked ball," muttered Monk.

They ascended via the Jacob's ladder and worked through the abandoned vessel.

The story of what must have happened was simply read.

From pilothouse to stern, the cruiser was deserted. Evidence of dry tea leaves in small porcelain cups, and half-smoked cigarettes told that the ship had been evacuated in a violent hurry.

Here and there, a boot was left behind.

"Whatever happened, they couldn't be bothered to stop and grab their kicks," Monk mumbled. He looked worried.

Doc Savage examined one boot. The leather was dry and horribly distorted, laces the consistency of punky wood. He handed it over to Monk, whose simian face frowned heavily as the boot sole crumbled under examination.

Doc next opened up the bilge and shone down a light. It was as dry as an empty water tank.

Next he examined the boilers, and their oil supply. What oil had been in the reservoirs had turned to a gummy substance resembling hardened tar.

"Blazes!" squeaked Monk, whose chemical knowledge told him that such a thing was virtually impossible.

"It is evident that this ship was attacked by a vessel bearing the greater portion of the Buddha of Ice," Doc decided.

Monk eyed the surrounding ocean. It was the hue of blue

jade. Without stooping, he absently scratched a knee.

"You figger the crew got overcome by the same thirst that hit us, and jumped into the brine, Doc?"

Doc nodded. "It is reasonable to assume that in their blind panic, they would seek relief in any water at hand. No doubt they drowned."

"Or sharks got 'em," suggested Monk. "Say, Doc, what if the raiders come back?"

"They will not. No doubt they have sailed farther north to seek more Japanese warships."

There being nothing more to discover, Doc and Monk scrambled down to their raft and made their way back to the waiting amphibian.

Back on board, they related their tale.

"That sounds like the work of my father," said Mary Chan. "He despised the Japanese."

"What sort of craft was at his disposal?" asked Doc.

"A junk of war," she replied.

"An armored junk," elaborated Mark. "With bow and sails marked by the sign of the Red Dragon."

"The Red Dragon is the symbol of the *Hung-Hutz*," echoed Mary. "My father is a power among them."

"The *Hung-Hutz* are a bandit organization also known as the Red Beards," Doc imparted. "They have been operating in the north of China since the days of the Red Terror revolution. They are no better than gangsters."

Mark and Mary Chan looked uncomfortable, but declined to contradict the bronze man's stated opinion.

"That junk won't be hard to identify, if we can spot it from the air," Ham suggested.

It was brave talk. Even in this time of conflict, the South China Sea was busy with maritime commerce. Spotting one junk among the many plying open water would take luck as well as skill.

That obstruction seemed not to bother the giant Man of Bronze. He ordered the hatch closed and began snapping ignition switches back to life. The still-warm motors crashed into a bawl of synchronized sound.

It was an easy take-off. There was only a modest amount of suction that had to be overcome in order to lift the big bronze bird off the water's surface.

Bearing north, Doc offered a thought. "Assuming they did not hove into port, the junk would not have gotten far in the day or so since the attack. We will head for the northernmost point they could conceivably have reached, and fly circles until we spot it."

As Doc flew north, he engaged the Chans in further conversation.

"Back at Pirate Island, you said that there was talk about what happened to the monk called Tang, in the Gobi Desert. What kind of talk?"

Evidently, the bronze man was interested in the origin of the Buddha of Ice, even if it only consisted of hearsay.

MARK CHAN considered his words a long time before offering speech.

"It is said that, in its original state, the Buddha of Ice was discovered in an arid part of the Gobi, where no water existed, and it rained but once or twice a year."

Mary Chan inserted, "Tang claimed he had found a piece of jade the color of mare's milk, which summer winds had uncovered from the sand. He believed it to be valuable and, having some skill in the carving of minerals, began to cut and polish it as a stonecutter would."

"The claim is that he took over a year to work it into the form of a sitting Buddha," said Mark.

Mary frowned. "But Tang's mind wasn't pious. He carved the body of a Buddha, but when he got to the head, he made it over into the semblance of a dog-eared devil. Or so my father told us."

"Tang was able to do this safely?" Ham wondered, curious.

"At the time, the Buddha of Ice was not yet awake," explained Mark. "It was dead, inert."

"Or perhaps slumbering," offered Mary.

"Preposterous story!" Startell Pompman exploded. "Utter rot! Listen to them spin that sorry tale."

"You shut up," Monk growled.

Spittle dribbled off the plutocrat's plump lips. "Pshaw! Mineral substances do not harbor spirits! Every educated man knows this." Pompman's derisive laughter shook his globular belly.

"So says the esteemed astrologer," Renny grunted sardonically.

The merry man's mouth abruptly snapped shut like a steam shovel. He went about polishing his pince-nez spectacles with fuming intensity.

"Continue," invited Doc, voice carrying above the faint drone of the three speed-cowled engines.

Mark Chan took up the tale.

"After Tang the monk got the Buddha in the shape and semblance he desired, he set out for China in an attempt to profit by it," he related.

"What his plans were at that point are locked up in his wicked mind," seconded Mary. "But during his journey, it chanced to rain."

"Uh-oh," muttered Monk.

"Only a few drops fell, but it roused to life the evil spirit that slumbered within the Buddha," said Mark.

Mary continued, "Tang was carrying the Buddha and he lifted his mouth to the sky to drink of the falling precipitation. But a curious thing happened."

"The more he drank," Mark said, "the thirstier he felt."

"When the rain stopped, he remained thirsty," Mary intoned.

"And when he looked at his arms, they were shriveled horribly," revealed Mark.

Mary nodded. "The Buddha had tasted its first earthly water. Its prodigious thirst was awakened. Since then it has known only thirst—as do all who come into contact with it."

Ham touched his throat as if the memory stung. Monk made tasting sounds with his suddenly-thick tongue. But neither made a move for water, for fear that it would be needed later.

Doc Savage said, "The properties you ascribe to this Buddha are not properties of jade. Nor of any known substance."

"We do not know where the material that constitutes the Buddha originated," Mark admitted.

Mary nodded. "Tang never spoke of that. He did not know."

Methodically polishing his glasses, Startell Pompman spoke up confidently.

"I know. I know exactly where the Buddha came from. That I do."

"Yeah?" said Renny skeptically. "Where?"

"From the stars, of course."

"Hah!" scoffed Monk. "More astrology."

"Nothing of it, sir," Pompman said huffily, gesturing with his beribboned pince-nez. "Do any of you gentlemen recall the comet that passed near the earth some three or four years ago?"

In the cockpit, Doc Savage's trilling began to sing. It drifted up and down the musical scales, seeming to fight the engine drone for supremacy. After a while, it became the dominant sound. Or so it struck the ears of all who were within listening range.

"The comet Giacobini-Zinner," said the bronze man, "passed by the earth in the latter months of 1933. One of the most dramatic Draconid meteor showers on record followed."

Ham asked of Pompman, "What makes you think this was a piece of a comet?"

Startell Pompman cleared his throat like a toad croaking.

"I study the stars. I constructed a horoscopic chart of the comet. What it told me suggested that a great calamity would befall the earth when it passed. I waited for said calamity, but it never eventuated."

Startell Pompman had all attention upon him. He seemed to greatly enjoy having an attentive audience for a change.

"I had not taken into consideration the possibility that a cometary fragment might have fallen to earth to work its evil ways three years after the fact," he amended. "For I was looking out for a purely celestial influence."

Renny turned to Doc and demanded, "Doc, what do you make of this bloated line of bushwa?"

"A cock-and-locoweed yarn, I call it," Monk snorted.

Doc Savage was thoughtful for a moment. "To this day no one knows what constitutes the essential matter which comprises the seemingly fiery comets which pass by the earth periodically. There are many theories. It may be that some comets are crystalline or possess a mineral nature. Meteors, after all, are most often rock or metal. It is entirely within the realm of possibility that a cometary core possessing an uncanny affinity for water has fallen to earth."

"Since ancient times, comets have a reputation for leaving disaster in their wake," Ham mused.

"Spoken by a man who understands the mechanics of the heavens," exclaimed Pompman, replacing his rimless glasses upon the predatory bridge of his nose. "Perhaps you know the derivation of the very word, 'disaster.' Originally, it meant the unfavorable aspect of a heavenly body. Sadly, such portents of severe events have been all but forgotten nowadays."

"How much of what you believe to be true, did you learn through spying?" asked Doc of the rotund astrologer.

"Ahem. A portion, I will admit. The rest is educated conjecture, arrived at using the time-honored methods of Solar Psychology."

No one made a comment on that line of thinking. Bewilderment crossed the faces of the amphibian passengers.

That was all.

Up ahead, Doc Savage batted the throttles to wring more horsepower out of the great air-slashing engines.

In the navigation compartment, Renny leaned over to Doc and breathed, "What do you think of the Chans' stories?"

"It is imperative," said Doc Savage, "that we locate Wah Chan's war junk and confiscate the Buddha of Ice, so-called."

Chapter XX
JUNK OF THE RED DRAGON

THEY RECEIVED A break.

As breaks went, it was decidedly mixed. And its repercussions proved to be unfortunate indeed.

By this time Monk Mayfair had been spelling Renny in the navigation cubicle. Monk was a fair navigator when he put his mind to it, and he evinced a desire to sit as far away from windy Startell Pompman as humanly possible, the latter having lapsed into a discourse on the planet Mars as it pertained to human events.

"Mars was the Roman deity of war," the astrologer was declaiming to no one in particular. "We are now in a period where the earth lies under the influence of Mars. Wars are abounding. Africa. Spain. China. Mark my words, red war will run riot for years yet to come. That is the awful power of Mars."

"That is the power of hot air," the hairy chemist muttered.

"To that canard," harrumphed Startell Pompman, "I will fall back on the famous aphorism reliably attributed to no less than that financial titan, J. Pierpont Morgan. To wit: 'Millionaires don't use astrology, billionaires do!' And it is my sincere conviction that I will one day be numbered among the latter legion of the elect."

After that, the corpulent capitalist fell into a fuming funk.

Doc and Monk spotted the speeding boat about the same time. Where Doc Savage was normally not demonstrative, preferring to observe and study before reacting, Monk bellowed out a sharp yell.

"*Y-e-e-o-w!* Lookit!"

He leveled a hairy arm that could bend horseshoes.

The others could not see it, so they demanded that Monk explain his outburst.

"There's a Japanese destroyer steaming as fast as it can go," Monk exclaimed. "And it's being chased by a fat Chinese junk."

"Rot," said Ham, frowning. "Impossible!"

"Take a look, shyster."

Ham was seated the farthest forward, so he stuck his immaculately groomed head into the cockpit. The dapper lawyer had brought along a pair of binoculars taken from a seat pocket.

They were approaching the tableau, so Ham got a good look.

It was exactly as Monk reported it to be.

The Japanese destroyer was flying south, throwing up a trail of salt spray that, even from this height, told that all her boilers were involved in the effort.

Hardly a nautical mile to her stern, a Chinese junk of traditional construction was in hot pursuit. It was of a five-masted type sometimes called a treasure junk.

From the turmoil of the latter's wake, it was clear that the junk did not depend upon sail power alone.

"Whatever they got on that ark," Monk observed, "the Japs are petrified by it."

"Do you blame them, you hairy mistake?" snapped Ham.

Monk grabbed the binoculars from Ham's manicured hands and trained them on the foredeck of the junk.

"Doc," the apish chemist reported, "I see some kind of a contraption on the bow deck. It's pointed forward."

"Describe it."

"Can't make it out. It's squat and fat like a pot-bellied stove. Looks like it might be made out of cast iron."

Doc took the binoculars from the apish Monk's hands. He spent a minute scrutinizing the device in the bow of the junk.

If he understood its nature, the bronze man did not divulge his conclusions. Handing the binoculars back to Monk, he said, "We will drop down and take a closer look."

Swinging the amphibian around, for they were about to pass over the junk, Doc dropped the plane in abrupt stages.

Engines moaned and changed key. Wind in the wings and what few struts the streamlined craft boasted whined and sang.

First, Doc Savage overflew the vessel. He slanted in from the west and banked the craft violently so that those sitting on the starboard side could see the junk clearly.

The first thing they noticed was the hull. It was painted a bilious shade of mustard. There was a weird design done in glaring scarlet on the high bows, which all recognized as the head of a Chinese dragon. It had eyes of some glittering substance that resembled mother-of-pearl, which were as large as meat platters.

Also discernible was an unfurled mainsail of straw-like matting with a splotchy smear of scarlet pigment, which undoubtedly was meant to represent the coiling anatomy of another dragon of the samc species.

"The junk of the Red Dragon," Mark Chan exclaimed.

"Our father's junk!" Mary Chan gasped. "It is him!"

But the bronze man's golden eyes were on the squat black thing crouching in the bow.

Seen more clearly, it resembled a cast-iron stove set on wheeled casters, so that it could be rolled about freely. Brass handholds studded the thing to control its movements. It bore some resemblance to the grotesque lion-like statues called by some "Fu Dogs," which guard Oriental temples from Canton to Manhattan's Chinatown.

The howling maw of the squat thing seemed to consist of louvers operated by a long white handle that was being manipulated by a man hunkered down directly behind the globular device.

It was taller than the operator by two feet or more. The latter seemed to throw the lever up, forcing the louvers to yawn open, then drop after a moment or two.

Only when the louvers were shut did he poke his head out from behind, evidently in order to study the stern of the Japanese destroyer.

Then he repeated the operation, taking extreme care to crouch behind the stove-like apparatus before he grasped the lever anew.

That much they saw, and no more, as they flung past the junk.

Suddenly wrenching the plane around, Doc Savage asked for water.

"I feel thirsty too," mumbled Monk, thick-tongued.

There was scramble for the canteens. Everyone drank, including Startell Pompman, who thus far had escaped any dry-mouthed affliction.

"My word!" he said upon drinking his fill. "That slaked me!"

"The Buddha is on the war junk," Mark Chan announced.

Doc Savage nodded. "They have it encased in a device designed to baffle its influence, except when a lever is thrown. They are attempting to bring the destroyer to heel by directing the Buddha's power at the fleeing vessel."

It seemed to be working. The destroyer began losing speed. Perhaps that was due to the crew succumbing to thirst and dehydration. Possibly the Buddha's influence was affecting the fuel-oil in the engines.

No effort was being made to fire upon the pursuing junk. This suggested that the crew had become incapacitated and unable to perform their duties.

The destroyer began laboring. As they passed over the vessel, they could see that the decks were a vortex of activity.

The next thing that happened confirmed Doc's earlier suspicions.

All at once, men in crisp black sailor suits began dropping

off the destroyer.

"Look at that!" exploded Monk. "They're abandoning ship!"

What started with a few dead men hopping over the sides turned into a rout. No boats were lowered. The Japanese sailors just jumped into the choppy waters.

"Like rodents deserting a sinking ship," rumbled Renny.

From their high vantage, it was more like black ants fleeing an anthill that was being flooded by rain. But the result was the same.

Within an amazingly short span of time, the destroyer's crew was floundering in the water. Some ducked their heads wildly, as if trying to drink up the South China Sea. The consequences were not pleasant. Swallowing salt water never is.

They did not have long to enjoy their misery.

THE RED DRAGON junk was soon upon them.

It slowed. The unwieldy cast-iron contraption was wheeled to port and pointed toward the meandering Japanese destroyer.

The effect was to cause the splashing seamen to splash about even more frantically. Soon they began to weaken. One by one, they slipped from sight, disappearing beneath the wrinkled surface of the sea.

This operation was repeated on the starboard side.

Others were run down by the junk's dragon-headed prow.

It took little more than three minutes, but in the wake of the Red Dragon junk, bodies floated in the South China Sea. Lead-colored sharks began to appear. The water churned, foaming white, then turned scarlet.

"Done for!" Renny boomed. "Every man jack of them."

"How horrible," gasped Mary Chan, looking away in horror.

Mark Chan said nothing for a very long time. All the color had drained from his ivory features. His narrow eyes were sick.

"My father hated the Japanese," he croaked out at last.

They had precious little time to soak in the gruesome events that had transpired below. The destroyer, unmanned, began to swerve crazily and, in the manner of unattended vessels on the high seas, began to carve foam circles aimlessly.

That alone told that no member of the crew had remained on board.

Doc Savage seemed undecided what to do next. He watched the ocean tableau with intent golden eyes.

Their situation was difficult at best. They could hardly land unannounced and attempt to communicate with the junk. Nor did they wish to encourage the dire fate that had befallen this latest ill-fated gunboat.

"Monk, see if you can raise them by radio," Doc requested.

The homely chemist gave it his best, but every frequency was filled with a blur of Chinese singsong talk.

"I can't tell who I'm talkin' to," he complained to Doc.

"Never mind," said the bronze man, who spoke all dialects of Chinese and grasped the problem entirely.

It was evident that they were pegged as an enemy by the crew of the Red Dragon junk. To attempt another pass would be to court disaster, for the crew of the raking ship was again jockeying the big iron device on its caster wheels, as if preparing to repel another pass.

The amphibian was equipped with dual controls. Monk sat in the co-pilot's bucket.

Doc directed, "Take the wheel, Monk."

Then he pitched to the rear of the aircraft, where numbered equipment cases were suspended in cargo netting, so that their volatile contents could better withstand the rigors of aerial flight.

Doc rummaged through these items. Clearly he was seeking a particular case. Finding it, he heaved open the lid and took out a thing that resembled an aerial bomb.

It was a long teardrop of a thing, constructed of aluminum, but painted black, with stabilizing fins. Affixed to the tail was a parachute of modest size. Doc unwound the bundled shrouds and prepared to deploy the device.

When he had the projectile ready to go, the bronze man rushed back to the controls.

"Monk, bring us around," he ordered. "Try to pass directly over the junk's stern."

The hairy chemist obligingly sent the amphibian into a sideslip, while Doc Savage yanked the pilot's-side window open. Slipstream came rushing in, cold and bracing. It disturbed Doc's fine bronze hair a little.

As Monk glided the big bird over the water, Doc rapped out, "Reduce airspeed. Now!"

Monk complied, cranking down the flaps and fishtailing the rudder to lose momentum.

The amphibian raced for the junk's broad stern.

Doc dangled the bomb-shaped device out the window. He mentally calculated altitude, airspeed, other factors, then let drop.

The parachute opened up of its own accord. It was not packed, thus there was no need for further action.

Doc's aim was excellent. The bomb drifted downward, swinging by its shrouds.

When it struck the poop deck, it erupted in a fabulous shower of whirling red sparks and lavender smoke. The display was amazingly pyrotechnic. It was not an explosion so much as a paroxysm of fumes and fireworks.

Before the smoke obscured it, the bomb appeared to be spinning in place like a firecracker which had been split in two and then set alight.

Crewmen surged in to investigate the violent display. They clustered around, clearly unsure of how to deal with the unexpected menace.

A figure larger than the others stormed up and gestured wildly with his arms. Someone found a coal shovel and plunged this implement into the heliotrope smoke, as if desperate to dislodge the hissing, spark-spitting fury before it could further detonate.

He came out a moment later, overcome by fumes and pawing at his eyes.

"Tear gas is mixed in," explained Doc.

The crew did not give up. Others came in, carrying various implements. Pry bars. More shovels. One individual even brought a huge monkey wrench, although what conceivable use it might be put to was doubtful.

It took them considerable effort, but at last they got the sparking, snarling, smoking nuisance over to the stern rail. With a final push with the crowbars, they heaved it over the side where it struck the sea with a great splash.

That should have been the end of it. It wasn't. No sooner had the device disappeared into the brine than there came another wild eruption, greater than the first.

It was as if contact with seawater had produced an even more violent reaction than impact on the poop deck had occasioned.

The crew of the Red Dragon junk began falling to, maneuvering the junk, fleeing as far from the devil of a device as possible. Clearly, they feared that they might be sunk.

But nothing of the sort happened. Great motors in the stern churned and began throwing spray everywhere.

Lurching forward, the junk got clear of the thing which was showing signs of settling down at last.

"It was a valiant effort," declared Startell Pompman ponderously. "Alas, it was also a failure. It must have been so written in the stars."

"I'll show you stars," snapped Renny, sticking one great globe of a fist under the plump plutocrat's predatory nose.

"No need for fisticuffs, my good fellow," Pompman said nervously. "You are among friends."

"Then keep your trap shut tight," invited Renny.

Startell Pompman settled in his seat and offered no further

comments. His mouth was an unsatisfied line.

"Where to now?" Monk asked Doc.

Doc Savage vouchsafed no reply. Instead he sent the big amphibian thundering back in the direction of Shanghai, motors a-howl.

But when they reached the portion of the South China Sea where they should change course for the city, the big bronze man continued flying south.

He offered no explanation of his intentions to his aides. This was understood to be characteristic of his personality. When the bronze man was ready to reveal his plans, he would do so. Not before.

Night began falling.

Chapter XXI

THE GENERALISSIMO

THE TIME WAS two days later.

A colorful individual stood under the furled sail of the great saffron-hued junk with the scarlet dragons splashed on its bows and five batting-reinforced sails.

He was a big man. Six feet would have caught him at about the eyes. And he had a build that was made for trouble, lean of flanks, a lot of weight crowded into arms and shoulders. Attired in a riotous costume that was equal parts Manchu caftan and Mongol padded tunic, he cut a fabulous figure. His feet were stuffed into sheepskin buskins of a type favored in the cold reaches of northern China. His face was a rude block of brass, weathered by harsh climates. Scars marched across it like tracks across a map of the Gobi.

He was called Wah Chan. This was not his original name. No one knew what that was, not even the crew of the junk which now lay anchored in a river inland of the rugged edge of the China coast, hidden deep from the prying eyes of the Japanese Navy.

Wah Chan strode the teak deck of his ship, supervising the lowering of the contraption that had formerly been stationed at the bow of his ungainly-looking craft.

It resembled nothing so much as a cross between a great pot-bellied stove and a Chinese lion. In fact it was exactly the former, both items converted for the containing of a thing that, whenever he contemplated it, made Generalissimo Wah Chan shudder inwardly.

"Be careful with those lines," he barked at his coolies as they wrestled with the block-and-tackle arrangement that dropped the cast-iron monstrosity into a waiting hold. "One mishap and we'll all be turned into human prunes."

He spoke rough Mandarin. The sinewy Orientals pulled and strained at their ropes while the ungainly black thing was carefully lowered into the hold.

Once its wheels touched the matting below, it was lashed into place and otherwise secured with heavy ropes.

More crewmen came and closed up the hatch, obscuring the contraption from sight.

Only then did Wah Chan exhale a long, gusty sigh of relief.

"Some day the devil inside that thing is going to break loose, and when it does—" he growled.

Wah Chan did not finish the thought. Instead, he fished a cigarette out of his shirt and stuck it between his wind-raw lips.

Rasping a match alight, Wah Chan applied sulfurous flame to the tip. He smoked furiously, grizzled brows knitting in thought.

Sunset was painting the anchored junk in hues normally associated with Arizona deserts—a weird mixture of purple, gold and scarlet that a superstitious person might dub satanic. Tidal water lapped at the gently rocking junk with steady intent.

Wah Chan had grown rich as the leader of the red-beard bandits who had roamed and pillaged the wilds of China in the days before the Japanese came. He had amassed in that interval considerable wealth. He could have retired, but in his own eyes, he was still a young man.

When the Japanese came, looting and killing, Wah Chan took offense at the encroaching upon his preserves. He reorganized his fighting men into an army of liberation. It felt good to do so. The bandit business had grown stale by that time. Only the taking of treasure still appealed to him.

It was wealth sufficient to send his two children to the United

States to be educated. That felt good, too.

But the life of a soldier of fortune—as Wah Chan preferred to proclaim himself—left no room to raise children. He was sorry when they had returned to Shanghai.

Wah Chan wondered where they were now. He had lost touch with them in all the excitement that attended the arrival of the monk who called himself Tang.

Sea breezes stirred the moth-holed sails, making the dragons pop and snap as if imbued with wavering life. For centuries, the junks of China were decorated with colorful flags designed to appease a cloud-dwelling dragon said by superstitious sailors to inhabit the skies. Wah Chan had improved upon that custom by daubing a scarlet dragon on the prominent parts of his vessels—dragons by repute favoring red above all other hues.

Years of evading capture by the National Chinese Army had sharpened Wah Chan's ears. He heard the soft catlike padding of bare feet steal up behind him.

Grasping his sword, Wah Chan whirled smartly. His dark, windy eyes narrowed at the one who had stolen up behind him.

"Is it a wise fox who does not creep up on the den of another fox," he muttered.

The individual who approached came to a complete stop, which sent the maroon folds of his robes trembling.

This was a man who possessed the emaciated physique of an Oriental to a degree that was breathtaking. He was not tall, but he seemed tall, so lean were his limbs. Only a thin coating of parchment-like flesh protected his muscles from the elements. The veins and cords of his wrists, his throat, and even his ankles stood out alarmingly.

Had an ancient mummy come to life to walk the Earth anew, he would have looked much like the monk, Tang.

Technically, Tang had been defrocked long ago. But he still wore the robes of his erstwhile trade.

There was nothing holy-looking about his face. It was sharp, pinched and devilish in his cast. His eyes were malevolent slits the hue of anthracite. His mouth gaped, a shapeless vent stuck with teeth that were snaggled and black as charcoal. Cheeks were lean and stringy. The ears at either side of his head seemed to come to canine points. The entire effect was unlovely. He looked like some grotesque, incredibly withered Oriental devil-eared turtle.

Tang made speech with a raspy voice that bespoke of perpetually parched vocal cords.

"The Buddha of Ice has been safely stored below?" he asked.

"Do you see it here?" Wah Chan returned. He was in league with this villainous monk. But that did not mean he liked him. They held enemies in common and these considerations had drawn them in close association.

Tang croaked out, "I see that you are troubled, Generalissimo."

"Three Japanese warships have felt our wrath."

"The wrath of the Buddha of Ice, you mean."

"You keep talking as if that crystal devil was imbued with evil spirits," grunted Wah Chan.

"I believe that it is," Tang intoned.

Wah Chan said nothing to that. He had his share of superstition carved into his soul. But he did not understand the Buddha—only its spell upon men. This was devastating to behold.

"Three Jap warships bested, and Tokyo is sending more destroyers and cruisers," said Wah Chan. "We cannot fight them all."

The withered monk said slowly, "It is high time we took the fight to the cities under thrall."

Wah Chan raised a weathered fist. "What are you suggesting? That we slide into a Japanese-controlled harbor and unleash the Buddha? It will kill a whole lot of innocent Chinese, as well as sons of Nippon."

"It is the price that must be paid to liberate China," intoned Tang. "Otherwise, it will become a vassal state of the Japanese silkworms who have infiltrated the north."

"If we scuttle the Japanese Navy, we cut off their supply lines and so keep reinforcements from being landed. That task has barely begun." The tone Generalissimo Wah Chan used suggested finality.

Tang made an unhappy mouth. Shadows hid his dark teeth, making him appear toothless. "That will not drive the enemy from our land. Only the Buddha's power can do that. We must not contain the Buddha. He thirsts for Japanese the way a spider thirsts for many fat flies."

Wah Chan shook his craggy head. "I'm not ready to shift tactics."

Tang fell silent. He seemed to be choosing his words carefully. When he did speak, it was to change the subject.

"The British Navy will leave us alone as long as we harry only the Japanese."

Wah Chan grunted. "True. So?"

Tang murmured, "I am remembering that airplane the color of brass. It was not British. It possessed no markings."

"I've been thinking of that myself," Wah Chan muttered.

"I know you have. I have been ruminating on it, also. I do not think it belonged to the Japanese, despite the fact that it dropped a queer aerial bomb upon us."

Wah Chan grunted. "That was not like any bomb I ever saw. It didn't do any damage."

"We were fortunate to rid ourselves of it, regardless, Wah Chan," intoned Tang.

Wah Chan blew out a careful stream of cigarette smoke, as if releasing his suspicions to the open air. "One man flies planes that color," he said. "Not brass, but bronze."

Interest flickered across Tang's seamed tortoise-like features. "Yes?"

"Ever hear of *Chun-tzu Ch'ing-t'ong*—the Personage of Bronze?"

"No," allowed Tang.

"No, I wouldn't think you had, being shut up in monasteries like you have, then exiled to the Gobi Desert. But he is a Yankee legend known as Doc Savage. By reputation, a man who takes an interest in other people's troubles."

"An enlightened soldier for hire, like yourself?"

Wah Chan shook his head heavily, "Not like me. Doc Savage does not go in for battle for its own sake—or for profit. Sometimes he fights other people's wars for them. Some new species of altruist, they say."

"Are you suggesting that this foreign devil has entered the cause of China?" croaked out Tang.

"I don't know. Maybe."

"Or could this *Ch'ing-t'ong te Nanjen* be on the side of the Nipponese?" pressed Tang.

Wah Chan slowly blew out another long plume of malodorous tobacco smoke, black eyes reflective.

"Doc Savage would never take the side of a conqueror," he decided at last.

"But the bronze one attacked us, did he not?"

"It's too soon to say what that was all about," Wah Chan said. "But maybe Doc Savage will present himself again, and the truth will reveal itself."

"Let us hope, Wah Chan, that the truth does not reveal itself in unpleasant ways."

"How I hooked up with you, I don't rightly understand," admitted Wah Chan wearily.

"The Buddha of Ice brought us together to make common cause. It was ordained that we do so. Once we have defeated the Japanese, we will ask the Buddha what it wants us to do next."

Wah Chan spat, "After this is over, you can have that vile thing. I will be done with it."

Tang's eyes narrowed like those of a hungry cat. "But will

the Buddha be done with Wah Chan?" he purred.

With that, Tang slithered down below, there to hold congress with the Buddha in the fat black stove surmounted by a grotesque Chinese lion's head with goggling eyes, whose ferocious mouth yawned open in a frozen howl.

Wah Chan shuddered again. Once, weeks before, he had eavesdropped and heard the wizened old monk talking to the Fu Dog in that parched voice of his, pausing often to listen, and having a regular conversation. It made spiders march up and down the Generalissimo's spine to hear it all.

Sometimes he did wonder if the Buddha of Ice were alive in some way. Tang insisted that it did not merely suck the moisture from a man, but his very soul, too. It was a disagreeable thought.

But what else could explain the fact that the Buddha of Ice was growing with each use? That its size had almost doubled since they had begun to harry the Japanese Navy?

Crushing his cigarette beneath one boot heel, Wah Chan decided to turn in for the night. With a final command to his night guard arrayed about the stern mast, he disappeared below deck.

Only the monotonous *lap-lap-lap* of tidal water against the stout hull lingered in the night air.

HOURS passed. The night was cooling down appreciably.

No sounds drifted from inshore; soft murmurings which the lapping waves made were lulling, peaceful, and conducive of sleep.

A scrawny Chinese crewman at the bow was having difficulty keeping his sleepy eyes awake. He had to pinch himself several times lest he doze off at his post.

He was known as Fragrant Fung, for he rarely bathed. Fung had been with Wah Chan a very long time. Men of Wah Chan who dozed on duty were often beheaded. He did not wish to trade his head and all that it contained for a few hours of sleep.

So he fought the drowsy feeling that kept stealing over him.

From time to time, the tiny squeakings of bats could be heard as they dived into clouds of flying insects for food. They avoided passing over the deck, for bat soup was a Chinese delicacy, and bats were easily brought down by rifle shot.

Distracted by the busy flying mammals, Fragrant Fung failed to detect a faint dripping sound not many rods below his post.

The gurgle of cove water covered some of these watery sounds. Too, they were faintly stealthy.

Junks ride high in the water, much like the caravels of old, so the idea of a man scaling the rust-caked anchor chain while dripping water was a little fantastic.

But one man *was* attempting the difficult feat.

The invader climbed hand over hand, pausing, not to rest, but rather to listen for breathing noises above. Also, he took time for water to drain from his trouser legs.

This man was huge, after the fashion of the Mongols of the north. His burly muscles bunched and writhed, proved more than equal to the feat of ascending the heavy anchor chain.

After another pause, he continued to climb.

Moonlight revealed his face. It was an unlovely visage. Scars crossed his cheeks. One ear was a mass of gristle. As if all those scars were not enough, he wore an eyepatch of beaten silver over his left orb.

Every finger was decorated with a heavy ring—more rings than any man would need to wear. They resembled booty, those rings, as if they had been plucked from the fingers of countless victims.

Possibly those heavy gold rings helped the stealthy one climb up the rusty anchor chain. One great golden hoop dangled from an ear. It danced with his every move.

When the man's head topped the rail, he peered about carefully.

Darkness clotted the barn-like superstructure. Deck hands were sleeping by a fold of the matting sail, which had been lowered, allowed to slat down on the deck, probably as a shelter from the chill night breeze. Some snored. Otherwise, they did not stir.

Cigarette smoke carried to his nostrils. One eye sought its source, discerned the burning coal of a cigarette as it was pitched into the drink.

Only then did the massive one climb over the teak rail and move in the direction of the lone guard, Fragrant Fung. He paused beside an overturned rowboat, hunkering down in an effort to avoid detection.

Fung chanced to be looking inland, thinking how good it would be to stand on dry land once more, and possibly patronize a fan-tan gambling parlor, when great copper hands seized his head in its entirety.

The grip of his assailant was like a vise, the many gold rings adding to that fearsome impression.

The guard attempted to cry out, but his lips were crushed beneath the iron-tendoned fingers. He could not utter a singsong syllable.

The big attacker gave a wrench and a twist. While the hapless Fung struggled to breathe, he was lowered to the deck, still fighting the insanely strong man who had overmastered him.

At length, his breathing ceased. Whether entirely or not was difficult to tell. No one stood near enough to tell.

The big boarder worked his way to a companionway and slipped below, unseen. His buskin-clad feet must have been soled with gum, for he made no sound.

He crept along the narrow corridors that honeycombed the junk's substructure, and found his way to the forward hold without rousing the slumbering crew.

There was a door. It was a ponderous affair of planks fitted together with wooden dowel pins. An iron bar served as a makeshift lock.

The intruder lifted this, and crept within.

The hold interior was so black it might have been a solid

substance. The junk was well maintained. No chink in its hull permitted moonlight to penetrate. The air was heavy with some pungent incense mixed with the foul, fleshy odor of unwashed bodies.

Light flicked out in the lurid darkness—a thin beam of radiance that might come from a pencil flashlight.

It quested about, disclosed cobwebbed rafters of teak over a chamber that was almost bare except for an inch-deep mass of refuse in one corner. The tongue of light came to rest on the huge lion-like Fu-Dog stove that had previously been stationed on deck.

The intruder went over this carefully with his fingertips, noting its construction involved caulking any chinks in the iron form with pitch, paying special attention to the great porcelain-handled lever that actuated the baffles that concealed the unseen thing within.

No attempt was made to throw the lever, or open the makeshift contraption in any way. Evidently the intruder was sufficiently familiar with the contents to avoid creating a calamity by doing so.

His inspection accomplished, the big Mongol returned topside. He exited warily, single jet eye searching for signs that the felled guard had been discovered. He had not.

Reconnoiter compete, the be-ringed one made his way back to the forward starboard rail and slipped overboard.

No one saw or heard his going any more than they did his coming. His silence was sepulchral.

The wet footprints that he left behind were already drying in the cool night breeze. Before many minutes, they would be gone, leaving no discernible sign that anyone had trod the deck who should not have.

An hour later, Fragrant Fung snapped awake with a start. He jerked to his feet, felt of his neck and was amazed to discover himself breathing.

Peering about the superstructure, Fung saw that all was well.

Just to make certain, he made a quick promenade of the forward deck.

All was as it should have been. Fung spotted a solitary moist footprint on the steps leading below.

Slipping down, he investigated, saw and heard nothing untoward. He prudently decided to return to his post forthwith. There were no other footprints similar to the single one to be found anywhere.

"I will say nothing of this," Fragrant Fung muttered to himself, again feeling of his throat. The sensation of being choked was still with him vividly. It was too much remindful of hanging to risk doing otherwise.

Chapter XXII

SAT SUNG, WAR LORD

DAWN BROKE WITH a garish splendor.

The crew of the Red Dragon junk roused itself and got down to the morning's business, hauling anchor, unfurling sail and making ready to depart for the open sea.

They were attired in shapeless trousers which resembled the lower halves of pajamas. One or two wore skirt-like garments which hung down outside their pants. Most wore the conical rattan hats that marked the Asiatic seafaring class.

While the scarlet sun burned off the last of the morning haze, they accomplished their tasks, thanks to thc ease with which the brown four-cornered sails could be lowered by just a few junk-men hauling on halyards.

Wah Chan strode the deck, refreshed from slumber. He wore a cartridge belt high above his waist, held in place by suspender-like straps. A spike-nosed automatic hung at his side.

"Make ready to sail!" he thundered. *"K'wai-k'wai!* Make haste."

Long bamboo poles were hauled out of deck storage and employed to push off from shore. This was accomplished with lean-muscled efficiency, for the Red Dragon junk was a flat-bottomed vessel, called a "sand boat," capable of navigating inland rivers and the high seas with equal aplomb.

Laboriously, the riotous junk of war worked out of the mud-yellow delta toward the wrinkled blue-green of open ocean.

The sea air stretching his reviving lungs, Wah Chan felt good.

The uneasy thoughts of the previous evening were dissolved by the sun's splintery rays, the tang of salt air, and the freedom of open water.

The emergence of the monk Tang from his austere sleeping cubicle below did not entirely dispel those dark misgivings from the Generalissimo's thoughts.

"The Buddha hungers for fresh souls," Tang intoned. He wore his habitual maroon robe favored by Buddhist monks throughout Asia.

"And he will receive them," Wah Chan returned. "Receive them in great numbers."

They set out, sails belling in the freshening morning breeze as the great ship made its way through the jumble of fishing junks, flower boats, and covered sampans that crowded the inland waterway. Numerous holes made the batting-reinforced sails look moth-eaten.

But looks are deceptive.

Once out in the Yellow Sea, the helmsman at the tiller pointed her dragon prow north. The junk dug her armored nose into the fast-running seas, dividing discolored swells with startling efficiency. With her poop deck riding high, she gave the impression of a craft about to knife into the lower deeps. This was an illusion that junk-type vessels present to the eye. In reality, they were amazingly stable craft.

The crew kept a weather eye for other traffic. The Japanese did not venture this far south, but with three cruisers falling into misfortune, there was no telling what they would do in response. Cruisers are expensive. And the loss of a crew did not have to mean the loss of a ship.

No doubt the sons of the Rising Sun would be sending aloft reconnaissance planes to search for those abandoned cruisers—or dispatch gunboats to put off fresh crews to replace the old.

Wah Chan hoped to encounter such craft, whether they went by air or sea.

The Red Dragon junk encountered only normal maritime traffic, however. Trade and fishing junks and covered sampans predominated.

Among the vessels plying these waters was a junk of unusual lines. Its lean hull and sails were as black as the wings of a night-flying bat. Round white eyes with black centers were painted upon the narrow bows, unsettlingly remindful of goggling octopus orbs.

A man with an eye for good sailing vessels, Wah Chan trained a spyglass on the lumbering vessel. He almost whistled in admiration. It was a good craft. Sturdy. It was on ships such as these that Chinese navigators had sailed from Cathay to as far as the Cape of Good Hope in ancient days.

While a sailing junk may look awkward to the unappreciative eye, they are fast for their size and formidable enough to range the vast Pacific. This one, Wah Chan saw, was rigged for navigating the prevailing winds of the South China Sea, which favored a port tack when sailing close-hauled. Thus the lugsails were hung to starboard of the mast for maximum efficiency.

Dropping his glass, Wah Chan returned to his objective, which was to tack north in search of proper prey.

He paid no more attention to the black-hulled junk, until possibly an hour later, when he noticed it was sailing behind them, off to the port stern, throwing up spume from either bow.

Mounting the poop deck, the Generalissimo brought his glass to bear upon it.

The pepper-hued junk was well manned. He could see a number of lean-limbed junk-men and conical-capped coolies going about their business. None looked Japanese, which was his only concern.

For Wah Chan did not put it past the Japanese Navy to commandeer a fishing junk and man it with disguised soldiers and sailors in hopes of overhauling him.

A great figure stood in the bow, like a sea rover of old.

Tall he was, and broad of shoulder. He might have been a

figure plucked from the days of Genghis Khan, the former ruler of half the known world. His clothes, from coat to buskins, were Mongolian. His face had that wind-burned gleam of copper that bespoke of the Gobi Desert. Numerous knife scars crisscrossed a face that was bold and full of unbridled humor. The silver eyepatch detracted not a whit from that impression. His good eye resembled an ebony pearl plucked from a treasure chest.

Here, thought Wah Chan, was a man cut from similar sail-cloth to my own.

The master of the trailing junk must have had very good vision in his surviving eye. He spotted Wah Chan scrutinizing him and gave back a hearty wave. Gold teeth shone in the morning sunlight and he burst forth with a laugh that boomed across the waves.

Wah Chan did not wave back. He had bloody business to conduct.

The junk of the Red Dragon was flying under half-sail. She was equipped with marine motors, but these were kept in reserve for pursuit and escape. Petroleum was not cheap or easily obtained along the Chinese coast. Not even if one were a reformed bandit chief turned enlightened freedom fighter.

Over time, the sepia-hulled junk, also under sail, crept up on Wah Chan's vessel.

Prevailing winds were favorable. Sails filled, stiffened. Sea-foam churned on either side of plunging bows. Soon it was a race.

The Red Dragon junk was larger, and possessed more sail, while the black vessel was smaller, more nimble. Her lean prow cut the waves like a plow. She began to gain headway.

The air was cool; the sun made a brilliant glare, but little heat. Despite that, Wah Chan began to perspire freely. He fell to studying the overhauling junk, and noticed a peculiar something about the construction of the thing. Junks, he full well knew, were slow craft, built like scows.

This one was different. The upper portion was unwieldy enough, but a foot or so above the waterline, the appearance of clumsiness vanished. It was plain that, under water, the craft had raking, fleet lines.

A frown roosted upon the Generalissimo's square face, and remained there unchanged.

Tang put in another appearance at this time, hands clasped inside the merged sleeves of his maroon robes. His eyes were squeezed into slits until they resembled walnut seams.

"Who are they?" he demanded.

"They have the look of river pirates," grunted Wah Chan.

"They should display their colors less boldly," spat Tang.

"They are nothing to us," retorted Wah Chan. Turning to his first mate, he called out, "Li! More sail!"

Men rushed to the bow, seized the halyard. The foresail ran up smartly, unfolding like a Venetian blind. Wind filled its batten-reinforced surface, took hold. The canvas swung on its forward-raking mast until it found perfect balance.

Now it really was a race.

WHATEVER it was that dwelled in men to challenge others when nothing more lay at stake than the thrill of besting another at his own game overtook Generalissimo Wah Chan.

He had business, but that business lay to the north. Both junks were headed north, in the direction of Shanghai.

The Yellow Sea was running high. Whitecaps churned into squirming life, only to collapse and vanish from view. The waves had a sharpness like rolling reefs.

Sailing close to the wind, both ships leaped and plunged like some strange species of seahorse. Prows gnashed whitecaps until salt spray spattered foredeck and sails, wetting everything. Impelled by cracking canvas alone, they strove for nautical advantage.

From across the choppy waves came the boom of the big Mongol's laughter.

Standing in the shade of the great mainsail with its gory, many-coiled dragon, Wah Chan raised a megaphone and called over to the other ship.

"What are you called, One-Eye?"

A booming laugh pealed back.

"Sat Sung, Master of the junk, *Cuttlefish*. Sat Sung, Warlord of the Yellow Sea."

"I have never before heard your worthy name," grunted Wah Chan.

The colorful swashbuckler spread his great arms expansively. Rings flashed on his fingers. "It is written in flame from the Canton to Macao," he boomed. "I am new to these waters."

"Where are you bound?"

The Mongol captain pointed north. "To Shanghai and beyond, where the Japanese lie fat for the slaughter."

Now it was Wah Chan's turn to laugh.

"Then I wish you good hunting, Sat Sung."

"Good hunting to you, too," boomed the self-styled Warlord of the Yellow Sea.

Lowering his megaphone, Wah Chan decided that here was a freebooter with style. Still, Sat Sung was a mere brigand, and no more. The Japanese Navy would make short work of him.

The race continued. The ebony junk was well maintained and her crew executed their captain's orders smartly. But, try as they might, the other vessel could not outpace the war junk of Generalissimo Wah Chan with its five great sails.

In her efforts, the bat-sailed vessel heeled over to starboard several times, coming dangerously close to encroaching upon the right of way belonging to Wah Chan.

Concern warped his weathered features. He scowled at Sat Sung. The big Mongol only laughed unconcernedly.

Three hours of this and Wah Chan had lost interest in the unwanted race. The other junk would have overhauled him by now, if that were ever to happen.

Wah Chan returned to his business—searching the waters off his bows for sign of Japanese vessels.

So it was that the Generalissimo missed what next transpired.

A flag was raised from the other junk. A jet-black ensign. It was a very familiar sight, but not one seen in Chinese waters. Nor in any waters for many generations.

Chattering madly was the grinning skull and crossbones of the Jolly Roger!

This defiant signal of intention was missed entirely.

Steel shields were lifted away from the ebony junk's bulwarks, exposing a row of iron cannon maws ranging from antique muzzle-loaders to comparatively modern breech-loading examples of naval gunnery. These were manned by an assortment of blue-turbaned Malays and bare-chested Dyaks. These worthies applied fire to old-fashioned fuses with long burning sticks of bamboo punk.

Gunflame belched loudly. Grapeshot expelled from exploding cannon peppered the straw-like matting sails, but were aimed too high to harm ducking and dodging junk-hands. One missed fire, and its gunners hastily flung open the breech and attempted to discover what was wrong with it.

Next, men lined the port rail of the other junk. They were members of the crew hitherto not in evidence. One was big and hulking with monster fists. Another carried a rapier-thin sword. A third was squat and had the hammered-down head and sloping shoulders of a Congo gorilla. Coolie hats shaded their faces.

Looking fierce, they unlimbered oversized pistols of unusual make, training them on the Red Dragon junk.

Red dots began winking along the rail. The sawing sound of machine guns of impressive caliber became audible. Their sound blended into a monster moaning. The Red Dragon emblems on the bows began to acquire punctures. Mother-of-pearl eyes shattered, fragments falling away.

Crewmen fell, screeching, their bodies flecked with minute

blood spots. They seemed only to fall, whereupon they went still. Curiously, no death agonies were in evidence.

Wah Chan came rushing to see what was transpiring.

He sped to the junk-men lining the opposite rail. Heard the unearthly moan of the machine guns—for that must be what they were—and realized that his crew was melting at their posts like scythed grain. His blocky jaw fell open.

Through rolling, malodorous clouds of burnt black powder, Wah Chan spotted the Jolly Roger flag flapping in the wind. He began cursing volubly.

On the opposite deck, the big copper-skinned Mongol boomed out his hearty laughter in uproarious peals.

Wah Chan had a reputation the length and breadth of China, and not just along the coast, either. Men knew him by repute more than by sight, for China is a vast and open country. His fame had reached sparsely-settled regions of the hinterlands.

But up until this time, no one had ever dared attack Wah Chan in open waters. Not even the Nationalist army, for the most part.

"What is the meaning of this!" he roared.

"Piracy!" boomed back Sat Sung, the laughing Mongol. "Prepare to be boarded."

"Boarded!" Wah Chan sputtered. It was ludicrous. Impossible! "No one boards Wah Chan," he howled back. "Wah Chan boards others!"

Ducking below, Wah Chan came back with a Browning automatic rifle, lined up the lean muzzle, began squeezing the trigger. It commenced whacking, the stock bucking and kicking against his padded shoulder.

The big Mongol laughed again, throwing his head back.

Then he noticed wood splinters jumping about him as lead bullets gnashed them off the hardwood rail.

Sat Sung ducked with alacrity, showing that he was no slouch when it came to reflexive speed.

"That will teach him to laugh at Wah Chan," the Generalissimo muttered fiercely. Calling over his shoulder, he bellowed, "Unworthy ones! Hoist the Buddha topside! Lively now! *K'wai-k'wai!*"

The crew gave it their best, but working under fire was no pleasant thing. Spiteful cracks warned of bullets snapping past, harrying them at their tasks.

Alone, Wah Chan organized resistance. From plunging stem to high stern of the junk, the marauders were concentrating upon the men at the block-and-tackle arrangement.

They were successful. No crewman who grasped a rope stayed with it long. Many fell. Wah Chan ordered others to take their places. Crewman leaped in response. These, too, were cut down easily.

It was almost as if the pirate crew knew exactly what was coming up from the hold.

At length, Wah Chan could see that the tide was turning against him.

"What is it you want, Sat Sung?" he demanded.

Came the reply: "Your fine vessel."

"Yours is just as fine," lied Wah Chan.

"More junks are needed than one. I am expanding my seafaring operations!"

"Against the Japanese?"

The massive Mongol pounded his chest with a gold-ringed fist. "Against any who resist Sat Sung, the Warlord!" he proclaimed.

Wah Chan thought furiously. Seeing that he was about to lose control of his warship—and what was contained in its forward cargo hold—he altered course.

"Why not join forces?" he called over.

"Against the invader?"

"Yes!"

"I will consider it," returned Sat Sung. "*After* you have been boarded."

Wah Chan shouted assorted imprecations and maledictions, some in respectable English. He ran out of them before he exhausted his supply of verbal bile and spleen, however, and was reduced to sputtering incoherent rage.

Suddenly the other junk was coming alongside. Braided silk cords tied to heavy iron grappling hooks were being flung toward his railing.

Wah Chan grabbed an axe and began chopping away at his own rail to dislodge the grapnels. Twice he succeeded. But he was only one man with one axe and his crew was hunkered down under the withering fire of the raiders of Sat Sung, some of which included assorted Malays and Dyaks blowing poison darts through long jointed tubes of bamboo. At least, the Generalissimo assumed they were poisoned. Any junk-man quilled with one or more darts instantly succumbed to something pernicious.

It proved to be an impossible situation.

Sails in rags, the proud junk of war began to wallow. So Wah Chan spoke the words he never expected to utter.

"I surrender to you," he said stiffly.

Sat Sung boomed out an enormous laugh. He gave the order to strike sails. Black canvas collapsed with blinding efficiency.

Then armed pirates came rushing up with long planks. These were set upon the pirate junk's rail and shoved skidding over the intervening chop to link the two abeam vessels. The crewmen began pulling on the grapnel ropes, drawing the two ships together.

"Prepare to be boarded!" sang Sat Sung.

So paralyzed was the mind of Wah Chan that he did not at first wonder what had befallen Tang the monk.

Then he heard clattering noises far below, and grew alarmed.

"That unholy fool is waking the Buddha!" Wah Chan hissed. "He will doom us all!"

Chapter XXIII
VIOLENCE ON DECK

THE FORMAL BOARDING of the war junk of Wah Chan was accomplished with near-military efficiency.

Coarse boards were laid across the gap separating both decks. To the ends of these were affixed rows of iron hooks and these made the boarding planks fast to the rails, where they were not crowded with attackers and defenders.

By this time Wah Chan had emptied his Browning rifle and was hastily ramming home his last remaining ammunition clip. He was in no position to go below for more. His chief concern now was the strange sounds coming from the forward hold.

But the Generalissimo had no time to attend to that. A cloud of wiry pirates swarmed over his deck, led by the fearsome Mongol, Sat Sung.

With a ringing war-cry, the mountainous Mongol mounted a boarding plank. He gave a running jump, and, with a broad-sword raised in each hand, vaulted the distance. It was a prodigious leap, clearing the span easily.

Sat Sung landed lightly on both buskins, ready to fight.

A modicum of resistance met him. Two crewmen rushed in, gleaming daggers held low.

The giant Mongol laughed uproariously. With the flat of each war sword, he slammed them both to the deck. He was so confident he did not bother to run them through. There was no need, anyway. Both were out cold where they lay.

Sat Sung's raiders piled in behind him. Separating, they

sought out other defenders, cutting loose with their ferocious little machine guns in order to clear the way. Resistance melted before them, unable to withstand such concentrated firepower.

Sat Sung moved on to his chief objective. A running leap carried him there.

Having retreated to reload, Wah Chan found the point of one of the one-eyed Mongol's swords fixing his bobbing Adam's apple.

"Raise hands!" he was ordered.

Wah Chan swallowed his shame. Surrender wasn't in his makeup. Reluctantly, he elevated his hands, the Browning rifle thudding to the deck uselessly.

The Mongol began cracking out orders. Wah Chan blinked. He did not understand the tongue. Was it Manchu or Mandarin? It bore no resemblance to Cantonese.

Only the trio of raiders who brandished the moaning pistols seemed to respond to it. They were rushing about, knocking down the last resistance, using their fists when their guns ran empty. Their knuckles appeared as effective as their bullets.

For buccaneers, they didn't appear very bloodthirsty. In fact, the absence of gore was remarkable. Normally, the junk's decks would be awash with it by now, making footing treacherous for boarders and defenders alike.

This raised vague suspicions in the back of Wah Chan's cunning mind.

"You are a very strange pirate," he accused.

"I am a *successful* pirate," rejoined the other. He was not laughing now. A grimness settled over his features. His solitary eye held a trace of worry.

Again Sat Sung gobbled out a string of words in the foreign tongue that was like nothing that had ever reached Wah Chan's well-traveled ears before.

Eying the rings on his adversary's fingers and the colorful costume, the Generalissimo added, "You are no Mongol. You dress like a Mongol, but Mongols are seldom so tall. Perhaps you are a freak of a half-caste."

"Perhaps," said Sat Sung, prodding Wah Chan back against the pilot house with his blade.

"What is your pleasure, cut-throat?" Wah Chan spat defiantly.

"Take us to the Buddha."

Wah Chan started. "You know of the venerable Buddha?"

The blade dug deeper. "Take us there now. No tricks!"

All of the great humor fled from the big Mongol. He grew deadly serious.

"You do not want to meet the Buddha," Wah Chan told him. "The Buddha is a thirsty Buddha. He drinks greedily of all men who come into contact with him. Worse, he sucks out their souls."

Wah Chan did not really believe all this. But he put everything he had into the warning. In the back of his mind, he was giving Tang time to do whatever it was that the wizened monk was about below decks.

He fervently hoped it would not spell the end of him, too.

The Mongol Sat Sung goaded Wah Chan at sword point toward the companionway and down into the gloomy, bullet-riddled innards of the ship.

His defeated pirate crew sat topside, huddling on the poop deck, under guard. They had been overcome with amazing ease.

"No trickery," warned the Mongol.

"I am out of trickery," returned Wah Chan. "Just as I am out of all hope."

Stepping below, they made their way through dim passageways and worked forward.

The Mongol seemed to know exactly where he was driving Wah Chan. That seemed impossible. He had never before been on this ship. Of that, Wan Chan was certain. Absolutely certain.

But the cocksure manner in which Sat Sung guided him, made Wah Chan doubt this own convictions.

The door of the forward hold lay just ahead. It stood shut, firmly in its jamb.

"Open it," commanded Sat Sung.

Wan Chan steeled himself, not knowing what to expect.

Lifting an iron latch, the Generalissimo threw open the door.

What he saw within the cavernous hold made the blood run icy cold in his veins.

The great iron Fu-Dog stove had been turned around on its caster wheels. Its slanting black baffles were now facing the door—not in the direction of the bow, as before.

A scrawny hand could be seen sticking out from behind the bulky cast-iron contraption. It was clutching the porcelain handle.

Seeming to come from the Fu Dog's ferocious louvered maw, the parched voice of Tang resounded hollowly.

"Back, back!"

"Listen to him," hissed Wah Chan. "If he throws that lever, we are finished!"

The Mongol needed no special convincing. He grabbed Wah Chan by the collar and yanked him back, booting the door closed. Not that it would do much good. Mere wood was no barrier to the power of the Buddha.

Wah Chan found himself being rushed up the stairs faster than his feet could normally propel him. He lost a slipper in the process.

Up on deck, Sat Sung called out to his men, first in that strange gobbling language, then in the various dialects of his corsair crew.

The gist of what he propounded was that no one was to make any rash moves.

"Was that the monk, Tang?" Sat Sung demanded of Wah Chan.

The Generalissimo's eyes bugged. "How did you—?"

Sat Sung shook the words loose and demanded, "Answer

me."

"Yes, that is Tang. He worships the Buddha. He will not surrender it. He would rather die first."

"Try to convince him otherwise."

Wah Chan made helpless hand gestures. "I know not the words to do that. His hatred of the Japanese is eclipsed only by his enmity toward all mankind. He loves no one, only hates."

Sat Sung stood silent while that settled in.

Lurking by the hatch of the forward hold, the grim-faced Mongol rapped with the hilt of one of his war swords. He did this twice for attention, then began speaking.

"Tang the monk! I am Captain Sat Sung, new master of this vessel. If you surrender, your life will be spared."

Tang's thin croaking voice was a long time in coming back through the thick planking.

"If I surrender," he croaked, "you will cut my throat and be done with me. Therefore I will not surrender."

"No harm," Sat Sung repeated. "I swear by the bones of my honored ancestors."

That solemn Oriental oath seemed to produce no effect.

"If you do not leave this worthy junk," Tang continued, "I will awaken the Buddha. Then we will all perish."

"He means this," warned Wah Chan, horny fists tightening.

Sat Sung seemed to accept that statement as fact. He began thinking swiftly. His single dark eye narrowed.

"If we retreat to our junk, what then?" the Mongol asked at length. His question was directed at his unseen enemy.

Tang's parched voice retorted, "Retreat and keep retreating. Leave my sight. And the Buddha will sleep—for a measure of time."

"How do I know that you will not awaken the Buddha once I have cast off?" Sat Sung countered.

"Because I hate the Japanese more than I despise wretches such as yourself," hissed Tang. "If I awaken the Buddha now, I will not survive to turn his wrath upon any son of Nippon. This I live to do."

Sat Sung considered this.

"Very well," he rumbled. "We are leaving."

Wah Chan looked dumbfounded. This Mongol seemed to possess too much knowledge. His strategy was perfectly sensible, given the existing conditions. But how had he come by such carefully-guarded knowledge?

"Get off my ship," Wah Chan spat.

Sat Sung turned to him, light glancing off his silvery eyepatch, his solitary uncovered orb very grave.

"Nothing was said about not holding you hostage," he said coolly.

Suddenly, jeweled fingers harder than brass took hold of Wah Chan's mouth, squeezing off all outcry.

Impelled by a brute strength that seemed indomitable, Wah Chan found himself being hoisted over the burly brigand's broad shoulder.

The sound of running feet assaulted his ears, then he was sailing through space to land on the pirate-junk's deck, as helpless in the Mongol's oak-thewed arms as if he were but a kidnapped bride.

The other pirates were not long in following. They withdrew their iron-fanged planks, cut the lines leading to the grappling hooks, and pushed off with long bamboo poles normally used to propel the junk along shallow river ways.

Soon, the two ships were separating.

Up to this point, the pirate junk had shown no sign of being equipped with modern gasoline motors. These came into play now. They made the water about the stern boil madly.

The bat-sailed pirate vessel hastily surged ahead and away.

OVER on the deck of the Red Dragon junk, the conquered crew began to pull themselves together. Bereft of their captain, they milled about aimlessly, shouted profane complaints and shook angry fists.

The Generalissimo watched them from the other deck, fulminating helplessly. Finally, Wah Chan's mouth was released. His hands beat horny knuckles against the big Mongol imprisoning him. All he accomplished was to skin them raw. The one-eyed giant seemed to have been constructed of fire-hardened teak beams.

"What is to be done with me?" he asked at last. "Ransom?"

Switching to very good English, the big Mongol said, "There is someone we wish you to meet."

This brand of educated English left Wah Chan gawking, speechless.

He was escorted to a cabin below. The door was thrown open and two nearly identical ivory faces took in the sight of him, breaking into shocked surprise.

"Dad!" cried Mark Chan.

"Father!" exclaimed Mary Chan.

They rushed into his waiting arms. Tears flowed.

Wan Chan now lapsed into pretty fair Yankee English himself.

"How did you find your way here?" he demanded. "Are you prisoners?"

Mary explained, "No, not prisoners. We have brought a man who is renowned in America, Doc Savage."

Wah Chan turned to stare at the impressive Mongol who called himself Sat Sung. Realization began dawning over his salt-weathered features.

"You?"

Doc Savage began removing aspects of his disguise. It was very artful. Yet it did not take very long to peel away the elements that had transformed him into a giant from the Mongolian steppes.

The last to go was the silver eyepatch, along with a dark optical shell that had covered his good eye. The orbs which were thus revealed glinted like the gold false teeth he plucked from his mouth.

The chemical stain that had turned his deep bronze skin to a greasy copper was all that remained.

"I wondered about that bronze plane," Wah Chan said thickly.

"The aerial bomb released a chemical in the water, coating your rudder board," Doc explained. "Your vessel left a distinct trail possessing ultra-violet properties, which was visible through special apparatus."

Wah Chan nodded. "That was pretty slick work, snookering us like that."

Doc Savage studied the Generalissimo. He saw a man with the outdoorsy look of an adventurer. His eyes had something of the aspect of a Manchu, but it was only a broad suggestion. Other than his wild attire, nothing else about him spoke of the Orient.

"Your true name is not Wah Chan," the bronze man stated quietly.

Wah Chan shrugged casual shoulders. "Washington Chandler is my full name. Just a tramp soldier of fortune who hit it off lucky in China. I'm an American with just enough Cherokee blood in me to pass for an Asiatic. Years back, I got a hankering for the East and struck gold."

"Other people's gold," Doc Savage pointed out.

"Now I fight the Japanese," Washington Chandler said proudly.

"With a weapon that is too dangerous to remain in an individual's hands," Doc reminded.

"Take that up with Tang. It's his devil now."

Mary Chan grabbed her father's sleeve. "Dad, what can we do? The Buddha of Ice is too powerful to control for long. We tried to warn you of this reality."

"We were doing great damage to the Japanese," Washington Chandler said defensively. "In time, we might have eradicated the entire Japanese Navy."

"Possibly," admitted Doc Savage. "But if they fire on your ship with their big guns, sinking you, the Buddha would go to the bottom. With calamitous consequences."

"I thought of that," Chandler grunted. "Don't think I didn't. But it was a risk I am willing to take."

"It was a risk that you did not think through," the bronze man said steadily. And here he launched into a short speech calculated to congeal the blood of all who listened.

"Whatever substance makes up the Buddha," Doc pointed out, "it is unknown to science. The evidence we possess is that it swells in volume in direct proportion to its absorption of moisture."

Chandler nodded vigorously. "I know that. The Buddha is almost half again as large as when I first joined up with Tang. Every dram represents an enemy life."

"If it were to fall into the South China Sea," Doc countered, "how are we to know that it would not absorb the *entire* South China Sea like a sponge, and grow correspondingly large?"

Chandler rubbed the back of his close-shaven neck slowly. It was clear that his mind did not dwell on ideas so grandiose.

Doc Savage went on. "And since the South China Sea is connected to the Pacific Ocean, can we be certain that it would not drink up the Pacific as well?"

The erstwhile Wah Chan paled. "I had not thought it that far along," he admitted.

Doc Savage continued his unnerving discourse. "Almost every sea and ocean on earth, except for the very few which are landlocked, is connected. Moreover, most of the surface of the earth is composed of water. If the Buddha were to fall into any large body of water, who is to say that it might not absorb every drop of water available to it? Conceivably enough for it expand to rival the size of the moon. Larger."

Chandler winced visibly. Then, as the bronze man's speech sank in, he groaned.

Doc Savage's words had the ring of definite knowledge. His

tone grew sharper, more compelling.

"It is urgent that the Buddha of Ice be captured and taken as far away from any body of water as possible. Now. Immediately."

"I see your point," said Washington Chandler, his eyes retreating into his skull, his chest shrinking. "Yet how do we accomplish that very worthwhile end?"

"If you agree to terms, I will grant you your liberty."

Washington Chandler looked from Doc Savage to the faces of his two children.

"I will abide by any terms you state," he said thickly.

Suddenly the craggy generalissimo looked as if he had taken the weight of the world upon his sagging shoulders. "I have been a foolhardy old man."

Chapter XXIV
MUTINY

DOC SAVAGE NOW began organizing a course of action to deal with the menace of Tang and his Buddha of Ice.

"It is vitally important that we wrest control of the Buddha before anything untoward transpires," Doc said emphatically.

The Chans—all three of them—nodded in unanimous agreement.

"It is only a matter of time—" Mark began.

"—before Tang turns the Buddha's awful power upon us," Mary finished.

Doc Savage addressed Wah Chan, now plain Wash Chandler.

"How loyal is your crew?" the bronze man asked.

"Extremely loyal," he said confidently. The former generalissimo hesitated. Doc detected this hesitation and asked, "But?"

"They hate the Japanese occupiers as much as I do—as much as Tang does. If Tang convinces them that banding together with him is in the best interest of China, they could be swayed in his direction."

"We must act before Tang can go to work on their minds," urged Doc.

"Agreed," the bandit-turned-freedom-fighter said simply.

"It might be best, then, to go topside and address them before Tang can get organized," Doc suggested.

They mounted a companionway and came out into the brilliant sunlight.

The seas were running high. There was a freshening wind that blew soapy scud off the wave tops and filled their nostrils with the pleasant bite of salt air.

Mounting the high poop, Washington Chandler reverted to his Wah Chan persona, his two children at his side. He filled his lungs with air, raised his voice to carry.

"Followers of the Red Dragon!" he exhorted. "Brothers of Wah Chan. Hear my speech."

Chinese crewmen began assembling on the other deck, not many rods away. One stood out.

This was a veritable tower of a Chinese sailor. The newcomer called for more than a passing inspection. He was a massive man, a colossus. His size made a pygmy out of the rest. His body was proportioned like a professional athlete, with wide, sloping shoulders, bunched with muscle, which tapered sharply to powerful compact hips and lithe legs.

His head, an upstanding shock of it, was perfectly white. The moon face was brown and healthy-looking, although sun-seamed. He was the helmsman of the Red Dragon junk.

This giant's voice lifted.

"Speak, Wah Chan. Are you injured?"

"No, I am well. My offspring are with me. Behold, the man and girl children of Wah Chan."

The crew of the war junk crept closer to the rail, the better to hear their captive leader speak.

"Those are yours?" the white-haired helmsman asked.

"True children of the Red Dragon," Wah Chan pronounced, putting out his chest. "Born of a Manchu princess, my wife."

"Why then are they captives with you? Why are you a captive?"

"I am no longer a captive. I have joined forces with Sat Sung, the Mongol raider."

"Against whom?" wondered one coolie.

"Against Tang, the wicked."

"Not against the Japanese?"

Wah Chan shook his head emphatically. "No, against the greater menace, which is Tang and his infernal Buddha."

This pronouncement brought dark muttering from the crew.

"The monk Tang has helped us slay many invaders. Now you turn against him," accused one.

"Not against you. Nor for the hateful silkworms of Japan. But against the unholy idol harbored in the hold of the Red Dragon junk."

This sudden turn of fortune caused bewilderment to ripple across the bland faces of the Red Dragon crew. Their slit eyes narrowed sharply.

Loitering nearby, Monk Mayfair muttered, "They're not buying it, Doc."

Lurking in the well of a companionway where he would not be seen, Doc Savage whispered, "We may have to resort to extreme measures."

"Yeah. Like what?"

But the bronze man did not answer. His metallic face was set in graves lines, however. This caused the apish chemist's narrow brow to furrow unhappily. It was never good when Doc's expression betrayed concern, a thing which rarely happened.

The crew of the Red Dragon junk had fallen into a cacophony of singsong conversation. They were eying the *Cuttlefish* crew, with their blue turbans and foreign garb. The crew of Wah Chan's war junk was all Chinese to the last man. But the *Cuttlefish* crew was a slovenly gang mixing ruffians from Malaya, Java, Borneo, Java and Siam. Worse, they looked exactly like what they were—pirates. This did not inspire confidence.

The towering helmsman broke loose from the clot of conferees.

"It is written, 'Who but the sages are free of faults?'" he asserted. "What would you have us do, Wah Chan?"

"Overthrow Tang. Quickly!"

"But will he not unleash his devil upon us?"

"If he is not stopped, Tang will unleash his devil upon the entire world," Wah Chan pointed out.

They fell into a huddle. Excited talk grew angry. Men spat and cursed. A brief scuffle broke out, the immediate result of which was that a dissenter was overpowered and flung overboard, left to strike out for land, if he could.

Finally, the helmsman stepped forth and called over.

"It has been decided that Tang may unleash his devil on any who are not crew members of this worthy vessel," he said flatly.

"Kai dai!" swore Wah Chan. "Helmsman, where is your loyalty?"

"It belongs to China."

This brought wild cries, clucks of agreement.

"Is there no one of you brave and loyal enough to eliminate Tang for Wah Chan?" demanded the bandit generalissimo.

No one spoke up. Their faces were as blank as copper gongs.

"Plainly not," murmured Ham worriedly.

"Oh, Dad," whispered Mary. "What are we to do?"

"It is no use," Wah Chan moaned miserably. His broad shoulders drooped. "They think Tang is their salvation, the savior of China. I have convinced them of this, now I cannot convince them otherwise."

Then an unexpected thing happened. The sailor named Fragrant Fung abruptly scuttled down a companionway. He was not noticed by the crew jammed along the rail, but his furtive actions were plainly visible to the watchers from the *Cuttlefish*.

Not many minutes passed. Sails cracked in the wind. The red flags flying from the mast as a superstitious protection against storms fluttered madly. Waves lapped at hulls, producing a discordant chuckling.

Wah Chan kept talking in hopes that Fragrant Fung would produce a miracle.

"It is a wise dog who knows his master," he announced.

"We are no longer your dogs," came the tart reply.

The trend of the exchange was not productive, but Wah Chan carried on, making more noise than necessary to cover Fung's surreptitious reconnoiter.

"I am recalling a saying I taught my children when they were young: *Chen chin pu p'a hao lien.* 'True gold fears no fire.'"

A junk-man spat back, "*Mi chin pi shaung*! 'Honeyed deceiving speech!' We skinned faces, and washed hands, turning our backs on banditry to defend China. Would you have us lose?"

"Chieh!" retorted Wah Chan. "Alas! If Tang—"

Came an outcry from below. Muffed by hull and deck planking, it seeped out into the open sea, a bleat of shock, fear and other emotions mixed with it. It was impossible to say who cried out, but the sound was high-pitched and sharp.

Then they heard the thud of a body. Not loud. The one who had fallen was not a large man.

"Sure hope that was Tang," Monk muttered.

"It might have been the other fellow," breathed Ham, making his lean sword blade sing in the air.

"If so," Monk said, "Tang might figure the whole crew turned against him. No tellin' what he'll do then."

In less than a minute, they had their answer.

A vague sensation plucked at them. At first it was not noticed. Then it seized them in its powerful grip.

It was thirst. Raw, raging thirst.

"The terrible Buddha!" Mary gasped.

"Tang has awakened it!" Mark cried.

Wah Chan took his children in his great arms and rushed them to the imagined safety of a companionway.

But there was no safety.

The armored hull of the junk of the Red Dragon was stout, but the terrible force emanating from the infernal Buddha was irresistibly strong.

They could feel it sucking the vitality out of them as if an unseen vampire were attempting to wrest their very souls from their bodies. The pirate crew sought the shelter of the lower regions of the boat. A few ducked into the auxiliary cabin in the high poop deck.

DOC SAVAGE shouldered his way topside. He was obeying the opposite instinct that comes over men facing certain death. Instead of seeking the questionable shelter of the cabins below, he made for the rail and vaulted it in an amazing space of seconds.

The bronze man struck the water like a javelin coming down. He made a larger splash than was his custom. That was the only sign that the bronze man was not exercising the full control normally part of his training.

The ocean brine swallowed him. He did not come up for air.

Minutes passed as the terrible suction-like force that projected from the Buddha of Ice continued to exert its sway.

Teak and timbers began to crackle and groan, no doubt in response to the leaching of residual moisture that was locked within them. Planks shrank, separating.

In a matter of less than a minute, the *Cuttlefish* showed signs of coming apart at the seams, so great was the dramatic force sucking moisture from it.

The crew of the *Cuttlefish* was cowering below deck, lighting joss sticks to supplicate their heathen gods. They expected death.

The Chinese coolies who were braced on the deck of the Red Dragon junk were likewise enduring the awful, debilitating thirst and suffering of victims of the infernal Buddha.

They were getting a taste of their own cruel medicine.

They milled about, sought water, bumped into one another in their panicky consternation. Some leaped over the rails. A flat-bottomed boat was pitched overboard, making a sloppy splash.

In the pell-mell confusion, no thought was given to Doc Savage, who had vanished beneath the turbulent waves. For, like dancing devils, the wave tops were leaping and jumping excitedly, too.

In the intervening minute, Doc had arrowed under the flat keel of the Red Dragon junk to surface on the leeward side. His silk line and grapple came out. He swung it lariat-style, snagged a cleat, and began climbing.

This the bronze man did without hindrance.

Realizing that Tang had pivoted the black-iron contraption that contained the Buddha toward the opposing junk, Doc had sought the protection of water. He had not known whether immersing his entire body in water would protect him. It was reasonable to presume that it might. It did.

The protective ocean had prevented the lethal influence from leaching fluids from his Herculean bronze form. When Doc had come up on the other side, he was positioned behind the open baffles and therefore out of range of the Buddha's unseen, thirst-inducing tendrils.

As the bronze giant climbed over the starboard rail, he was unimpaired.

Doc moved toward a companionway and began to feel his way down. It was careful work. If a sound or outcry betrayed him, the Buddha could be pivoted in instants and trained upon him. He wore no protection, having shucked his outer garments during the improvised swim.

Shedding his clothes meant that Doc had lost any gadgets he carried concealed upon his person. He had saved the grapple and line, because he knew he would need them for the climb.

Moving slowly to allow his eyes to adjust to the gloomy conditions, Doc Savage made his way to the sturdy door that sealed off the hold. He came to the door. It was shut.

Before it lay the gnarled thing that had been in life Fragrant Fung.

It resembled a dog that had perished and been left to dry out in the sun. Fung looked as if he had been dead a month or more. In actuality, life had departed barely ten minutes ago.

Doc stepped over the remains and sought a chink or opening

in the door that would permit vision. There was none. A space under the door might have allowed him to insert his periscopic device, but that too was no longer on his person.

Doc began testing the door, to see if it was latched from within or not, when the commotion from above deck changed character.

Before, it had been frantic confusion. Now it darkened, grew excited in a high-pitched, angry way.

Snatches of words reached the bronze man's keen ears. He heard enough to understand that the danger was about to become even more perilous.

That decided him. Setting his metallic back against the panel, Doc Savage exerted sudden pressure. Hinges squealing, the door caved. Doc burst into the hold.

Tang was revealed, crouched behind his black-iron contraption, hunkered down as if in abject terror of the thing he had unleashed as well.

He narrowed hard orbs. Spying the oncoming Man of Bronze, Tang emitted a wild screech. He grasped the stove with bony claws and gave the thing a violent spin.

The black hulk rumbled on its caster wheels and the grotesque head of the Fu Dog came about, revealing its yawning maw. Doc Savage, caught half way between the door and his objective, faced the full power of the Buddha of Ice!

Even steeling himself for it, the bronze man was unprepared. Something like a cold wave of shocking power struck his nearly nude body full on. He sealed his mouth, lest it be dried out.

He dared not stop. Retreat was too risky. Doc could only move forward.

He never reached the Buddha.

Instead, a distant cough came from beyond the hull, in the direction of open water. It was followed by a whistling noise. The sound terminated in a dull detonation. The vessel rocked wildly. This impact felt as if the entire stern of the Red Dragon junk had been blown apart—as possibly it had.

Angrily, Tang grabbed for the brass handholds bolted to the stove's heavy back, redirecting his clumsy weapon toward the spot where he thought death was coming.

It was a blind guess. But the action turned the power of the Buddha away from Doc Savage for the moment.

The bronze man lay supine, fighting with every fibre of his being against the overpowering thirst that had washed over him.

Although stripped down to the black silk bathing trunks he wore in the event he needed to take to the water unexpectedly, Doc was not entirely unprotected.

Long ago, he had prepared a concoction, a pasty mixture that could be applied to the body. When immersed in water, a chemical reaction would keep a swimmer warm. Doc had perfected this in the remote Arctic, where he often sojourned at his Fortress of Solitude. Up there in the frigid waters, he tested it until the greasy preparation offered the correct degree of protection from the debilitating cold of polar conditions.

It happened to be coppery in hue, and thus doubled as part of his Sat Sung disguise.

Earlicr, Doc had applied the thick paste over much of his body, not knowing if it would safeguard him against the Buddha's influence by sealing the pores. To a degree, it had. Doc had been severely dehydrated, but he lived.

With measured stealth and strength, the bronze man climbed to his feet.

Hidden behind the terrible engine of destruction, Tang the monk continued jockeying the Buddha this way and that. Came another cough. A whistling.

Another explosion tore the junk. This one seemed to carry off the mainsail when it hit. Wood shivered. Heavy objects tumbled about on deck. The staunch hull shivered under tearing blows.

Doc Savage pounced on Tang, found his scrawny neck and began the chiropractic manipulations which invariably induced unconsciousness.

It was not an even contest. However, Doc Savage's prodigious strength had been depleted. Tang was a wizened bag of bones with an evil tortoise face framed by canine ears. His body was almost devoid of flesh. His ribs stuck through the skin, arm and leg tendons standing out like taut strings when they moved.

Yet outward appearance can be deceiving. Tang's catgut-like muscles were imbued with the raw power of fanaticism. He scratched, snarled, and attempted to bring his snapping teeth to bear. All in vain.

Hissing like a trapped animal, Tang succumbed to the unrelenting pressure of blunt bronze digits.

Doc held the monk's head in his great cabled hands longer than usual, before he was certain that Tang was no longer conscious. Then he lowered him to the floor.

Creeping around to the back of the ebony machine, Doc found the lever that actuated the louver-like mouth baffles and dropped it with a clang.

The thing sealed itself up. The power of the Buddha of Ice was once again contained.

Clumsily, having to feel his way, Doc exited the hold and regained the deck.

What he beheld did not surprise him. He had gleaned the truth from the excited shouting of the confused crew.

A Japanese naval gunboat had appeared on the scene.

Its forward deck gun was being swiveled on its carriage, round muzzle still smoking. This pointed squarely at the junk of the Red Dragon. Blue-uniformed sailors stuck fingers in ears, ducked at the waist.

As Doc took in the unnerving and unexpected sight, the gun coughed anew.

Having no choice in the matter, the bronze man vaulted the port rail and threw himself into the water ahead of the screaming shell.

Chapter XXV

FIST MEDICINE

THE SWIM BACK back to the *Cuttlefish* was a living agony. So great was Doc Savage's thirst, that he had to fight the strong urge to swallow brine. While not always fatal, this would have injured his system, leading to greater dehydration, and crippled him for the trying battle ahead.

In his weakened state, Doc sank a time or two and seemed unable to draw upon his reserves of strength. Too, his ability to hold his breath for extended periods was no longer in evidence. Once, he seemed to struggle to stay underwater.

Sewn into the waistband of his swimming trunks was a packet of tablets, protected by oilcloth. Doc retrieved this and swallowed two of the pills. They were concentrated tablets of chemical. When mixed with saliva, they released oxygen into the system, permitting breathing without the need for lung respiration.

Finally, Doc made it to the hull, but lacked the physical strength to ascend it. He had regained possession of his silk line and grappling hook, but using it was out of the question.

Doc called up, "Monk! Renny! Lend a hand!"

Not long after, several heads looked down over the starboard rail, spotted Doc's head bobbing at the waterline.

"Doc!" howled Monk.

"The crying thirst stopped," Renny grunted. "Was that you?"

Doc nodded. "Throw a line. Stand ready to haul me aboard."

Monk and Renny blinked in unison, scarcely believing their

ears. It was a rare day when Doc Savage required help. Obviously, the bronze man was severely dehydrated.

They found a coil of Manila line, fashioned a noose big enough around for the task and dropped it. It splashed beside Doc, who took it up and dropped it over his head. When it was snug under both arms, he drew the knot tight and signaled.

Together, Monk and Renny yanked the bronze man's splendidly muscled body up in measured jerks. It was tough work, due to Doc's dead weight, but they succeeded.

Helping their bronze chief over the rail, they stood on the warped planking.

"What happened?" demanded Monk.

Doc related the story in short sentences.

"That Jap gunboat just hove up," Renny thumped. "We're in for it now!"

Another shell had burst on the war junk, this time reducing the high poop structure to kindling.

Renny rumbled, "Just a matter of time before they sink that old scow."

"The Buddha has been sealed in its watertight container," Doc said quickly. "But it's unlikely to survive a pounding."

"If that ark sinks—" Monk muttered.

"—say goodbye to the world," Renny finished.

Ham Brooks came up then, his face several shades paler and drier that it had been a half hour ago. For some reason, the leaching effect of the Buddha had sucked all the color from his handsome features. Even his eyes appeared dry. He kept squeezing them as if to moisten his parched eyeballs.

"Doc!" he yelled. "Some of the crew of the other ship slipped up to our stern in a dink. They're trying to board us!"

Doc leaned over the rail in the direction of the stern. He spotted one of the flat-bottomed boats that had been stored on the Red Dragon junk's deck. The little shell was bumping against the hull, filled to the gunwales with scrawny amber men.

"As if we don't have enough trouble," Monk grumbled. "What now, Doc?"

"Fight them off. Don't use your supermachine pistols unless absolutely necessary. Otherwise you will draw fire from that patrol boat. I will go below and attempt to raise the Japanese gunboat captain by radio."

"Then we'd better get cracking," Renny boomed, making mauls of his gargantuan hands. Mightier fists had not existed since the days of John Henry, the famous railroad steel driver.

As they surged after, Doc's men encountered Washington Chandler and his two nearly identical offspring, creeping up from below, looking haggard and bewildered.

"What has happened?" he demanded.

"Your mutiny boys are stagin' a comeback," Monk growled. "We gotta beat 'em off the stern before they take over this tub!"

"Rush them!" Chandler snapped. He had in one horny hand a club the size of a baseball bat, of wood so hard and heavy it resembled iron.

Together, they raced back toward the stern. Just in time to witness heads lifting over the poop deck, vicious as ferrets.

Renny was the first to reach the scene. The narrow-eyed crew of the Red Dragon junk swarmed over the spot like flies. Grunting explosively, he smashed at a twisted, sallow visage with one knobby-knuckled fist. The other lost his grip, splashed into the water below.

Renny drove his other fist into a wiry belly so hard he could feel his knuckles grate on the ridged backbone.

Others scrambled over. Their torsos were bare, and each wore a gaudy sash of silk into which was thrust an astounding array of weapons. Four of them had three foreign pistols apiece, while the fourth had only two, but made up for it with a short, wide sword that resembled an ordinary corn knife. All had knives with long, needle-like blades. Once their hands were freed of climbing purposes, they began producing the latter from their sashes.

The stern overflowed with junk-men. Excited, crackling, unintelligible yells were everywhere.

Immediately, the aft deck became a storm of activity.

Monk and Ham picked out foes, began whittling them down. Monk grasped heads, two at a time, and endeavored to wrench them off shoulders. He almost succeeded with one. The other he flung back into the water, that being the surest way to settle him.

For his part, Ham sent his sword cane leaping ahead of him like a dancing blade of platinum. He used it to stab and prick at sword-wielding Chinese. They wielded heavier blades, and a few brandished stabbing daggers, but Ham had but to scratch a wrist or cheek and his foe quickly dropped his weapon clattering, and followed it down. The sticky anesthetic at the blade tip ensured that result.

Seeing how successful Ham's strategy was, Monk bounded into a clot of boarders, batted blades from hands, then gathered them up in his burly arms, and presented the squirming, complaining bundle to the dapper lawyer. Ham obliged him by jabbing his blade into frantic waving arms and legs, until the hairy chemist found himself holding a pile of slack sailors, whereupon Monk dropped them unceremoniously onto the wood planking and went in search of a fresh batch of victims.

Howling, Wah Chan waded in. His club lifted. A parchment-skinned head broke under the club with a sound like a rotten cantaloupe.

A rifle stock whistled through the air. The Generalissimo hurled himself backward just ahead of it. But the walnut butt flashed again, caught his wrist, knocking the club high into the air and to one side.

Wah Chan was soon enveloped by a frenzied vortex that seemed to consist of screeching, snapping pigtails. Mark Chan plunged into the melee. Fist blows made a flurry of smacking sounds. Foes fell. Most failed to rise again.

MORE Chinese came, a snarling cloud of them. The attack of thirst followed by the short swim had not deconditioned them as much as might have been expected. They showed great nerve and agility.

Many wielded the traditional skull-splitting hatchets favored by Tong assassins. They came on, whirling their weapon wildly.

Two Orientals landed before Renny, bristling with steel. One spat a crimson stream of betel juice into the big-fisted engineer's face, then clucked something to his companion.

"You rats!" Renny complained. "Fight fair!"

While Renny pawed the red fluid from his eyes, matched blades sought his vitals.

Came a *swish!* A thump. The half-blind engineer suddenly stumbled over something that rolled away. He wondered if it was one of his own detached fists.

Renny gaped. The body of another invader sagged over and struck the deck with a dull sound. The thing he had stumbled over was its head—jowls sagging, eyes rigid, like marbles stuck into pursy brown sacs.

"That's that!" hissed Mary Chan. "Wah Chan's junk-hands keep their swords sharp—and Dad taught me the art of the short blades. No hatchet-man can withstand it."

More startled than he would have believed possible, Renny seized a length of twisted fibre line, snubbed it about a crude cleat, trailed the end to the starboard rail. He used the line to sweep a flood of invaders off their bare feet, then made certain they stayed down by rapping them on jaws and close-cropped skulls with his massive fists.

A semi-naked tawny body hurled at him, seemingly out of nowhere, preceded by an arc of madly slashing steel. Blinded by the spray of betel juice that had been dripping into his eyes, Renny bounded backward, close to the deckhouse. His assailant struck, missed, and lost his thin blade as it dug into the tough wood and broke. The fellow gave vent to a howl that had the piercing quality of a steam calliope.

Renny hit him in the throat with his fist, paralyzing the yell into a gurgle, caught him as he fell, then bore down on a second snarling Celestial with the body held before him as a shield. The newcomer lost his balance and fell.

Renny dropped his senseless burden, pounced on the fallen man, kicked the sword away from his clutch, and pitched him over the rail. He heard the body crash, screaming, into the side of the hull as it tumbled toward the heaving water.

The sound mingled with a thudding rush along the deck. Renny turned, grunted, "Holy cow!"

The towering white-haired Chinese sailor who served as the helmsman of the junk of the Red Dragon loomed before him. Breath wheezed through a flat nose that had been smeared across an unlovely physiognomy. Fat lips twisted into a strange grin. He clucked out a threat of some sort.

Renny closed with him. And quickly received one of the really big surprises of his life. Handling the wiry seamen had been child's play. Not many of them had weighed more a hundred and twenty pounds, many of them less. They were catlike bags of skin and bones.

The colossal Chinese was different. Muscles of tempered steel lay under the coat of leathery brown skin.

Renny ducked, launched his gangling frame forward like a battering ram. His head, turtled between his shoulders, landed in the giant's paunch. The other rocked back, but kept his feet. Grasping hands reached out for the astonished engineer.

The big fellow's arms closed inexorably, crushed the air from Renny's protesting lungs. He had the strength of Samson. The pressure of his bear-like hug was prodigious, bone-crushing. Renny's ears began to ring, and through that sound he could hear his own sturdy ribs crackling in protest.

A numbing pain shot through the big engineer's back, and his legs suddenly felt like lead casks.

Faintly, as from infinite distance, Renny heard the stuttering crash of gunfire, and nearer, from a spot toward the bows, frenzied movement. Then everything was lost in the struggle.

It was not a nice fight. The big monster drew his head down. Renny jerked his head back, heard the betel-reddened teeth snap viciously where his jugular had been.

After that, Renny lost no time in twisting a fat ear, which stunk of sweat and perfume. He hung on, beating a furious tattoo with fists, elbows, and knees. They went down in a struggling knot, rolled wildly about on deck.

Renny got a fist free, drove it repeatedly into his opponent's bulging paunch. With each blow, his opponent collapsed a bit, deflating like a balloon. When he judged the time right, Renny bounced to his big feet, caught his foe by the slack of his pants and ran his snowy head against the ornate superstructure. That did the job.

When the great bulk stopped wriggling, Renny pitched it over side, straining slightly with the effort. The dunking quickly revived the giant, but he was out of the fight for good.

Renny whirled, staggering weakly, eyes swimming under a film of crimson.

The first thing he noticed was the Japanesc gunboat. It had drawn near. Seeing the commotion, it had turned its attention away from the junk of the Red Dragon, whose superstructure was a shambles, in any event.

The rail of the gunboat became a line of ugly red tongues that licked at them repeatedly. Submachine guns!

"Holy cow!" Renny bellowed to the others. "Flatten!"

Wah Chan grabbed at Mark Chan and pulled him down, positioning his own body to absorb mortal lead.

Monk and Ham reverted to their wartime training. They sought immediate shelter, unlimbered their supermachine pistols and hosed the gunboat deck with mercy bullets, seeking to silence the chattering weapon. But the range proved too great to accomplish much.

Eyes anxious, Renny searched the vicinity for Mary Chan.

She was in the act of kicking a Chinese sailor who had her

by her hair. Two others were intent upon the hapless junk-man's rescue.

Renny started in. Then came a stuttering blur of sound. Two of the Chinese boarders on the stern pirouetted about and went overboard, shapeless bundles of arms and legs.

"Holy cow!" he blurted. "It's a young war!"

Another stream of rapid-firer reports erupted over his head, louder and more sharply staccato. The high, ornate poop was suddenly outlined like an electric flasher sign by the winking scarlet spears of gunfire. Wood chips and splinters became a biting cloud around them.

Two more Celestials melted, torn apart by submachine-gun lead.

Then Renny flattened as a dozen machine-gun bullets stung his shoulders in lightning-like succession, ripping through his shirt. They felt like hot needles. Renny no longer wore his chain mail undergarment due to the very real risk of falling overboard and drowning due to its unwieldiness.

There was no other place to go. The big engineer groped for the fibre line he had used earlier. He yanked it along, found Mary Chan, and seized her by the delicate waist.

They went over side in quick order. Their combined weight proved too much for the line. It parted with snarling *snap!*

RENNY'S ungainly frame landed on the gunwale of the flat-bottomed boat. The keel-less craft flipped over as smoothly as though it were on hinges.

The water was cold, benumbing, liquid ice.

They bobbed back to the surface in short order. The girl was an otter in the depths. She shot ahead. Renny followed more slowly, not sure if he had been seriously wounded or not, at the same time trying not to splash.

There were Chinamen in the water. Babbling, they rushed him.

"Still active?" Renny thundered. "Try some old-fashioned

fist medicine!"

Another battle ensued. Gargantuan fists smashed out. Soon the big engineer and his foes disappeared in a welter of foam.

Renny went down with them in depths that were chilling and clear as crystal. An automatic coughed twice under the water with a twin concussion that threatened to rip his eardrums apart.

Renny clawed to the surface in time to drive a bony mallet of a fist against the temple of a snarling, spitting Celestial. The fellow vanished soggily.

Two more came up, their faces distorted masks. Renny kicked briskly at one. His clothes had filled with water, impeded his movements. The blow did no harm, merely pushed the Oriental out of sight. The other lunged, a long knife in his talon-like hand.

The Chinese miscalculated the length of Renny's arms. Too late, he struck. Renny's fingers closed about the pipe-stem wrist and it broke with a hollow, crunching sound. Squawling, the man sank.

Mary Chan surfaced, squirting water from her inviting mouth. "Very thirsty," she said, grinning bravely. "But I did not swallow."

Above, the racket of machine-gun fire gave another ripping burst. Then abruptly, all gunfire died.

Renny waited, ears straining to make out distinct sounds.

"It may be safe to climb back up," Mary suggested hopefully.

"Don't bet on it," rumbled Renny cautiously.

A moment later, Doc Savage's head appeared at the rail and looked down.

"I have convinced the Japanese gunboat captain that further violence will not be necessary," the bronze man informed them.

Chapter XXVI
CAPITULATION

MARY CHAN CLINGING to his neck, Renny ascended the fibre line hand over hand, making it look easy. For one possessing such viselike fists, it was. Only then did he realize that his shoulder wounds were mere bullet burns.

Apparently there had been few fatalities in the fight; the fellow whose knife-arm Renny had broken had gone down and failed to reappear.

Doc Savage gathered his men together in the shadow of the rakish mainsail.

"I have surrendered this vessel to the Japanese captain," he announced.

Ham frowned. "Was that wise, Doc?"

"A cessation of hostilities will buy us a chance to reason through the matter without further bloodshed. Too, there is the dire matter of the Buddha of Ice. To continue fighting, risks the sinking of the Red Dragon junk, and unforeseeable consequences."

Monk bunched rusty paws, simian features seemingly making a third fist. Renny glowered. Ham jointed and unjointed his sword cane as if unsure what to do with it. But all recognized the undeniable wisdom of the bronze man's decision.

"We must prepare to be boarded," Doc added.

A tender was put down from the cruiser. It was filled with Japanese Marines in olive drab, recognizable by the sea-anchor emblems on the front of their steel helmets. They came with bayonets fixed on their very modern rifles.

The captain of the gunboat was a compact little man with a knob-hard face possessing skin like a drumhead drawn taut over projecting facial bones, and very polite manners. His crisp dark-blue uniform and polished boots showed a lot of snap.

He introduced himself, speaking swiftly in a tone that was characterized by a series of hissing inflections.

"I am Captain Kensa Kan of the Imperial Japanese Navy, on permanent assignment to patrol these waters. Pleased to make your acquaintance, Savage-*san.*"

The captain bowed formally.

Doc Savage returned the greeting with an infinitesimal nod of his head.

"You have convinced me to cease shelling the other vessel," Captain Kan said crisply. "Kindly explain your presence in the Yellow Sea and your actions of recent days."

Doc Savage had evidently anticipated the direct question and considered his response in advance.

"We are engaged in a scientific expedition," Doc replied in perfect Japanese.

Astonishment at the bronze man's fluency in his own language caused Captain Kan's flat features to flicker. "To what definite purpose, might I inquire?"

"A dangerous discovery had fallen into the hands of a Chinese bandit who goes by the name of Wah Chan," Doc explained.

Kan's impassive face darkened. "We know of Wah Chan and his gang of devils. Where is he?"

"Wah Chan is my prisoner," replied Doc, not exactly lying.

"In the name of the Emperor, I claim custody of this anti-Japanese criminal."

"It is not Wah Chan who matters here," said Doc, sidestepping the demand. "But the discovery that he had in his possession."

"Please to continue, Savage-*san,*" invited Captain Kan.

"A full explanation would be difficult and perhaps border on the incredible," Doc told him. "For now it is vitally important that the other junk not be allowed to sink."

"I see," hissed Captain Kan, who only thought he understood. "I will have a shore party board the other junk and investigate."

"That would be exceedingly dangerous," returned Doc, choosing his words carefully.

"Why so?"

"The discovery is one of almost unbelievable destructive power."

"You refer to the thing that has been sinking Japanese war vessels?"

Doc nodded. "The same. Its true nature and dangerousness are not yet fully understood."

This statement caused Captain Kan to consider his position carefully. He retreated to speak to an aide. They conferred briefly.

"Are you saying that it is too dangerous to board the junk?" Kan asked after returning.

"Yes. Definitely. You may be familiar with the dangerous emanations of radium. This substance is far, far worse in its lethality."

"But to sink it is unwise, you insist?"

Doc said, "Not merely unwise, but far more dangerous than to board it unprotected."

"I do not fully understand."

"That makes two of us," returned Doc, stalling for time.

Captain Kan turned his narrow gaze in the direction of the junk of the Red Dragon. It was a wreck. The fantail was a splintery mess. One mast lay athwart the deck, the Red Dragon mainsail lying like a dirty brown blanket across the starboard side.

The junk was listing. Smoke poured from three spots. No fire was visible, but that only meant that conflagrations smoldered out of sight, threatening the entire vessel.

"I regret to inform you that I have received orders from Tokyo to sink that junk at all costs," purred the Japanese captain.

"It appears that you may be minutes away from accomplishing that task," Doc pointed out.

"Yet you say there would ensue a calamity?"

"Of the highest order."

Captain Kan appraised Doc Savage's metallic face for long moments.

"Which can be avoided," the bronze man added.

"How so? Speak!"

"Allow us to board the junk and secure the thing before it disappears beneath the waves."

"It is a weapon, obviously?"

"Obviously," Doc admitted.

Captain Kan lifted his head off his shoulders. "Then I am honor-bound to claim it for the sake of the Japanese Empire," he said crisply.

Doc shook his head firmly. "The substance has been found to be uncontrollable—uncontainable as well. To send a boarding party would be to doom every member of that party, and possibly all of us, should the dreadful power hiding in the other hold be accidentally unleashed."

"If it is so dangerous, how is it you think you can control it?"

"We have learned enough to believe that it can be safely secured. But if the junk sinks, all hope is lost."

"Hope for whom?" asked Kan.

"Hope for the world. For no nation is any more or less at risk from the thing that lies in that other junk's hold. All are equally in danger."

"You have a reputation for honesty, Savage-*san*," allowed Captain Kan.

Doc inclined his head in acknowledgement.

"But I cannot trust you above the orders of my Emperor," Kan snapped decisively. "I will send a boarding party. You will accompany us. If what you say is true, you will safeguard my Marines."

"I am willing do that," allowed Doc Savage.

"You have no choice in the matter, being my prisoner. Now where is Wah Chan?"

"He has not been seen since the battle with the crew of the other junk," replied Doc truthfully.

Abruptly, Captain Kan rapped out guttural orders. Marines were dispatched to the innards of the junk.

They began hauling out crewmen of assorted nationalities, herding them at bayonet-point onto the foredeck. They were not polite about it. The Malays and other Asiatics lined up like brown owls perched on a telephone wire.

Surveying the blue turbans and Malay tunic costumes, Kan demanded of Doc Savage, "What manner of ship is this? These men have the look of pirates!"

Doc explained dryly, "We hired them in the South China Sea. References were not available."

Captain Kan's tight-skinned face hardened. "U. S. neutrality in the affairs of other nations has been proclaimed and guaranteed by your Congress. Has it not?"

Doc nodded. "We are not here for any reason other than the one stated."

"It would be a deplorable state of affairs if developments should prove otherwise," purred Kan, his eyes unreadable.

Mark and Mary Chandler were brought into view, and introduced as American geologists. Of Wah Chan, there was no sign. The Japanese failed to recognize him, for most of his Manchu garments had been torn away in the battle with the boarders and without them, he looked like an American. Furthermore, the battering his face had received obliterated all resemblance he had to a Manchurian man.

He was introduced as Washington Chandler. This passed without question or comment.

"Where is Wah Chan?" demanded Captain Kan of Doc

Savage.

"It is conceivable that he fell overboard during the struggle," Doc suggested. "Many did."

This did not satisfy the Japanese captain. He scanned the faces of the assembled crew. His tightening expression told that he did not like what he saw.

Kan faced Doc Savage, who towered over him. The officer took pains not to stand too close to the bronze giant.

"Take your choice," he suggested. "It is merely a question of joining your ancestors now, or living longer, with my word that you will continue to enjoy good health if you follow my orders satisfactorily."

HAM BROOKS sidled up to Doc Savage. Ham understood enough Japanese to have followed the trend of the exchange. Under his breath, he said, "Doc! If they get hold of that hellish Buddha, they will have a weapon with which they can have their way with any nation on earth!"

The dapper attorney spoke Mayan, the tongue they used to communicate with one another in secret.

"No doubt," Doc replied in Mayan.

"How can we stop them?"

"If necessary, they must be allowed to do so."

"What?"

"It would be the least dire alternative," explained Doc. "If they decide to sink Wah Chan's junk, the consequences will be too terrible to contemplate. The entire earth turned into a ball of mud, or perhaps a desert."

Ham stood tongue-tied, a condition rare for the sharp-tongued barrister.

Monk sidled over. "We can take these monkeys, Doc!" he growled.

Doc Savage shook his head definitely. "We are outgunned by the gunboat. They would blow us out in the water in retaliation."

Renny cracked a set of knuckles with a sound like far thunder rumbling. "I'm for trying anyway."

"You are forgetting something," Doc reminded.

"Yeah? What's that?"

"The Buddha's Toe. If they search thoroughly or, worse, sink this vessel, that outcome will be just as unpleasant as the other."

A chill settled over the skins of Doc Savage's men. Ham actually shivered.

Renny Renwick suddenly looked around, his equine face growing longer.

"That reminds me," he rumbled. "What became of Startell Pompman? I don't spy hide or hair of that bloated windbag."

"It is something to wonder about," Doc Savage admitted, his tone grim.

"Do you suppose he got loose in the fracas?" wondered Monk.

"It would be almost impossible for a thorough search of the vessel to fail to uncover him," Doc pointed out reasonably.

"Well, good riddance, I say," sniffed Ham. "He has been a thorn in our side all along."

"Let us hope that is all he proves to be," Doc said, eyes strangely still, as if concern had caused the ever-active metal flakes in his golden eyes to cease whirling.

Chapter XXVII

THE DANGEROUS ONE

THUS FAR IN the affair of the Infernal Buddha, one person had played a relatively inactive part.

Corpulent C. Startell Pompman, the prodigious plutocratic importer-turned-astrologer, had been confined to a cabin which was securely locked deep in the bowels of the pirate junk, *Cuttlefish.*

He had been largely a captive eyewitness and eavesdropper to the amazing stratagem perpetrated by Doc Savage in his quest to seize control of the Buddha of Ice.

Three days before, the bronze man had flown south, communicating all the while to British authorities, requesting that a certain junk last seen in the South China Sea be located.

When it was, and its position conveyed to him, Doc had overflown the junk, which happened to be the vessel recently commanded by the late Dang Mi, otherwise Hen Gooch.

Doc had dropped a message by parachute-equipped canister onto the afterdeck. Once it was read, he had landed and set out by rubber raft to board the *Devilfish.*

There he had made the pirate crew a fair proposition. If they accepted him as their captain and sailed north to China, he would see that they were richly rewarded.

The pirates, some already fretting about their future, had wholeheartedly agreed. There were a few dissenters. The first mate, a worthy named Datu, pointedly suggested that Doc make these malcontents walk the plank.

Instead, Doc let Datu off at the next habitable island to reconsider his attitude toward human life.

This was after the bronze man had transferred his men, the Chans and Startell Pompman over to the seaworthy pirate junk. Whereupon, Doc had ordered the vessel's name changed in order to avoid unpleasant encounters with ocean-going authorities. This nearly occasioned a mutiny, it being thought evil luck to change a ship's name. A compromise was soon reached, and the name *Cuttlefish* was brushed over that of *Devilfish* in bold Chinese characters. The difference was not considered significant enough to carry the argument forward.

Pompman had languished in chains for some of the time. That was for show, more than anything else. There was no place for the fat man to escape to, and Doc wanted the crew to understand that Pompman was a prisoner and not deserving of respect.

Once he was confined to his cabin, the chains were removed. There, Pompman took his meals and listened avidly to any and all sounds emerging from above deck.

It was during the melee in which "Sat Sung" had made an unsuccessful attempt to commandeer the junk of the Red Dragon that the crafty Pompman had contrived his escape.

He resorted to an old trick. It still worked in movies, but in real life it was unlikely to gull even the unwary.

It happened that the crewman who took Pompman his meals was not an avid moviegoer; possibly he had never been to a theater in his rough-and-tumble life.

Pompman simply lay in his bunk, gasping for air and seizing his own throat as if choking—or perhaps overcome by an incalculable thirst.

"Air!" he gasped out in the Malay tongue, the word conversely meaning water.

The crewman, seeing this display, thought that the weird power was loose again.

"You alleesame thirsty?" the man demanded in Pidgin English.

"It must have gotten loose," gasped Pompman with feigned difficulty. "Where is the box? It must have been jarred open."

As it happened the crewman did not know exactly where the box was. But he had a fair idea. The only sensible place to look was in the captain's cabin.

Doc Savage was busy with the battle and could not be consulted.

Dropping the prisoner's bowl of rice and fish, the cook hastened to the captain's cabin. He did not think to lock the door behind him.

ROLLING off his bunk, Startell Pompman hurried after him. His shoeless feet pattered along the planks with surprising softness.

It was while fighting with the door lock that the cook felt the belaying pin that cracked his skull open. He fell, his blue turban unraveling like a scarf.

Using the seaman's tool as a pry bar, Startell Pompman made furiously short work of the padlock, splintering the door in the process.

He barged in. For all his girth, he was strong.

Rummaging about the cabin, Pompman's efforts at first went unrewarded.

Then he spied the stratosphere suit that was hanging in a closet. It was the only garment ensconced therein.

Eyes gleaming behind his pince-nez nose glasses, Pompman reached into the suit's open neck and began fishing. His questing fingers encountered a small metallic object. He brought this forth. It was a brass key.

A key meant a lock, and he naturally began a search of the cabin. The plump plutocrat examined the cabin's inner walls and floor without profit. He frowned heavily.

Turning his attention to the captain's bed, he discovered that it sat on a curtained hardwood platform. Bending awkwardly, Pompman flung the curtain aside, exposing a demon's mouth whose recessed gullet proved to be the aperture of a lock.

Eagerly, he thrust the key within, gave it a turn. The demonic face opened in the fashion of a small door, revealing a stout safe with a modern dial combination lock.

By now, Startell Pompman was perched on the gently rocking floor. Rubbing his pudgy fingers together, he presently demonstrated that his education was not limited to affairs of ordinary commerce.

First he gave the dial a testing spin. Pressing an ear to the steel door, he moved the dial back and forth, while listening for the clicking of the tumblers.

It took some time, during which Pompman paused often to listen for warning sounds coming from the deck above. Satisfied, he resumed his furtive activity.

Perspiration crawled from every facial pore, so great was his concentration. Eventually, the tumbler mechanism surrendered. He yanked the porcelain handle. The door opened, disclosing a crackled-finished blue metal surface. Pompman suppressed a bubbly gasp of unbridled joy.

The sought-after box was enwrapped in a fat wad of oilskin—evidently a precaution should the rocking of waves disturb it.

"Zounds!" he breathed. "Pluto, Mercury and Mars."

Carefully, Pompman began to excavate the stout steel strongbox. He set it on the floor. Next, he began assembling the suit about himself. It took considerable effort and time. More than once he began mouthing maledictions in his frustration.

Soon enough, Pompman scraped and wriggled his doughy bulk into the confining outfit like a pleased hippopotamus.

When he was firmly stuffed within, he placed the fishbowl-style helmet on a shelf and, by a clever manipulation which involved ducking under the globe and pulling it toward him with his flabby womanish hands, succeeded in getting it to drop over his head.

Bolting the flange to the metal cuirass on his shoulders was the most difficult part, but there were only two catches, one on each side his the neck, and at last he got this final bit of business done.

"Egad," he puffed. "My stars!"

Picking up the box with supreme care, Startell Pompman strode out into the corridor, looking like a denizen from another realm navigating unfamiliar territory.

A profound change now settled over the wide features of the man of affairs. Hitherto, he had resembled a well-fed merchant. Now there was something stark and predatory in the lines of his bloated face. There was the proverbial blood in his fat-sheathed eyes.

This changed abruptly when he heard the first dull cough of a deck gun. A whistling sound approached. Although unversed in the arts of modern naval gunnery, Startell Pompman recognized the sound signals of an approaching shell.

He froze in his clumsy boots, waiting. There was no use running; the suit was not designed for flight. Nor did hiding appeal to him. The shell, when it landed, might strike and demolish any part of the vessel. No point in blundering into danger when standing still might be the safest course of action.

When the detonation came, the pirate junk did not respond, other than to roll slightly in the swells. Excited cries came from topside.

It soon became clear that the target was another vessel. Years spent as an Oriental importer had made Startell Pompman fluent in various dialects—Mandarin, Cantonese, even Annamese. He quickly gathered that it was another junk that had come under attack by a Japanese gunboat.

Other activities quickly followed. Abruptly, members of the pirate crew began tumbling down the hatch of the main cabin.

Startell Pompman sought shelter. He found it in the same place that Renny Renwick had earlier hidden during the mad affair—in the junk's indescribably filthy bilge.

Here, in darkness, sounds were more muffled and it was difficult to make out snatches of frantic conversations. Too, many of the pirate crew spoke languages with which he was not familiar.

Startell Pompman waited, perspiration of impatience coursing down his fat features, soaking the clothes he wore under the bulky protective suit. It was very hot and he had to take care not to move about too much, for he feared tearing the suit, whose seams were greatly stretched in the effort to contain his voluminous bulk.

Eventually, a strange silence fell. The coughing and booming of bombardment eventually had ceased. The rattle of a machine gun came and went during this interval, too.

It sounded safe to emerge.

Then, and only then, did the bloodlust return to Startell Pompman's eyes. Laboriously, he climbed out of the bilge and tramped his way to the companion which led topside.

Chapter XXVIII
THE UNTHINKABLE

DOC SAVAGE WAS making explanations to a skeptical and stiff-necked Captain Kensa Kan.

"Below in my quarters, there are protective suits," he related. "These will enable a man to approach the dangerous device aboard the Red Dragon junk without risking harm."

"What do you propose, Savage-*san?*"

"Since you insist upon accompanying me to the foundering junk," responded Doc, "we will each don one of these special outfits and enter the hold where the dangerous thing is."

Captain Kan considered this for some moments.

Doc Savage showed a trace of impatience when he said, "The Chinese have a saying: *Ch'in-shu, kuang yin ssu chien.* It means: 'Kinsmen, time is like an arrow.'"

"Meaning that it flies," said Kan.

"Exactly."

"Produce these suits, then," Kan demanded.

Doc sent Mark and Mary Chan to get the weird coverall suits that they had worn at the beginning of the chain of events that had brought them to this dangerous juncture.

Under armed escort, the Chandler twins found the black atmosphere suits that had been custom designed for their slender forms.

When they brought them topside, Captain Kan took one in hand and gave it a thorough examination. When he came upon the manufacturer's label with words sewn in Russian, he turned red in the face and began sputtering.

"What is this? Russian!"

"The suits are versions of those worn by Soviet high-altitude balloonists. They offered the greatest protection possible," explained the bronze man.

Kan said, "Either garment will fit me, but what about you?"

"A special suit of my own design is stored in my cabin. I will wear that one."

"We will see," said the captain. He gobbled out harsh orders and two Marines began assisting him into one of the black suits. Due to the airtight construction of the rubberized outfits, and the oxygen apparatus that had to be fitted, this was a task requiring more than one man. Even with help, it took some time to do it.

To an aide, Kan barked, "Yakamashi-*kun!* You will don the other one."

Doc Savage objected, "Too many men will complicate the operation unnecessarily. And there is still the risk involved."

"I will undertake any risk to obtain this weapon, Savage-*san,*" Captain Kan rapped out. "But I will decline the risk of falling into your capable hands, should I accompany you alone."

That settled the argument. Doc Savage fell silent. His eyes were sweeping the junk's deck, the surrounding seas. He chanced to look up. A low bank of storm clouds—thunderheads—were approaching from the south.

Monsoon season was near its end. That did not mean the threat of the violent summer rains that sweep this part of the world was entirely over.

"We had best get going," Doc advised. "It appears that a line squall is approaching."

"Ah, so it seems. Two of my men will accompany you as you retrieve your personal suit." Kan gave the orders. Two stone-faced Marines stepped out of line and produced the lean-barreled automatics with which Japanese soldiers are equipped.

Under those converging muzzles, the bronze man was escorted to the main hatch.

Doc stepped around the ornate superstructure and wrenched to a halt.

For up from the interior, stomped an imposing and unexpected figure.

Doc's trilling came, wild and excited. He was so startled he failed to realize he was making it and the exotic sound ran unchecked for some moments.

There stood his stratosphere suit, bulging at the seams—the bespectacled head of Startell Pompman encased in the transparent fishbowl helmet!

In his gloved hands, the plutocrat tightly grasped the blue strongbox with the crackle finish!

Pompman's thick voice boomed through the loudspeaker apparatus.

"No one make any untoward moves, if you please. It appears that my stars are in the ascendancy!"

The strange outburst struck the ears of the main contingent of Marines, who were out of sight of the tableau. Captain Kan ordered three additional Marines to investigate.

They charged along the deck.

"Stop!" Pompman warned. He repeated his cry in Cantonese, Mandarin and the Hakka dialect of South China. Evidently, he did not yet realize that the soldiers were Japanese.

"Again I say, halt, or I will open this damnable Pandora's box!" he bellowed.

Doc Savage rapped out swift words in the language of Japan. This had no effect on the charging Marines. They came on, bayonets fixed.

Realizing the danger, the bronze man gathered the heads of the two Marines guarding him in his great iron-fingered hands and brought them together with an audible *bonk!*

They collapsed. Doc let them fall to the deck unceremoniously.

Seeing this, the charging Marines changed course and attempted to run the bronze man through.

What transpired next happened with the speed of streaking lightning.

Doc Savage's great bronze fists lashed out. He blocked one stabbing steel bayonet with a wrist, removed the blade from its mounting and tossed it over the rail. Then he slapped the man so hard his helmet flew off, chin-strap parting.

This display of ferric strength and superior reflexes caused the remaining pair of Marines to switch tactics out of self-preservation.

They elevated bayonet-tipped rifle muzzles, fingers squeezing triggers. Gunsound came.

Doc dodged. Had there been only one man, conceivably Doc might have avoided injury. One bullet jerked splinters from the superstructure. The other burned along the bronze giant's unprotected side. Reacting, he twisted, stumbled.

In the act of falling, he threw himself into the hatch. The sound of his bronze form careening down the companionway stairs came like a great commotion.

When Doc landed, all sound ceased.

In Japanese, the victorious Marine cried out, "Honorable captain! Doc Savage is dead!"

Cursing volubly, Captain Kan came running up. He was not happy.

When he popped around the superstructure, Kan saw no sign of the bronze giant, but the unexpected sight of Startell Pompman transfixed him as through he had encountered a being recently deposited on earth from the moon, or some farther sphere.

His hand flashed to his holster. A startled expression twisted his face when he realized the holster was sealed inside his suit. Sputtering angrily, he grabbed for the sidearm of a nearby Marine, yanked it from its holster.

Kan took careful aim at Startell Pompman's bloated shape.

Pompman again bellowed, *"I warn you, sir!"*

Then he raised the lid....

THE Marine nearest the big plutocrat never had a chance. He had redirected his rifle in Pompman's direction.

The lid lifted only a fraction of an inch.

The sea air hung heavy with moisture. Almost immediately, it commenced to thicken and swirl, as if a fog was descending upon the becalmed junk. But this was a fog that behaved with singular intent. It rushed toward the open box.

The Marine with the pointing rifle released that rifle abruptly. He had no choice in the matter. His hands, from finger bones to tendons, suddenly lost all moisture. The dead weight of the rifle literally yanked his dry, mummified hands off at the wrists.

The eyeballs in his head turned to white raisins. His jaws slacked, and the tongue flopped out like a mummified snail.

The Marine was dead before his mummified face smacked the deck.

Captain Kan was more fortunate. He was wearing his atmosphere suit, although it was not entirely sealed. He merely suffered a sudden unaccountable shock of thirst. Recognizing his peril, he backpedaled, returning to the bow where the prisoners were clustered. He screeched out frenzied orders, the words tumbling together in an avalanche of sound.

Startell Pompman advanced, holding the container lid cracked just enough that the power of the Buddha's Toe was operating. His eyes were avid with power, his features sweating profusely, like a man enjoying strenuous but pleasurable exercise.

The sound of his boots on the deck planking resembled warning drums.

"My day has come!" he crowed. *"I control the power of the Buddha of Ice. When my natal horoscope was first cast, it foretold that this would be the most auspicious day of my entire life!"*

Doc Savage emerged from below. A noticeable change had taken place. Over his head he had affixed a gas-proof hood, as transparent as Cellophane, which sealed at the throat by a thick rubber band. His bronze skin was greasier than before, and its hue was more coppery. Even his hair was smeared with the stuff. The only part of him that did not partake of that coloration was the tip of his right forefinger, which was a dull, dark bronze.

The bronze man was moving rapidly, while still adhering to the stealth that marked his deep training. He was barefoot, and attempted to creep up on Startell Pompman from behind, unawares.

But no man is perfect—not even Doc Savage. The art of stealth requires that other conditions be right. They were not.

His own shadow betrayed the bronze man's approach. There was no helping it. Doc was a giant and he cast a Samson-sized shadow. This intercepted the light falling on the spherical helmet.

Alerted, Startell Pompman turned ponderously, saw his Nemesis.

Grinning, he directed the corrugated box at Doc Savage's exposed bronze physique.

Doc halted. His flake-gold eyes, which rarely missed any detail no matter how minute, discerned something of import.

"Pompman," he cautioned. "Seal the box. You are in grave danger."

"Do you take me for a dunce and dumbjohn, sir?" Pompman sputtered. *"I am in control of the situation, and I will not relinquish that splendid mastery."*

"You cannot hope to control the thing in that box," Doc asserted. "It must be destroyed."

A lumbering human pachyderm, Startell Pompman bawled, *"Destroyed! The power to sway nations? Poppycock! Balderdash, I say! Why, there isn't a government under the stars that would not pay tribute in the billions of dollars to avoid the Buddha's unslakable influence falling upon their waterways and reservoirs. Can you imagine it, sir? The power to make a dust bowl of any sovereign nation lies in my grasp. Fabulous fortunes will be levied by me, for I possess an earthly authority greater than that of Jupiter himself."*

Face working, the pompous plutocrat pushed the blue box at Doc Savage.

"Fall!" he bellowed. *"Why don't you turn into a mummy, damn you!"*

"I have found a counteractant to the Buddha's influence," the bronze man told him firmly. His lips did not move, however. He kept his mouth closed as much as possible, as a precaution should the gas-proof hood prove insufficient to the task.

Seeing that Doc Savage was somehow standing up to the awful influence, the astrologer opened the box a trifle wider.

It was his undoing.

The act of flexing his left hand caused a stretched seam to pop on that sleeve. Doc Savage had spied the weakened seam, attempted to warn the crafty man of the peril.

It was no good. The blue box cracked wider. A tearing sound reached Pompman's ears. He recognized its import. His eyes grew round. Then they shriveled into white blobs in his surprised skull. His rimless spectacles dropped from his retreating nose.

In an instant, the visible part of Startell Pompman's anatomy—his round head—had collapsed into the papyrus visage of a mummy. He stood rooted, already dead, held in place by the enveloping stratosphere suit.

Then, like a tree chopped to the tipping point, he began toppling.

Fate is a fickle female. Startell Pompman might have fallen backward, or to either side. Either would have been calamitous.

Instead, he fell forward. Forward—still clutching the fatal box!

The expired astrologer happened to land atop it, causing it to snap shut. The power of the Buddha's Toe was cut off. But it was a near thing.

Doc Savage pitched forward in an attempt to claim the strongbox.

But Captain Kan came storming up, flanked by a pair of Marines. He flung off the hood of his black coverall suit, which he had prudently donned during the confrontation. The neck thus revealed was the hot hue of flame.

Excited words blew off his lips. "So! You lied! The death device was concealed on this junk all along."

Removing his own protective hood, Doc Savage came erect. He shook his head firmly.

"I told no lies," he stated. "What is contained in that box is only a fragment of a larger relic. That most dangerous piece must be recovered from the Red Dragon ship."

Captain Kan eyed the bronze man for an indefinite period of time. His eyes squeezed shut until they were almost closed, the exposed slits resembling the seamed edges of twin walnuts.

"Please to hand me the box," he said at last. "Carefully."

Doc Savage rolled the desiccated cadaver that had been Startell Pompman off of the steel box. He grasped the latter, holding it firmly shut, and came to his feet.

For a moment, his flake-gold eyes quested about, as if seeking a safe place to which he might carry the dangerous container. But there was none. His face set in firm lines.

Having no choice in the matter, the bronze man presented it to Captain Kan.

"I accept this important treasure in the name of my Emperor," Kan said in a pleased purr.

"What about the other fragment?" inquired Doc.

Captain Kan was a long time in answering. At length, he said, "Since you are so eager to acquire it, I suggest that you don that outfit and go aboard the other junk to recover it."

"Alone?"

"Alone. The safety of your men and your—ah—scientific crew, will be my guarantee that there will be no further treacheries."

WORDLESSLY, Doc Savage knelt and began disassembling the atmosphere suit from the still corpse of Startell Pompman. It was amazingly small, like a deflated balloon. No one failed to notice how shriveled up was the corpse of an obese man who had been full of vitality only moments before. It was unsettling.

Doc managed most of the operation, but requested that Monk help him with the gauntlets and clumsy helmet.

"We've been holdin' back, Doc," Monk whispered in Mayan.

Doc undertoned, "Make no moves unless necessary. Kan now controls the Toe."

Doc carefully removed an emergency patch from a slit pocket and clapped it over the ruined seam that had caused Startell Pompman's grisly undoing. He clapped this in place with a spring clamp designed for this purpose, one of several affixed to the suit's broad tool belt.

Lastly, the marvelously clear helmet was set on Doc's shoulders.

When the bronze man was fully encased, he switched to speaking Japanese, and said, "A boat will be necessary to convey me to the other junk."

Captain Kan gave the orders to assist Doc into the waiting tender. This was done by lowering him by a sling of hempen ropes. Monk and Renny did the honors.

The tender was run over to the Red Dragon junk, which had taken on water, and was listing. But junks are such marvelously seaworthy craft that this one looked as if it would float until the end of time.

When Doc reached the bow, he was forced to climb via the anchor chain. This was a ponderous and difficult process, but the bronze man negotiated it as if he were a spider climbing its own web.

Captain Kan watched with intense eyes, but no expression.

Then he gave the tender crew a short downward chop of his hand.

They pushed off.

"Hey!" Monk howled. "They're stranding Doc over there!"

"Merely applying necessary caution," said Captain Kan thinly.

All watched until the tender had moved to a safe distance. Then Captain Kan shot a significant glance in the direction of his aide, Yakamashi. The latter blew a blast on his whistle.

A Marine produced a flare gun from his kit and pointed it skyward. He pulled the trigger. A rocket shell was sent screaming into the darkening sky.

At the point at which Doc Savage was clambering over the rail, the gunboat coughed a shell in the direction of the wallowing junk.

It whistled briefly. Struck. Subsequently, the Red Dragon vessel's stern was blown away, going entirely to pieces.

Chapter XXIX

THE BUDDHA AWAKENS

PANDEMONIUM BROKE OUT on the deck of the pirate junk, *Cuttlefish.*

Mary Chan gave vent to a screech of surprise. That started it. This brought heads swiveling from the spectacle of the exploding Red Dragon junk.

Monk Mayfair took advantage of the unexpected distraction. He bunched hairy knuckles, hauled off, and knocked Yakamashi off his puttee-wrapped boots. Then he grabbed the Japanese by the front of his uniform tunic, lifted him over his bullet head, and flung the hapless sailor bodily in the direction of Captain Kensa Kan.

Captain Kan lunged for his scabbard, which was leaning against a deck cannon, drew his military sword, and charged after the apish chemist.

Temporarily without his sword cane, Ham Brooks harvested a *parang* short sword off the body of a fallen pirate, and came rushing to Monk's defense.

An argument ensued over whether or not Monk needed defending. Monk pushed Ham away. The dapper lawyer stuck out his handsome jaw and glowered.

A slash of Kan's sword settled the conflict for the moment. It took a nip off of the edge of one of Monk's ears. Monk vented a howl of wrath, clapped a hand to the injured ear.

Ham stepped in, caught the next sweep, parried it expertly. Kan drew back and hammered fiercely at the dapper lawyer in retaliation. Sparks flew off clashing edges.

Thereafter the air rang with steely sounds as the two drove their clanging blades at one another. Accustomed to a lighter, fencing-style weapon, Ham appeared to be at a disadvantage. He quickly recovered his aplomb and hacked furiously against Kan's slashing counterattack. The engagement began going against the captain.

A Japanese Marine attempted to intervene with fixed bayonets.

Monk tripped him and sat down on his chest until the man's boot heels ceased beating frantically against the blood-smeared deck.

Renny had been hovering near a fallen length of bamboo. It had the look of a discarded Malay blowgun. The big-fisted engineer bent, scooped it up and sighted down the fat tube. His pleased frown told that he spied one of the feathered darts whose tip had been earlier dipped in the same anesthetic that coated Ham Brooks' sword cane blade.

Placing one end of the blowgun to his mouth, Renny filled his capacious lungs and expelled them in the direction of another Marine, who was attempting to brain Monk. The apish chemist was still seated atop his fallen foe.

The dart struck the Marine in the cheek. He had started his downward blow. Then he stumbled. Roused, Monk batted the rifle butt aside and grabbed for an ankle, pulled his antagonist down, and changed perches.

This foe did not struggle under the weight of the hairy chemist. A puzzled expression crawled over Monk's unlovely countenance.

"That one's already out cold," boomed Renny. "Get up and join the durn fight."

Monk bounced to his feet and slapped the nearest Marine so hard that teeth flew out of the latter's mouth.

The contingent of the Emperor's Imperial Marines suddenly discovered that their thinned ranks meant that they were now outnumbered. Their sagging faces reflected their consternation.

Wah Chan pushed his way out from the clot of prisoners. Suddenly there was a sword in one hand and a Malay *kris* in the other. He began making short work of the nearest Marines, literally chopping their rifles from their hands.

Those who could, whisked swords from scabbards.

Pandemonium was now in full cry.

It filled the skies, too. For one of the swift-moving violent line squalls that trouble the Yellow Sea was rapidly descending upon the scene. A pelting rain began falling. Wind picked up, making it slant at angles to the waves. Seas churned.

Gore had made the foredeck slick and slippery. Pounding rain now mixed with the sticky crimson fluid. Keeping erect became a problem for the combatants.

Amid this fierce confusion, Wah Chan organized the pirate crew of the former buccaneer junk, *Devilfish.* His leadership qualities showed themselves now. He rallied the corsairs about him and made a run at the Marines, pushing them toward the bow.

A fresh shell screamed from the Nipponese cruiser, made kindling of another section of the Red Dragon junk. Evidently there was a powder magazine stored below, for the detonation was immediately followed by a greater explosion. Masts and sails of the great war junk erupted in all directions at once.

In the act of throttling a squawking Marine, Monk's head swiveled toward the blast. His mouth yawned open cavernously.

"Doc!"

"Holy cow!" Renny rumbled thickly. "He's done for!"

Hearing this, Ham Brooks's head jerked around. His guard momentarily down, he felt his *parang* being knocked out of his fist. It skittered along the gory deck.

Eyes bright, Captain Kan placed the tip of his blade against the lawyer's exposed throat.

"Victory lies in my grasp," he purred throatily.

DOC SAVAGE was not yet done for.

During the fight aboard the *Cuttlefish*, he had managed to work his way into the hold as the first shell splintered the foundering junk's stern. The craft was listing dangerously. The bronze man's previous forays to the Red Dragon ship, combined with his remarkably retentive memory, had saved him precious time.

Water from separating hull planks had begun squirting from numerous chinks, pooling in the hold. Tang lay where Doc had left him, still insensate as a result of the bronze man's wizard-like knowledge of human anatomy.

Doc proceeded to wake him up. Loss of life was something he always sought to avoid. No matter how evil the monk's past deeds, Tang deserved a chance to live, if not to repent his ways.

Vising him by his chicken-like neck, the bronze man manipulated nerve centers until a coarse-textured groan was elicited. Tang's eyes snapped open. At sight of Doc Savage, they became livid with fury.

Cracked nails clawed for Doc's regular features, but were defeated by the glassy helmet of his stratosphere suit.

Setting Tang down, Doc went next to the Fu Dog that encased the Buddha of Ice. It appeared intact, a swift inspection showed. There was no break in the pitch-caulked seams which insured it remaining watertight.

Doc Savage was considering his options when Tang sprang to his feet and made a mad lunge for the porcelain handle which actuated the Buddha's baffles.

Encased in the waterproof suit, the bronze man did not hear the splashing of Tang's sandaled feet in the rapidly-filling hold.

With a croaking imprecation, the wicked monk seized the handle, wrenched it upward.

Doc Savage was hampered by the bulky suit, but he tramped

around and seized Tang about the waist, lifted him off his feet and with his other hand calmly dropped the handle again.

In the seconds between the raising and the lowering of the handle, a peculiar phenomenon could be seen. The water sloshing about the floor of the hold actually lifted, as if pulled toward the encased Buddha by magnetic attraction.

Once the baffles were shut, the liquid settled back to a normal level. Still, it was an uncanny thing to behold, and it momentarily mesmerized the bronze man, whose interest in strange new phenomena was without equal. He stared at the uncanny thing, his metallic face intent with a kind of wonder. There was a whirling in his golden eyes that bespoke of fascination with the unknown—a thing that drove the bronze man in his more risky exploits, of which he never spoke.

The trilling sound that was often prodded out of him in moments of extreme emotion could barely be heard outside the confines of the sealed bubble of his helmet. Nevertheless, it was present—a tiny, wondering thing in the face of the uncanny Buddha from the stars.

For once, even Doc Savage was awed.

Tang had grown limp in Doc's grasp, possibly due to the brief period the Buddha had been exposed to open air and had exerted its power. Suddenly, he began wriggling in an alarming manner.

The whistling of an incoming shell finally registered through the remarkable substance which comprised Doc's helmet.

There was nothing to do but run for it.

The helpless monk under one arm, Doc pitched toward the exit companionway. A rare alarm animated his flake-gold eyes. They swirled like twin storms of dust-fine metal.

The impact of the shell came before Doc Savage reached topside. He was thrown from his feet, almost lost Tang, gathered him up and tried to grope his way back to the deck as the wounded junk began rolling and heeling drunkenly. Such shrapnel as flew were mostly of wood splinters and failed to penetrate the many-layered suit.

A cascade of rushing water flooded down to meet him.

Doc Savage knew then that the Red Dragon war junk was doomed.

For a long moment, Doc hesitated as if struggling between two equally perilous courses of action. His metallic expression wavered as he calculated his options. Doc seemed genuinely torn.

Finally, he made his choice.

Scrambling to the questionable safety of the deck, the bronze man flung a final glance back at the black-iron contraption that was all that preserved the world from the power of the infernal Buddha.

It was rolling about the hold, careening crazily on its unsecured wheeled casters, louvered lion's mouth stuck in a fixed position.

The junk gave a sharp lift to port, and the wheeled thing bounced off a bulwark, toppling over with the resounding clang of a church bell dropped from a great height.

The sound made Doc suspect that the watertight shell had been breached, but there was no time to think about that now. Not if he wished to preserve his life. Still pulling the limp Tang along, the bronze man fought his way up through the inrushing ocean, a task seemingly beyond even his terrific strength.

Chapter XXX
THE BUDDHA GORGES

THE JUNK OF the Red Dragon sank swiftly from view. The superstructure remained intact as it was swallowed from sight in the pelting monsoon rain. This was witnessed by the survivors aboard the *Cuttlefish,* as well as those on the Japanese gunboat, which had caused her destruction.

Doc's men were struck speechless. It was difficult to tell if the moisture running down their stricken faces was a product of the clouds, or their own eyes. Perhaps it was both. They hung over the rail, stark eyes raking the turbulent seas.

Finally, Renny groaned like sailcloth tearing.

"I don't see Doc!"

His sword still prodding Ham Brooks' exposed throat, Captain Kensa Kan said, "So! The brazen devil is dead. Very regrettable." His tone suggested otherwise.

"You'll really think that, if the Buddha breaks free," Ham returned sharply.

Perplexity crossed the Japanese captain's bone-hard face. "Buddha?"

Mark Chan spoke up. "The Buddha of Ice."

"The most horrible thing that ever fell to earth," added Mary Chan.

"The thing in the steel strongbox has only a fraction of its awful power," Mark imparted.

One eye on the superstructure fast disappearing beneath the waves made frenzied by the pelting rain, Captain Kan shrugged nonchalantly.

"Small matter. It is lost now. I have what I require for my Emperor. Now, please to surrender once more—unless you wish to see this man's throat sliced open." Kan prodded Ham's pulsing throat anew.

But the eyes of Doc Savage's men refused to leave the spot where debris of the great junk of war floated. Their gazes were fixed, their faces strained.

When the choppy waters regathered at last, there was no sign of survivors.

"That suit can double as a diving rig," Renny thumped hopefully.

"If it wasn't breached," moaned Monk.

They watched and watched, but no sigh of life did they perceive.

Over on the gunboat, another tender was being lowered into the rain-stirred brine. It was not going well, due to the whipping winds and ocean churn.

"Reinforcements coming," Renny warned.

"I could use the exercise," gritted Monk. But when his eyes went to Ham Brooks, they looked sick.

Wah Chan loomed nearby. He was still clutching two mismatched blades. They were smeared with scarlet and dripping freely.

"What are we waiting for?" he growled. "Invitations?"

"We ain't riskin' Ham's life," Monk snapped at him.

The Generalissimo barked back, "What difference does it make? Once those reinforcements get here, we're all going to be summarily executed anyway. Kan can't afford to let any survivors live to tell the world that the Japs murdered Doc Savage."

"Don't say that!" Renny said angrily. "We don't know that Doc is dead. Yet."

Just then, a body bobbed to the surface, floating face downward. It resembled a twist of meat caught in a maroon blanket.

"Tang!" pronounced Wah Chan. "His Buddha finally got him."

"This means *it* is loose," whispered Mary Chan. "And the Buddha will drink his fill."

His clenched fists like ivory bones, Mark Chan remained silent. There was nothing more to add.

All eyes went to the maelstrom of water that marked the spot where the junk of the Red Dragon had gone down to a watery grave.

"Why are you all looking like that?" Captain Kan demanded, his mood partaking of the aura of fear that had settled over the prisoners. "What do you expect to transpire?"

No one replied. For in truth, they did not know what to expect. They only knew that it would be very, very terrible.

IT was.

The zone of disturbance grew more turbulent. That was not unusual, or unexpected. Ocean conditions were deteriorating. The monsoon winds commenced churning a filthy froth mixed in with fragments of the lost junk.

Then the rain began to slant strangely.

It had been beating down in a northeasterly direction, but now it seemed to be twisting, reorienting its pelting, as if obeying some Chinese storm god that had been roused by the recent violent activity of humans.

Even Captain Kan noticed this peculiar phenomenon. He paled. Everyone paled. A few turned literally green.

A sizzling bolt of lightning turned the cloud cover into a luminous greenish-white sheet. A cannonading of thunder rolled across the rain-pimpled water's surface like giants bowling.

Then the Yellow Sea began bubbling and churning prodigiously. This unexpected activity appeared to be centered at the Red Dragon junk's last known location.

Something lifted into view. It was white, yet translucent as crystal. A diamond-hard dome of a thing, it swelled, or seemed to.

It was difficult to tell if the phenomenon of the rising of the infernal Buddha of Ice was the result of its lifting to the surface, or the swelling of its size as it greedily devoured the Yellow Sea.

Conceivably, it was both.

The forehead of the thing appeared first. Steadily, a face lifted into view, literally emerging from the swells.

In size, it appeared monstrous, fully as large as a temple Buddha. The towering face was long, sinister of lineaments. The eyes were knife slits, the ears pointed like the ears of a dog, the mouth a cruel slash. All of crystal, cold and impersonal like some being from the stars.

Those who had known him in life recognized those canine features.

"Tang!" grunted Wah Chan.

"It was whispered that he carved the head of the Buddha of Ice to resemble his own visage," Mark breathed.

"And it is true!" whispered Mary.

The glassy head hoisted completely out of the water. Only then did it become apparent that it was not merely emerging, but swelling. The chin lifted above the waves, then the shoulders, then the upper chest. A mangled piece of iron fell from one shoulder—all that was left of the prison that could no longer contain it.

All the time, it grew and grew and grew like an elemental force of unstoppable power. Where it had emerged from the chop, its glassy surface was slickly moist. But as soon as it reached open air, this dried. Even being lashed by rain, it would not stay wet. Multitudinous raindrops entered the thing, leaving the surface looking like dry ice.

A coldness emanated from the glassy behemoth, radiating outward in waves, touching all with an icy dread that made their marrows congeal. It was a coldness that was remindful of the airless reaches of interstellar space.

"What is that monstrosity?" demanded Captain Kan.

No one answered. No one had the words. It no longer mattered—none of it. The Buddha of Ice had broken free of its fragile iron prison and was devouring all that it could.

Around it, rain swirled in frenzied circular motions, the raindrops themselves behaving like living things, as if eager to become united with the Buddha.

"Why ain't I thirsty?" Monk muttered, feeling of his throat.

"Wait for it," Renny grunted.

There was nothing else for them to do. Their fate lay in the hands of unknown forces.

The Buddha loomed twenty feet over their heads. Then thirty. Forty. The turbulent waters made it impossible to judge, but no doubt the Yellow Sea was rapidly evaporating—if that was the correct term for it—as the Buddha absorbed it at a frightening rate.

"One thing for sure," Wash Chandler grumbled. "The Japs won't take Wah Chan alive!"

Captain Kan heard this outburst over the wind and rain and howling of the surviving pirate crew.

"Wah Chan! You!" He reached for his sidearm, only to remember that it was holstered beneath his atmosphere suit. His small eyes crossed in frustration.

Ham Brooks came to life then. He seized the advantage, grabbed for the hilt of the threatening sword. He got it and struck Kan against the head, using the flat of the blade, then knocked him down with bunched knuckles.

That should have encouraged a fresh melee. But no one had any stomach for that.

Eyes popping, jaw slackening, they watched the Buddha swell and swell and swell until its face was larger than any tropical full moon they had ever beheld. The sheer magnitude of the thing gripped them in a profound silence, all thoughts of life or death, survival or imprisonment, fled their stunned consciousness.

Their fate lay in the hands of the Buddha that could not be contained.

Washington Chandler took his children in his arms, hugged them tight. Mary Chan was weeping to think that her life—if not *all* life—was drawing to a conclusion.

Renny made impotent fists of his monster hands. Monk and Ham exchanged confused glances, as if they did not know whether to hurl at one another a final farewell insult, or to simply say goodbye.

Members of the *Cuttlefish* crew began to moan, *"T'ung! T'ung!* All is lost!"

Another blue-white bolt of storm lightning arrived. It seemed to crack open the very sky, split the night with a reverberant thunder that promised to go on forever. For an unforgettable instant, it illuminated the entirety of the Buddha, showing its icy interior.

It was the size of a skyscraper now, its cold, opaque orbs fixed on distant points. It seemed to be looking out over the whole wide world like a conquering deity. All who witnessed this phenomenon felt like helpless ants.

Abruptly, when it seemed as if the dreadful Buddha could not grow any more massive, an unexpected thing transpired.

Its crystalline countenance shattered, as if struck by a massive but unseen hammer. The vile canine visage looked momentarily startled. No doubt that was an optical illusion created by the myriad fissures which suddenly veined its austere countenance.

Yet it presaged a greater event. Everyone expected something. No one knew what. Then the Buddha of Ice exploded into a million gleaming shards of starlight!

A deluge rivaling that of Noah's flood swept across the deck, washed the unprepared over the rails and into the Yellow Sea. Pirates. Marines. Only the Chans and Doc's men, coming to one another's assistance, held fast to rails and cannon and bulwarks.

Panic overtook the survivors now. There was pandemonium. Elemental chaos. Those possessing weapons clutched at them—a mistake. They, too, were swept overboard. Those without, sought to grab for railings and other lifesaving projections. Some managed to hold on for dear life.

UNNOTICED in the pelting downpour, a small rubber-encased grappling hook jumped out of the water at the bow, bit into the rail, and a knotted silk line grew taut. Up this, Doc Savage climbed onto deck, flake-gold eyes surveying the scene.

No one challenged him.

The bronze man slushed along the deck until he found the crackled-finished steel box containing the Buddha's Toe and took possession of it. It had been set deep in a coil of line, which kept it from upsetting.

Throwing off his helmet, Doc called out in Mayan. "Monk! Ham! Renny! Take control of the ship!"

As it turned out, there was not much ship to take control of. Virtually everyone had been knocked off their feet by the deluge that attended the abrupt and miraculous disintegration of the Buddha of Ice.

Doc got his men together. Everyone had made it. The Chans were also safe.

Wah Chan had Captain Kan by the scruff of his uniform collar. The latter's uniform cap had been lost and his shock of coarse black hair, straight and stiff as wire, was disclosed.

"You are now a prisoner of China," the Generalissimo grated.

Captain Kan looked whipped, but he hissed, "You are forgetting my ship, and the sailors who man it."

"I'm not forgetting anything," Wah Chan hurled back. "They're over there and you are here with us. Savvy?"

Captain Kan said nothing to that. His dark eyes remained confident. He seemed to believe the odds were still in his favor. For the gunboat crew was getting itself organized and attempting to finish putting off the shore craft.

"If necessary, my crew will sink this junk, even with my unworthy self on board," Kan assured Doc Savage, who had joined them.

The bronze man considered his words. They carried weight.

"Terms?" asked Doc.

"You can't expect fair terms from that cur," Wah Chan complained.

"Terms," repeated Doc grimly.

Fire snapped into Kan's dark eyes. His chin came up. "Surrender the box and permit me to disembark. I will spare all your lives."

"How can we trust you?" asked Doc.

Captain Kan squared his shoulders, lifting his gaze as if giving an admission that he did not want to utter. "I beheld what you all did, Savage-*san*," he admitted. "The so-called Buddha was in truth too dangerous to dwell on the earth, just as you warned. Far better for the world that it was destroyed. Satisfied with that result, I only crave something to carry back to my superiors, with which to save face."

Doc was thoughtful. He removed the gauntlet of his stratosphere suit, revealing a cabled bronze hand.

"In my country, as in yours, it is customary to conclude an agreement in a friendly manner." Doc put out his hand.

"Ah, so."

Smiling with thinning lips, Captain Kan shook it firmly.

Doc touched the dull bronze tip of one finger to the Japanese's clasping hand.

A strange expression crossed Kan's features. His eyes rolled up in his skull and his knees gave out. He collapsed on his feet.

Doc caught him, lowered the man to the deck.

"Fainted!" grunted Wah Chan, studying the captain's slack features. "Why, that milk-livered so-and-so! He couldn't take it!"

Doc shook his head. From one forefinger, he removed a dull

cap of bronze, resembling a thimble cunningly made over to look like a fingertip. This was tipped with a tiny hypodermic needle, which fed off a gland reservoir containing an anesthetic chemical. Pressure actuated the contrivance. Doc had donned it before leaving the *Cuttlefish* in the event it would prove useful later. It had.

Monk asked, "What do we do now?"

"Yeah," grunted Renny. "We're still outgunned and outnumbered by that gunboat crew."

Doc said, "We will inform the vessel by radio that Captain Kan has suffered a spell and needs emergency medical treatment. If they let us go, we promise to provide it."

"I get it!" Ham snapped. "You'll give them the antidote to the dope in that trick hypo."

Monk grinned broadly. "Pretty slick, Doc. But will they buy it?"

AS it developed, the Japanese crew did. They had all witnessed the Buddha of Ice and its downfall, and were in no mood for further experiences of that sort. They got busy pulling their countrymen out of the water, along with assorted Malays and Dyaks.

While they all watched operations, Renny put several questions to Doc Savage.

"How did you escape the Red Dragon junk?" he rumbled curiously.

"I managed to drag Tang into the water before the junk went down," explained the bronze man. "But we, too, sank due to the atmosphere suit. I dared not remove it, or the Buddha would have drained me dry, as it did Tang."

The bronze man looked genuinely sorry that he could not have done more for the wicked monk.

Continuing, Doc related, "The weight of the suit and oxygen tanks took me to the bottom. Just in time to witness the Buddha of Ice explode in size, throwing off the pieces of the shattered ship like a chick hatching from an eggshell."

"Some chick!" Ham exclaimed.

"It was reasonable to hope that being immersed in water would protect us from the Buddha's influence, but its increasing size counteracted that protection," Doc said. "When it became clear where matters were headed, I shed the tanks, which allowed for a safe return to the surface."

"Well," Monk said, "I'm gonna be havin' nightmares about this day until I'm old and gray like this ambulance chaser here." He jerked a hairy thumb in Ham's direction.

"That reminds me," Ham returned. "The next time you see me in a sword fight, you stay out of it. Or you won't live long enough to sprout gray hairs!"

Monk made a show of rolling up his sleeves. "You Harvard Yard fencing master! Next time I see you in a scrap, I'm comin' in on the other side!"

Ham grabbed for a discarded *parang* and tested the edge with his thumb. It was like a razor, so sharp that he had not felt it slice in. A dribble of blood came.

"I have a good mind to skin you for a throw rug," Ham gritted.

Monk roared, "Wave that thing at me and I'll hammer your head so far down, it will look like you grew a third shoulder!" he vowed.

Violence clearly impended. Mark and Mary Chan exchanged worried looks.

Renny inserted, "Pay them no attention. This is their way of blowing off steam."

Doc Savage attended to the wounded, beginning with Renny's lead-lacerated shoulder. His medical skill soon became evident. Lastly, he patched his own bullet-scored side. When the bandages came off, a week or two hence, the scarring would be invisible.

The exchange of rescued pirates for the slumbering Captain Kan and various Marines was conducted with quiet ceremony.

Doc Savage solemnly handed over a charged syringe to the officer who took possession of his superior, along with instructions brushed onto parchment in perfect Japanese.

"By the time that stiff-necked captain wakes up," Monk beamed as the Japanese took their leave, "we'll be out of these troubled waters."

THEY sailed for Pirate Island that evening. A sickly yellow half-moon dominated the clearing night sky, and seemed to follow them south—south to the South China Sea.

During the voyage, the Chans had many questions.

"It is obvious—" said Mark.

"—that the Buddha of Ice possessed a limited capacity to absorb water—" continued Mary.

"—hence, it exploded when it had gorged its fill," finished Mark.

Doc shook his head. "By all evidence, it *imploded,* releasing all of its trapped moisture and constituent elements back into the atmosphere, after it reached its crystalline breaking point. As you know, in nature crystals grow in a near-organic manner—sometimes to gigantic size. The Buddha was no different in that respect."

"But no one could have known that beforehand," Mark said simply.

Doc Savage was silent a very long time. It was not his nature to boast, or take undue credit for accomplishments that were not his. He was a genuinely modest man.

Noticing Doc's discomfort, Renny prodded him to speak.

"There's something you're not telling us," he suggested.

The bronze man took a moment to assemble his thoughts.

"It was reasonable to imagine that there might be a limit to the Buddha's capacity to absorb moisture," he said at last. "No way existed to demonstrate such limits without risking inconceivable consequences. To test the theory might have been scientifically sound, but bad policy."

The bronze man fell silent. He seemed to be embarrassed by his failure to best the Buddha by his own efforts.

Monk Mayfair, who was perhaps closer to the bronze giant than any of the others, sensed that there was more to be told.

"Something happened down there, didn't it?" he offered.

Doc Savage nodded. "The outcome of the apparent catastrophe was entirely in doubt. It was as reasonable to assume disaster, as it was to trust in salvation. But there was no calculating which eventuality would transpire. There is a certain helplessness one feels in those circumstances. In such times, an appeal to the Deity makes as much sense as any futile action."

Mary Chan gasped, "So you prayed...."

"Sure," croaked out Wah Chan. "The psychology of powerlessness made it the only sensible course of action. I've been in tough spots like that. Nothing to be ashamed about."

But Doc Savage was not finished with his account.

"Many people who face death in such circumstances describe a kind of peace that falls over them when the end seemed unavoidable." Doc paused. He colored slightly, as if unwilling to unveil his deepest thoughts.

Everyone looked at the bronze man in rapt expectation.

"No inner peace came over me," he admitted at last. "Instead, my thoughts went to all of you, and my cousin Pat back in New York, and the millions of people worldwide who would perish. A deep anger arose within my being. A fury such as I never before experienced. It took possession of my senses. In my frustration, I made for the Buddha. Intending to do what, I do not know. Lash out blindly, possibly. But as I approached it, a flash of lightning illuminated the thing to its very core, showing its crystalline inner structure. It appeared to be internally fragile. A compulsion to give it a final and, presumably futile, expression of human anger came. Employing my foot, I struck out with all my might at the stump of the missing toe, where it appeared weakest."

Ham gasped, "The devilish thing went to pieces just after

that last lightning bolt!"

Doc nodded. "It imploded after I struck it."

"So it *didn't* die of its own thirst, after all!" Monk squeaked.

Doc Savage continued to look uncomfortable. The degree to which he employed the personal pronoun alone told how jarred he was.

"The answer to that question is known only to the Almighty," he admitted. "The Buddha might have reached its upper growth limit at that coincidental moment, or later. My kick could have jarred its structural integrity at an opportune time. There is no way of determining the truth of the matter."

Wah Chan frowned fiercely. "I don't see what all this mumbling and stumbling is all about. You kicked the damned Buddha and croaked it dead. Just like Jack the Giant-Killer! You preserved the whole blessed world and everyone on it. They'll give you a ticker-tape parade bigger than Lindbergh's reception when you get back to America!"

Doc Savage looked even more uncomfortable than before. During his strange upbringing, emotion had been schooled out of his makeup. This did not mean that he lacked natural feelings, but rather they were under rigid control. That superb self-possession had been shaken loose a bit.

"It would be best if we never spoke of this affair again," Doc said sincerely.

Wah Chan glowered at the bronze man incredulously.

"What's the matter? Don't you like being a hero? Ain't that how you make your living?"

Renny boomed, "Shucks, Doc doesn't want to take the credit when it's due him, and he plumb doesn't want any when the facts are in doubt."

But Doc Savage put it another way. "The world would not believe our account in any event. Telling it would further nothing useful."

As those plain words soaked into their brains, the rains gradually eased off to a gentle pelting. The practical sense of

Doc's speech was undeniable. There was no more discussion.

After a while, Wah Chan wondered, "What are you going to do with the Buddha's Toe?"

Ham Brooks said, "Doc has a special place for dangerous discoveries like that."

"Nix, shyster," hissed Monk, elbowing the dapper lawyer in the ribs. "Keep our secrets secret."

The apish chemist was referring to Doc's Fortress of Solitude, in the Arctic, where he maintained a vault of deadly devices confiscated from enemies, devices that were too dangerous for further development and experimentation.

Ham rapped Monk smartly on the head, saying, "Be thankful I don't run you through, you grotesque baboon."

Monk batted the offending cane away. "Tap me again like that and I'll shuck an arm off you!" he growled.

Doc Savage offered, "The Buddha's Toe is clearly unfit to be studied in any locality, no matter how remote."

Wah Chan did not dispute that. "So what are you going to do? Drop it in the South China Sea and let it go the way of its bigger brother?"

"Sound reasoning," Ham offered.

"A less risky idea would be preferable," returned Doc.

BUT they could not get it out of him until they reached Pirate Island two days later, to reclaim possession of their tri-motored plane and let off the surviving corsairs, with pointed reminders of past promises to abandon their former piratical ways.

Doc led them into the jungle.

"We encountered this spot during an earlier foray on this isle," he explained.

They came to what at first appeared to be a jungle pool, except that it was very black and still. Insects drowsed lazily over it.

Ham unsheathed his sword cane and probed its placid surface with the tip.

"Jove!" he exclaimed. "The tar pit!"

"I believe it to be the safest repository for the Buddha's Toe," said Doc.

The bronze man had rigged the crackle-finish container with a silk line that he had attached by spirit gum to the lid.

Cautiously, he set the container onto the viscous asphalt surface, and stepped back to observe what happened.

Slowly, the box sank from sight in the inky stuff. No one looked sorry to see it go. With infinite care, metallic fingers paid out the line.

After considerable minutes had passed, Doc gave the silk cord a sharp tug. They knew the box lid came ajar when the tar made a noise like the cracking of a tree split by Arctic cold. The oily surface suddenly became a dry black cake.

"I'll be damned," exclaimed Wah Chan. "It sucked all the moisture from the tar!"

Doc nodded. "No one will ever be able to extract it, probably."

"Well," grunted Renny. "That's that. Guess I can get back to that rubber plantation job now." He suddenly eyed the three Chans—or Chandlers as they were calling themselves now. "What do we do with you folks?"

Wash Chandler had evidently been giving this some thought.

He jerked a thumb at his broad chest. "Me, I'm retiring. I've been through the Chinese civil war, the invasion of Manchuria and a damn rebellion in the south. I have had enough of being a Chink freedom fighter. Let the Chinese fight their own ragtag battles. I'm taking my kids back to America to settle down. I stashed a lot of loot back there, and I think I'll set them up in business. They should do right fine. Regular breed of the Red Dragon, both of 'em!"

That seemed to satisfy Doc Savage, for he made no objection. Whatever Washington Chandler's past deeds had been, he had ended his career as Wah Chan fighting to prevent China from becoming a Japanese puppet state.

That night, as Doc and his men readied their tri-motor for

departure, there was a final ceremony of farewell.

The erstwhile pirates of the former hellship *Devilfish* gathered on the beach to watch them take their leave.

Doc repeated his lecture about staying on the straight and narrow. After all that they had been through, the corsairs seemed to have taken it to heart once more. A few volunteered to join Doc's band of altruistic adventurers, but the bronze man politely but firmly dissuaded them from that notion.

One enterprising buccaneer reminded Doc of his promise to reward them all richly.

Doc informed them that, by radio, he had set in motion pardons for their piratical pasts from the British government, and that henceforth none of them need fear the hangman's noose. Provided that they abandon all banditry.

After some discussion, the crew agreed that their lives were reward rich enough for any retired freebooter.

And so it was agreed. They assisted in ferrying the Chans to the waiting plane.

As Doc's tri-motor smashed along the swells and took to the air, the former cut-throat crew rushed to the blade-and-bullet-chewed foredeck of the renamed *Cuttlefish.*

One final time, they lifted their bright blades in salute. A yellow moon looked down upon them like a blandly benevolent deity.

"Doc Savage!" they hailed. "Doc Savage! *Doc Savage—Scourge of the South China Sea!*"

About the Author

LESTER DENT

LESTER DENT'S ANCESTRY was Scots-Irish, his people having migrated to Missouri by way of Bullitt County, Kentucky, Ohio and Illinois. It is said that there were Dents at Jamestown, during the early days of that Virginia colony. Coincidentally or not, there were Savages numbered among the founders of Jamestown, too.

Lester came into the world on October 12, 1904—one year and one day after the October 11, 1903 demise of Richard Henry Savage, the American war hero who would later inspire the creation of Doc Savage, the Man of Bronze. Born in La Plata, Missouri, Lester was the offspring of pioneer stock, his father, Bernard, having owned ranches in Oklahoma and Wyoming and Nebraska, one situated near Savageton, Wyoming. His mother's people were Norfolks, of Missouri. Dent Family members were said to have served their country in the Revolutionary War, and took up arms on both sides of the Civil War. But the record shows that Lester's paternal grandfather, Marquis Lafayette "Marcus" Dent, fought for Missouri on the Union side. Lester's maternal grandfather, John Thomas Norfolk, also wore Union blue. He hailed from Ohio.

Lester once joked, "My grandfather was a pot-washer in the Civil War, and his grandfather was a pot-washer in the Revolutionary War. I'm probably in the wrong business." Bernard Dent was a member of the notorious Pot Gang, whose wild exploits in northeast Missouri have passed out of memory and into legend.

As a boy growing up in the half-tamed West, Lester spent a lot of time around cowboys, soon discovering that their bunkhouses were brimming with exciting pulp magazines. And so he encountered the heroes of his day. Dent never lost his taste for pulp fiction and when he drifted into that field in 1929, Lester claimed that he was in it for the money, but people who knew him best, knew different. Dent went on to create a raft of memorable pulp heroes, but none as great or as enduring as Doc Savage, who was said to be a combination of Sherlock Holmes, Tarzan of the Apes, and Jesus Christ—and who had more than a little Dent blood in him.

About the Author

WILL MURRAY

WILL MURRAY WAS born on April 28, 1953—exactly fifty years to the day after the birth of his namesake paternal grandfather. His synchronistic arrival set the tone for a life as unusual as might be expected. His maternal ancestors were undiluted Irish—his mother's people having tended their turf fires on the same patch of County Kerry for some 2,000 years, while his paternal bloodline—improved according to legend by contact with the Spanish Armada—included Maurice Bransfield, a Civil War-era Indian scout who participated in Seige of Atlanta, and his son, William, a barber infamous for braining a contingent of British soldiers who invaded his shop during the Troubles and living to tell of it. Corkmen, they were. The Murray branch hailed from Roscommon.

With ancestors such as those, perhaps it is no wonder the 1953 edition Will Murray took to heroes at an early age, discovering Superman, Batman and others at the age of eight. This was back in the Christmas vacation week of 1961, when comic books cost twelve cents. Although he participated in no American rebellions, Murray did contribute to the Marvel Comics renaissance of 1961-69, purchasing the earliest issues of *The Fantastic Four*, *The Amazing Spider-Man* and *The Incredible Hulk*, thus insuring that the multi-billion dollar Marvel Entertainment Group had a long and prosperous future ahead of it. This also ignited his imagination and inspired his creative drive.

Doc Savage came into his life when Murray was 15—the

precise target age for Doc readers established back in 1933—when, enthralled by James Bama's arresting cover to *Dust of Death,* he purchased his first adventure of the Man of Bronze. This January, 1969 encounter signaled that Murray was moving on from comic books to real literature. Now he writes Doc Savage, collaborating posthumously with Lester Dent, the writer who first breathed vibrant life into Street & Smith's seminal superman—who may or may not have been Irish, but sure handles himself like a true son of Erin.

About the Artist

JOE DeVITO

JOE DeVITO WAS born on March 16, 1957 in New York City's famed—or infamous—Hell's Kitchen neighborhood. Family legend has it that due to an impending blizzard, 1957 was the only year New York's St. Patrick's Day parade was held on the 16th rather than the 17th. His mother held him up to watch the parade, and he has had the "Luck of the Irish" ever since. As part of a large Sicilian family living in a predominantly Irish neighborhood, this was a good thing to have.

Coming from an artistic family did not hurt either. DeVito's mother could have been a professional artist had she not chosen to have six kids. Being the fifth of six children, Joe is eternally grateful for her decision. His mother's brother, Joe (after whom the artist was named), was both a priest and a very talented oil painter. But it was primarily Joe's older bother, Vito DeVito—also a professional painter and sculptor—who ultimately influenced him most.

Vito, seven year older, first introduced Joe to comic books and super heroes, *Famous Monsters of Filmland* magazine, all the great monster movies, and most important of all, the original 1933 movie, *King Kong*. Already a certified dinosaur fanatic who knew how to spell "Tyrannosaurus" before he could spell his own name, Joe DeVito's first viewing of *King Kong* changed the highly impressionable four year old's life forever. The sense of atmosphere, wonder, adventure and danger, combined with his natural love of dinosaurs and fascination with monsters, was irresistible.

It is no wonder that, in a mind so prepared, Doc Savage found a very welcome home several years later, after Joe's family had moved to Berkeley Heights, New Jersey. Upon graduating from Parsons School of Design and getting an apartment in Hoboken, Joe stumbled upon a used bookstore that had the entire run of Doc Savage paperbacks for 25 cents each. He was instantly attracted to the James Bama covers and bought them all. Later, Joe found out that it was Bama who painted the box art for all of the Aurora monster models he bought as a boy, King Kong in particular. In just a few short years, Joe found himself painting the covers for the new Doc Savage novels written by a guy named Will Murray. Life had come full circle. Is it fate, or the Luck of the Irish?

Printed in Great Britain
by Amazon